PRAISE FO

THE BLOOD GIFT DUOLOGY

"Davenport sticks the landing . . . [blending] science fiction and fantasy tropes in her ambitious, action-packed conclusion to the Blood Gift duology." —Publishers Weekly

"An adrenaline-racing and action-heavy sequel, *The Blood Gift* is an exciting sequel with plenty of villains, gods, magic, and violence while also balancing themes of loyalty, love, belonging." —The Fantasy Reviews

"The plotting is an intricate mix of action, intrigue, and betrayal, with a fast pace and a high body count. . . . Thankfully, this is book one of a proposed duology, because revenge is a dish best served cold." —Booklist on *The Blood Trials*

"Davenport debuts with an ambitious epic that blurs genre lines, setting futuristic technology against a historical fantasy backdrop. . . . This invigorating debut marks Davenport as a writer to watch." —Publishers Weekly on *The Blood Trials*

"An action-packed adventure paired with luscious worldbuilding makes *The Blood Trials* an enthralling, unputdownable read. Davenport is a force to be reckoned with."

—KALYNN BAYRON, BESTSELLING AUTHOR OF *CINDERELLA IS DEAD*

"If you want to be on the edge of your seat, find another book, because this one hands you a blade, shoves you right into the action, and demands you start running if you want to keep up. It is action, mystery, and heartfelt character—all balanced perfectly on the tip of a knife."

—SCOTT REINTGEN, BESTSELLING AUTHOR OF THE *NYXIA* SERIES

"Each bloody scene has depth and leads to more answers that compel you to keep reading, which was one of my favorite aspects of Davenport's writing."

—*LIGHTSPEED MAGAZINE*

"*The Blood Trials* is an ambitious debut by N. E. Davenport that had me on the edge of my seat the entire time and constantly guessing. This story beautifully tackles some difficult themes that resonated with me deeply and imagined the main character that I fell in love with."

—BOOKISH BREWS

Also by
N. E. DAVENPORT

THE BLOOD TRIALS

✦

Written as
NIA DAVENPORT

OUT OF BODY

THE BLOOD GIFT

BOOK TWO OF THE BLOOD GIFT DUOLOGY

N. E. DAVENPORT

HARPER Voyager

An Imprint of HarperCollins Publishers

THE BLOOD GIFT. Copyright © 2023 by Enishia Davenport. All rights reserved. Printed in the United States of America. No part of this book may be used or reproduced in any manner whatsoever without written permission except in the case of brief quotations embodied in critical articles and reviews. For information, address HarperCollins Publishers, 195 Broadway, New York, NY 10007.

HarperCollins books may be purchased for educational, business, or sales promotional use. For information, please email the Special Markets Department at SPsales@harpercollins.com.

Harper Voyager and design are trademarks of HarperCollins Publishers LLC.

A hardcover edition of this book was published in 2023 by Harper Voyager, an imprint of HarperCollins Publishers.

FIRST HARPER VOYAGER PAPERBACK EDITION PUBLISHED 2024.

Title page background image © Vidady/abode.stock.com
Circular ornament © Andrey/adobe.stock.com
Map illustration by Nick Springer

Library of Congress Cataloging-in-Publication Data has been applied for.

ISBN 978-0-06-305854-5

24 25 26 27 28 LBC 5 4 3 2 1

To my wonderful readers who've shown so much enthusiasm for Ikenna's journey and who've connected with our favorite Murder Girl; to anybody and everybody who needs to rightfully rage at injustices; and to those who dare to dream big when the world tells us we shouldn't

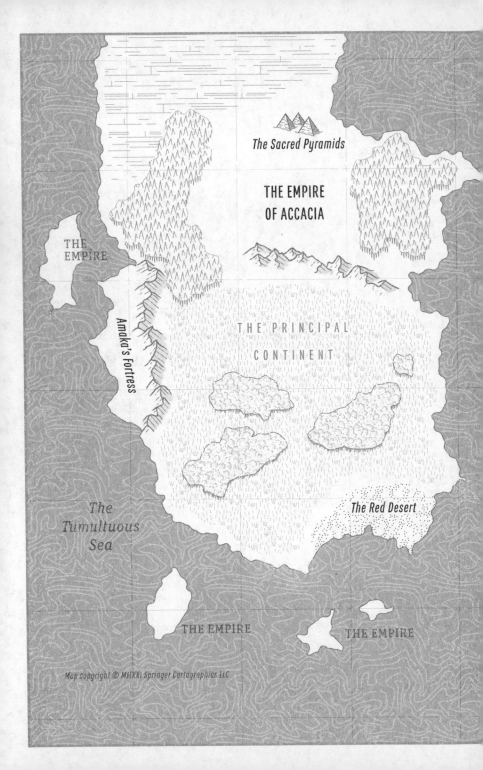

1

I SIT IN A MOUNTAINSIDE cafe, sipping a godsawful microstate whiskey, and watch my targets across the room. There's twelve in total—eight women and four men. They're in a reserved section roped off from the public, having a party. An ebony-skinned woman in her mid-fifties with flawless, gene-manipulated beauty and striking gray eyes that remind me ruthlessly of a certain other bitch I've been trying not to think about raises her glass and starts the speech for a toast. I mark the subtle elegance about Edryssa Cyphir—my desired target—and also the gruffness that makes it clear she could handle herself in most fights. Probably any fight.

Just not a fight with me.

Lady Edryssa keeps her oration short and sweet. I thank the Pantheon for the boon because it means less time I have to sit in a far corner of the cafe, imbibing disgusting liquor, and waiting to make my move. The speech ends; glasses clink; sparkling wine is guzzled.

Drink more, I urge everyone, *and make this a cherry walk.*

There's a moment where I swear I see emptiness in one of the party-goer's eyes, and I get excited. Did that really just pseudo-work?

But the tan-skinned man that's built like an armored transport places his empty flute on a table nearby and turns to the spread of food beside it.

I guess not. Damn! What's the use of having a stockpile of power if you don't know how to make it work *every time* you want it to? Whatever extra boost the goddess gave me in Khanai only worked unerringly long enough to get my team out. Almost immediately after it fizzled, though, and now it's wholly erratic. Sometimes it barrels into me with enough force that it literally knocks me on my butt, and other times it's lukewarm, stubbornly remaining at its old, usual—and unuseful—levels. Right now, it's the latter. I shake my head.

Guess things are getting done the tougher way.

I remain at my cramped table, continuing to drink whiskey that had no business being barreled in the first place and looking as if I'd been simply people-watching—as one often does when they're dining alone—until the fanfare of the party stole my attention and now I'm ensnared with watching them have a good time.

I could make my move right in the eatery. I could stand up, walk over to the group's private section, and do what needs to be done. But the cafe is full of people, and it probably wouldn't be a good look to commit a slaughter, in a foreign nation, in front of a slew of witnesses. And while I don't give a shit about how it looks, I have others around me who insist we at least try to do things right.

So I gotta wait.

And wait.

And fucking wait some more.

Irked, I slip out of character for a second and allow myself a quick, cathartic scowl.

I stay out of character longer than I should when low laughter floats into my ear.

"Go to hell," I mutter to Caiman through my nanomic.

"Patience is a virtue, Amari." He chuckles.

"This cafe is propped on a cliff," I remind the jackass. "I technically still owe you a push."

That shuts him up. For now. I swear the gods specifically crafted Caiman to get under my skin—even when we're in a truce and aligned to the same side.

"Focus. Everyone. This is serious." The new voice that hisses into my ear is, of course, Reed's.

I roll my eyes. "I can multitask."

"Amari." My name is a reprimand. A censure handed down from a commanding officer. I bristle, and if the op at hand wasn't so important, I'd blow it. *"Fuck you,"* I snarl quietly into the mic. "I'm not your subordinate anymore so get your tone together when you talk to me."

"This isn't the place for your ego," Reed snaps back. A beat passes then he curses. "Your point is valid, however. I guess. So, my apologies."

I try to remain irritated, but my mouth twitches, a thing I know the bastard can see because he hacked the establishment's vidcams and routed their live feed to his and the rest of our rogue cohort's Comm Units. "It is your bad," I say, keeping my voice hard. *Lots of things are your bad.* Darius Reed and I still have offenses to air out after what happened in Khanai, and until we do, it's actually *him* I want to shove off a cliff, not Caiman.

"Party's ending," Dannica chirps in her forever-present, supremely unnatural, peppy tone.

"Time for *our* bash to begin." I can practically hear the eager grin on Haynes's face as he says it.

I refocus on the party and watch good-byes breeze off lips and air kisses be passed in Lusian fashion. Gray-eyed Edryssa Cyphir, who gave the toast, leaves first. I track her as she slips out a narrow door along a wall inside the private section. Like I said, she's the person I'm after, but to get to Lady Edryssa, I've gotta go through her cronies first.

Those cronies, the other seven women and four men in the room, begin leaving via the back entrance precisely five minutes after Edryssa departs.

I swipe my Comm Unit over the mini monitor embedded in a corner of my table to pay for my subpar whiskey, stand, and head out the front entrance of the cafe.

"Let's see if they leave together or all go separate ways," I say into my mic.

"Let's hope it's the former so this'll be a piece of pie," Greysen says.

"From your lips to the cosmos's ears," I mutter. Otherwise, my crew will have to break off into teams and go after the dons of the Cyphir Syndicate separately. Which we can do, but confronting all of them at once will make more of a statement that Edryssa won't be able to ignore.

I exit the cafe to a bright midafternoon sun and swiftly hook a left to walk around back. Like I knew she would be, Edryssa is long gone when I get to the secluded transport lot. All the intelligence we've gathered on the Lady of Lusian says she never lingers in a place long enough for enemies to put a bullet between her eyes. Her dons aren't so paranoid, fortunately for us. The eleven fucks loiter in a holding lot that's paved with the same aquamarine flagstone that lends a shine to most of the city's streets, chatting casually beside a row of gleaming, top-of-the-line luxury transports, the best their blood money can buy.

I step behind a mass-carry rig that looms over me and keeps me completely concealed.

"Everyone in position?" Reed asks through the mic.

Each of us returns a quiet affirmative.

I'm the first one to move into view of the dons. They all turn to me, looking murderous at my intrusion. One of them, a short, stocky man with black hair, growls a curse in Lusian. "Who the fuck are you?" he barks in the same language. "Do yourself a favor, sweetheart, and turn around."

"Nah. I think I'll pass." I take a step closer to the dons.

That's when the others join the fun. Reed, Dannica, Haynes, Caiman, Greysen, Liim, and Dane (the last two are the other Alphas who were convinced by Caiman's little speech in Khanai) appear in the lot. Together, we've got the Cyphir pricks boxed in.

I'll award them points for not bothering to ask further questions or sling further threats. Their blasters are out and pointed at us half a heartbeat after we train ours on them.

"Why don't you do yourself a favor and put those away. We'll be quicker on the draw," I promise the dons.

The idiots don't listen. They start shooting, and every last one of them crumples. Lucky for them, we're shooting stun bullets instead of UVs. *Unluckily* for them, stuns still leave you in agony while twitching on the ground.

I stand over the head of the man who shouted at me. "Edryssa. I'd like to speak with her?" I make my demand politely in flawless Lusian to give him and his people added assurances that I'm serious and not fucking around. The insistence that foreigners do business with them in their native tongue is a weird summit to die on, but when in Lusian, as the saying goes, you bow to how the Cyphirs—who hold the City of Thugs in an iron grip—do business if you want to accomplish anything with the sons of bitches who run it.

Maybe not the snappiest phrasing.

The don glares up at me as he twitches. I'm almost impressed. It speaks to one hell of a fighting spirit that he isn't howling in pain—or pissing himself—by this point. I blow him a kiss as a reward.

"Edryssa will have your head and the heads of all your family," the man rasps.

I shrug. "Every one of my kin is already dead, so that threat lands nowhere. And there's no way in hell the Lady of the City could have *my* head. Your boss isn't that good." I trade my stun blaster for a gun housing UV bullets. I stoop and press the barrel to his temple. "I'll ask again, but then there won't be a third time. Edryssa? I want a meet?"

He's either supremely loyal, supremely moronic, or supremely just doesn't give a crap about dying because he turns his head to the side and spits on my boots. "Trash doesn't get to meet with Edryssa, and I at least know the trash around here. Who are you? Nobody, I bet. Kill me. If you don't, Edryssa will for wasting her time with you when I take you to her."

I ram the barrel of the blaster into his temple. Then I brandish a second one loaded with UV bullets and shoot him in the thigh. "I don't like being insulted. I think too highly of myself to put up with it." I jerk my head toward the Mareenians, who have his counterparts restrained. "Ask my friends. Also, I can promise you Edryssa definitely wants to hear what I have to say. If you agree to take us to her right now, I'll spare every miserable life in this lot, make it worth your *and* Edryssa's while. I hear you can make any deal with the Cyphir Syndicate if you can wrangle their respect and you've got enough credits." I shoot him in his already blown apart thigh. This time, the bravado deflates out of him, and he wails. Smiling my best homicidal smile, I wave one of my guns at his restrained peers. "Clearly, I've proven you need to respect me. Let's take the fact that I'm rich enough to make your boss forgive this incident on good faith, shall we?" I spear him with one of Dannica's saccharine-sweet smiles.

"*You whoreofabitch*," he growls up at me.

Haven't heard that as one word before—*I'll need to tuck that one away.* I shoot him a third time in the injured leg. He wails louder. "Every time you insult me, my trigger finger acts on its own accord. When I run out of bullets . . . well, I quite get off on stabbing people who aggravate me over shooting them. I'm simply trying to exercise some restraint here while showing a little courtesy, you dick." I aim the blaster back at the shredded mess of a hole in his thigh gushing blood. "How much damage do you think one leg can take before you permanently can't use it anymore? Hell—before you bleed out? Don't worry, I'm not going to kill you because I need you alive. But I can mangle you very, very, very badly, patch you up, and then do it again until you say yes."

"Why don't you go fuck with somebody else?"

"Real classy, throwing your people under the transport there." I kneel beside him again, and poke him in the center of his mushy wound. He hollers in pain. "That was for them. We both know I'd be wasting my time with one of the other dons because they aren't Edryssa's number two. They don't know how to contact her directly. They'd all have to go through you to get to her anyhow."

He seems surprised I know all this. But what good would we be if we couldn't run a little reconnaissance and do it well? It didn't take us long to figure out Edryssa Cyphir steers a tight operation. She has to when she's a wanted woman in every territory on the Minor *and* Principal Continents except the city we stand in, which technically isn't a recognized, formal municipality at all. Yes, a tight operation and one hell of an arsenal: Edryssa has some serious nukes and a sizable enough merc army guarding Lusian and herself inside its borders that no power on the Minor Continent, at least, wants the headache of really quarreling with her about it either. Further affording protection is the fact that the Cyphir Syndicate is the largest, longest-lived underground crime organization across Iludu, so its web and its power run deep.

Incidentally, these are also the exhaustive reasons why she's a woman who I need to, regrettably, sorely have a chat with.

Speeding up that end because my patience is blackfrost-thin on a good day, I poise my finger above the don's injury. He shudders. I take that as my cue that his resolve is breaking. *Fantastic.* I drop my hand to my side and slide my blue-steel dagger from its concealed spot at my hip. I let the tip of the Khanaian blade hover a centimeter above the open wound. The don throws his hands into the air. "All right. All right. All right! I'll send a Comm to Edryssa. Tell her you want a meet. See if she'll accept."

I lower my knife a fraction toward his thigh. I let its tip graze the exposed pink, bloody, shredded muscle with splinters of bone stabbing through. He hollers again. "*Make* her accept."

He breathes heavy, having gone ashen, and breaks out in a sweat. "Okay."

He drags his wrist up to his face, punches a message into the screen, and then drops his arms. "It's done," he says, heaving.

Less than a minute later, his Comm Unit beeps.

"What does it say?" I ask, on edge, as he reads Edryssa's response.

"She says to have my transport take you to a meet. She also says to start picking out homegoing lilies for your funeral." He spits the words, regaining some of his former courage. "Edryssa may kill you before one word is spoken, you know. I hope she does."

At that, he gets my special smile, and I can practically feel the blood coming from his wound run cold.

"That won't end well," I advise savagely. "Tell her I said if she tries anything foul, *she'll* need the lilies. *You too.* So will every single one of her people with the misfortune of being in the vicinity when she angers me. Afterward, I'll level her whole, precious organization. I guarantee it's a job I and my squad here can easily get done. So, make sure you impress on Edryssa it's wisest to play nice."

2

ACCORDING TO OUR INTELLIGENCE-GATHERING, Lady Edryssa's second goes by the name Bastien, he's a close cousin, and he's stood at Edryssa's side for the eighteen years she's steered the Cyphir Syndicate. Loyal Bastien sits across from me in his spacious, private transport, seething. I can tell he wants to murder me in the worst way, but at this point, who doesn't? Half of Iludu is gunning for my head. Guess it's a special charm I have.

I nod where Bastien's applying pressure to his thigh with a square of medgauze. "The shots were clean. They missed your femoral artery and the gauze has regeneration salve. You can get over them now."

He glowers at me more intensely. He doesn't have time to say whatever insult he's about to hurl my way because, finally, the transport is pulling up to our destination. He turns his full attention to the elegant townhouse I glimpse from the window. About three dozen armed guards are positioned outside its entrance. The transport comes to a stop in the circular driveway they're fanned out around. The transport's doors shoot up, and Bastien gingerly steps out first. He barks to the guards in Lusian that the arrived visitors are unfriendly. Then he moves out of the doorway and tells us unfriendly types that we can emerge.

The thirty-six guards line up on both sides of my team and march us single file to the townhome's entrance.

"This seems like overkill." Dannica, who is directly behind me, snorts.

Bastien, limping alongside us, shakes his head, not the least bit amused. "We both know it isn't. In fact, it might be *underkill* given the info dispatched to my Comm Unit during our ride on exactly *who* you lot are." He jerks said device her way. "Edryssa never agrees to a meeting blind. She's done her homework, and you all are pain-in-the-ass Mareenians. Worse, you're scumshit Praetorians. Well, *ex*-Praetorians, right?" The bastard winks at Dannica and me, a smug smile curving his lips, which he's a nanosecond away from having carved off his face.

"Careful," I warn him, soft and deadly. "Unless you want two maimed legs."

Brave on the side of stupid now that he's surrounded by a slew of hired guns at his beck and call, he shrugs and ignores the threat.

"The eight of you are currently wanted by your government for desertion and treason," he blabbers on, telling us shit we already know. "That second crime relates to harboring *her*." He stabs a finger at me, and now that he's revealed he knows who I am, rakes me with a look that's pure repugnance. But amid all the surge in bravado, he can't quite conceal the terror that washes over him.

I serve him a third helping of my winning homicidal-bitch grin to keep him on his toes. In case there are vidcams transmitting live feed of the grounds to the Lady Edryssa, I flick the same unleashed look toward the house. I need this asshole and his boss to truly, deeply, intensely understand that I was dead serious before. If they try to fuck us over, or murder us, for our assault on Bastien and his fellow dons, *they're* the ones who won't be walking away from the scuffle.

The guards lead us into a foyer that's as elegantly styled as the outside of the home. The floor is a subtle black marble, the walls are satin white, and a few pieces of abstract holoart, which never doesn't cost a fortune, illuminate the walls. We walk past a wraparound cherrywood staircase that leads to a second landing and venture deeper into the first story of the townhome. Like I'm sure the rest of my squad is doing, I catalog everything I see and construct a mental map of the circuitous route we take to our destination.

We turn a right corner, and one of the guards pushes open the door to a sitting room. Edryssa perches on a settee beneath the lone window. A quick glance behind her confirms that she was, in fact, watching our arrival; the window looks out over the front lawn. Then I fix my attention back on the Lady of Lusian. She's changed attire since leaving the seaside cafe where she and her dons celebrated her fifty-sixth birthday. Earlier, she wore a floor-length violet gown with a plunging neckline that showed off ample breasts, and strappy, gold sandals. Now she wears a black sheath whose hem slants right above her knees. Her pumps are the same lush black. So is her lipstick. The only splash of color about her are those eyes, the undiluted gray of which still (irksomely) unnerves me, and her coily, shoulder-length platinum hair. Her hair color is definitely the result of gene mods; no people on Iludu own it as a natural shade. I wonder, briefly, if the unsettling hue of her eyes is due to the same thing because the peoples that populate the Free Microstates normally have eyes that trend varying shades of brown and brown only. Then I let the errant thought go because scrutinizing Edryssa's physical traits is not why I'm here.

I do, however, prudently dissect what she's wearing. Or rather, the color she's wearing. The intel we collected on Edryssa Cyphir says she's a dramatic woman who likes making statements. Also, according to the intel, when she wears black, it means whoever she is meeting with should prepare for their funerary rites.

Just as we expected.

I break the line the guards try to keep us Mareenians herded into and swagger to the center of the room. I stare Edryssa down, giving her a look as murderous and as fearless as the one she's giving my crew. "The black is nice on you," I say in casual conversation. "But these days, red is more the shade I prefer. I don't necessarily like sending people to their crypts, but I do really, really, *really* enjoy spilling blood. And when I get pissed off, I do it well, so please don't piss me off while we're in this room. Or maybe, please do? My time in the Free Microstates has been boring thus far. I could use a few shits and giggles to enliven my stay."

Behind me, Dannica chokes on a laugh. I throw a quick glance to check the pulse of everyone else. They all, Dannica included, stand on alert, marking every detail, every exit, every potential threat in the room. If Edryssa did her homework on us, as Bastien said she did, then the Lady should know that the thirty-six guards she has in the sitting room are laughable. The eight of us could take them. If this ends in a fight, they, Bastien, and their boss will be the ones headed to their funerary rites. Not us.

Something I'm sure Edryssa knows because the guards haven't yet moved to gun us down and they've kept a respectful distance since we've arrived.

"You attacked my dons," Edryssa all but snarls.

I shrug. "I hear you only respect displays of strength. Or is that wrong? I needed a meeting, and I figured that was the easiest way to get one."

"Did you also figure you'd like to die?" Her expression is pitiless. Ruthless. And yet her disposition remains ever elegant and matronly. I think I like her. A lot.

"If we want to play a game of threats, that's fine. A waste of time, but fine. Let me help you out, though: I'm hard to kill," I return. "Most Praetorians are. So are most blood-gifted. As it turns out, I'm both."

"So *I hear*." Her eyes narrow on me and sweep down my form. "You're a pretty girl. Arrogant too." She huffs a laugh, and some of the tension deflates from the room. "You remind me of myself in my youth.

I think I could get on well with you, Ikenna Amari. Unlike with your prick of a grandfather. He was a self-righteous ass who'd never sully himself with the likes of me." I stiffen at the mention of Grandfather and the insult to him. I didn't think I would be surprised by anything today but have to admit she got to me. I quickly have to check my temper from exploding and losing any ground I've gained with Edryssa. Also, she's right. Grandfather would never be standing in a Cyphir safe house. He'd consider the offer of allyship I'm here to broker a stain on his honor and beneath him. Well, I'm not Grandfather. I have no hope of being a tenth as good as he was. So I've only got doing things my way left, and Ikenna would absolutely be looking to negotiate a deal with a criminal boss if it was advantageous. Besides, I think at the specter of Grandfather's memory and its disapproval that tries to lambaste me, Edryssa is no different from the Tribunal, or the Blood Emperor, or even the Khanaian royals at this point. Those three have blood on their hands and are neck-deep in morally questionable choices.

"What do you want from me, girl?" Edryssa asks me frankly.

She's cut straight through the bullshit, so I do too. "Enough weapons to go to war, a stockpile of tactical tech, and bodies." Edryssa practically owns the black market trade. Nothing gets passed under the table without Edryssa knowing about it and getting her cut, so my request for the first two things should be easy. As for the last thing, I've already noted the small army kept on retainer. I want use of those men and women when the time comes.

Edryssa blinks. The only indication that my request truly stuns her. Then, the ghost of a smile plays about her full lips, which I *know* have tempted countless men into damning themselves. "What are you planning, Mini Amari? The full of it. I want to know exactly who I'm doing business with and what business exactly I'm doing before I, *perhaps*, begin to entertain such a large request."

"Ikenna." The word of caution comes from Reed. He's stepped up to my side and holds himself stiff. He and I have had the argument about approaching Edryssa no less than five times. He's of Grandfather's type of thinking. But the team took a vote, and his opinion lost.

I grind my teeth and try not to give Reed an annoyed look. The eight of us are here as a single entity, and the team needs to appear as a strong unit.

Edryssa picks up on what's between us all the same. Her knowing eyes swish from me to the man at my side who can't just fall the fuck back and stay quiet until we get out of here. Edryssa rises from the settee and walks to where we stand shoulder to shoulder. She halts directly in front of Reed. Not me. "Darius Reed." She says his full name as she sizes him up. "Half Mareenian, half Khanaian, from the file I've got on you, and one hundred percent Verne Amari's mentee, I see."

Reed stiffens more—if that's even possible.

She tuts. "You darken my city. You attack my people. You demand I grant you an audience. I graciously do it, and you have the audacity to further pile on the insults and look down upon me from your supposedly moral high ground in my own damn home?" When she finishes, her glistening black lips curl back in a snarl that she doesn't try to contort into anything except savagery. "My people and I may not be able to kill all your crew before you wipe us out, but I bet if we focus our efforts on *one* of you, we could rid this world of *one* rude, pompous dick before we went down."

"Would you really relinquish your life and your people's lives to make a point?" I ask tightly while wanting to jab Reed in the throat.

Edryssa's laugh is husky. Nearly an incensed purr. "Maybe. I'm petty."

Ugh! Damn Reed to a hellpit. He's purposely trying to sabotage my efforts here. I curtail the burning desire to *stab* him in the throat for it.

And still, I say to Edryssa, making sure she's aware: "I'm petty as fuck too. Which means you can focus all the guns you've got on this"—I hike my thumb at Reed—"admittedly pompous dick. But also, he's one of my people, so know it'd be a wasted effort. He'd live. I'd make sure of it. And you and your people would still be dead. So forget about him, and let's keep this conversation between us women, eh?" Then, I add quickly, to achieve that desire and get her back on the track I want her on, "I came here because I want the Blood Emperor dead. As everybody on the Minor Continent should want. As *you* should want because while the Minor Continent's current ruling forces feel you're too much of a hassle to oust from controlling Lusian, the Blood Emperor doesn't feel the same. His endgame will be complete dominion over all incorporated and unincorporated territories on the continent—which includes this city, if that isn't clear. Which gives you and me a shared interest. I intend to follow in my grandfather's footsteps and go after the Blood Emperor. This time around, an Amari *will* end him. But like your intel apprised you, I'm wanted by my government, so I have no one but these few to aid me when I do. And while I and my crew have been trained extraordinarily well, we don't have the juice to go against the Blood Emperor and win without the backing of some type of army." Even Grandfather had that. If I can convince Edryssa to lend me the private corps she's got, it won't be near a large enough force, but it'll be a start. Grandfather's old allies among the western Microstates we've petitioned have been either ageist pricks convinced a displaced squad of "children"—no matter my blood-gift—can't topple the Blood Emperor, or flat-out cowards and fools who think they can avoid Nkosi laying siege to their states altogether if they follow Khanai's lead and yield to the Empire up front.

Which is how a syndicate boss has become part of my grand, quickly crumbling-to-shit plans.

Full shock colors Edryssa's face as her focus sharpens on me. The faces of Bastien and every guard in the room mirror their boss's expression. "I—" Edryssa snaps her mouth shut. I should get an award; I've rendered the great Lady of Lusian and the fearsome Cyphir Syndicate speechless. "I've changed my mind," Edryssa says when she finally strings together words. "You *are* a lot like him. Your methods might differ, but you've got his hubris in stars. His balls too." She makes a show of study-ing her long nails, which are painted black, of course, and filed so they almost resemble talons. "If I agree to aid you, what will you give me?

"What *can* you give me?"

You get to keep your prized city. It should be enough, I want to snap. But, as Grandfather taught me, that's not how the game is played—and it doesn't matter if you're playing it with a formally recognized states-man or a crime boss.

"Name your price in credits," I say. "I'll transfer them immediately."

The Lady of Lusian's answer is throaty laughter. "Did you know that this very morning, the price your Tribunal has on your heads quadrupled? For you, sweet dear, it's shot up to twelve billion cred-its. For the Rossi heir, it's ten. For the other fucks with you, five bil-lion a kill. If I were after credits," she says flatly, "you would've arrived at this meet staring down three hundred of my best marksmen, and your brains would already be splattered against my walls." She shuffles forward a fraction, giving me air kisses on both cheeks. "Perhaps the number would've been a tad overkill, but you sons of whores *are* Prae-torians. I didn't rise to be Lady of the Cyphir Syndicate by leaving room for error. When I want someone dead, I make a way for them to be dead. And when I want money, I get money." More sultry laughter floats behind that last statement, but her gray eyes stab into me like pitiless blades.

I keep my posture loose and bored at the smooth threat she deliv-ers. The bitch is definitely trying to goad me here—an attempt, with-out doubt, to one-up me after my earlier promise of a swift demise if she struck at Reed. However, I don't rise; the best way to deliver a *fuck you* back to someone like this is to simply not react. So I say nothing. Only sneer, as if whatever attack she thinks she can martial is of no consequence to me.

Edryssa's black-painted lips purse into a line of irritation.

I win.

I smile, smug, and toss dramatic air kisses at her cheeks to drive my victory home.

Her irritation magnifies.

Edryssa and I are kindred spirits, really. It's clear she isn't used to losing at these games and that she's the sort of woman who is used to being the biggest, baddest, pettiest bitch around. *Too bad.* She can have the crown back after I vacate her city.

I almost want to cackle at her puckered lips, which haven't yet smoothed themselves out, but that might push her a smidgen too far over the edge. I only want to keep the Lady of Lusian on her toes and continue to force her respect.

So instead, I say, cordial and courteous, "I thank you for the information. We actually didn't know the price on our heads has been hiked." I keep my face a smooth mask when I admit that truth, giving away nothing. But internally, my mind boggles at the gargantuan price tag. That kind of surge is going to be a damn pain in our asses. It's about to get harder to move through the Microstates while keeping a low profile, and it'll likely result in an uptick in the endless teams of idiot mercs and bounty hunters looking to track us down and collect the payoff.

Shit.

Shit.

Shit.

I curse myself for not anticipating it.

"What are you after, then, if not credits?" I ask Edryssa, nonplussed, playing the game.

But the Lady of Lusian returns me a knowing smile. "I admire women who claim beauty *and* cunning. What I want is something a lot more valuable, Ikenna Amari. If I aid you, I want to be able to step out of the shadows. I want me and Lusian to have a true seat at the table of Iludu powers. Whatever bounties any government has on my head, I want gone. I also want Lusian to be recognized as more than a criminal settlement that *thinks* itself a city within the cluster of Free Microstates that span the north. I want it recognized as a microstate itself, with me as its . . . I think I like the title of Lady-Sovereign."

I lose my cards face; I couldn't look *more* gobsmacked. "You're either joking or high. I can't give you any of that. I have zero authority to pull off what you're asking."

She bends toward me, her lips stopping a hairsbreadth from my left ear. "I think you underestimate yourself. Verne didn't foresee holding so much sway over the rest of the world and its workings when he first sought to thwart the Blood Emperor either. Yet, after he succeeded, that is precisely what happened. All of Iludu, save the Accacian Empire, worshipped him and lauded him and were ripe to hand him anything he requested. Especially if he couched it as being for the good of the Minor Continent and for the sake of holding off any renewed war by the Blood Emperor. Let's say you are more successful than even he was and you actually manage to kill Nkosi this time around. You'll be a goddess among men to the whole of the Minor Continent, perhaps even Accacia. It'll submit to whatever you ask of it, and then you will be able to give me what I seek."

This time, restraint goes out the window. I do cackle. "You're senile, old woman."

"I'm *experienced.* Aging and wisdom go hand in hand. Live long enough, see enough suns rise in the Iludu sky, and you, *young girl,* will get better wits about yourself too. You might even know the good fortune of becoming like me: forward thinking. But none of that is the point. What's pertinent for you to weigh here is if you don't hold that same belief about what influence you might come to yield, then really, dear, what do you have to lose by agreeing to an *old woman*'s delusional requests?"

Well, she's got a point there. It should be an easy assent on my part. And yet, I'm still given pause because I can't help the feeling that saying yes to Edryssa, even if she is insane as all fuck, is like saying yes to Hasani, the hellish god of the After. That I'd be unwittingly helping

Edryssa weave some unknown trap around me that she'll spring closed at an opportune time later.

Told you this was a terrible idea, I hear Reed quip in my mind.

I cut my eyes at him, and sure enough, the thought is plain on his face. Bastard.

I ignore him and the fact that, damn it, I'm seeing way too late that he's probably right. Not that it matters, though. Everything is moot until it isn't, so in for a penny . . .

"You have a deal," I tell the Lady of Lusian. We need Edryssa after failing to secure the support of any other microstate. Having the arsenal and the combatants to go after the Blood Emperor is all that matters. It's the *only* thing that matters. And I'll agree to hand Edryssa the whole shitting world—whether I'm capable of actually delivering on the bargain or not—if it gets me what I need to cleave the Blood Emperor's head from his neck.

Besides—if she tries to double-cross me, at that point I'll just do the same to her.

3

"TODAY WAS A HOOT!" DANNICA says after a swig of ale.

Haynes tips his bottle her way. "Most action we've seen in the last three months. I gotta tell you, I'm smitten with the Lady Edryssa. Boss Woman isn't a priggish ass like those fucks out west. And she called Reedsy-boy a hoity dick and threatened to hand our man his balls." He slaps his thighs, sniggering.

Caiman, who's sitting around the fire pit with us, shakes his head. "You pair are too gleeful for drama."

Haynes smirks. "I wouldn't expect a pampered prick like you to understand, War House Boy." It takes more than one snarky comment to get the big westerner riled up, so his words lack any real hostility. Haynes does, however, poke at Caiman a little more. "But those of us used to getting our hands dirty actually enjoy a little hard work."

Caiman rolls his eyes. "You're a real shithead."

Haynes shrugs. "Takes one to know one."

"I don't think I like you very much," Caiman tells him point-blank.

Haynes booms a laugh. "I don't think I care very much. We aren't here to be friends. We're here to achieve a shared goal. That's it."

The *here* in question, in the most literal sense, is a spacious safe house in Lusian. Given that the city is a haven for thieves, murderers, and mercs (as long as they're spending tons of credits within the zone that ultimately get pocketed by Edryssa), it's been a pretty secure spot to lie low while we lick our wounds and regroup from our prior spectacular failures to gather allies in the north.

"We shouldn't be *here* at all," Reed says curtly. In typical Reed fashion, he holds himself soldier-stiff as he strides onto the veranda and butts into a convo that didn't previously include him.

"Well, we are," I drawl, irritated that he's still harping on my decision to ally with a criminal.

"Not for much longer, *fortunately*." He folds arms corded with muscle across his broad chest and leans against one of the lounge chairs around the fire pit. He's changed into a short-sleeve, gray cotton shirt that clings to his upper body in a way that makes me order myself to stop ogling him and shift back to imagining collapsing his larynx. "*Your* business in this godsforsaken city is concluded," he says to me, making it super easy to obey the command. "In the morning, I'll start making preparations for us to move out," he says to everyone. I grit my teeth, but manage to hold my tongue. Until he shifts back to irritating me. "You had no right to promise Edryssa what you did, Amari," he just has to tack on. His tone is chock-full of a dress down, and *he* has no fucking right.

"I didn't give her anything—none of what I 'gave' matters!" I cry, my calm disintegrating. "I'm powerless! Let her think I'm not and can actually broker the ludicrous thing she asked for. Especially if it gets us what we need when nobody else will give us the time of day. So really, who gives a shit?"

"Who gives a shit? All those people who haven't committed to us . . . thus far," Reed says tightly. "None of Legatus Amari's former allies have opted to aid us *thus far*. But we've only visited the far north's western powers. We've yet to visit the Eastern Microstates, and how do you think they'll take this new union you've just formed? As usual, you jumped the gun and are being . . . well, *you*. You're so thickheaded and brash at times, I swear to the Republic." He takes a deep breath. "Edryssa might be cracked in her request, but not for the reason you've figured. She was spot-on about one thing: if you do accomplish what your grandfather didn't—actually killing the Blood Emperor—every other power in the world, save Mareen, maybe, because it'll still likely be gunning to terminate us all, will bend to whatever you ask of it. And Edryssa doesn't strike me as the type of women who'd easily let you slip out of a deal. Does she seem like it to you?"

"I—" Well . . . no, she doesn't. But I refuse to admit that to Reed. "What does it matter if I never have the *chance* to defeat Nkosi?" I counter instead. "Without an army, *none of this matters*," I remind him. "Yes. If I pull things off, I'll have a lot of power. But I need to get there first! Chiefly, I need a sure path to kill a particularly hard-to-kill bastard. What Edryssa wants is a problem for later. Much later."

Reed rubs his forehead. It's a simple gesture that shows he's tired, and for some reason, it pisses me off further.

"Fuck you and your judgment," I snarl. "We voted. I didn't decide this course alone. Why am I the only one getting shit for it?" Before I know it, I'm out of my seat and standing an inch away from him. I'm fuming for some inexplicable reason, and my hands are clenched at my sides . . .

Well, actually, no.

The reason isn't inexplicable. Deep down, I know why I'm so heated. It isn't about Edryssa, or Reed questioning my choice to make this deal with her. This is about Khanai. About the bullshit Reed pulled there. About the fact that after I saved his ass, he had the gall to question if I was a monster. Had the gall to face me down and prepare to try to exterminate me like I was some creature unfit to live. Then, the ass questioned my loyalty. My allegiance. "Fuck. You," I spit out again, glaring at him.

"You need to get it together," he snaps back. "This isn't the time or the place for you to spin out of control over . . . over . . ."

"We *both* know what the god-shitting-hell it's really over!" I shout. "And *you* know it's warranted. It's why you can't even finish that sentence, Reed."

A thick vein pops out of the right side of his neck. It cuts savagely through the Republic's four-pointed star that's inked on his skin, which has bronzed under the far north's long days. "I apologized, and I'm here with you. As part of *your* team. Can that be enough for now? Can we quash it for now? We have an op. An enormous fucking one. With the literal world riding on it. Please step outside of yourself for one second, Amari, and focus on the bigger picture."

I open my mouth. Then snap it shut. I have enough presence of mind to know whatever I say right in this moment is going to hurtle things from bad to worse.

Haynes clears his throat, throwing Reed a pleading look.

When Reed simply returns him an immovable, above-reproach one back, it's Dannica who hops up and wedges herself between Reed and me. She throws her arms out and forces us both to take a step back from each other. "Maybe this *is* the time and place. We can't keep on like this. The two of you can't keep dancing around this issue." She turns to Reed. "It's huge, dude. What you did was super screwed up, and it's not something that can just be pushed aside 'for the op.' There's always an op. More important, Ikenna's human. And you questioned that humanity. So it isn't fair to expect her to just get over it. I wouldn't just get over it. I'd be as massively pissed as she is and I'd remain her level of pissed until we hashed it out. Which you two haven't done.

"So *do* it."

After ripping into him, she swivels to me. "And after you two do it, *then* Reed becomes right. You need to drop it, Kenna. For good. If you want him here and with us on this op. We need to be functioning as a true team. A tight unit. A family—how Gamma always does things. It's how we've always gotten through the toughest ops. It's how we succeed when the fight is stacked all the way against us."

"Dannica is speaking truth," Haynes says from his seat.

Of course she is. But I'm not in the mood for truth right now. Neither is Reed—he and I continue to glare at each other.

Dannica throws up her hands. "You two are insufferable. If you want it to come to the alternative and can't be sensible adults about things, fine." She spins away from us and faces the rest of the squad around the fire pit. "We vote on the matter," she says to Haynes, Caiman, Greysen, Liim, and Dane. "Like we've done with everything else thus far. Hands for Kenna and Darius getting their shit together."

Caiman flashes me a shit-eating grin. "Oh, this is too good. A-plus amusement, Amari."

He gets served my I'm-about-to-stab-you glower for that remark.

He chuckles and shoots his hand in the air—his middle finger raised to me to emphasize his vote. "What Dannica says is legitimate, though," he says, shifting into seriousness. "We do need to be functioning more as a close-knit unit from here on out. The task—all the tasks—before us are no less than insurmountable. And they're too damn important."

Greysen's hand goes into the air behind Caiman's. Haynes gives Reed a stubborn, inflexible look of his own as he raises his hand too. Liim and Dane vote the same way as the others, the two Alphas looking mostly impassive at, albeit exasperated by, our drama.

With the vote having been cast, Dannica turns back to Reed and me wearing one of her saccharine-sweet smiles, her violet eyes twinkling with smugness. "You two don't have a choice." She points to the inside of the safe house. "Go fix your shit."

REED AND I stand on opposite sides of the great room, gaping at each other, looking lost.

Despite our face-off outside among the group, I'm pretty sure neither of us has any idea what to say now that we're alone with the directive to *fix our shit*.

So we simply keep staring in silence.

The ridiculous behavior makes my lips—damn them—twitch at a
memory I absolutely should not be recalling. But I can't curb the mad-
ness, because the last time we mirrored this stance plays out in vivid,
loud clarity in my mind. Instead of being in Lusian, I see the two of
us back in Mareen, in the subterranean level of the compound, during
the trials. I see me on one side of the open doorway to my transient
quarters, him on the other, and we gawk at each other after unwittingly
screwing the night before. I want to yell in frustration at the memory
even while laughing myself dead because that previous foolishness is
part of the reason we stand here looking like bigger morons now.

I keep the laughter and the screaming locked away, though. It ends
up being Reed who utters sound first when he asks: "How do we get on
the same page, Amari? I apologized and that isn't good enough for you,
so tell me what it is you need from me to make it right."

"Nothing," I say and make sure I articulate every syllable so it's
clear. "I don't need *anything* from you."

He drags in a breath, pinching his nose. My treacherous lips twitch
again, this time almost twisting into a smile, because I'm pretty sure he
did that same exact thing while being exasperated with me for something while I was his neo and he was my transition officer during the
trials.

"You aren't going to make this easy, are you?"

I fold my arms across my chest, not giving any ground. "Absolutely
not."

Another inhale. "Can we at least try to interact like reasonable
adults?"

My answer is more staring.

"All right, Amari. You win because Dannica smacked me upside the head with a serious truth. We do need to be operating as a tighter team. I'm sure our dysfunction is part of the reason we've been botching things so egregiously thus far. So I'll ask again: What do you want me to do? Grovel?"

"Finally, we get somewhere," I say.

"Are you serious—"

"All of the priggish, sanctimonious bullshit is out of your tone when we talk about this, and that's a good start," I say, cutting him off. "But I'm not quite done being a bitch, because you also deserve for this to be as hard as I can make it. You don't get to be disgusted with me and then *not* make groveling a part of your fucking apology. So, yes, please grovel, Reed. You sure as shit don't get absolution without it."

His jawline flexes, the tanned skin covering it pulling sharply against its proud angles. I expect a lecture about how I'm stubborn, or immature, or arrogant, or rash, or all four of those things he's called me before. What I don't expect is for him to cross the room and come near enough to touch me. He reaches out a hand, and I stiffen. He does as well and tucks his hand tight to his side. I can't describe the look he gives me as anything other than tortured, which is bizarre. "I'm an idiot," he says. The truth, but also bizarre to hear him say it aloud. "An idiot who thought it'd be better to leave things as they were, with a sizable distance between us, instead of making things more convoluted by explaining my actions in Khanai in depth.

"But what you believe were my reasons is wrong."

"Meaning?" I grind out, not liking one bit this vulnerable territory things are veering toward.

He shakes his head. "Amari, I wasn't thinking—"

"Don't bullshit me!"

"I'm not. I *wasn't* thinking that about you."

I bark out a laugh. "I never figured you the type to sink low enough to need to retcon shit." I take a step closer to him, almost pressing us together.

"What do you mean?"

"I mean you're a liar. It was written all over your face: You were about to *kill* me. Or at least try. You stood there and told everyone else to board the jet so you could. You weren't going to leave me behind in Khanai. Not the girl who you saw to be blood-gifted. To have the detested gift of the enemy. To be heinous and a monster herself. And who—"

His mouth crashes into mine. I startle, confused and sure I've been flung into some kind of warped alternate dimension because *what the hell?* I plant my hands on Reed's chest to shove him away. But he closes his hands on my waist—holding tight, fitting perfectly into my curves, his fingers brushing the top of my ass—and hauls me closer, crushing me to him and deepening the kiss. My treacherous body molds against him, and then it throws itself wholeheartedly into the kiss, returning his blitz attack that has successfully knocked me off-kilter. Somehow I pull away instead of grinding myself into him further, cobbling together a modicum of sense and remembering that I'm furious. I tell myself that my fury is the only reason I'm heaving and breathless when I break us apart. I glare at Reed, damning him to all the hellpits that exist in my head. I want to stab him after that kiss. For making me react like I did to it. For making desire for him flare in me after what he did in Khanai.

I wipe a rough hand against the back of my mouth. "You hate that you're still lusting after me, don't you? That's why you were really so bent out of shape in Khanai. It wasn't just disgust with me. It was disgust with yourself. For still wanting me. For still wanting to fuck me." Nausea roils in my gut as I spit out the truth. I'm sick at him, and I'm sick at myself. Then, there's the visceral hurt, as knifing as I felt in Khanai, at his response to me. To knowing all of me. Everything I fully am.

Reed reaches a hand between us, and that hurt quadruples. I brace for him to nudge me away. But his hand lands on my right shoulder. Then it moves, almost nervously and ever so carefully, to cup my cheek.

"None of that is what I was feeling or thinking, you insufferable woman. Yes, I was shocked as hell to see that you were blood-gifted. Yes, it sent me reeling and questioning everything I thought I knew about you—and myself. But disgust was never anything I was feeling. Dis*trust*, yes. Betrayed, yes. Terror, fuck yes, because it was gods-shitting frightening to see what you can do. But not disgust. Not once. Do you want to know what I actually felt? What I couldn't stop thinking? It was that more than anything, I was terrified *for you and for myself*. I was terrified for us as a doomed pair. Because you've got one thing right: I was prepared to kill you before flying home. I stood in front of you and got my shit together enough to be able to do that. Because it was my duty, and according to everything I've been taught and that I know to be true, it should've been the necessary thing to do. The only thing to do because of what you are.

"But still . . ." He takes a deep breath and pauses. "I stood there and struggled with it. I was going to do it—I won't shit about that because you deserve the whole truth. But it was never because I was disgusted by you. I was going to do what duty called for me to do, what I thought was necessary. I hate that this went through my mind, but I thought you might be on the side of the enemy, and it was either spare you or help damn our country and the rest of the world. Help make more children, like myself once, orphans when the Blood Emperor had you on his side and ripped through the Minor Continent on his second War of Aggression. So, yeah—I was going to kill you. But it was also going to kill me when I did it. It was already killing me just thinking about it and mustering the resolve. Because I . . ."

"Because you what?" I say it so quiet, I'm unsure if he hears.

"You know why."

"I'm not sure I know anything," I say hoarsely.

"Back in Khanai you told me to get my ass on the jet home you procured for me. You didn't say for the *team*. You specifically said for *me*. I know because I've replayed what went down between us hundreds of times in my head since it happened. Why was that so important? For you to get me, specifically, home?" He says this all as a challenge instead of giving me a straight answer.

"This isn't about me explaining my actions. It's about you."

"Wrong, Amari. It's about both of us. It's about me *and* you."

There is no me and *you,* I almost say to be ornery, but know it's an utter lie. One that tastes like acid on my tongue—so unlike his tongue, which had just been in my mouth—and sears my throat when I try to spit it out. "You got me home off the mountain," I say lamely. "I owed you a debt. I was repaying it."

Reed leans into me and dips his head down as if to kiss me again. Yet, he doesn't. Instead, he lets his lips hover a fraction from mine, never sealing the distance, and I can't decide if it's a relief or one more maddening thing in a long list of maddening, confusing offenses.

If I crane my neck just so, I could end this confusion.

My lips tingle with the thought and the urge to follow through. I gnash my teeth instead, refraining from doing what my witless body wants.

"Now you are bullshitting me," Reed says. When he speaks, his lips finally, blessedly brush against mine—though it's too fleeting, too tempered, and too damn featherlight.

I have no idea what to say to his accusation. I have no idea what he wants me to say. I'm not even sure I know words at this point . . .

Moreover, how the hell did the tables get turned on me? How did this become my interrogation as much as it was his?

It's about both of us.

It's about me and *you.*

I drag in a breath. I think about taking a step back. Several steps back. But doing that feels like admitting defeat, retreating, and letting Reed win at something—what, I'm not sure—but I refuse to do any of those things. Also, I can't shake the feeling that Reed and I are on the precipice of something that'll fundamentally shift what we are to each other. I can't quite discern if it's something disastrous or something magnificent, but I am hit with a deep-seated knowing that if I take those steps back, I'm soundly walking away from whatever the impending change is. Furthermore, I've lost my damn mind, apparently, because I find I don't want to move an inch. I can't shake the reckless, intoxicating urge to want to know where things will lead if I stay planted. If I stand my ground with Reed and face whatever has existed between us since the very start—since my bar fight with Radson, if I'm being honest.

If I lean *in*.

"Fuck it," Reed says against my lips. He lays his left hand against my cheek, cradling my face in his palms, and touches his forehead to mine. "Fuck it all." He kisses me again. He pours *everything* into it when he does, sucking oxygen from the room. He pours the shit in Khanai into it; he takes the fear and resistance to killing me he claims he had and shapes that into feelings that pass from him to me—big, life-altering, existence-upending feelings. I'm left breathless with my heart smashing against my chest.

Reed rears back to stare in my eyes as he tells me: "Even though I was prepared to do whatever needed to be done, all I wanted to do from the time I saw you safe and whole in Khanai when you descended the keep's steps, and then even more so after you freed us from pending execution, was drag you close and just revel in this." He reinitiates the kiss. And it's nothing like how he's kissed me before. It's urgent and scorching, yet slow and tender and intimate and gentle—so freaking gentle. Like I'm the most fragile, precious thing in the cosmos, which he almost lost, and he's handling it from here on out with extreme care. My eyes close then cross behind my lids. My toes curl in my boots as I embarrassingly melt against him. Before I'm aware of them doing so, my arms encircle his neck. They pull his head down more, soldering our lips together as tight as they can fit.

We stay like that for a long time with Reed pouring the apology and explanation he verbalized into the kiss, and me accepting it, welcoming it, and devouring it. I drink in everything he gives me, and I never want it to cease. But I do pause for a second to admit something vital. "To be honest, this is all I wanted to do to you after Khanai too. Though, I was prepared to murder you as well if you tried to come for me."

He huffs a laugh that vibrates against my mouth, still pressed to his. And, regrettably, because we need to have a different sort of convo now, I finally do step back. "So where does this leave us?" I ask evenly, trying to resurrect my emotional shields, which lie in shreds.

Reed clears his throat. A light pink tints his cheeks. I blink, not believing what I glimpse. Is he—no way am I seeing a blush on Darius Reed.

"I don't know." Reed's soft voice cuts into my astonishment. "I've never done something like this before."

I snort—which isn't the most attractive or mature reaction. But everything about this moment is surreal and bewildering and my brain has pseudo-short-circuited. "That makes two of us," I say, like an adult who can use words.

Reed's thumb traces a line along my chin. "So we figure it out as we go. I gather that's about all we can do from here because there certainly is no going back."

"No," I agree. "There certainly isn't." Then I grumble, "This is all Dannica's fault."

Reed bobs his head. "KaDiya meddles too damn much." Then, because he's Reed, he says, "We should probably set some type of operating protocol. You know, since we'll be interacting in this, um, new capacity." He blushes again. "And a professional one too." He falls quiet for a moment, as if in deep and discomfited thought about what that *protocol* should be. When he clears his throat, pink lingering on his cheeks, a smile tugs at my lips because I'm pretty sure this is the first time I've seen Reed exude anything other than absolute confidence. I mean, the man calls me arrogant, but Darius "the Great Protégé" Reed isn't too far behind.

Done with the soft stuff and shifting back to wiseass Ikenna, I give him an exaggerated wave of my hand, laughing at him, albeit good-naturedly. "You really can't help yourself, can you?"

He switches back to being incredulous about 90 percent of the shit I say. He stacks his spine and draws himself up tall. "Order and defined rules of decorum are always necessary for people like us. We're soldiers first. And now, we're also politicians of a sort. Diplomats, at least. It's about more than me and you. We have an entire team with us. It's too easy for waters to get muddy and to fuck things up without rules and stringent protocols. We can't run the risk of our personal stuff endangering other people's lives. Especially not with the fights we've decided to pick."

"That's the most romantic thing I've ever heard."

"Ikenna—"

"No, you're right," I tell him, finally growing serious. Yet I can't help throwing him one last cheeky grin before I have to pivot all the way into business mode. "It's just so much fun giving you a hard time. And as grovels go, you did a decent job, by the way." I tack on an audacious wink. He huffs another laugh.

Then we turn to the boring stuff and start hammering out how to draw hard lines between *Ikenna and Darius*, as we explore this thing between us that has my chest feeling pathetically light, and *Amari and Reed*—the soldiers and leaders we need to function as within our larger rogue cohort to pull everybody alive through what's looming ahead.

I don't know which one is going to be harder.

4

LIKE SHE'S ONE OF THE hardass academy instructors inspecting us to see if we pass muster, Dannica gives us a once-over when we walk back outside. Whatever she observes makes her snap a nod of approval our way. "Good. You made up." Then a wicked smile curves her face. "Though I did expect you to take longer. Don't tell me you were quick on the trigger, Reed? How *rude* to do our girl like that!"

"*Dannica*," Reed growls in annoyance beside me.

She throws him an impudent wink from her lounger in front of the fire pit.

Haynes's laughter roars around the enclosed courtyard. Beyond the veranda sits a rock garden with a retractable star roof for constellation viewing and 360 holovid walls reflecting the deceptively tranquil, shining sands of the Silver Desert in the far south. The Wonder of Iludu in massive panorama form was Dannica's choice for our viewing pleasure because my cohort sister is a jerk who thinks she's witty. The

Silver Desert and its Trinity Pyramids supposedly mark the site where the Pantheon first entered and then got cast off Iludu.

"*Maybe we should start heaping reverence upon the gods since our Kenna-boo is sort of like one of them. We wouldn't want to get smited,*" the heifer had said after telling the wall which visuals to project, and we'd all looked at her like she was sloshed off something highly illegal that soared you past boosters.

"I thought Gamma had a nonfraternizing policy," Haynes says to Reed while sporting a shit-eating grin.

"Good thing we're no longer really Gamma," I say before Reed deigns a response I'm sure he'll flub.

Haynes hoots louder. "Touché, Amari. Bang up thinking, by the way. I knew you were my kind of girl the first day I met you." He laces his big hands behind his head and leans back on the hind legs of his chair.

"I hope you fall," Reed mutters.

Haynes cracks his knuckles, dripping conceit. "With my impeccable athleticism? Not a chance, my good man. But you, oh dignified and mighty cohort lead, have definitely fallen—*plummeted*—so, so, *so* far from that saintly grace you like to nudge on the rest of us."

I snort. I know Haynes is only ribbing Reed, like the asshat often does, but it irks me that Reed's getting tossed a heap of crap for merely being human.

"Reed hasn't fallen from shit," I deadpan. "Case in point: our boy remains too noble to kick that chair and circumvent your *athleticism* . . .

"But I'm not."

I move blood-gifted quick—swifter than the speed his supposedly impeccable athleticism and biochip-enhanced reflexes afford him. One second Haynes is still cackling and the next a stupefied expression slams onto his face as he crashes to the floor.

Dannica howls. "You had that coming. Me, I stopped while I was ahead. Kenna is no doubt the type of woman who'll relieve you of your balls for messing with her man."

"I—" I have no idea how to respond to Dannica's bald statement, so I just don't. Besides, if I do, I'll only give my soon-to-get-punched cohort sister and brother more ammunition to keep up the bit. I'd prefer to sever their inanity, permanently.

To that end, I stare down venomously sweet at Haynes as he's sprawled on the gray slate. "Whatever is or isn't going on, or is starting up, *or whatever*, between me and Reed isn't your concern."

Haynes glares at me and then starts guffawing all over again because apparently he's got a death wish. While speeding toward his early demise, he leaps to his feet, rights the seat, and plops back in it. "I like your thinking *and* your style."

"Gods, you are such a dickhead! Do you ever let up?" I ask, half serious and half reeled into his bullshit, fighting a grin.

He blows me a kiss from the chair. "Nope. This gig will get too dark and depressing otherwise. Gotta hold on to joy some kind of way, girl."

I dip my head, conceding the point.

"Speaking of holding on to positivity," Haynes says, pulling on a serious air so quickly I almost catch whiplash, "being on Gamma squad, what it was, what it stood for, calling it that, was one of those joys-among-the-muck sort of things. If we aren't calling ourselves Gamma anymore, at least for the time being, can we get a different name?"

"I'd actually like a name too," Dannica says.

"Me too," Greysen, seated across from Dannica and Haynes, chimes in a little awkwardly. "I mean . . . I wasn't a part of Gamma before, but I agree about the name thing. I want a squad name. Having one has kind of been engraved in us since we were cadets at Krashen Academy, and it feels weird not to have one, even if we've technically temporarily broken from Mareen."

"We should have a formal name. It's good for camaraderie and forging bonds and all that," Caiman expresses from beside his childhood friend. "The piss-fuck Tribunal at least got that part right when designing the system."

Liim grimaces at Caiman's lambasting of the Tribunal, despite having chosen to go rogue with us. However, he also snaps off an affirmative salute to the new Rossi War House head, the Tribune of the Republic whom the Praetorians in Alpha have historically and traditionally always been most loyal to, above all the others, signaling that Caiman has his support and his blaster in whatever he thinks is best. Dane, who shares Liim's features of light eyes and painfully porcelain skin—hallowed traits of the Republic and Alpha Cohort—serves Caiman a salute of allegiance too. Yet, to the latter's credit, no dumb grimace precedes it.

"It's so neat we're all aligned!" Dannica gushes. Haynes laughs. "So what'll it be?"

For some reason, she and everybody else in the courtyard turn to me. "What the fuck are you looking at me for?" I flap my hands at them. "You all came up with us needing a formal name. Everybody knows things like formality and protocol can pretty much kiss my ass."

Reed coughs. "Yes, we know, Amari." I swivel to him, prepared to do battle over that quip, even though I'm the one who opened the door, but there's no disparagement cast my way. There's only a jesting spark to his blue gaze and a mirthful curl to his lips. Seeing that particular look on him gobsmacks me more. It's . . . peculiar and unusual and something inside me goes ridiculously mushy and light at it. That something decides it likes the look on Reed and wants to see it turned my way more often. It's similar to how I've seen him with Dannica and Haynes. Casual. Relaxed. Easy and friendly. *Intimate.* I cock my head his way as if to acknowledge that look, make it clear I know what it means, and then return a look that says, *So we're really doing this, huh?*

Reed doesn't miss a beat. He picks up on everything the subtle motion projects and inclines his head back to me, reaffirming what we decided inside the house. *Yeah, we are.* His eyes keep dancing. His mouth keeps its sportive curl.

My chest tightens, recognizing a thread of a nascent bond beginning to form between us. It's tenuous and fragile and could probably—will probably—snap at any moment, given who he is and who I am and the fact that we can't seem to coexist without wanting to strangle each other. But for the briefest of moments, I find myself considering what things might look like between Reed and me if the fledgling bond stays in place. If instead of eventually fracturing, it strengthens, grows, takes firmer roots.

Yet another thing I don't have a name for kicks up in my chest at the thought.

I scowl. Reed gives me a quizzical look. I clear my throat, not knowing what I'm ready to communicate back. So I let it ride.

I turn from him and speak to our group. "We'll never have a name if I've gotta come up with one," I let the crew know. "I'm no good at stuff like that. If we're kicking ass, I've got you. With hyperintellectual stuff, somebody else is going to have to steer."

"Give her a couple of days to think on it. She'll come up with suggestions," Reed declares.

"I could have a year; the answer would be the same," I inform him after he's talked over me. "But *you* can take a couple of days to think on it and come up with suggestions since we're speaking for folks."

"It isn't like that," Reed returns carefully. "Can you trust me to explain later?"

There's a weight to the request that halts me from demanding he explain himself right then. One of the rules we decided on is to do better discerning the talks (and disagreements) we need to have in front of everyone and the ones we don't. "Okay," I say, trying out the new way.

"Thank you," Reed says as Caiman curses up a streak.

When I turn to Caiman, he's reading something on his Comm Unit, expression carefully unreadable. "What is it?" I ask.

He lifts gold eyes to meet mine. "It's about the increased bounty Edryssa mentioned. I put out feelers to gather details on when it was upped and compile a list of fresh teams looking to claim it. You won't like one of the answers I've obtained." He grimaces and passes me an odd look that I'd describe as gentle if it were between anybody other than him and me. It's wholly unnerving when I have no clue what he's referring to.

"What won't I like?" I say and brace for whatever it is.

"The name attached to the order."

"Spill it, Caiman."

His weird look remains. "Rhysien . . ." he says. "Selene Rhysien, not *Sutton* Rhysien, is the person on record as issuing the exorbitant bounty. More importantly, it doesn't replace the Tribunal's bounty; it's an independent one that's backed separately by Rhysien War House's treasuries. It seems Edryssa conveniently left that tidbit out for us to discover ourselves," Caiman adds darkly.

"Come again?" I say, a cold fury dousing me at merely hearing Selene's name.

Caiman projects what he'd been viewing on his Comm onto the courtyard wall beside him. I scan it and recognize it's a capture-or-kill missive bearing Rhysien War House's seal. All our names are on it, along with our pictures and the credits each of us is worth. The latter aligns with precisely the numbers Edryssa quoted. At the bottom of the missive, Selene Rhysien is the name that's signed as the payer who'll verify fulfillment.

Reading her name there makes the rage triple. Selene killed my grandfather, which means I will always despise her and want her dead. However, some part of me clings to the possibility that the girl I called my sister for eleven years hadn't been informed that the legacy pendant she gave me, saying I was her family, was an agent to poison me. Selene could've believed she was gifting me a simple necklace. That it was made of iridium metal could've been orchestrated by Sutton, her father, behind her back. Otherwise, *how*? How could she hand it to me? How could she so readily and so easily be party to the harm the Tribunal intended for me? Yet, I see her signature on the bounty, plain as day. It emphasizes what she likely knew, makes every facet of her deceit glass clear. If I had any doubts in my mind before, I have zero left. How could she *not* know? How could she not be 100 percent apprised of and involved with *all* of Sutton's schemes if she's still doing his dirty work?

My hands clench into fists. "Sutton, specifically, wants us, *me*, hunted down and dead." I start speaking out loud what we've all been trained well enough to gather from a separate bounty. As I continue, I refuse to allow my voice to sound anything except unaffected and even. *I will not show the fresh gouge that's been inflicted.* "Further, he wants his War House to receive glory for what the greater Tribunal has been failing at. That's why there's a second bounty. Selene's name is on it because he's using me for another test of her loyalty to him." *A test that she's capitulated to, again.* The rage boils over, scorches my veins, and I'm unsure which I'm angry about more: the proof of Selene's all-encompassing duplicity or the fact that she's finally let her father break her down and is becoming more and more his puppet.

I so badly want to march to the wall where the missive is displayed. Smash my fist into Selene's name. It's not her face, but I need to hit something. Yet I keep my hands tight to my sides. I cannot be that much of a mess in front of the squad. Look as gutted as I feel. Seem that weak. But *godsdamned* if several daggers, one for each of the years of our supposed friendship, don't bury savagely into my chest. Like they do every time I think about Selene, pangs of anguish tear through me.

I stand in the middle of the courtyard fighting not to vibrate with dual rage and grief. But the attempt doesn't matter. The team glimpses what I try to conceal anyway. I see it in Dannica's, Haynes's, and Reed's sympathetic stares. In Caiman's and Greysen's winces. In Liim's and Dane's scrubbed expressions.

No use pretending I'm unbothered anymore. "I'm going to my room for the night. You know where to find me if something important comes up," I mutter and stalk off. I hear Reed and Caiman call my name. I don't turn around. I slip inside, away from everybody, so I can stop holding my shit even remotely together and enjoy the freedom to be a mess, if only for a bit. Yes, it's sloppy. Yes, it's immature. Yes, I need to do better if I wish to lead here.

But I head upstairs and ignore what's sensible anyhow.

Selene was my sister; she betrayed me on multiple fronts. It *hurts*.

5

I ENTER THE SUITE I'VE been using and make a beeline for its most important fixture: a well-stocked wet bar in the entry salon. I don't aim to get shit-faced, in case something unexpected pops off. I do really, really, *really* need a drink—or three—to take the edge off, however.

I scan the numerous decanters resting on the marble countertop that's the same dark purple as the floors. I'm thoroughly irritated when I remember there's no whiskey. Well, there's none with the light amber hue of Mareenian whiskey, which is the only whiskey worth drinking or that's worthy of the name. I refuse to choke down whiskey grown, distilled, and aged anywhere else in the world a second time in less than two days. Lamenting the lack of good liquor, and making a note to procure some, I settle for Lytheian rum. It's not nearly as blissful, but it's still pretty decent stuff. I pour myself two glasses, being good and skipping a third. Afterward, I leave the rest of the decanter on the wet bar, because I know myself, and walk to the adjoining bedroom.

I collapse onto the bed and down one of the glasses. The boosters in the rum don't hit quite like the ones in Mareenian whiskey, but they pack their own patented dropkick, and it's glorious. I allow myself to revel in the suspended moment of numbness and induced ecstasy. For a precious second, *nothing* is wrong and *nothing* matters; I get to let it *all* go—Selene's betrayal, Grandfather's death, Zayne dying on the mountain, losing the Gyidis, being on the run from Mareen, none of Grandfather's allies choosing to aid us so far, my squad possibly facing our impending demise when we confront the Blood Emperor—every burden I have evaporates. The only thing left behind is the goofy smile on my face as I sway on the cloud-soft mattress. I wait until the wonderful feeling is almost gone—my system nearly having purged it and cleared it out—then I toss back the second drink.

Before I know it, the decanter I left on the bar is in my hand and I'm lounging on the bed taking a swig directly from it because *fuck it*. I really don't want to deal with reality, or the unknown, or fears, or grief, anymore today. I'll go back to being mature Ikenna who keeps her shit together in the morning. I should be allowed a night to unravel. Hell, I should be allowed *several* nights to unravel, given everything. But a night is all I can reasonably excuse.

I hiss and glare at the decanter I've drained to half empty, thinking about hurling it across the room. "Stupid, fucking rum," I mumble. I shake the decanter. "You're not doing your job," I growl. "I shouldn't still be re-drowning in all the shit I don't want to think about. You're supposed to wipe it clean for an extended period." *And I also shouldn't be talking to a piece of glass, so maybe the rum is doing its job? And maybe I'm just too much of a mess to be helped.* Stubborn and intent on snatching the prolonged numbness that's eluding me, I fit the decanter to my lips and guzzle the remaining contents.

The room tilts, like I'm trapped inside a crooked portrait, and I smile triumphantly. I salute the decanter. "Great. You listened, soldier. Op accomplished."

I drop the drained container on the nightstand, unbuckle my

weapons belt, grown obnoxiously heavy, and slam it down there too, then unload the rest of the stifling weapons weighing down my person. Free of everything, I lie back on the cushy pillows that litter the bed and just *breathe*.

Good sex and a good buzz work gloriously in tandem for relaxation, and I briefly muse that a City of Thugs with a reputation for decadence must have impressive brothels with equally impressive males. But then I immediately think about Reed and how we're supposed to be . . . whatever the hell we are. And if we're a thing, no matter how undefined we remain, I'm pretty sure our recent convo slipped us past it being acceptable for me to casually hook up with somebody else— even if I'm paying for it. *So does that mean I ping Reed when I need a good screw?* All the rum I guzzled has me giggling at the thought. If I summoned him in this state, he'd turn up so not amused. Plus, has the thing we're in even evolved to the place where it wouldn't be completely bizarre and inappropriate for me to ping him? I giggle again, lingering in my current absurd, shallow thoughts so I don't have to go back to wallowing in the heavier ones.

Then, because I'm me and I have all of half a break at the best of times, *and* because if Reed *is* my boyfriend it makes no damn sense not to reap certain perks, *and* because I'm not doing muddled if we're about to be involved with each other—and probably because I've had a whole decanter of rum in under an hour—I grip the Comm Unit strapped to my wrist and shoot off a Comm to Reed.

I'm horny. Are we in the spot where we can just fuck yet without it being weird or awkward like last time?

There's a knock at my door precisely one second after I send it. The video feed from the door's camera appears on my Comm Unit. Reed stands in the hall looking down at his own Comm Unit.

I jump up and walk to the salon to open the door. "There's no way you got my ping and responded to it that fast," I say to Reed, who's looking at me with a stupefied expression.

He waves his Comm Unit at me, brows furrowing. "You'd be right.

I was already on my way here to check on you after giving you some space. I got the message right after I knocked."

I blink. "Oh." Yes, the word slurs. As did the others I spoke to him.

Reed, of course, gloms on to it. "Are you drunk?" I stiffen at the rebuff behind the question. Though I saw it coming. Still, it irks me.

"Yes," I snap. "Aren't we in for the night? I'll be in top shape by sunlight. Really, before the sun rises."

Reed pinches the bridge of his nose, and it's another action that rankles me.

"Why were you coming to check on me?" I demand, now more than irritated that he's shown up. "I don't need a babysitter. I can handle things."

"We all need backup," he says. He looks at me like his answer should've been obvious. "It's something I'd do with anybody on my squad. You were upset when you left the courtyard. Also . . ." In a move I don't expect, he reaches toward me and tugs me against him. "It's something I'd do for my girlfriend too. And obviously, given your state, it's something I needed to do for *you*."

He tucks me closer against him. It's an odd feeling, having some-body offering comfort like this. Caring about me like this. It startles me and makes a good bit of my anger dwindle even as I mull over if I'm all right with him offering the gesture. There's a different closeness and intimacy in Reed's extended comfort than what I'm used to, when Selene or Zayne had done the same thing in the past. It's not necessar-ily more of either of those things. Simply wholly different because the bond forming between Reed and me is wholly different from the bond I had with my former friends. With them it was about camaraderie and a bond as tight as siblings'. With Reed . . . well, we seem to exist in a space that's entirely new, foreign, and confounding.

"So . . . we *are* applying a label to this?" I ask so I can start untan-gling things. In hindsight, it's unwise. Because, *shit*, merely asking the weighty question starts to shatter my high.

"Labels work for me," Reed says without reflecting. "I like labels. I like clear definitions and clear terms. But I realize you were birthed of pure chaos, so if something as formal as labels makes you uncomfortable, we can forgo them too."

I'm not prepared for such a direct answer. In fact, damn him, his earnestness smashes through near the rest of my buzz. I swat his chest, throwing up a buffer of playfulness to keep things from growing heavier and blowing the drunk I worked so hard to get. "I was not birthed of pure chaos, thank you very much," I let Reed know. Okay, when I think on the circumstances surrounding my birth, I actually was . . . *and goodbye inebriation.* "Labels are fine, *boyfriend*," I say to Reed, grouchy and wanting to disprove what he thinks he knows about me. "I can do clear definitions and clear terms too."

He snorts. "So you must be a different Ikenna than the one I met in the trials, and the one who was the cadet that punched a Praetorian in a bar."

"Funny," I retort. "You must be a different Darius from the trials because I didn't know you had any sense of humor."

He cocks his head to the side. A twitch of a smile plays about his lips. "Darius, huh?"

"Yeah," I say, wondering what's so comical.

"That's the first time you've called me that," he murmurs.

I realize he's right. "That's your name," I say casually, trying to keep things from turning *more* cumbrous than they need to be, though I'm spectacularly failing. "We agreed to be Darius and Ikenna away from the squad, didn't we?"

"We did. And we should be." His voice drops an octave. I don't know why in the gods-created hell it makes me shiver because it's pathetic that I do. I've got more swagger than that.

He catches me around my waist and skims featherlight fingers up my spine. I shiver again, and this time whatever swagger I think I've got gets smashed to pieces because I don't even care about my reaction anymore other than to press my body closer against him, remembering that I was formerly horny, and pray to the gods that if he did read my message, he's game, even if that's not the reason he turned up.

"For the record," he rumbles, as if reading my mind, "yes, we're in that place if you're ready for us to be." Although he throws the final decision back on me to cross a line in our relationship, his desire for it is clear in the smokiness of his voice. It's made extra clear in the bulge in his pants pressing against me.

My answer should be an immediate yes. But now that he's here, standing in front of me, and I can actually go there with him . . . I know, without a doubt, that it'll be a yes to so much more, and I'm not sure I'm ready to take *that* plunge. I'm not sure I want to carry that particular burden. There are so many pressing on me already. I've lost everybody who's meant anything to me, and I'm on a campaign that I'm terrified will come with more inevitable losses. If I pull Reed closer, if I make him and the thing between us mean *more*, then I risk losing another person who means everything to me—and if that happens again, I don't know that it won't shatter me this time.

Reed lets me go and steps back before I can decide on a sure answer. "Though we aren't doing anything of that nature right now." He collects my hand and starts pulling me toward the wet bar. "First, we're getting water. Second, you're drinking it. After that, we're going to talk about why you're drunk."

"You're pushy," I say as he drags me across the room, yet I'm also relieved. "And my intoxication is already shot to shit after our deep-ish chat, thank you very much." I pull away from his grip and plant my feet in the middle of the room while crossing my arms over my chest. I realize belatedly it probably makes me look like a petulant toddler instead of an adult.

He ignores my grandstanding and continues to the bar on his own. He grabs a bottle of water from the fridge beside it, unscrews the cap, and walks it over to me. "Drink it anyway."

"I don't need the water," I mutter. "I never do. My highs never last for longer than a handful of minutes after my last drink. An unfortunate side effect of my blood-gift. My system purges liquor and boosters at warp speed."

I drop onto the chaise beside me, highly disgruntled about that.

Reed sits, too, and nods. "Good to know," he says, like it *is* a good thing.

"I hate you," I say. Might as well see this acting juvenile thing all the way through.

"Do you message everybody you hate that you're horny and inquire about their services?"

I scowl.

This time his mouth does more than twitch in amusement. He full on laughs at me. "You're absurd."

"I'm fucking spectacular," I let him know.

"You are," he says without an ounce of snark. Before I can really process his reply—or the ardent tone he delivers it with—he shocks the hell out of me further when he catches the back of my neck and kisses me deeply. I melt into him. I suddenly no longer care that my high is blown because this is better. The gust of desire that flares makes Reed, and the kiss, and his hard body beneath mine when I straddle his lap, all that consume my thoughts. *Perfect.*

Sex with Reed doesn't have to make things deep, I tell myself. Although, from what I remember from the last time, *deep* is something Reed can do quite well. I flush at that thought and grind myself against him a little more. This can simply be good sex. Really good sex. We don't have to let emotions make it bigger or get all entangled in feelings. It can stay about pure enjoyment. The self-indulgent part of me latches on to that flimsy reasoning and I run with it, fully intent on seducing Reed for self-gratification and to worm out of having a talk about real stuff. I rock against him, laser-focused on a mission, and break our kiss to lick down the side of his neck. Indulging in my stealth op a bit since ink is hot, I select the right side, where his inktat rests, and kiss my way along the soft skin that the gleaming, black four-pointed star of the Republic adorns.

"I intend to do this same thing to your Xzana bands," I inform him, moving my hips so that neither of us can escape the sensation.

Not that anyone wants to escape this. I moan and he groans, tangling his hand in my hair and kissing me fiercely.

That's it. Be reckless with me. This is exactly what I need.

"Clothes. Off," I say, reaching for his zipper to help him obey the order quicker.

Except he doesn't obey. Instead, his hands firmly grip my arms and lift me off him. He deposits me back on the cushion beside him.

I cock my head, affronted.

"You're not getting around my request that easy," he says. "This doesn't go further until we have an actual proper conversation about what I asked."

"Who the hell remembers what that was?" I move to straddle him again, and he sits me back on the chaise.

"You're kidding, right?" I say, incredulous.

"Ikenna," he replies. "Open up to me, please."

"I'm *trying* to! You're the one delaying things."

He gives me a look. "I didn't mean like that."

"I did, and it will be so, so much better than talking. I promise you. I can do glorious things with my tongue that forego producing speech. Let me," I say, sultry, "and your dick will thank you for it later." I cup him, and for a minute I think I've won because his head falls back against the chaise. His hand curls around mine as if urging me not to let go.

"You're impossible and stubborn and you drive me insane, you know that."

"So that means: 'Yes, Ikenna, no more talking. Let's fuck'?" I ask, squeezing his dick harder.

His hand tightens on mine and with a visible effort he drags my hand away. He shifts on the chaise so he's facing me and collects my face between his hands. He stares at me intently with a tortured yet determined expression. "Let me do this," he grits out. "I don't want to just fuck you. If we're in this, we're in this for real. If you want me, you get everything that comes with me. You get me caring about you and not being dissuaded when you attempt to keep me at arm's length. That's not how I operate in a relationship, and it's not how I'm about to operate with you. I won't and I can't, so don't expect me to."

I stare at him, speechless, because I have zero idea how to respond. Then, something rips a raw admission out of me. "I don't know if *I* can operate like that. It's . . . a lot. Maybe more than I can handle. You want to know why you found me drunk? The revelation about Selene started my ill mood, and then it magnified into something more overwhelming. The truth is: most days I have to distract myself from waking nightmares and grief that doesn't end, and tonight it became especially brutal. I shut myself away in here and then I couldn't stop thinking that *everybody* I love, everybody who meant anything to me, everybody I was close to is either dead or lost to me in some other way. My grandfather, Zayne, *Selene*, Mustaph, Enoch, Brock. All of them. Now I'm planning to go after the Blood Emperor, an insane, murderous madman that even Grandfather couldn't kill. But for some outrageous reason, I think I can. I'm about to try the impossible. And it's not only my ass I'm dragging into the shitstorm. It's you, and Dannica, and Haynes, and Caiman, and Greysen, and Dane, and Liim. But what if I get one of you killed? What if some of us don't come through it alive? *Or none of us do?* It'll be more deaths that I caused, and while I'm trying to come to grips with the gut punch it'll deliver if it happens . . . with you . . ."

"It'll be different.

"Downstairs, you told me what you were thinking the whole time when things went to shit in Khanai. You know what I was thinking in the Prisoners' Keep, when you were fighting Enoch, and I saw you injured and bleeding and about to die on the floor? My heart stopped and I lost it. I was frantic with grief and terror and utterly powerless to stop what was about to happen. That's why I did whatever made me commune with Amaka. *You're* why I uttered a mad prayer to the Pantheon. When one answered, and told me I could save you, I gave the scary bitch whatever she wanted from me. It didn't matter what it was. I said yes because I couldn't lie on the keep's floor and watch you die. It was for the rest of our squad, too, but primarily it was for *you*. You're the one I needed to ensure made it out of the keep and stayed alive. You're the one I needed to ensure made it home. If any of the others died, I would've been devastated, but if you died . . . I would've been beyond wrecked. Between the increased bounty that will have nearly *all* of the planet, not a manageable fraction like before, gunning for us and how hard it's been to collect allies to our side, it's hitting me tonight in triplicate just how much of a certain-death op we're on.

"So I had a few drinks to cope."

After it all spills out, I drop my face into my hands. I rub my forehead, trying to lessen the throbbing that's kicked up. With my high all the way gone, all the fears, worries, and torrential grief have re-erupted full force.

"Speaking of which—I need more liquor," I mutter and rise from the chaise to go retrieve it.

Reed pulls me back down.

He doesn't say anything at first. Just gazes at me with an intensity that makes me suck in a breath.

As he does, his fingers trace the planes of my face. They skim down the length of my nose. Along my cheekbone. Across my jaw. Then, the pad of Reed's thumb finds its way to my bottom lip. I catch my top lip between my teeth when it does. "What's the deal with you?" he asks. "The real deal."

"I don't follow," I say, playing stupid.

"Your file from the trials . . ." he responds hesitantly. "I reviewed the profiles of all the aspirants at the start of each term. Yours . . . it included the psymedics' notes from your exit evals. According to them, you have an extensive tendency toward destructive behavior when faced with adversity. Your bar fight with Radson wasn't your only ill-conceived brawl after the Legatus's death. You had a scuffle with an academy instructor. The notes also mentioned binge drinking." His says it all matter-of-factly, with zero judgment in his voice, which is . . . surprising. It helps me not lose it on him or feel teeny-tiny small hearing my exhaustive shortcomings laid out.

"You were our co-lead," I respond, keeping my pride to myself. "I guess I should've guessed at all the information you were privy to. How come you've never mentioned it before?" The question isn't an accusation exactly. But I'd be lying if I said it didn't rankle to find out he's known so many intimate details pertaining to me from the start, while what I know about him is still so slim.

"I wasn't trying to not disclose it. But you also can be really extra about things, and by 'extra' I mean homicidal, so I didn't know how well you'd take knowing I'd read your file. Especially since we slept together, which made it all the murkier and potentially explosive for you. But I do owe you another apology. When we slept together, even if unanticipated, it did change things. I should've been up-front about stuff. I'm sorry I wasn't, and I'm a jackass for the choice."

"Is it just me that you easily apologize to or is this another one of your routinely noble character traits?" I ask it as a crack, but also, I'm so curious to know.

Reed shrugs. "Can the answer be both?"

I roll my eyes. "I wasn't aware you were such a charmer either. The thing you said before the apology made it sound like I'm a walking nanogrenade. I'm currently trying to decide if I'm offended, the 'I'm sorry' not withstanding," I let him know.

"That's what you choose to zero in on? Well, you aren't a nanogrenade, just so you know. Nanogrenades deliver controlled damage to a contained area. You're more like a Centauri Starsploder."

I cock my head, serving him a savage narrowing of my eyes. "So you're saying I blow shit to hell?" I grin, not even trying to keep feigning supreme affront.

"You would take that as a compliment." He breaks into his own grin. Somehow we've slipped into an easy banter.

"I like this," I tell him bluntly. "I mean us being like this. Like we are right now," I clarify.

His thumb retraces its former path along my bottom lip, and I remember that it's been resting in the center of it all along. I catch the tip of the digit between my teeth, playfully.

Reed's cobalt stare darkens. "Me too."

I circle my tongue around his finger, then suck on it. "Sure you wanna keep talking about my shit? My mouth really is very, very, very skilled at funner things."

He closes his eyes for a moment and mutters something about the cosmos testing his discipline, when it comes to me.

When he opens his eyes, he drags his hand away from my mouth with an expression that can only be described as regretful. "Later. *Please keep that same energy later.*"

I shrug. "It might be gone. Serious conversations about how much of a disaster I am sort of douse the horniness."

"You aren't a disaster," he returns softly.

I bark a laugh. "We both know that is a lie."

He adamantly shakes his head. "It isn't. You've been through a lot of misery and trauma in a very short amount of time. I know Praetorians with years under their belt who'd be in worse shape after everything with Verne, the Tribunal, and then Khanai, not to mention the brutality of the trials on top of it all, which you had no time to really recover from. All things considered, you're doing pretty well. And you were the one who got us out of the keep and saved our squad from execution, so there's that too."

"You make me sound better than I am."

He flicks a glance up at the ceiling. "Are the cosmos imploding?

They must be if you're not eating up a compliment. Your ego is almost as colossal as Rossi's."

I punch him in the shoulder. "Now you're definitely insulting me and killing my horniness. Don't liken me to Caiman. We're *nothing* alike. He's spoiled and entitled and thinks the planet should preen over him; he just sometimes happens to be decent alongside all that."

"I have a comment, but it might destroy what I'd like us to eventually get around to doing later, so I'll keep it to myself."

I glower at him. "Wise man."

Then I stop stalling and answer his initial question because I know he won't forget things or drop them. He might feel I'm spoiled, entitled, and arrogant, but he's a demanding, pushy, too virtuous pain in my ass. "Sometimes, it gets to be too much, and I feel like I'm drowning," I say about why I default to reckless Ikenna whenever I'm spiraling. "In those times, I opt for not feeling anything at all. I self-medicate with numbness and triage myself with oblivion. If I drink enough liquor with boosters, it usually gets the job done. And I snatch the brief reprieve, no matter how fleeting, because that's the only way I can seem to find the strength not to crack."

Again, I wait for his judgment. Or disappointment. Or embarrassment. I wait for him to tell me Grandfather was tougher. Grandfather handled bad rows with more grace and with a dignity more becoming of an Amari, a fighter, and what the Republic's best, a Praetorian, is supposed to display. But I don't get any of that. Instead, there's something much worse reflected back at me in his eyes.

Sympathy greater than what I glimpsed in the courtyard.

I get angry at myself for being so pathetically weak. For allowing a vulnerable moment to show. Sitting in front of Reed, as he looks at me the way he does, I feel bare, and raw, and exposed. I feel brittle. And self-conscious. "I don't need your pity." I spit the words.

He shakes his head. "It's *empathy*. There's a difference."

He pulls me into his lap and just holds me. "Now that you've explained it," he says, "I get it. With the rank we hold . . . the things you'll see and do over your term of service . . . the people you'll lose . . . the ones you can't save . . . the orders that are murky . . . we all have to find a way to cope."

"What do you do?" I ask, needing to know more about him. Needing to not be the only one exposing all the inner, private corners of themselves. "How do you cope?"

"By being me, as you put it." He holds me closer and rests his chin on my shoulder. "I control what I can in every capacity that I can. Because there's going to be things that go to hell and spiral out of my control. There's going to be orders I get that I might not like yet duty demands that I follow, and I don't get to decide otherwise. There's going to be people who die that I'm powerless to save. I learned that lesson the first time around with my parents, and too many additional times during my own trials. Then there were the casualties on the ops that came afterward. I had to swiftly figure out what to do not to crack. My remedy was to let the things you call obnoxious be my pillars: Unwavering principles. Iron discipline. A commitment to duty and protocol and decorum. Because all of that makes sense to me and all of that I can one hundred percent control. It gives me an area of my life that won't go to shit.

"Everybody who doesn't hold our rank walks around with the mistaken notion that it's a glamorous existence. Yes, we have wealth, respect, prestige, some degree of power, and influence in the Republic—or we did, at least. We also deal with a lot of muck. You've got legacy lines and war houses constantly sacrificing children to vie for better status or to retain what status they have. Then, you've got us, born of common stock, who willingly offer up our lives for a *chance* to be chained to the rank—to live, eat, breathe, and bleed only in service to the Republic. And we do it because it's the only way for us non-legacies and non-scions to rise above the shitty conditions near everyone else is left to exist in.

"My parents were labourii miners. We lived in squalor. Leaving

Rykos for the academy was the first time I knew what it was like to have consistent meals," Reed says quietly. "When I was eight and arrived in Krashen City, to the splendor of the academy and the northern base, it literally changed my whole life. I felt bad about leaving my parents behind to live how they did, but I was happy for myself. Then, I learned of their deaths soon after, and I thought it was my punishment. The cosmos paying me back for being a selfish jerk. I lived a long time after that actively doing everything I could to be miserable. I didn't think I deserved to experience joy in any capacity. Once I set my mind to it, I got real good at being miserable. If you read my exit evals, there's an in-depth write-up on my earliest years at the academy and how the psy-medics I met with three times a week diagnosed me with depressive and post-traumatic disorders. I didn't start to get better until Verne stepped in and began mentoring me." He looks at me, his eyes serious yet somehow soft. "If you're a disaster, I'm a disaster. Nobody with our rank can claim not to be. Hell, I don't actually think anybody in the entire Republic can claim it. The way things are currently done . . . it's to the detriment of everyone. Verne realized it, and it's a big part of why he fought so hard to start to make sweeping changes in the Republic."

And why he's dead, I think.

We sit quietly for a long time after Reed finishes speaking, I lost in my thoughts and he lost in his own, I suppose.

My mother died before I was cut from her womb so I never knew her, and Grandfather didn't leave me until I was nineteen, technically an adult. I can't imagine being the age Reed was and losing a parent, let alone two at once. If I'd lost Grandfather at that age, I don't know what I would've done. I would've been so lost. So afraid. So unable to process any of it.

My heart squeezes, meeting the man beneath the surface Reed is allowing me to see. I twist in his lap to face him and wrap my arms around not only current Reed, but the poor eight-year-old boy he'd been. I hug Reed tight, and completely get his predilection for duty, protocol, and decorum now. I deal with the shit that threatens to drown me by diving headfirst into further chaos, and he deals with his shit by rooting himself firmly on the side of order.

Considering we're both fucked up, I'm sure there's a lesson to be learned here. Probably one that encompasses the great Republic being shitty on multiple fronts.

Reed tangles his hands in my hair and kisses my temple. "I don't think I've ever had that conversation with anyone. Thank you. It was cathartic." He exhales heavily, like he's releasing something cumbersome that he's carried for a long time. His breath is comfortingly warm against the side of my head.

I kiss his jaw and the day's worth of stubble lining it. "Ditto," I say. "I guess you were onto something. Talking it out actually felt good. So thank you for forcing me to."

We stare into each other's eyes, possibly really seeing each other for the first time.

I don't know who moves first. Maybe we move at the same time. All I know is that I find myself angling my head toward him as he does the same toward me. Our lips meet, and it's a lot like the kiss in the great room. Gentle. Tender. Ardent. It tugs at emotions I've never felt about someone before and terrifies me anew. The nascent bond between us strengthens a little bit more, which is also petrifying. But after our conversation, I decide I don't care. In fact, I want it to be scary. I refuse to let fear dictate my life or the decisions I make with it. I've never lived that way before and I'm not about to start now. It's never been who I am. Mareen, the Tribunal, the Blood Emperor, what occurred in Khanai . . . none of it gets to change *me*, or break me. None of it gets that power.

I give up control, and it feels wonderful.

It feels even better when Reed abruptly flips me so I'm on my back and he's leaning over me, pressing light kisses to my neck. He starts below my earlobe and travels downward to my collarbone. I gasp, surprised, but eager for where this is hopefully headed.

"Am I being rewarded for sharing my feelings?" I ask with a raised brow.

His answer is to tug aside the collar of my tactical shirt and kiss lower than my collarbone. His lips work along the swell of my right breast as he squeezes my nipple through the fabric then lazily rolls it between his fingers. "This is a demonstration exercise. If you want to use alcohol to drop into oblivion, that's cool. I understand. But let me show you there's a second option you might find more appealing. You're very good with your mouth, but I'm very skilled with mine too."

He drags my shirt and sports bra down lower so my breasts slip free. He palms the one he's already been kissing and closes his mouth around the nipple. His teeth graze it for a glorious flash of a second that makes my head drop against his shoulder. Then he starts doing expert things with his tongue that make stars explode across my vision as my eyes cross.

I cry out when he stops kissing my nipple and pinches it, on just the right side of pain. He collects my hands in one of his and firmly holds them in place above my head. His teeth and tongue graze the sensitive spot on my neck where my pulse flutters. "Am I being convincing or do I need to try harder?" he asks in a voice that's pure conceit.

The only answer I'm able to give is an embarrassing whimper. My horniness screams at me to let the blow to my pride ride and not interrupt things with some quip to restore it, but my ego grabs for a wiseass response. Luckily for the former, my brain continues to short-circuit and can't think of anything because Reed goes back to doing amazing things to my breast. He pays slow, torturous homage to one and then the other. His teeth clamp down on my left nipple. I hiss in a breath, then shiver when he licks the second small hurt, then snarl at him to do it again when he tries to switch things up.

He glances up at me through thick, dark lashes with a look that's pure male smugness. "I'll take all of that as a yes. The first time we did this," he says, "things got a little wild. Is that your default preference? Or was it a one-off?" He doesn't return to what he was formerly doing.

Only waits for me to respond while sporting a grin, as if he knows him not touching me is the only way I'm going to be able to figure out what words are again.

Admittedly, it's challenging, but I force my brain to string together sentences because the bastard is gloating a little too much here. "I was born in chaos, remember," I return, managing a crack along with speech. "What do you think?" I offer that as the answer, refusing to admit that I've never had sex like what happened in my room during the trials *ever* in my life before. Whatever was going on with my blood-gift under the Blood Moons had me out of control that night, but also, I can't entirely blame events on the moons. I was 100 percent into what was happening, and I could've put the brakes on at any time. But I didn't want to. I wanted to career full speed ahead over a cliff with Reed.

Needing to repeat the same thing (and snatch my pride back), I prop my right leg up for leverage and take Reed by surprise, flipping our positions. As he lies beneath me, I squeeze his dick. "One: same question? Two: I thought I told you I wanted your clothes off."

This time, he lets me pop the top button of his pants and drag down his zipper. He follows the order and shirks his shirt. I quickly unbuckle his weapons belt, toss it aside, and push his pants and skin briefs down ripped thighs that make my mouth water. He kicks the pants aside, and together, we make just as quick work of my clothes.

"I like pleasing my partners," Reed says. In clear demonstration, he strokes me lightly, sinking two fingers inside my wetness, then works maddening circles over my clit that make my thighs clench as I damn near cum on the spot. "I'll go with the terms you set," he states, much too in possession of his faculties while mine are hanging on by a thread.

I grab his wrist, pull his hand away before that thread cleaves. "Nuh uh," I return. Like I've been itching to do since the first time I saw the damn things, I dip my head and lick along the thick, beautiful stripes of Xzana bands that adorn his equally stunning chest. I take my time, like he did on me, and draw his torment out. "You don't get to assume the noble and collected act in this," I tell him when I'm done. "Telling me you're fine with what pleases me isn't good enough. I want to know what really, truly gets you off too." I run the pad of my thumb over the head of his cock, applying just the right pressure to start wringing answers out of him.

He makes a guttural noise and digs his fingers into the back of my neck. I give him the most wicked smile I've got. "Now we're getting somewhere. How do you want to fuck me, Reed? How do you want me to fuck you? I think you like how rough we got the last time. Personally," I say, moving my hand slowly up and down, "I loved it."

"The last time . . ." His breathing is ragged. "The last time got out of control a bit much."

I squeeze his cock again. With greater applied pressure. Wetness beads on the tip of his dick. I drop my mouth to it and lick it away, lightly scraping the tender skin with teeth, returning the favor he paid to my nipples. He makes the guttural sound again and I feel a warmth spreading down from my belly. His hand flexes on my neck then grips it tighter. "A loss of control is good sometimes. It's therapeutic," I say, glancing up at him.

The hand that's not on my neck digs into the velvet cushion he's lying on.

"You love being reckless, don't you?" he says, panting.

I lick across the head of his dick again. "It's exhilarating. Come be reckless with me when we're being *us* and we're like this." I take his entire dick into my mouth, letting the head hit the back of my throat. I squeeze his balls as I suck up on it hard. Reed rasps. Whatever he says, or tries to say, slips out unintelligible. I smile and keep working him because I'm going to win this tussle. I squeeze the base of his dick as I suck it and speed up my pace. Reed groans, and his hand goes from my neck to the back of my head. He grips my hair and pushes my head farther down.

"This isn't how things were supposed to go," he heaves in a helpless way that almost makes me take pity on him. "I was supposed to be getting *you* off."

I pause for a second to tell him, "You will. But right now, I'm *demonstrating* how very, very good it feels to loosen the reins." I go back to my task and soon I'm rewarded with a victory. His hips lift off the chaise and pump wildly. He grows rigid as steel in my mouth and snarls. His hips move even more frantically. Faster and more out of control. When he says my name it's hoarse, and just as frenzied as his movements. Then he's spilling into my mouth and I'm sucking him harder. Swallowing everything he gives up.

Afterward, he yanks me up his body so I'm back at eye level with him. "My turn," he growls. He flips us and pins me beneath him. In a move reminiscent of us briefly sparring in the gym during the trials, I try to buck him off me. He presses into me more firmly and holds me in place. I fight to reverse our positions until he slides those damn two fingers inside me, adds a third one, and his touch makes my limbs turn to jelly. I moan, wrapping my legs around him, and letting him have the high ground. His mouth closes over the erratic pulse in my neck. He bites the spot, then licks it, switching back and forth between the two, while his fingers continue pumping in and out of me. I thrust my hips up to meet his movements. I snarl when his fingers leave me and demand he puts them back in place. He throws me an arrogant smile, wholly ignoring me, and kisses his way down my stomach and along my inner left thigh before moving to the right one. Finally, blessedly, gloriously, he settles his head between my legs and starts doing really unfair things with his tongue that should be outlawed. When his thumb presses down on my clit, I lose the battle not to come apart. The room, *me*, the world, the cosmos—*everything* explodes. It detonates, leaving me panting and breathless, and then slowly stitches itself back together.

For too long a time, all I can do is lie on the chaise boneless and dazed. My brain forgets how to think, much less form words. I slowly gather my wits and some sense about myself. "I—" I still can't form speech. Motherfucker. Whatever game we were playing, I think Reed just one-upped me and won it. That can't stand. It's a matter of principle. I force my brain to re-form from the pile of mush that Reed and his mouth and his hands melted it into. I rise to a sitting position and straddle Reed on the couch. I press my palm flat to the center of his chest and shove him onto his back. I slide down his dick, purposely and excruciatingly slowly, trapping Reed with me in every ripple of pleasure as I take in his impressive length, adjust to his exquisite width. He grips my hips as it drags a moan out of him. I do it again. And again. And again. Smiling each time his head rolls back and another moan escapes. He made me come apart. His ass is coming apart too.

But my planned siege doesn't go off smoothly. Reed lets me stay in control for all of two minutes before he wrests it from me. He doesn't switch our positions. He lets me stay on top. But he thrusts his hips into me and pulls me down on him forcefully, controlling how things go. For a moment, I abandon my campaign. Hell, I forget what it even freaking is. Pleasure racks me and my entire system short-circuits until I'm tumbling in his hold. I drop my head to his shoulder and bite down, crying out. *Oh fucking gods.* I'm pretty sure I scream his name. Several times.

"Don't stop," I beg. Damn near whine. His pace is merciless, just like before, and just how I told him I liked it. His hands are ironclad on my waist, chaining me into place so I don't have a hope of wiggling away or reversing positions. Not that I'd want to. How we are, what he's doing, is perfect. I revel in it for a time before remembering that this is about me, but also not about me. And I have a goal. There's something I want out of him too. That steel wall of self-control, I want it shattered, always, when he's inside me. I don't bother trying to gain the upper hand by physically switching our positions. Instead, I try a new tactic. I let him stay in control and set the rhythm and pace; I let him drive into me exactly how he wants and how he's surmised I want. I clench my walls around him as he does, wringing another groan out of him, and I drop my head to his ear. "This is good," I croon. "This is really good. But remember how you fucked me back at the compound? I spun out of control and so did you. You asked me what I wanted. How I liked it. I want that. Fuck me like that, Darius." I clench around him, tighter than before. As I do it, I fit my mouth to his throat and bite down. My nails on one hand dig into his back. With the other hand, I reach behind me and squeeze his balls.

A cry rips from him. "Godsdamned warring gods, Ikenna!" Something unleashed, and vicious, and dark, something that doesn't care to possess an ounce of restraint, flashes in his fierce gaze. And I know I've won. I brace for it, greedily.

His pace finally, deliciously, goes from frantic to breakneck. He stands up, securing my legs around him, and somehow we get to the bed. He sets me on my feet then turns me around so I'm facing away from him. His hand skims along the top of my spine and prods me forward. "Bend over," he says roughly in my ear, spanking my ass.

I do as he asks.

He splays one hand flat between my shoulder blades, pressing me into the bed. The other hand grips my neck and then he's slamming into me to the hilt, over and over and over again. He resumes the relentless pace from before and he doesn't let up. His movements are as wild, and unrestrained, and out of control as I wanted them to be.

"Yes," I choke out. "Yes."

I push my backside into him in sync with his thrusts, giving as good as I get. I know I've got him entirely when he goes rigid and gives up any semblance of trying to keep or regain control. He falls into me, his chest covering my back. He breathes my name and buries his face in the crook of my neck as I grind furiously into him. My name becomes a refrain that my ego decides it relishes. I always want to hear my name fall from Reed's lips in this hushed, reverent tone, as if he's kneeling for prayer in the temple of a goddess.

He makes the guttural sound that I've come to crave hearing too, grabs my hips, and pumps into me hard. One. twice. Three times. On the fourth, he's growling and emptying himself inside of me. But even as I feel him filling me, his hand reaches around and his fingers find the spot that makes my knees shake. Like the bastard he is, he slicks two fingers and starts to thrum back and forth until I, too, am having a hard time breathing. When it hits me, I hiss sharply, and he allows me to regain my composure before rubbing me again with those two wet, calloused fingers.

Reed does this to me enough times that I stop having the ability to count, and finally I have to push his hand away. He collapses onto my back and just breathes afterward. Silent. I twist around in his hold and pat his chest. We don't say anything, and I wonder if this is what it means to feel happy.

6

EVENTUALLY, BECAUSE I'M ME, I say, "You know, that felt good, not to be so restrained with things."

It takes Reed a minute longer to catch his breath, and it's my turn to grin at him with a smugness that's all feminine finesse. He shakes his head and rasps a laugh. "I swear you are so cocky."

"I've got good reason to be," I say and scoot up into the bed, pulling him along with me. "Are we going to do the 'you leave rigidly' thing this time or are you staying?"

He cocks an eyebrow. "You want me to stay? You don't really seem like the cuddle afterward type."

"I'm a girl that's full of surprises," I say. "So, for the record, I am. Asking."

"Great," he says. "Because I want to stay."

"Good," I tell him, then lay my head on his chest.

His arm curls around my side.

I have a moment where that action scares the shit out of me. I consider pulling away or telling him I've changed my mind and he should leave because him holding me like he does seems more intimate than the sex and is glaring proof that we're growing closer. But then I remember I'm giving a colossal, fucking, nerveless middle finger to any fear and stay as I am.

Besides, I feel a lot more balanced with Reed near.

"Thank you for checking up on me," I tell him quietly. "And you're right. You absolutely do amazing things with your mouth, and other body parts, and they're a stellar alternative to getting wasted." Being with Reed certainly accomplished oblivion, and it was like one, long free fall I didn't want to end. Whereas with boosters, it's the feeling of being dropped into absolute darkness and a deprivation of senses except for a synthetic, fleeting hit of false ecstasy. With Reed, it definitely wasn't fleeting or synthetic. It was all real, and as I snuggle into him in bed, even though the mind-blowing sex is over, the feeling of ecstasy and the high from it linger. I'm not sure what this means or if it's strictly healthy or not, but I say fuck it and simply allow myself to steal a moment of joy, solitude, and peace before I go back to the neck-deep muck in the morning.

And since I'm indulging myself, I shift in Reed's hold and prop myself up on one elbow. "Turn over," I order.

He gives me a weary look. "Why? What are you up to now?"

I purse my lips together, refusing to reveal what I'm thinking. Half the fun will be his reaction. "Just do it."

"Tell me what I'm getting into first."

"Do we have to go to battle again?" I ask with mock exasperation, the thought of a round two tugging my lips into a smile. A hungry thrill shoots through me, but I have something else in mind other than actual sex. Well, at least not actual sex straightaway.

"That was enjoyable," he concedes. "But you won't win a round two."

I smirk, full of arrogance. "Whatever. Lie to yourself if you must." I poke his bicep. "Turn over. There's something I want to do.

"Trust me," I add.

"Always," Reed murmurs then immediately flips over, both his words and resulting action making my heart squeeze in my chest. But I don't go mushy; I'm after something important at the moment, something I need to get my fill of, and won't be dissuaded.

Reed, lying on his stomach, places his stunning back on full display. The smooth skin, the corded muscle beneath it, the beautiful Xzana bands inked there. I trace my fingers over the thick, black swirls that mark his Khanaian heritage and that he wears proudly on his fair skin, which would've passed as wholly Mareenian before our microstate travels. But he's never tried to pass. He boldly and loudly proclaims his Khanaian heritage with the bands inked on his skin. I brush reverent fingers over them, and a sound halfway between a snarl and a purr rips from Reed. Smiling, I lower my lips to his back. I kiss and lick and worship his Xzana bands there like I did earlier with the ones on his chest, sating a need I've hungered after since the first time I glimpsed his ink, and then opting for gluttony.

Reed shivers beneath my lips, and when he sinks into the bed, I take that as my cue to take my time in the fun I'm having. Some time later, Reed moans. "You are killing me," he says, voice low and suffused with sex. "Are you done yet?"

"Nope," I say and continue enjoying myself. "I've got a thing for sexy, muscular backs. Asses, too, and you have a great one."

"I know," Reed quips, the response suffused with a bald cockiness that he usually has too much grace to display like the rest of us do.

I snort, grip a tight globe, and give it a squeeze, letting my nails score the silky flesh with just a little sting—since during our earlier session we've seemed to have mutually decided we like a bite of pain mixed with the excruciatingly pleasurable. Reed hisses when I do it. *"Republic's sake, Ikenna!"*

Being extra bad, I abandon kissing his back for a minute and bite his ass.

"Shit," Reed barks. Then, in one breath and the next, I'm on my back and he's on top of me, plunging into me.

I wrap my legs around him and grip that glorious ass, reveling in it and the luxurious feel of him rock-hard—like silk draped over steel—as he thrusts into me fast and relentless. Entirely unrestrained, and this time I didn't even need to coax it out of him.

"I love this you," I tell him, grinning and digging my nails into his ass. Watching this man's control shatter in real time is a treat I relish. I nip his throat, and he grunts. "Can this be the Reed I always get when we're like this?"

He drops his forehead to mine, still fucking me hard. "You can have whatever you want. Whenever you want it."

I raise my hips to meet him, thrust for thrust. "When we aren't fucking and you're not so pliable," I pant, "and you're being difficult about something, I'm going to remind you that you said that."

He erupts in a slow, satisfied, male laugh. It zips along my skin and heats my blood. I grip his back and clutch him to me. "Deeper," I demand. I want him buried as far inside me as possible. I want to crawl into his skin. I want him to crawl into my skin.

"I'll deny ever saying it if you try to use it as ammunition." Almost as if in punishment, he drags himself out of me agonizingly slow, leaving the head of his dick perched at my entrance. I whimper.

"It'd make me a pretty piss-poor soldier if I didn't use every weapon at my disposal," I return when I can talk again.

He laughs, self-satisfied and immodest. "You're deadly enough on your own without added tools." He smacks the side of my ass then slams back home inside me. I erupt in violent tremors, and I'm not even ashamed that I do because so does he.

I ride the orgasm out as he does the same, relishing that Reed still pumps away inside me as he cums.

A new orgasm starts up after the last. Then another. And another. Until it's one long cascade and it's impossible to tell where one ends and the other begins.

The world shatters apart again. *I* shatter apart. Still trembling, the entire length of me tingles, *thrums*, with a jarring yet intoxicating, discordant energy. My scalp, my fingers, my toes—every inch of my skin buzzes with the things that *feel* larger than my body can actually contain, and perhaps larger than the universe, possibly the cosmos, can contain. The tingling erupts into roiling, scorching fire, singeing me down to each individual molecule. Without warning, or me actively calling on it, a terrifying flux of power rams into me. It floods me, as furiously as it did back in Khanai when I got a boost. My blood turns molten, and my body vibrates like it's about to combust. Hard as I try, I can't curtail any of it.

I brace my hands against Reed's chest to push him away, to warn him, because I don't know what'll happen if I surge like I did before while we're fucking. Can I somehow hurt him?

Before I have a chance to do anything, Reed's eyes meet mine, widening in an awed-like fashion, and he goes completely still inside me. That's when I see it and understand his expression. I glance down at my hands, braced against his chest, and they're limned in soft, red light. Like an inner glow beneath my skin is oozing out into the world—searing and viscous and crimson, like blood. More horrifying, there's slivers of gold glimmering among the red—like I thought I saw in my blood when it spilled out of me up on the mountain. I frantically scan the rest of my body and—*all of it is swathed in the same crimson-and-gold light.*

What in the hell?

What in the fuck?

What is going on with me?

It's worse than my eyes that night after the cage fights under the Blood Moons. The red glow isn't just contained to one part of me. It's leaking out of all of me!

I touch my eyes because I'm not wearing eyefilms. I ditched them after Khanai.

"Are they red too?" I ask, my voice trembling and hoarse and barely a whisper.

Reed swallows thickly, his throat bobbing.

"Yeah." His voice sounds as wobbly as mine did.

"I—" I shake my head. My hands drop away from his chest. I clench the sheets beside me. "I don't know what this is. Or why it's happening."

Are there Blood Moons out tonight? They could've risen. I wouldn't have glimpsed them; we'd placed steel coverings over all the upstairs bedrooms' windows for security.

I scoot away from Reed and roll over to the side of the bed where my Comm Unit got abandoned on the end table. I grab it and check the current phases of the moons. They're full orbs, as they were when my eyes went berserk during the trials. But tonight's astronomy chart doesn't report Blood Moons. I rub my eyes, having no idea, then, why the fuck they and the rest of me are glowing right now.

Swiftly, I build up the walls, become a fortress, and drag my hand away from my face. I lift my eyes to Reed and brace to see the disgust, and the hatred, and the revulsion for who and what I am reflected back at me. I promise myself I won't go off the rails and murder him for it when I do. I'll take that cut, that viciously deep wound, with a semblance of grace and try not to carve out *his* literal heart.

When I look at Reed, his expression is—I can't actually discern it to be a singular thing. There's confusion there, and astonishment, and a million and one questions, and also a little bit of fear, and oddly— worry. For me? What I don't see is repugnance, though. I loose a breath because the rest isn't so bad. I can deal with the rest.

"You don't look repulsed," I say, confused, grateful, and astounded all at once that he doesn't.

He comes to the side of the bed I fled to and have been sticking to, letting him stay on the opposite half, keeping a clear line between us. Trying to respect that he might want it that way after seeing what he did and being rattled. He collects my face in his hands, the crimson glow still wafting off me, illuminating his skin. He kisses the bridge of my nose gently. Like someone would do who thought the receiver was the most precious or fragile thing in the world. It makes me want to cry at how tender and careful with me he's being, given the situation. "I meant what I said downstairs, *and* what I said in Khanai. I was ashamed of my behavior then, and I still am now. I won't repeat it. I won't be a bigot. Regardless of what you are, what power you possess, what you can do, *or* if you're glowing like some damn scary goddess incarnate. *I know you all the same. I know Ikenna.* I'm going to judge you for *who* you are, for the person I know you to be, and not base it on anything else. Okay?"

I nod, turning my right cheek into his hand, and kiss the inside of his palm, driven by something that he could've broken inside me, but didn't. "Okay."

As I heave the word and a starsload of tension and impending heartache evaporates alongside it, I realize I was wrong. So comically, cosmically, grossly wrong when I thought admitting I wanted him to stay the night was the thing that would send us into some new, deeper territory, forge a weightier bond between us, and make Reed mean perilously more to me. Whatever sturdier links fell in place then are paltry compared to the massive roots sprouting inside my heart after our conversation. And after witnessing Reed seeing all of me, possibly the full scope, including the terror and the heinousness, and then coming *to* me, instead of reeling back. He crossed the invisible divide I put before him. Then he kissed my nose like he did and said what he said and is cupping my face so damn tenderly right now and—*oh fucking gods.* This is what I should've been afraid of. This is what I should've been *terrified* of.

But it's too late now.

I lay my head against Reed's chest, momentarily closing my eyes, inhaling his scent. It's a mistake that becomes a second sundisc detonating in my chest, shredding it. Reed smells exactly how he tastes— like the icy, ferocious, steady mountain storm we survived during SSEE mingled with the crisp, cleansing, and pristine first snowfalls of the year in Khanai. Unmistakable traces of blaster smoke and steel cling to him too. And the fact that I can parse each of these things out . . . I am in such a huge, heaping pile of shit with this man, who I could stay lost in the smell and the feel and the taste and the heat of until Iludu itself stops spinning. After everything that's gone down in this room, if he's ripped away from me like everyone else in my life who's mattered—*It can't happen*, I tell the cosmos savagely. I won't *allow it to happen*, I vow to myself, determinedly not returning to the place Reed found me in when he appeared at my door; *that* state won't win me any battles.

I need to remain levelheaded and confident and sharp because it *is* within my power not to add Reed to the people I lose, so long as I master how to *always* have that power. To do that, I need to not wallow, or second-guess myself, about anything. Instead, I need to do what I do best: figure out a way to punch forward and triumph.

7

THE NEXT MORNING, I GAZE at Reed snoring lightly in my bed, one arm thrown over me and holding me tight, and remain rooted in the same conviction. A fierce, protective instinct rides me hard. *I will burn the world down*, I promise Reed and myself. *I will annihilate the world for him, for us, for the team if it comes to that.*

"I think I'm in love with you."

I say out loud an undeniable fact that I've got too much pride to say while he's awake—at least this soon.

I smack my forehead, so far out of my element. I've never done love before. I've never done giving a shit about anybody other than myself in any romantic capacity before. So I do what I do best: I ignore my feelings like hell to sort out later. Or never. I slip out of bed, leaving Reed behind in it, grab my Comm Unit off the nightstand, slip it on my wrist, and cross to the bathroom. I take a scalding shower to bring myself back to center and stop being pathetically mushy, and then grab enough food from the kitchen to feed a small unit, because after the energy expenditure of last night, both from the sex and the surge, I could eat everything the synthesizer is stocked to spit out.

Reed strides into my room's salon as I'm setting the food, which I suppose I'll share, down on the coffee table.

"Good morning," he says, voice still groggy with sleep and too damn sexy for it.

I look him over—and completely forget what the hell I was formerly doing because he's entirely nude, his Xzana bands, and other things, on full display. I focus on his bare chest; it seems the safest place to stare that won't ooze my brain out of my ears. Gods, am I wrong. The onyx-black ink against his ripped chest, biceps, and abs makes me wet my lips. "If you want to have a conversation that doesn't end in me dragging you back into the bedroom, you need to put on clothes," I order Reed.

His mouth quirks up at the corners. He leans against the archway, folding muscled arms over that damn sinful, powerful chest. Nobody should have a chest like that. It's unfair. His biceps flex with the movement, and my eyes snap to them. I give him my best unimpressed scowl, even though, okay, I am *really* impressed. "There's no way that flex was an accident. Let me find out you're as vain as the rest of us and your humility is a big, phony lie."

He huffs a laugh. It's a rich sound that dances along my bones. I like when he laughs, and I love the light that suffuses his eyes, turning them from a dark cobalt to an electric blue.

"Shirt. And pants. Now," I say. "I've got important things to do today, like fueling up on the food I just got for us, holing up in the training gym, and trying to see if I can replicate surges similar to last night, *on purpose*, every time I call my power forth. I figure repeated experimentation via trials and failure eventually's gotta lead to success, right? So I need to get to it and make effective use of my time before you hustle us in the air to head east." I wave my hand in his general direction while gazing at a spot on the wall beside his head. "You need to get dressed because I can't get distracted—" I snap my mouth shut, refusing to utter *by the walking temptation that's your gorgeous body.* I've got more self-respect. Maybe?

Reed chuckles again and points to his pile of clothes and weapons belt on the floor by the chaise I'm standing in front of. "That's actually what I was coming in here to do."

"*Right.*" I snatch his things up in a ball and throw them at him. He snatches them out of the air. He doesn't need to cross to my side of the room while he's naked. He can stay far, far away. Otherwise, it's asking me to exhibit too much restraint.

"I'm gonna head to my room, shower, and change," Reed says, pulling on his pants (damn) and then, tragically, his shirt. He moves to my side, hauls me into his arms, kisses me long, and slow, and thorough. He pulls back and fingers the damp fishtail braid I gathered my hair into after my shower. "But since you brought up food, I can come right back."

Thinking of showers and having him near enough to feel the heat of his body make me recall the fact that showers have walls. And Reed does really, really impressive things against said walls.

I inwardly sigh, lamenting the work we both need to accomplish.

"While you're figuring out how to kick the Blood Emperor's ass," Reed says, yanking me back to the reality of what really matters, "I'll spend the latter half of today beginning to address our other problem too."

I grimace. "You're going to have to be more specific than that. We have about, oh, a godsdamn dozen."

"The most recent one." Reed sighs. As he does, I glimpse the enormous tension, the heavy concern, the extreme fatigue. The exacting stress that's bearing down on the entire team, but that Reed's usually particularly good about not letting show.

"Are you good?" I ask quietly. "*Truly?* I know these are new waters, new challenges, and new responsibilities for us all." I lay my head against his chest. Kiss the spot that his heart beats beneath, massage out the knots in his back that my fingers brush against as I hold him, offering what repose I can.

He kisses my temple, keeps his lips pressed to my head, inhaling and exhaling slowly. "I am now. *Thank you*," Reed says, sounding a lot more unflappable.

"Any time," I respond. Yet, I can't decide if his rapid shift is a good thing or a bad thing; if that iron control locking back into place is a mark that *he's* better or still a disaster. It speaks to how shitty of a predicament we're in, that we will *always* be in as long as we're soldiers, but what can you do? We're literal children of war, born and bred to fight. To do battle. So that's what *we* do, and we take the punches that come with it and keep going. Children of war don't have the freedom, or the luxury, to do anything else.

We must recall this inescapable quality of who and what we are at the same time because we step away from each other in unison, mutually allowing the few precious minutes of peace we've stolen to shatter.

"The world is currently full of multiple raging firestorms that we've got to put out," I say once we do. I'm not sure if I'm trying to reemphasize the necessity to Reed or myself. Maybe both?

"Right," Reed says, though his voice is tinged with regret I don't examine closely, lest I fold and decide we're never leaving this room to battle those firestorms. He clears his throat, then returns to our former discussion, helping steer us back to business. "Caiman compiled a pretty exhaustive list of who all have decided, or might decide, to try for the exorbitant bounty. The best course to deal with the amplified teams is to take the proactive route: track everyone down who's targeting us and kill them. If we neutralize enough threats up front, then we turn coming after us into a high probability that it will end in certain death. That should dissuade a good portion of any would-be pursuers," he says, every inch of Grandfather's protégé, a master strategist with a fierce mind for combat. "Mercs and bounty hunters take on dangerous work, but they aren't morons; their sorts generally opt for the easier payoffs. Which means we need to make sure the message that gets spread is that we are a hellish payoff and that anybody who comes after us won't ever see it . . . because dead men don't see. As it happens, there's a few squads based in Lusian. I'm going to take Dannica, Caiman, and Greysen with me to go terminate them. Haynes, Dane, and Liim can stay back with you here and help make sure the house remains secure until we depart." The ruthless, lethal, terrifying version of Reed that I first witnessed during SSEE and then beheld back in Khanai, too, peeks through by the time he finishes. If that's the man who's going hunting later, I extend a starsload of pity to his unfortunate quarry.

I never get the off-hand joke about his duality out. I form the first words; the violent tremors that throw me across the room sever the rest.

There's ringing in my ears. Warm blood slicks my neck. I probe the gash in the back of my head it seeps from and assess the injury as mostly shallow. I brace my hands against the wall I hit when the floor shook. Use it to heave myself up. I blink until the fuzziness clears from my vision. The chaise is turned on its side. The coffee table's glass has splintered, its metal frame mashed against the door to the room. The food that formerly lay atop it is strewn all over the place. A few feet away, Reed is springing to his feet from where he fell, blaster in hand by the time he's upright.

"What the hell was that?" I say, brandishing my own gun while pulling my blood-gift closer.

"We're too far north for landquakes; it had to be an explosion," Reed says, heaving breathlessly. He sprints to the door, hurls the coffee table away, and jabs the control panel so the door slides open. I move to his side, and we emerge into the hallway in step with each other.

My sweep of it reveals the second landing, as far as I can see, is intact. Caiman and Greysen rush from the former's room, weapons out.

Dane, who has this morning's surveillance shift, steps from the monitoring room cradling his left side with one hand, blaster in the other. He immediately starts giving a report. "The courtyard was the site of the blast. About ninety-seven intruders poured through the shattered star roof right after. Liim, Dannica, and Haynes were in the kitchen; they're okay and currently fighting. We need to get downstairs STAT."

"Well, then," Caiman growls, already spinning for the stairs. "Today's a lovely day for motherfuckers to die."

The five of us reach the wrecked courtyard and join Dannica, Haynes, and Liim in the fray of battle. Our guests wear the same nondescript black tactical gear we Praetorians do; seven among them, curiously, have masks. I complete a quick recount of enemy bodies and tally no additions to the initial ninety-seven that Dane quoted. Whoever they are, they sure as godsdamn know who they're dealing with because they brought along enough manpower to outnumber us twelve to one.

Too bad the assholes still suck at math. Or rather, they spent too much downtime counting their big payday, and now this idiot crew of bounty hunters is about to pay penance for this deplorable miscalculation.

Before fully throwing myself into the ass-kicking, I glance around to take a quick pulse of my team, just to be sure we do have the upper hand. Dannica, a scary-ass crackshot who gives Selene a run for her credits, is already having way too much fun with a pair of glossy silver D-Phoenixes, her fingers a blur on the triggers as she mows down a good ten bodies in under four seconds—all of them dead-center head shots that make me remember to stay on her good side. Haynes, Greysen, Caiman, Liim, and Dane are making short work of pumping bullets into their chosen targets too. Reed's gun has vanished. He, amazingly, has holstered it, as if it was a hindrance.

Clearly, he doesn't need *any* weapon in a fight.

He's positioned in the center of six men, outstripping the lot in bulk and hand-to-hand skills, dropping one after another with only his

fists or, in one case, a well-timed kick that snaps a neck. When necessary, he has no problem dragging a man in front of him as a body shield.
He's engaged his opponents in combat that's too close range for their
long, blocky assault blasters to be of any use. And from the wicked, relishing gleam turning his blue eyes an electric cobalt, I surmise he opts
for melee for the sheer adrenaline rush of forcing sorely outmatched
men to be his partner in a Xzana dance that nobody can quite master
as good as him.

The pulse check is complete in a handful of seconds and then, sure
my people have got things covered on their end and don't need an assist,
I select my weapon of choice for a little party of my own. There's a pair
of glorious D-Phoenixes tucked against my back, but fuck all that noise.

I'm the type of girl who thrills at the idea of bringing a knife to a
gunfight.

I snatch my sleek Khanaian dagger off my hip, yank a triangular Mareenian push dagger out of the holster strapped to my thigh,
and launch into the thick of it. As I do, I briefly drop the knives only
to catch them by the blades, letting the metal nick my palms, before
flipping them up and re-grabbing their hilts. Now I'll have an endless
supply of pointy things to help dead these fuckers with, although I'm
pretty sure I can handle myself without needing my blood magic.

To prove that point, I swipe the blue steel in my left hand across
a neck, opening up the first bastard I gift with death from ear to ear. I
spin to my right and with a vicious side kick knock the assault blaster
out of the hand of a second prick just before he squeezes off a shot. "You
thought," I croon, and take special pleasure in burying the silver push
knife in his chest because the asshole was aiming to splatter my brains.
I drive *both* knives into the same spot again, through the breastbone
this time, into his heart. He drops instantly, the life snuffed from his
green eyes before his body hits the ground.

I don't get time to yank my blades out of his chest cavity before I
need to pivot and face the rest of my swarm of attackers.

Magic it is, then.

I form blood spikes in my hands and hurl them in rapid succession, forming a fresh spike in less than a heaving breath, as soon as its predecessor leaves my grip. The blood weapons sail at their targets, each one embedding unerringly as a kill throw.

Brain; carotid; heart.

Brain; carotid; heart.

Brain; carotid; heart.

It's not a displaced calm that I sink into with the rhythm. It's a roaring frenzy—my pulse whooshes in my ears, I *feel* my blood thrumming in my veins, and the ignited bloodlust plunges me into an exhilarating high that surpasses the usual adrenaline of a fight. Especially since the team hasn't seen any true action since Khanai. For a Praetorian—or whatever we now are—that was a lifetime ago, for a good brawl is necessary for any warrior. So I don't hold back. I pull more of my bloodgift to the surface with savagery, letting it roil in delicious molten waves through my veins and spill out of me as I fight. The thrill is interrupted when I quickly take another check of my team and see the opponent Reed's battling snatch off his mask. The blood spike I hurl tears through someone's eye instead of the center of their head. I stumble because the guy fighting Reed is fucking Lykas Chance.

Fucking scum.

The Alpha Cohort lead stares Reed down with his trademark rampaging fury, smug that he's revealed his identity. Reed displays astonishment for a millisecond before recovering and twisting to the right to evade the stiletto Chance attempts to bury in his gut. The narrow knife catches Reed in the side. Reed might be deadly fast, but when Chance is motivated, so is he. The pair trade blows. Reed rocks Chance's chin back with an uppercut. From the look of them, they've been fighting for a while. Blood stains both of their fists, their faces, and other parts of their bodies. Chance's right eye is swollen shut. A gruesome purple bruise covers Reed's entire left cheek. Neither sway on their feet as they circle each other or look like they're losing stamina any time soon. They're Praetorians, among the *best* of the best; they could keep the fight up for hours if nobody lands a truly debilitating or lethal strike.

Chance continues to opt for trying to do it by carving Reed into pieces. Reed continues to go weaponless so he can break Chance apart with his bare hands, a pointed sneer directed at the Alpha lead when his fist rams into Chance's torso with a force that I'm certain breaks bones.

Locked in combat, Reed battles like his hensei: half on instinct, half methodically. I can practically see Reed's mind moving as he and Chance have out what's been a long time coming, from what I gathered during the trials. Chance (it chafes to admit this) fights more similar to me: he lets entwined instinct and rage carry him the bulk of the way, only falling back on critical assessments when he must. My heart shoots into my throat when Chance's stiletto slides into Reed's abdomen. I start for them—Chance is about to die, swiftly—but pull up short to slice through the jugular of one of the masked fuckers who gets in my way. He dodges the swing too easily for a bounty hunter, who wouldn't have heightened agility from a biochip. Only Mareen possesses that tech, and the Tribunal would only ever allow a Mareenian *Praetorian* to receive one. The knowledge steals my attention away from Reed and Chance's tussle. I focus solely on the masked combatant. He doesn't dodge the second swipe of a blood spike. I open him up pectoral to groin, do enough damage to leave him in agony, though not enough to kill him, yet. I kneel beside the guy after he drops and jerk off his mask, confirming he's a Praetorian. Not another Alpha. One from Epsilon. One whose face I know. He's the eldest brother of Selene.

I snarl and smash my fist into an eye that's the same gray as hers. *"Are Praetorians behind all of the masks?"*

He isn't wailing from being split open lengthwise; I'll award him those points. He loses them when he spits in my face.

I punch the other eye, sure to shatter the socket. "Answer me."

While I'm sure of the answer, given his and Chance's presence plus my own Combat Trial, confirmation is never *not* a wise route.

His clenches his jaw.

I shrug. "We can do this the messy way. Your sister and father owe me blood debts. I'll start exacting payment with the Rhysien heir." A blood spike rips a vertical line identical to the former down the opposite side of his body. The groin, it gets extra attention. He screams, finally.

I smile. "I understand you may not be able to talk anymore; I'll accept simple nods. Are the masks Praetorians? Let me guess: the Tribunal can't spare an entire cohort during war, but it assigned a small team to lead mercs after us?"

He supplies nothing. Holds out. And now greater magic is needed. This Rhysien fucker won't let me have fun and simply stab my way to the info. I repeat the questions while threading compulsion into them.

His eyes go vacant, face slack, and he tells me yes to both.

I ask a third before I'm done: "Your sister: Is she behind a mask? Is she here?" It's likely Sutton placed her among the Praetorians as another test.

A new yes leaves the Rhysien heir's lips. I let out a rage cry, *a war cry*; the bitch is near. Within reach. I slide back into bloodlust, though somehow managing to retain just enough presence of mind and a conscience to drop the compulsion. I wait for Selene's brother to gain full awareness then drive the blood spike into his chest cavity a fraction below his heart. It still isn't time to kill him; it *is* time for Selene to stop being a fucking coward and face me. She has crimes to pay for. I stand, scanning the intruders who remain fighting. I don't see the lone curvy figure wearing a mask hurtling toward me. Instead, Selene's locked in a scuffle with Caiman, and he's kicking her ass.

Upon spotting her, I don't grin. I don't snarl. I don't make a sound. Simply grip blood spikes and prowl toward her, keep the path between us clear.

The sweet killing song from before returns:

Brain; carotid; heart.

Brain; carotid; heart.

Brain; carotid; heart.

Each body around me that I tag as *enemy* and *obstruction* goes down.

While I'm tangled in the maelstrom, in the pitiless need to *kill everything*, a surge comes with the same viciousness from the prior night, and this time it fires up right *on time*. I give myself freely over to it. Blood spikes fly from my hand in a faster blur, a tide of crimson crashing upon a beach of bodies like grains of sand spread out around me in every direction as I stride through the center of the sea of red death.

Brain; carotid; heart.

Brain; carotid; heart.

Brain; carotid; heart.

Keep the path clear.

It becomes the *singular* song I know.

I keep advancing, projecting at Caiman that he better not kill her before I get there and can do it myself. Near them, I register Greysen surrounded by three Praetorians; the idiot has clearly figured out what they are because he's pulling punches, attacking in a way meant to incapacitate, not murder. He takes a blaster shot to his upper body for it. Caiman, on a shout, pivots from Selene and rushes to Greysen. The Praetorians around Greysen are on the floor and death-still in seconds once Caiman reaches them.

I keep killing as I track all this. Keep closing the distance to Selene. No longer facing an opponent, she snaps her attention my way, must sense the new threat. She stiffens, fear evident in the set of her body. *You should be scared. You're about to die. Very messy,* I throw to her with a glare that promises it won't be quick either. My rampaging bloodlust, the hazy rage, howls that she should at least die over several long minutes.

I'm nearly to her, two new blood spikes in hand. I don't fling them across the space that remains, though. *Nah. We're doing this shit up close and personal.*

I gauge forty feet. Thirty. Twenty. Fewer than ten.

Frantically, she raises a blaster.

I smile, finally, and it's ruthless. Pitiless. *That won't help you,* I mouth, and I'm standing in front of her in a blink.

Her eyes widen at the inhuman speed of the movement. My gruesome smile stays in place. "I've learned some things since you last saw me. Lots of things," I repeat meaningfully, closing my hand around the blaster to snatch it from her hold. Instead of keeping her eyes locked on me, they flick to something over my shoulder. *Or someone,* I surmise too late. A needle jabs into the base of my neck. An iciness spills between two vertebrae and spreads vertically. I try to lunge at Selene anyway. My spine locks. Spasms. The piercing coldness flushes through my veins, and the surge vanishes. Any ember of my blood-gift is gone when I reach for it. A wave of nausea and rapid dizziness hits me. I snarl, "What the fuck was that?" They're the last words I squeeze out before falling to my knees, panting, gasping.

"You're not stupid, Ikenna. You can guess exactly what it was. I've learned some things since we were last together too. So has Rhysien Labs, motivated by the fact that we're at war with monsters like you," Selene says, standing over me.

I flinch even as I sputter a "fuck you" because the words wreak the havoc they intend. They skewer me with the fact that her choices and actions aren't only about bending to her father. She believes I'm what she's accused me of being.

She knows me. She *knows* me. Better than anyone. We've trained beside each other, and we've had each other's back for longer than a decade. How does any of that not matter? How could she deem me automatically evil and a threat? Sutton and the rest of the Tribunal holding firm to the belief, I get. But Selene should've been the one person who refused to think the worst of me, who went to battle *for* me, like I would've done for her.

Yet my former friend continues to do the opposite as she bends down to where I kneel, hatred flashing in her eyes. She reaches for me, and I don't know if it's to capture and drag me to Sutton so the Tribunal can execute me, or if it's to terminate me for him in the courtyard.

I never find out.

First, a merc hits the ground beside me with a hole in his head, the syringe he stuck me with clattering against the stone.

Second, Selene flies through the air and lands on her back.

Dannica presses a boot to her ribs, D-Phoenixes aimed between Selene's eyes. "Whatever you thought you were about to do, you're not. The only reason you breathe is because Kenna deserves to fuck you up and I won't take the kill from her."

Selene grabs Dannica's calf, yanks her off her feet. The former scrabbles backward and stands faster than the latter does. Selene's eyes dart left to right—to Reed, Caiman, Greysen, Haynes, Dane, and Liim. I realize my squad's surrounded me.

That my actual friends have my back.

Selene looks to hold her ground against all . . . and turns and runs for the hole in the courtyard wall. When only Chance, carrying her brother, sprints after her, I understand why she retreats. The numbers they came with are decimated.

I struggle to push to my feet. I struggle to wrench my blood-gift back to existence. I can't do either. *Iridium in a liquid form. That was the injection.* I'm getting really sick of Mareen and its serums.

"Go . . . go after them! Go after . . . her!" I manage to get out. "I'm fine . . . only . . . iridium. It . . . will wear off." At least, I hope it will. I have no idea of its effects and lasting damage in the different form. There's a moment where I'm stricken with panic. Because what if it doesn't wear off? What if my gift is permanently stripped?

What I forget is that I'm not alone, and my panic recedes just a bit as Reed drops down on my left side, Dannica on my right. They pick me up and shoulder my weight between them. "They're not what's important," Reed says. "Making sure you and everyone else is all right and getting someplace undetectable if the Tribunal knows our location are what's key now. Especially if some of us are weakened. Do you want to be on the receiving end of a drone strike? I sure as hell don't."

"We'll catch up to them later. We'll get you to *her*," Dannica promises.

I nod. It's all I can do in my state. I suck in several angry breaths and try to calm down. Slowly, my breathing evens. The iciness in my veins recedes. A moment later, it disappears. With it gone, I feel my strength return more and more until I'm able to straighten and stand without aid. I probe for my blood-gift. It's not near the surge levels of before, but it's usual currents thrum beneath my skin.

"I'm back to normal," I tell the team. It eases a pang to behold their looks of relief after what Selene said.

As I gaze at them, I take a welfare inventory, post-fight, guilt creeping up for not completing the scan sooner. Nobody bears any critical wounds or severe hemorrhaging. Reed's cuts no longer bleed. Dane merely has a bruised cheek. Liim's taken a simple flesh wound to his left bicep. Greysen took only the single blaster hit about five inches below his left pectoral, but from the minuscule amount of blood that's left a tiny wet spot against his black shirt, I'm assured his nick is shallow too. With the enhanced healing conferred by their biochips, all four guys will be good as new in a couple of hours. Dannica, Haynes, and Caiman aren't injured.

"I wouldn't ever call you *normal*," Caiman says.

A few of us laugh, me included. "Good," I say. "We're all in decent shape, and we took care of most of the assholes." Maybe Selene got away, but that's still a victory.

"*We?*" Dannica laughs. She gapes at the dead bodies as if seeing them anew and shakes her head, looking thunderstruck.

The rest of the squad project similar expressions my way.

Well, Haynes looks flabbergasted *and* annoyed. "What the *hell*, Amari?" He jerks a thumb at one of the piles of corpses strewn about the courtyard. "This is the first time we've seen a good fight in months.

You wrecked it for the rest of us and stole most of the kills for yourself."

The meaning of his complaint registers in my mind, making me gawk at the bodies like the others stare at me. "I didn't do the bulk of this," I say, laughing nervously, unless . . .

Did I?

"There were ninety-plus bastards who came after us. That made more than enough to go around. How many really could've been me?"

And then I hear that song ringing in a corner of my head.

No . . .

"I got in about four good kills before there were just no bodies left," Haynes gripes further in his thick-as-sap western Mareen drawl. "*None.* Zilch. Zift. *Ze-ro.*"

"I deaded like six," Dannica says, gloating. "But still not enough. He's right, Amari. You were a stingy bitch who robbed the rest of us of a good time. Well, maybe not Reed. He was a beast as always. The perfect fucker."

"This is another thing that's not important," Reed cuts in. "We need to move out, right now. We've spent enough time standing around." His fingers already fly over his Comm Unit, presumably coordinating exactly that, as he pulls on the coat of a leader. "Let's at least pretend we had Praetorian training, okay?"

Everything he says is spot-on. It's what I should've remained thinking about, impressing the urgency of getting us moving alongside him. Yet, my mind can't unstick from Dannica's and Haynes's revelation.

"Reed. What's your body count?" I ask, wanting to do the math to determine how many of the ninety-four corpses I killed.

While waiting for Reed to answer, I try to recall the specifics of my fight. I try to slow the blur of blood spikes singing through the air and blood splatter and corpses in my head so I can interrogate each individual frame and piece together a kill count. But the bloodlust I plunged into is too great. It's another thing that leaves me bewildered and altogether disconcerted when standing on the other side of it. The last time I felt that everything except the fight fell away, to where I was no longer an individual participating in it—where I *was* the fight—was when I faced Chance in the cage match during the trials and he spewed words that made him seem guilty of killing Grandfather. That memory felt like how it had been now, just like it had that prior night under the presentation of Blood Moons: an unstoppable, all-consuming, roiling eruption consumed me and made me *need* to decimate everything marked *enemy* in my path.

"Twelve," Reed says without looking up from his Comm Unit. "Can we focus?"

"I'm about to," I say. "We do need to coordinate relocation, but first—I don't know. Shit. I just need to know everybody's counts so I have an accurate picture of mine. This is my first time surging in a fight since Khanai, and I feel—it seems like I'm more than I was. If I'm going to understand what I can do, I need to know, okay?"

The word "evolved" brushes against my mind in the queenly and commanding, and altogether petrifying, voice of Amaka, the goddess of blood rites. I don't use the term out loud, though. The mere thought of it sends prickles up my neck. It's a glaring reminder that I did what should be impossible and communed with one of the Pantheon back in the Prisoners' Keep in Khanai. And not only did I do that, I agreed to a foolish bargain where I accepted Amaka as my patron goddess; I accepted her favor, and I submitted to being her *Blood Daughter,* her *Chosen*; I yielded to *evolving*—and I have no godsdamned inkling what any of those terms mean other than seeing my power grow. Which I wanted . . . but—

I look at the scores of bodies. I caused most of this chasm of death. The courtyard runs red with blood, spilled primarily by me.

We're at war with monsters like you.

Selene's words return. They aren't so easy to dismiss as merely narrow-minded and hateful and treacherous anymore. A chill slithers up my spine. The very monsters that I broke with the Republic and Khanai to take down—the Blood Emperor of Accacia and his murdering pack of bastard Red Order warlords—are infamous and feared the planet over for visiting this scale of death, this type of carnage and destruction and massive bloodletting, on their enemies. My stomach clenches with the comparison, bile searing the back of my throat. I wanted to be able to wield a surge in a fight. I aimed to increase my kill capacity to protect Reed and the rest of the squad. But . . . I look at the slaughter around me again, and consider, no, *fear*, what it'll ultimately mean to master the surges and use them as a weapon. What might it transform me into if and when I do?

"Tell me your stats?" I ask Greysen hoarsely, dreading the rest of the team's answers.

"Two," says Greysen.

"Seven," Caiman offers.

I nod numbly at Dane.

"Four," he says.

"My count is six," Liim says last.

Together, my squad felled forty-one men. That means I took out *fifty-three*; it's more than what seven fucking Praetorians, biochipped warriors who are the elite of elite soldiers, accomplished in the same amount of time.

Less, I think. *I took a minute to look things over, remember?*

The courtyard, the world, the whole *gods-shitting planet* wobbles on its axis. At least, I feel as if it does. My head spins, and I nearly vomit as pangs ripple through my gut. *Tonight was definitely a time where my power skyrocketed.* And after the scale of carnage I've wrought by myself, I'm not sure if I should be elated or sick that I was able to wield my blood-gift with such potency a second time in warfare.

As if in answer, my nausea ticks up as I wonder: What did the goddess do to me? What precisely did Amaka make me evolve into? What does becoming her Chosen and Blood Daughter entail?

They're questions I should've been seeking answers to from the start, I realize. Vital, possibly life-upending, and absolutely dangerous intel I should've been more prudent about carving out time to collect, regardless of the chief mission commanding my attention.

What the hell *did I allow the goddess to turn me into in that dungeon?*

From what I can see from my squad's faces in response to my kill count, it seems pretty clear that Selene had it right:

A fucking monster.

WE TORCH THE SAFE HOUSE with the bodies in it.

After scrubbing any trace of our presence in Lusian—including any bread crumbs revealing where we'll head—we leave the city in under an hour, the territory as burned as the house we can see smoldering on the horizon. Our destination is the small eastern microstate of Braxxis, where Reed thinks we'll be successful at collecting allies next. The craft we take there is lent to us by Edryssa, at my request; it's the start of the Lady of the Cyphir Syndicate making good on our bargain. In appearance, it's nothing more than a private-commerce, heavy-haul cargo jet, big and blocky and ugly. But since Edryssa's people use it for smuggling black market products while evading governments, the craft is *nothing* as it appears. Like the military stealth jets Praetorians are used to flying, the loaner ride is impenetrable, equipped with its own stealth mode, fast as shit so we can outrun whoever and whatever in a fight, and, my personal favorite attribute: it's outfitted with a ton of firepower so we don't need to flee like little bitches if we run into trouble.

Yes, I wanted some good faith when I suggested the switch to traveling in one of Edryssa's modified crafts that from intel I knew she possessed, but I also wanted to fly in badass style. With a swarm of bounty and merc teams likely hunting us, this new mode of transport is much better than the previous—and more easily trackable—leisure crafts we'd been chartering. Not to mention one would leave us as sitting doves in an air scuffle since they have no cool guns.

I quash my giddiness over the jet when I spy Liim standing beside a window watching flames and smoke paint the sky. There's no mistaking his haunted expression.

"What's the matter?" I ask. "You good?"

Obviously, he isn't.

He damn near flinches at my voice, doesn't answer, keeps his eyes on the window.

I easily read what's going on: the trials left me intimately familiar with shell-shock following horror. "Is it me? What I did back there?" I find the guts to ask, fighting a flinch myself. I prepare to reconvince him, along with the entire crew listening, that I am not the enemy.

However, Liim startles at the blunt question. He turns partially to where I'm sitting on a plastic crate, blinks, goes back to staring in the direction of the fire, even though it and the safe house have shrunk out of sight.

"Whatever it is, we've gotta talk this out, man," Haynes, seated on the crate next to me, says quietly. "If you're a part of the team, you're *a part* of the team. We have to stick with being a tight unit; we can't give room to internal distrust. We'll implode if we do."

I release a breath after Haynes speaks up. I release several others when Reed, then Dannica, then Caiman, then Greysen speak similar remarks because it means none of those five abhor me.

Dane—the other ex-veteran Alpha—keeps his face carefully blank. I don't allow it to get to me. Five-to-one—or a possible five-to-two—isn't terrible. I can live with it.

At first, I assume that Liim will simply continue to opt for Dane's approach and choose punctuated silence. But then he hangs his head and says, "No. It isn't you, Amari. *You* didn't kill Praetorians back there.

"But I *did*."

Okay. Whoa. That's loaded. It's the answer I didn't see coming, and I'm unsure how to respond.

Liim slides his hands into the pockets of his pants and curses heavily while I'm trying to figure out what a leader would say to ease his evident torment. "Which one was it? Did you know them personally?" I ask as gently as I can, thinking maybe talking it out, and simply *getting* it out, might help.

"I did," he grinds out. "I shot the other Alpha who showed up with Chance. I didn't mean to. Didn't even really think before I did it—was acting off adrenaline and fight instinct when we faced off." When he laughs, it's rough with the type of guilt that can hack away at you, piece by piece, until there's nothing left. "I knew going into this our path would inevitably pit us against brothers. But—*I don't know.* I guess I wasn't quite prepared to see *my* brothers die at *my* hands, you know? We—he—*I* should've done something different. I could've knocked him out. Broken bones. Aimed for a place that would take him down but leave him breathing."

His torment—witnessing the death of a brother and believing you caused it—hits so close that I grind my teeth and pass Liim a grimace of sympathy.

"And you would've ended up in the same predicament that Greysen found himself in when he almost got himself killed," Caiman says, not sharply, but firmly. A brief look passes between him and Greysen. Greysen sets his jaw and Caiman scowls back at him with irritation, an unspoken argument clearly passing between them. Caiman's expression smooths and then he turns back to Liim. "Look, man. You didn't kill a comrade. Sutton Rhysien, others like him, and the Republic's entire, long-standing fucked up ways did. The three

Epsilons I killed and the Alpha you killed died for one reason, and one reason only: Sutton Rhysien is a power-hungry fucker who sent them on a self-serving suicide mission," Caiman says, reemphasizing the conclusion we came to after mining the Comm Units of the dead Praetorians.

The lifted data revealed their merc partners were comprised of several crews hired by Selene, and the Praetorians themselves were issued orders from Sutton, independent of the Tribunal. Basically, he rounded up seven soldiers who might've made a difference elsewhere to help Selene execute *his* greedy agendas: Lead mercs to us. Use their greater number to take us out and forgo the extended time it might've taken with bounty hunters. Then let him and Rhysien War House get credit for the swift, successful action so he could secure his apparent bid to become Legatus. It was all on one of the Epsilon's Comm Units as gloating transmissions between the soldier and Selene's brother.

Idiots.

One thing I know: *No fucking way and under no fucking circumstances does Sutton get to become Legatus.*

I want to descend into rage just thinking about it, yet I don't. This isn't about me and *my* agendas; it's about one of the team grappling with *their* heavy shit.

"You should be upset," I catch Reed saying to Liim. "Though not at yourself. Direct the energy at the right person and don't let guilt eat away at you. Caiman is right: Sutton is the one who got all of those Praetorians—and the mercs—killed unnecessarily."

"It isn't just Sutton that's the problem." Dannica throws out what we already know. "Bullshit orders like his and like what we got in Khania could've been, and have been, handed down from every Tribunal."

Nods that speak volumes go around, and I'm sure we're all thinking about what has to come, what we've formerly agreed needs to come, after getting rid of Bastard Number One, who plagues the world.

That's when it hits me, and I don't like the realization. *Are* we all on the same page about killing the Tribunes after the Blood Emperor? I finally think about how Reed, Dannica, Haynes, and I had that precise conversation after my Pledging Ceremony when I became officially a Gamma with them. We've never had it with any of the former Alphas; the exact phrasing *we are going to murder Tribunes* has never been applied to our end goal. I clear my throat.

Might as well figure it out sooner versus later.

"Just so we're all on the same page," I start. "Sutton and the others—they die at the end of this, right?" Given my display back at the safe house, it's maybe not the most ideal time to slip back into Murder Ikenna, but it seems like the only in I might have to bring it up without it being awkward or weird.

Caiman stares at me. Blinks. Then laughs his ass off. "How long have you been holding that in and weighing if you'll have to convince us or not? Yeah, Amari, we know they die. They're merciless Tribunes." He snorts like a jackass. "The only way they're giving up power is by having it pried from their cold, dead hands."

Greysen, Liim, and Dane don't speak up against it either. The latter two don't look so eager about it, but they do nod with a grim, knowing resolve.

Your friends and compatriots being 100 percent on your side to commit a bloody coup shouldn't be so heartwarming.

It has a nice mushy feel to it—right up until Caiman's unswerving support, once again, drives a guilty blade into my gut.

Would he still be 100 percent behind me if he knew who really killed his father in Mustaph's throne room?

I shake off wondering, though; I can't let myself grapple with it right now. One: dealing with my shit isn't what's of immediate importance, and two: the team has to remain a tight unit; we can't afford to fracture when so much is on the line.

I put my hand on Liim's shoulder and give it a squeeze. He doesn't look up at me, but he doesn't shrug it off either. We all fly through the air in silence.

And maybe that's the best we can do for now.

"WE SHOULDN'T BE headed to Braxxis." I finally decide about another thing I've weighed in-flight. Reed gives me a look, as he should, because we're only about ten minutes out from entering the nation's airspace.

"One: I'm sorry to ruin your plans so last minute. Two: Hear me out. I've been mulling over something since the subject of Rhysien got me thinking about it in depth. Even if he can't get away with sending more Praetorian-led merc teams and losing more good soldiers, I think the Rhysien bounty alone considerably complicates our plan to collect allies in the east, especially allies like Braxxis." I continue mulling it over in my head, already sort of arriving at an alternative.

Haynes gives me a quizzical once-over. "What's up, Amari? Why?" He's not dismissive—he's genuinely asking me, and I appreciate the respect.

"What's up is fifty-two billion credits is a lot of currency. The sum isn't significant to a nation like Mareen, or even Khanai and Lythe. Neither is it anything to somebody like Edryssa and her flourishing city of Lusian. But a great many microstates are meager in square kilometers *and* treasuries. That's especially true in the east where—"

"The statesmen we approach might be tempted to detain us and add handsomely to their exchequers," Dane finishes, perched on a crate like the rest of us inside the jet, which only has a pair of seats in the cockpit.

I snap a grim salute to the redhead from Alpha, who graduated from Krashen two years before Reed, Dannica, and Haynes.

"At least, *try* to detain us," Liim says. "Until Ikenna bloodies them up with her magic juice."

I give him a tight grin.

"The bounty." Reed closes his eyes and rubs them for a second. "I should've thought of that."

Greysen grimaces. "So where does that leave us? We've exhausted the west, have only one—*criminal*—ally, and are flying into a potential trap."

"For fucking Republic's sake," Caiman curses from his seat beside his friend. "Can't we catch a break?" He lifts his golden eyes to the cosmos, as if it will genially reply *yes*, and hand us the easy trek through the muck.

Liim clasps Caiman on the shoulder. I don't know if I'll ever be true friends with the blond from Alpha after his bigotry in Khanai before the Prisoners Keep, but he's come a long way from being a dickhead, and I do have to appreciate how fiercely loyal he is.

"But you must have arrived at a solution?" Dannica asks. As always, she remains in perpetual high spirits even when the occasion calls for the exact opposite. She waves at me from her place next to Haynes. "You don't look as if you've eaten shit you can't digest like the guys do. What do you got, Kenna?"

Reed leans forward at her assertion, peering at me intently. "Do you have something?"

"Ska'kesh," I answer, positive it's the safest choice. "The monarchy is rich as shit. They already compete with all of the big-three powers on the continent in that respect. Which means they don't need Mareen's money. More, they're not going to be inclined to help Mareen: Ska'kesh royalty *hates* them as much as the Lytheian Hearth Mothers do, if not more."

"Right," Reed says. "It's why Ska'kesh declined attendance at Mustaph's sham of an ally summit."

"Exactly," I say, careful not to let my thoughts linger on the man who has, *had*, been like my uncle since I was a little girl. Still, the reminder drives a million sliver-thin, but no less lethal, stiletto blades into my chest for the brief spell I do dwell on Mustaph. I shake off the ache, trying my best to ignore the vicious sting of Mustaph's betrayal.

"Plus," I add, fastening my thoughts firmly and singularly on Ska'kesh, "if anybody will lend more than a scoffing ear to what we're trying to do, it might be the Queen-Sovereign, Tariyal. Grandfather often spoke highly of her and with great affection. Like he and Mustaph, Grandfather and Tariyal were more than allies." And with any hope, she hasn't lost her entire godsdamn mind and decided to throw her lot in with a murdering despot, as Mustaph has.

I keep that last part to myself.

So much for not lingering.

"Moreover," I say, continuing to make my case, "I know you believed Braxxis was a sure bet, Reed, and want to get a 'legitimate' ally to help coax the others into backing us. But if your belief holds true, then that's another reason visiting it can and should wait. We've already caught whispers that Accacia's warlord Ajani has been quietly working his way around the Minor Continent while his liege and others of the Red Order war with Mareen, extending the same offer to key states as they did to Khanai. Ska'kesh has got to be high on Ajani's list to court. We can't let Accacia collect it *and* Khanai to its side. With both aligned to the Blood Emperor's cause, Accacia will truly become unbeatable." I pause, looking around the cargo hold—all eyes are on me, intent. "And consider this too: How many smaller nations do you think will persist withholding from simply kissing Accacia's feet and beseeching mercy to forego a fight that seems unwinnable? The Blood Emperor could have near the whole of the Minor Continent under his heel in a matter of days if Ska'kesh repeats Khanai's choice. Which puts us in a race against Ajani where Ska'kesh is concerned. We need to win over its Queen-Sovereign before that motherfucker does."

After I've laid out the plan, nobody responds for a second. Their grave expressions make it evident they're turning it all over in their minds too.

Reed scrubs a hand along his jaw, which now sports a near perfect, natural five o'clock shadow after skipping the daily shave I've seen him treat like a sacrament these past three months. The gesture makes me expect the gleam in his dark blue gaze to be grim. Only . . . it's not? I stare back at him as mystified and perplexed as the way he's looking at me. What the hell is up with him right now?

"One," he says, breaking the silence, "great idea." He snaps me a salute that boggles me more since I swear there's admiration behind it. "And two," he says, voice crisp and baritone, "you've been lying your ass off, Amari. You absolutely do not suck at strategy because you sound one hell of a lot like Verne on this jet."

I snort, incredulous. I will never live up to any of Grandfather's heroics or his genius. I'm merely grappling to do the best I can to haul us all through the multiple, catastrophic solar storms brewing on the horizon. The apocalypse that my friends are somehow willingly sprinting headlong toward alongside me.

But he's serious. The others are nodding, agreeing with him *and* my plan.

"O . . . kay," I say. "On to Ska'kesh?"

Reed is already moving toward the cockpit. "Definitely."

THE WESTERN MICROSTATES HAVE LONG disbanded their monarchies. Therefore, the individual countries have no true palaces as state buildings. Rather, it's all senatorial halls and private ancestral estates that act as seats of power. So Ska'kesh marks the first time that I've stood in a bona fide palace since fleeing the Gyidis' home in Khanai. Doing so gives me a strange sense of déjà vu. Which is nothing compared to the unsettling dread of being back in a throne room.

I try not to let the stiffening of my spine show as I swat away the unease, the guilt, the shame, the rage, the terror . . . all the emotions I tumbled through the last time I stood in a similar space with the Blood Emperor's warlord, the royals that were like family, and the Tribunal that betrayed me. I display a pathetic model of what a solider, a Praetorian, *an Amari*, is supposed to be, and I fail at my attempt to stay rooted in the present. My anger boils at the memory of too recent traumas, and now the rose quartz walls of the Ska'kesh throne room fade into the jade walls of the Grand Monarch's. In my head, I see Ajani, Enoch, and Mustaph standing in a line before me, with the Tribunes shackled and kneeling a few inches away. I'm plunged back into the awful moment where I learned the truth of what happened to Grandfather, why it happened, and what violence my Tribunal was visiting on me. I see red, and with the surge of anger, the extra power Amaka bequeathed me roars to life without me intentionally calling on it, *again*—because apparently it does what the fuck it wants to do when it feels like doing it.

But I have no time to bemoan the chaos inside me. This flare-up is more volatile than back at the safe house and it knocks the breath from my lungs as my heart rate increases, my skin blazing as if I've been plunged into a roiling volcano. My vision blurs, and I blink to clear it while fighting to curtail any outward signs of what's happening at the worst possible time. I'm supposed to be acting triumphant here, which I wasn't out west. And to do that, I need to stand in front of the Queen-Sovereign and convince her to see a young woman who is several decades her junior and barely out of an academy and make her believe it's a good idea to place faith—and her nation's welfare—in my hands.

Not give in to a post-traumatic episode or fly into a murderous blood rage.

As it is, Tariyal already sits on her throne looking me and the others over with a lukewarm expression that chips away at my confidence that we will find friendship here.

"*What's the matter?*" Reed, who stands next to me, asks in a whisper that's for my ears alone.

The question sends panic crashing into me. If he's caught something amiss, does Tariyal glimpse it too?

I drag in a slow, hopefully inconspicuous deep breath. After three more controlled inhalations, the flare becomes easier to handle, and I give thanks to Grandfather for having taught me the power of something as simple as breathing exercises to remain calm under duress.

I wrangle my shit together right on time because a millisecond later, Tariyal waves us forward from where we stood for inspection by the entry door, finally giving us permission to approach the dais and address her.

Keeping to manners, we sink into bows when we near the throne. "Thank you for receiving us," I say after straightening. "We—"

"I know why you've come."

The Queen-Sovereign has pursed her lips in distaste. She's a woman of seventy-two years, yet a stranger might place her as having lived no more than forty turns around Iludu's sun. Her hair, which stops in line with her shoulders, is sleek as oil, glossy, and raven black. Her amber face bears only a few age lines, and the ones that are present add to her beauty rather than detract from it. She's dressed in a sapphire and rose quartz crown, a cream pantsuit, and nude heels. Everything about her is perfectly poised and refined, and while Edryssa automatically gives off the air that she's a woman who can hold her own in a fight, Tariyal's mien expresses the Queen-Sovereign would never need to fight in the first place. I stand before a woman used to having people bow at her feet, and thank her for the honor of being given leave to do so.

Everything I assess about the woman who's ruled Ska'kesh as its absolute monarch for the last fifty years makes me choose what I say next with extreme care. She won't value or be charmed by my capacity to commit violence. Manners and perfect court etiquette is what someone like Tariyal will demand if I think to gain her ear, support, and respect. I know because Tariyal carries herself in a similar way to Queen Akasha, Mustaph's wife and the woman who's been like an aunt from the time I was little. And the surest, swiftest way to lose Khanai's Queen Consort's respect and charitable will is to be rude. Discerning all of this, I bow to Tariyal a second time, dropping low enough in the gesture that my knees brush the floor. "Please hear us out, Your Grace."

"I do not need to," Tariyal says before I can get more words out. "The individual microstates may be ruled as independent territories, but in the spirit of friendship and entente, those of us in the far north exchange information that we find to everyone's benefit to be aware of. Our western sister states, Pellu, Yi'ssin, and Suhare, you've visited already. Now you've come to me."

Of course she's talked to the west, then, and she knows of their staunch refusal to lend support. So the real question is: do her words mean to inform us that her answer is the same as her counterparts?

Shit. Shit. Shit. If we don't get Ska'kesh . . .

Then we need to be on guard now, because a trap is about to be sprung. Was I so enormously wrong about the rich microstate? *No.* I can't immediately jump to that conclusion, as Tariyal has displayed nothing concrete to support it. Besides, Grandfather once told me Tariyal is as tough as any Tribune in negotiations. It made him admire her a great deal. This may simply be that.

I pray.

"The Blood Emperor—" I start, trying again. "He—"

"I know what you'll say where Nkosi is concerned as well. I was Ska'kesh's Queen-Sovereign during his last war, when my people got pulled into a bloodbath we couldn't avoid. Believe that I understand the threat the Blood Emperor poses to us all. Perhaps better than any of you. The problem, young Amari, is you play at a dangerous game. One your grandfather himself couldn't entirely win. What makes you think that you'll succeed where he failed? More importantly, why should I have faith that you will? That is what you're asking me to do if I support your endeavors. If I align myself with you against the Blood Emperor—and, it seems, Mareen—it'll place Ska'kesh in an untenable position should either survive your strikes." Tariyal has expressed the same reservations as the leaders of the west did.

I need to come up with a different answer this time. Something inspiring more confidence. Something that will eclipse the terror Nkosi ground into the Minor Continent with his last war. Something that will pull a necessary yes out of the Queen-Sovereign.

The cosmos-damn problem is, my mind offers up nothing that's good enough.

Because, in truth, Tariyal revealed how utterly mad and hopeless and headed for disaster my scheme is when she asked how I could ever excel beyond Grandfather—a man who had no equal, a man who was larger than life, and a man whose feats I don't have a hope of matching, let alone exceeding. Blind hope that I can pull off the impossible is all I've really been operating on since fleeing Khanai.

"I—"

The only thing I've got left is to spit out the truth. Which certainly won't win over Ska'kesh's royal. So now I stand at the base of her rose quartz dais, mute, pathetic, and looking like the incompetent child she'd be a fool to aid. Hell, maybe I am exactly what the west accused me of being.

"Ikenna is blood-gifted like the Emperor." Caiman speaks up, offering Tariyal our usual response. Pulling on the coat of an effective statesman, he bows deep and reverentially to the dark-skinned woman who is also a foreigner—a thing his father would never do. "I've seen what she can do," he says in earnest after he straightens. "All we Mareenians here witnessed it. She has a power that may rival the Blood Emperor's. That's what'll make her succeed where Legatus Amari failed. He wasn't touched by the gods.

"Ikenna is."

Tariyal's olive eyes sharpen on Caiman. Recognition glints within them as her stare flicks from his golden eyes to his golden hair and then settles on the porcelain skin of his face. "You come from high Mareenian stock too. I know your features and that particular lordly mien you carry about yourself. Haymus Rossi is your father, yes?"

At the mention of his dad, Caiman turns a shade paler. "He was. Though I am not sure why that matters here." Despite his attempt at a detached tone, agony he doesn't bother to conceal—or maybe it's just so great that he can't curb the tide spilling out of him—twists the features he and Haymus shared.

"It matters," Tariyal says curtly, "because Verne Amari was the only Mareenian I favored or trusted. The rest have always turned up as rotten fruit when sliced open, even those of your people who try to appear unblemished otherwise." She sweeps a pointed stare over Reed, Dannica, Haynes, Greysen, Liim, and Dane, who stand in a line between Caiman and me. Then she looks back to me, scrutiny sharpening as if trying to cut away exocarp. I stand up straighter as she says, "Verne left you rich enough to relocate anywhere in the world and live as royalty without strife. Yet, you stayed in Mareen before your fugitive status, you continue to remain and rely upon Mareenians, and you're picking a fight *for* Mareenians?" She shakes her head. Sighs. "It seems Verne imparted to you more than wealth. Like him, you are loyal to those who are undeserving. Why?"

Many of her words are a throwback to Mustaph's in his throne room—inciting another disquieting wave of déjà vu. But the Grand Monarch didn't get it then, and Tariyal doesn't get it now. If she were anybody else, I wouldn't subject myself to having such a personal conversation with a stranger. At least Mustaph was family and had a right. The Queen-Sovereign isn't and doesn't. Yet, she does because I'm asking for her allyship. So I've got to speak, true and earnest, expose the inner fiber she surely spoke the questions to examine. "Mareen, despite the rot that needs to be excised, is my birthplace. It is the country and home that reared me, for better or worse. That is why I stayed after Grandfather died. *Because it was my home.* My friends with me," I say to her second inquiry, "have proved as loyal to me as I have to them. We're on the same side, we want the same future, and there's no people I'd trust more to guard my back. Finally, as I told you, I'm picking a fight with Nkosi for *everybody.* *The entire world.* If you want to know how I feel about the citizens of Mareen being embroiled in a war, specifically: simply put, there are people in the Republic that I actually give a sh— *care* about their living or dying."

Tariyal's only response is to sit silent, eyes pinched at the corners in consternation.

"I will not talk with you further regarding anything in the others' presence," she declares abruptly. She waves her hand at us, motioning to guards by the door to shuffle us out of *her* presence. "I will, however, consider your request and arrive at what position Ska'kesh will take on the matter," she adds as six men advance. "I'll reach out to you after I've deliberated, and you and I will speak privately."

"How long will it take for you to decide if you wish to stand against mass slaughter?" The very unreverential question leaves my lips before I can snatch it back.

Tariyal draws herself up atop her throne, and her eyes pinch tighter in anger.

Beside me, Reed cuts a look at me, and I give him one back that says: *I know. My bad.*

I contort my mouth into an apologetic, deferential smile that's aimed at Tariyal. "My apologies," I say to the Queen-Sovereign. "Forgive me." I bow, and hopefully I've done enough to smooth over the insult.

"Your grandfather was a lot better at diplomacy," Tariyal says in a voice that's dropped several octaves and unmistakably warns caution.

"I know. Grandfather was better at everything. I strive to be even a fraction of the person he was. Sadly, I've only been taught to fight—he was taken from me before I could learn the rest of what I sorely needed from him. But I'm trying."

It is as pretty a speech as I've ever made. And, for what it's worth, Tariyal seems to buy it—or, at least, accept its humility (and pointed reminder that my grandfather was murdered). She nods in acquiescence to my words. "You may remain in Ska'kesh while you await my answer," the Queen-Sovereign says. "Know that my extended hospitality is *solely* due to the friendship I had with Verne."

Trying to recover some ground, I touch three fingers to my heart and dip my head—a Ska'kesh gesture of thanks.

Tariyal only smirks, my display of respect for the cultural customs of her nation not thawing out the imposing Queen-Sovereign one bit.

So much for pretty speeches.

10

"HOW IS IT YOU KEEP finding the criminal sector in each city so easily?" Reed scowls as he surveys the latest place with questionable persons I've dragged him to.

"I didn't try with this one," I say defensively. "I only asked the transport to take us to a bar in a section of the city with minimal crowds. This is where *it* chose to bring us."

Moving around low-key is necessary while we've got a fifty-two-billion-credit bounty on our heads. Who wants to deal with the headache of recognition? And I'm sure Queen Tariyal won't be as blasé about us Mareenians dropping a trail of corpses while we're in Vynn, her capital city.

"If we go by the Queen-Sovereign's assessment, we're the same level of unsavory as these good folks." From a center seat of the dusty, circular booth we're clustered in, Haynes looks over the bar's other clientele, shrouded in shadows in their own dark booths. The individuals, mostly men, appear as seedy and shifty as the shoddy dive and its bedraggled employees. Most of them are light-years past trashed (not that that particular observation is a mark against their character. I advocate public drunkenness. Private drunkenness too. Really—I laud inebriation in any place. Who doesn't love a good, heady buzz?). Rather, it's the other activities they're engaged in that, admittedly, support Reed's criticism. Upon entering, a tall, lanky fellow tries to pickpocket Haynes by brushing past him and initiating a tap-to-tap transfer of credits from Haynes's Comm Unit to his, and a male asks Dannica her going rate for the night when she goes to fetch us drinks and a platter of food from the bartender. Haynes is more gracious about his incident. Dannica breaks the man's nose. Then Reed reminds her we need to maintain a low profile, and afterward turns to me to express his annoyance at us being in "this shithole" at all.

"I mean, technically, our Tribunal is comprised of sheisty fucks," Greysen says. "So . . . can we really blame Tariyal for thinking even worse of their trained killers?"

"Didn't say that we could." Haynes chuckles. "Just making an observation."

A man with red hair, alabaster skin, and a nasty slash across his right eye staggers into the back of Caiman's seat. He rights himself, and his hazel eyes momentarily—and suspiciously easily—clear of heavy intoxication as he gives us a once-over in our gear. He sizes up the nondescript black tactical shirts, pants, and boots, takes in the crisp, pristine condition of our garb, and I see the moment he decides we're easy marks who have wandered into the wrong side of town. A greedy, already victorious gleam shines in his brown stare. He cranes his neck and looks over his shoulder to a table across the room. Four bastards nursing ales are seated at it. One of them nods to him, then, like the rest, pretends not to be watching us.

"Whatever you and your friends are thinking of doing, don't," I warn him. "It'll end bad for you."

Ruddy Guy gives me a toothy grin that holds no pleasantries. "I'm not sure what you're talking about, sweetheart. But I do know you and your friends are dressed in mighty fine digs for these parts. Vynn isn't all cliff-top splendor. Us down-cliff folk are a different breed, and we don't like you sorts coming around throwing your fanciness in our faces." He hawks up a wad of spit that lands on the ground beside our booth. "Most of youse know better. Did you forget the Divide and that you've got no business here? Plus," he stabs an index finger at Dannica, "the gal broke one of our noses. I don't care if you're queensguard or royal servicemen types." He rakes an unimpressed gaze over our clean military gear. His next smile is vicious. "You pampered pricks only play at being fighters. You're all soft. The best down-cliff brawlers can take one of you any day." He cracks his knuckles—like a first-class, corny jackass.

The noise of chairs scraping the floor sounds off to the right; the four men at the table he glanced at stand and begin making their way to us.

"You think we're from the palace?" Haynes asks, amused.

"Stand down," Caiman says to the men darkly, and I roll my eyes because he's imbued all the authority of a war house head into his voice like it means anything here. I guess he can't help it. Speaking in that manner is unequivoically who he is.

"Go away," Dannica snaps. "Before you embarrass yourself. The dickhead I punched in the face deserved it. He mistook me for a whore," she says, wholly insulted. Then adds, "I mean, there's nothing wrong with whores; they make an honest living. It's the amount that he tried to offer me and the attempt to get handsy before he even paid that got his nose broken. I don't like cheap bastards, and I don't like touchy bastards." She pauses, thoughtful. "And so I guess I don't like any of you motherless sacks of shit."

The man's face lights up with red splotches.

Reed clears his throat then stands from the table. "Time to go," he says to the group.

I know he's right, and it's what our response should be if we're keeping a low profile . . . but I can't help staring at him with incredulity. Everything in me wants to punch the jerk talking hot shit in the face like Dannica did his buddy. I know the others do, too, and I think about how I robbed them of that release the last time there was a fight.

I wonder how Reed isn't feeling it too.

The urge must be written all over my face because Reed throws me a look that's both pleading and exasperated. "We shouldn't cause a ruckus."

"Who is causing a ruckus?" I ask, innocent. "We're all just sitting here."

He folds his arms over his chest. "You know damn well none of you are trying to avoid a fight. Especially you."

"What's that supposed to mean?"

He gives me a pointed look. "So I'm asking *you* can we get out of here before things go to hell?" *Before you careen off the deep end* is the unspoken subtext. Something about it grates on me, and even though we hashed things out in Lusian, I suddenly desire to see if his sternum can survive a boot-clad kick. Are you supposed to want to assault your boyfriend? I've never been in a real relationship before, but I'm pretty sure that's not how healthy, *normal* ones operate. Then again, I don't suppose anything about Reed and I will ever be normal. I'm blood-gifted, he's a Praetorian, and together we're trying to kill one tyrant and then go murder a crop of bigoted fucks who command a republic . . . so there's that.

I notice I'm unconsciously flexing and relaxing the muscles in my leg, as if getting them warmed up to greet Reed's chest.

As I contemplate a lover's quarrel, the other men reach our booth. "It's cute that you think you're leaving," Ruddy Guy says.

"We're trying to do you a favor. You *really* don't want to venture down this path," Reed advises. "Go find somebody else to harass." His tone takes on commanding authority too. It doesn't hold Caiman's war house—heir pomp, but it's very much the steel voice of a general giving orders.

These idiots should listen to us.

They don't.

They spread out around our table to box us in. Menace and confidence that they've got us beat, even if they're outnumbered, wafts off them.

"Seriously, last chance. You're not going to get the fight you're spoiling for," Reed tells them coolly. "Let's go," he urges us.

"You're no fun." Dannica sighs but stands. Haynes, Caiman, Greysen, Liim, and Dane do too. It takes a cosmic effort, because I don't ever fucking back down from a fight, especially when bastards are being, well, bastards, but I stand too. Since everybody else has, keeping my butt planted in the booth would only prove Reed's chafing point.

Reed goes to move past Ruddy Guý, careful not to touch him. The dumbass takes that decision away from Reed and reaches out, grabbing Reed's arm as if to yank him back. Everything that follows happens in literal seconds:

Reed slams his palm into the asshole's windpipe and he crumples.

The rest of his buddies forget about any of us and rush Reed.

Reed doesn't kill anybody, but he does break many bones and leaves them moaning in anguish on the floor. It makes me forget my former annoyance with him because my mind turns to oozing smutty thoughts when it's all over. Seriously, whose wouldn't? Reed doesn't end up with a scratch on him and couldn't look any hotter. I cross to him, smooch his cheek, and tell him, "You, boyfriend, are sexy as hell when you're kicking ass."

Reed mutters something about me being insane as the guy with the broken nose wheezes so hard it sounds like a party favor.

Dane chuckles down at the fools sprawled on the ground. "Y'all were warned. Many times."

"I told you y'all couldn't afford to play with us," Dannica says.

Haynes blows the fucks a kiss as we leave.

"SHOULD WE STAY in this sector for lodgings or go someplace else?" Greysen asks once we've settled inside a mass-carry transport that seats a maximum of sixteen. Dannica and I are on the front row she claimed. Reed, Haynes, and Liim are in the middle. Caiman, Greysen, and Dane occupy the next to last row in the far back. For now, we're hovering idle a block away from the bar while we pin down the wisest choice for accommodations. We were supposed to be deciding on lodgings *in* the bar while also taking care of nourishment, but then dickheads had to go and be dickheads.

"I'm thinking somewhere else," Caiman says. "Or else we need different gear so we don't stick out as not belonging in this sector so much. We need to not look like soldiers if we stay." His nose wrinkles in distaste when he says it.

"What the hell should we look like, then?" Dannica asks, looking as aghast about the prospect of a change in appearance as Caiman. She's seated sideways, head turned to see everyone, the same as I am.

"Common thugs?" Caiman offers and almost has to choke out the words.

Haynes leans forward and flicks the upper curve of Dannica's right ear. "We could find you a getup that a proper brothel girl would wear."

She turns fully around and sinks her fist into the middle of his meaty neck. "I'm sure you can help with that," she says as he grunts. "But no thanks."

"We don't necessarily need a change of attire," Reed says thoughtfully. "I think we only need to shift the vibe we're giving off. If we appear more as a merc crew than an organized military unit, that should do to help us keep a low profile. People sit up and take notice of soldiers, no matter what military they belong to. Mercs . . . folks overlook if they aren't specifically seeking them out for a job."

I twist around further in my seat to look at us and realize Reed is right. We've ditched the formal maroon coats and stiff slacks of Mareenian Praetorians, but we're still *carrying* ourselves like Praetorians. Like proud soldiers. Like people who belong and demand and enjoy the benefits of existing among the upper ranks of society. Mercs wouldn't function like that. They'd be more gruff, less polished, and a hell of a lot less entitled than the lot of us. We still walk and move like we expect the world to fall at our feet, because in Mareen Praetorians are as high as it gets next to war house scions, and the world there *does* bow before Praetorians.

Then something dawns on me that makes my face split into a wide grin.

"What are you thinking?" Reed, seated directly behind me, asks warily. "That smile can't mean anything good."

I give him a teasing look. "I'm just wondering if you can pull this off. Mercs move with a great deal more of a relaxed air than you. They aren't shackled to protocol, and most don't give two shits about *decorum*. You sure you can don that swagger?"

Reed snorts. In one of his own—rare—displays of jesting, he gives *me* a look that could beat out Caiman for the Arrogant Bastard of the Year Award. (*And* Reed is a hell of a lot sexier and less obnoxious when he does it.) "I can pull on whatever kind of swagger I need. I'm versatile, and I was trained to be better than the best. I'm extremely good at what I do, so yes, wiseass, I can."

I wink, keeping the banter going. "We'll see. You seem a bit too . . . priggish about most things to me. So much offends your noble sensibilities."

There's a glint that ignites in his blue gaze. It's laced with an edge that's entirely wicked. The right corner of his mouth quirks, and if he were anybody else the upturn of his lips and the fiendish gleam in his eyes would make me think a dirty response was coming behind them. But he's Reed. He'd never stoop to levels that are . . . well, mine. So I'm sure it's just my mind that's re-dived into the gutter. Proving the inclination right, his brief playfulness snuffs out, and he turns back to utterly serious. "Depending on how long we end up stalled out in Vynn with the Queen-Sovereign stringing us along, it may be best to remain in this sector and set up a safe house here first," he says to the group. "We shouldn't stay in any one place more than a night at most; so if Tariyal drags things out too long, we might need to relocate to several different sectors before it's all over. That means we need to leave options open for future use that we haven't already visited and been sighted in."

"I have a suggestion about lodgings," Haynes says. "Err . . . since we're on the topic of brothels."

"*We* were never on the topic," Dannica asserts. "*You* pestered the rest of us with your fixation. For Republic's sake, *move on!*"

Haynes puffs out his chest. "You'll thank me in a minute for being well versed in most brothels across the Minor Continent."

Dannica pokes him in the middle of his left pectoral. "That's nothing to ooze pride about, genius. It's pathetic to need to pay to get laid."

"Really? I'd call it upstanding since I pay the fine women I procure for their services beyond their weight in credits. My usuals adore me for it."

"You have *usuals?*" Dannica says, shaking her head.

"Praetorians travel a lot. I have needs."

"You've got something."

"As entertaining as this is," I cut in, "can we get back on track? Haynes, what were you about to say about lodgings?"

He huffs. "I would've already said it had Dannica not butted in with her unsolicited opinions. There's a high-class, excellent brothel a couple of blocks south. You wouldn't think so from its location, but the owner once told me rent is cheap and this seedier sector gives her business cover. I promise the trimmings inside compete with Mareen's priciest spas. We can secure rooms there if we want to remain here, and I know the owner well enough that I trust her not to give up information about who we are and our presence while in residence. Part of why she can charge a year's worth of my stipend per visit is that her clientele knows that she and the pleasure experts she employs keep secrets about who visits the brothel house well."

Dannica just shakes her head again. "If I was your mother, I'd smack you. A year's worth of a stipend on your dick is insane."

"I don't know . . ." Liim says. "How pretty are they?"

"See? We all have our vices," Haynes responds unapologetically. "Besides, we get more money in a year's stipend than the average person accrues across a lifetime. I have the credits to spare."

She does smack him upside his head then. "You're an idiot." She looks at Liim. "You're both idiots."

Dane and Caiman blush.

"All of you? Gods!"

Haynes takes it in stride, but raises a brow. "Do I harp about your habits?"

"That's different. Nice gowns are a necessity for a girl when she's outside of uniform."

"Sure—but *hundreds* of those frilly things? You only have one body to place them on!"

"And you only have one dick. You don't need to have amassed an apparent few hundred places to stick it."

I lose the battle to stay neutral that I've been fighting since their antics started. I want to act like a leader and not get involved in their absurdity, but I can't help it when I cackle at the two of them.

Reed doesn't look nearly as amused as he asks us all, in a pinched manner: "Is it the group vote to head to Haynes's brothel?" He looses a breath. "If it checks out as well as Haynes says it does for security, as such high-end places usually do—not that I frequent them—then it's admittedly a pragmatic option."

I cackle louder at the completely scandalized way he looks, agreeing to our next safe house to be a brothel. "Edryssa and her syndicate-run City of Thugs that I chose last go-round doesn't seem so bad, now, does it?"

Reed massages the bridge of his nose. "Between you, Haynes, and sometimes Dannica, Gamma might need an extreme overhaul when we get back home and everything stretching before us is done."

"Nah," I counter. "You love us. Who'd keep you on the right side of fun if you cut us loose?"

"Set destination to Belladonna Gardens," Haynes, extremely giddy, tells the transport, leaning forward toward the control panel up front. "Wait until you see the sex rooms," he says to the guys. "They're an exquisite playground."

My ears perk up, and, all right, I'm intrigued. I've become really, really interested in passing the night in a brothel with Reed.

My Comm Unit vibrates and an alert of a waiting message from the Queen-Sovereign, who I didn't expect to hear from so soon, flashes onto the screen.

Sobering, I inform the squad Tariyal has reached out and read her Comm out loud: she is summoning me, and only me, back to the palace.

"Let's hope her answer is what we want," I say when I finish.

Haynes nods in agreement, but settles against his seat, scowling. "I don't like you separating from us and going back there alone. Especially not after the Lusian ambush and who led it."

"I second that," Liim says.

"Same." Reed nods to Dannica. "Take KaDiya. She can track your location and set up a sniper's nest. I still don't like it either, but backup will be near enough if you need it."

I accept Dannica tagging along so *they* feel better.

The Queen-Sovereign just wants me, but she's the one who better be prepared for what it means to take on Ikenna Amari one-on-one.

11

INSTEAD OF BEING LED TO the throne room by Tariyal's brown-skinned, slender guard, I'm escorted to a grand sanctuary with rows of wooden pews bearing black velvet cushions. The palace's worship house is occupied only by Tariyal, who kneels at the base of an altar, and a child priestess in iridescent black robes standing before the Queen-Sovereign when we enter.

"I didn't catch your name?" I say to the guard genially, trying for statesmanship, as he walks me down a center aisle decorated with a night-black runner. Clearly, there's a color scheme here, and I assume there's some religious significance to it since Tariyal is dressed in a black gown that matches the priestess's garb in luminosity.

"You don't need it," the guard snaps.

All right. Grade One Asshole it is, then.

We halt our march when we reach the pew closest to the altar.

"Sit, *Mareenian*," he says like he's speaking to a canine instead of an actual person.

I gnash my teeth, envisioning ripping out his throat like the dog he's treating me as, but keep my cool.

See? That's called growth.

Keeping to mature, calm Ikenna, I obediently and respectfully drop onto the pew, then quietly wait for the queen to finish her people's practice of daily devotions to their monotheistic goddess, the Celestial All-Mother.

The young priestess with raven hair and raven eyes bends to kiss the crown of Tariyal's head as her queen sings a soft hymn about a beneficent higher being, one that sits above the Pantheon, who grew the heavens and universes and stars and planets and life itself in her womb to birth the whole of the cosmos. Tariyal finishes her song, then the Queen of Ska'kesh kisses the lowly priestess's feet. The priestess blushes a furious red beneath her amber-brown cheeks, kneels, and collects Tariyal's hands. She kisses the queen's knuckles in return and lifts her sovereign to her feet.

"The Celestial All-Mother accepts your devotion of song," the young girl says in a melodic, high-pitched voice. Her small stature and baby face place her at no older than perhaps nine or ten turns around the sun. We Mareenians train up our youth to be soldiers of the Republic beginning at the age of eight turns around the sun. From Iludu history studies in the academy, I know that in Ska'kesh, young girls born with black hair and black eyes—the combo an extreme rarity among their people—are revered as being touched by their Celestial All-Mother and given the option of entering priesthood on their eighth born day. The special, All-Mother-blessed little girl curtsies to the queen, and Tariyal bows back before turning and gliding to the pew where I wait.

"Mareenians cut ties to any religion long ago," Tariyal says after she sits beside me. "To your moral detriment, I'll add. But tell me, child, what about the particular Mareenian beside me? Do you ascribe to a higher power who holds providence over us all? You must, if you're Pantheon-blessed, no? Is Amaka, the daughter of my All-Mother, the god who holds your devotion?"

The question catches me off guard. Yet, I immediately discern it's a definite second test. The Queen-Sovereign is looking to be pleased by one answer, and another sort will be used to prove every (admittedly rightful) misgiving the rest of the world holds about the Republic and its citizens. I could lie, tell her exactly what she wants to hear. But will she know? I've learned enough about her to be positive that if she surmises the falsehood, she'll mark it as one more character defect and hold it against me. So I gamble on the truth, while selecting the way I convey it with care.

"I don't embody my people's common tendency to either disparage the gods or ignore they once existed entirely. I don't necessarily profess myself to be a *devotee*, per se, of any god or goddess either," I hedge. "I am not predisposed to be a person of devout faith, as, in Iludu's past interactions with the gods, that has come with submitting oneself to be part of somebody's flock and living at the gods' behest and will, not your own." As I say it, I try not to think about the fact that I recently gave Amaka a vow to do precisely that. It's a problem I'll sort out later—or never. I clearly still haven't shed the character flaw of just ignoring huge shit I don't have a clue how to deal with.

For now, though, I continue answering Tariyal's question. "As you said, Queen-Sovereign, I am blood-gifted. So I do harbor . . . not a reverence, but a healthy, smart dose of fear for the gods. It's foolhearted not to acknowledge their existence and the blessings and curses they left behind. I also don't carry Mareen's usual bigotry that marks anything having to do with the gods as a polluted thing that needs to be exterminated. I mean . . . I turned out all right." *I think.*

"Interesting stance," is all Tariyal says when I've finished. Her voice is flat and gives no indication of whether I've warmed her with my response or not. Tariyal's really set on making things excruciating, isn't she?

This win, if I get it, I'm gonna really have to work for. I go ahead and start the uphill battle now. "Your Majesty, I'd like to impress the gravity and importance of—"

"Verne held a similar religious philosophy." She cuts me off with the pivot to Grandfather's beliefs. "Though the Legatus was quite smitten with Kissa." She chuckles, her tone laced with a tenderness and adoration that signify a close intimacy between Grandfather and Tariyal *and* being smitten herself. I turn in my seat to peer at the Queen-Sovereign straight on. She's a woman I've never met before now, but clearly, she and Grandfather had a relationship beyond diplomatic channels. Were they two old, dear friends, like he and Mustaph? Or something more? Was she a lover? Something tells me the answer might be closer to the latter.

"Your grandfather and I sat in this same spot, discussing such things under the wide-seeing gaze of the All-Mother, many a time before you were born. Your mother, Maiika, was sometimes present beside him. I knew her from a child up through her teenage years. I tried to woo Verne away from the Mareenians, who never deserved him. Our shared friend Mustaph did too. But Verne, and as it seems, you, was simply too attached. I'll admit I'll never know why that reprehensible place, for someone like him, was what his heart decided was home." The girlish gaiety about her when she had previously spoken of Grandfather and laughed vanishes. Her demeanor turns somber, and furious, and grieving. My stomach clenches, Tariyal's darkened mood piercing me like a bullet. A sea of grief I have been managing to keep walled off these last few months—mostly—floods me. And tangled with that first emotional downpour is the fact that Tariyal also mentioned having known my mother for many, many years.

"How long were you and my grandfather . . ." I pause, not sure how to word it without overstepping. Then again, is overstepping even a thing here? Tariyal opened up these personal channels, and he was *my* grandfather.

"Verne and I were lovers for a decade," Tariyal says while I'm deliberating. Her expression twists with more pain when she admits it. She balls her right hand into a fist and slams it noiselessly down on the velvet cushion between us. "Damn it. I'd suspected that godsforsaken Republic killed him. Mustaph contacted me a few short months ago to confirm it. I gave that insufferable man an alternative, you know," Tariyal says, radiating anger. "But your grandfather and his stubborn, staunch allegiance to country and kin made him decline my marriage proposals each and every time. All he had to do was say yes. I was going to lay the world at his feet. He would've had riches and power several times above anything he amassed as Legatus. He would've been Ska'kesh's King-Sovereign during my, *our*, reign. He could've built out his legacy here. Why didn't he?" Tariyal asks the question in a whisper, staring down at her now open hands, palms up to the sanctuary's shining black ceiling, as if they hold the answer.

Okay . . . Tariyal was in love with Grandfather to the extent that she tried to make him a freaking king? A real, shitting king. Her king.

I can only look stupefied at the knowledge, my jaw nearly hitting the floor as I gaze upon a woman who is heartsore. Is that why she asked me here? So we could speak alone and she could get all this off her chest, share the pieces she had of Grandfather with his surviving kin to process heavy grief?

You should've taken the damn offer, I silently hiss at Grandfather. True to his form, he turned it down, though. I'm certain for the precise reason Tariyal gave: he would've likened accepting her proposal to turning his back on Mareen. On the Republic that was home, heart, and kin for him. He would've *never* abandoned it. He never *did* abandon it. He *continuously* loved it. Even when so much of it refused, so ardently, to love or safeguard the hero it had back.

The Queen-Sovereign is right. He was an insufferable, stubborn, fool. It's clear in Tariyal's voice and gaze that she, Ska'kesh's mighty Queen-Sovereign, would've loved and respected and protected him as he deserved. Then, he'd still be alive.

But so much else would be different. Most importantly, you may certainly not have been sparked into existence in the form that you are.

This version of you wouldn't've existed in that alternate future because we wouldn't have had each other against the world in the way that we did and you wouldn't have had Mareen and Krashen Academy. So you wouldn't be you. And all of that is precisely how it was supposed to happen. Because you, Ikenna Amari, child of my name and my blood and my kin, are my greatest treasure to prize and safeguard. You were meant to exist and be great. To change the world. To surpass me and cement our family's legacy as fierce fighters and stake claim to the war house we deserve someday.

I hear his maddening and unyielding response in my mind, knowing that if Grandfather were alive to speak it, it is without doubt what he would say. I swear to the gods his voice is so clear and solid and real—and firm—that if I didn't know better, I'd think his damn ghost were stalking the planet—and me—making sure things still were going the way the master strategist and combat arts hensei wanted them to go.

I scowl back at spirit Verne. *Fuck all of that if it preserved you. To hell with even me.*

"Did I offend you with something I uttered?"

Tariyal's stiff question snatches me out of my argument with an infuriating, too selfless dead man, who had always placed too much stock in me when *he* was the great warrior, the great hero, the great mind. The one who needed to survive and who the world needed to survive.

"No," I tell the Queen-Sovereign politely. "Not at all. It's just . . . disconcerting to speak of my grandfather. I miss him, too, and have taken his death hard," I admit. And though I sorely don't want to talk about Grandfather anymore, I can't let topics involving him drop just yet. Tariyal also mentioned knowing my mother, and I wonder . . . if she accompanied him on visits to Ska'kesh like I did on visits to Khanai, did Tariyal grow close to my mother as Mustaph and the rest of the Gyidis did with me? Some confounding urge, perhaps born of the pain of losing so much, ignites in me to know more about a woman I've built an emotional fortress around myself to evade thinking about.

Sitting among the pews of the sanctuary, that fortress crumbles.

"Since you mentioned her, can you tell me about Maiika?" I ask Tariyal, curling my hands into the velvet cushion beneath me and gripping it so tight my fingers groan. "What did you know of her? I . . . I don't know very much."

Merely asking the questions feels like a vulnerability. Like purposely and stupidly leaving my flank exposed. I grip the cushion harder. I also wait for an answer, instead of abruptly expressing I've changed my mind about knowing, because I couldn't turn back from the path I've ventured down now even if I tried.

"I suppose Verne wouldn't have expressed much about Maiika. He wouldn't have had many good things to say, and he possessed too much grace to speak ill words to a child of her dead mother."

It's another thing she says about Grandfather that knocks me off-kilter. "I . . . don't understand what you mean," I hazard, unsure I now want the knowledge I'm asking for. When I was little, before I entered the academy at eight and stopped asking about my mother to sever the weakness of *aching* for something that was missing and I'd never have, I'd bring her up to Grandfather routinely. He'd grow stiff and say to ask him questions when I was older and could understand difficult answers better. I assumed the stiffness was due to the grief any parent would be awash in over losing a child. But what Tariyal says alludes to something much different.

Tariyal's brown eyes soften with clear sympathy and discernment. "Are you sure you want this story, child?"

No. Yes. Maybe?

Amaris are strong, Ikenna, I hiss to myself. *We aren't cowards. So stop being one.* "I do," I answer Tariyal resolutely, calling on strength for whatever I'm about to hear.

"Your grandfather could be a hard man to love. I learned that myself firsthand, and it is why he and I eventually parted ways. I loved him, infinitely. Although he was kind and generous and wonderful, I always knew in my heart that he'd never feel quite as strongly about me as I did him. His precious Republic was first and foremost, always his true love—even above Maiika. I'm sure you experienced the same as your mother and I did with him. Verne—"

"No, I didn't." My voice cracks out harsher than I intend it to. I can't help it. I know Grandfather wasn't perfect. I've placed him on a pedestal, *hero-worshipped him my whole life*, but I've also never viewed him as not being human. He was a man, and mere men are bound to have flaws if even the all-mighty gods can't get their shit together. But still, what she says about Grandfather can't possibly be true. I know him, and I know how he felt about family. "Grandfather *always* placed me first. In everything. Including the Republic," I tell Tariyal. What I don't voice is, *in fact, he died for me*, because that's too intimate a detail. Yet, it's another reason why I unswervingly know what she says about him and my mother is all wrong. He put me before Mareen and his own life. His own survival. When the Tribunal found out about my blood-gift, *he chose me*.

Tariyal regards what I say with shock. Not as if she doesn't believe me, but as if she's astounded. A bittersweet smile eventually curves her lips. "Then Verne grew from where he was when we were lovers, as a parent at least. He and Maiika were never close. He wanted things of her she wasn't willing or built to give. Similarly, she wanted things that Verne wouldn't hear of."

"The part of what Grandfather wanted from my mother, I know of. He wanted a formidable soldier. He wanted another Amari Prae-torian. He wanted to continue building his legacy with her and work-ing toward his war house. He got none of that from Maiika because, as you said, she was weak. She wasn't built for war. When the Blood Emperor's warlords came for her to strike at Grandfather, she let them butcher her with no evidence of a struggle. That *is* a pitiful trait, and if it's any indication of the type of woman she was, then I understand why he might've always pushed her to shed it," I say in Grandfather's defense. "A man like him was never without his enemies. The Amari name *itself* has never been without its string of rivals since Grandfather ham-fisted the Khanaian surname onto the Republic's Praetorian roster. Perhaps if Maiika had been more suited for warring, she would've found a way to survive. Or flee. Somehow. I won't condemn my grandfather for championing strength."

Your mother was of softer stock than you or me, adds Grandfather's voice. On the rare occasions he did speak to me about my mother, it's what he would say. Not scathingly, as Tariyal's recount of their dynamics hints, but simply sorrowfully. It was the few times I witnessed Grandfather allow himself to display being gutted about anything. *She didn't have the stomach, the strength, or the right disposition to excel at what Mareen prizes most, above skin color and above lineage: war games, combat prowess, and strategic cunning. But you do, my girl, and you're exceptional at it.*

Yet Tariyal is shaking her head. "Perhaps. It doesn't change the travesty that Maiika . . . she withered a great deal under the pressures of life in Mareen. She detested living there. She viewed it as something she needed to escape and frequently fought with your grandfather about his desire for himself and her to remain within the Republic. She begged him several times to allow her to leave. Verne wouldn't bend. Her fleeing Mareen would've been a stain on the Amari name and the prestige he'd worked so hard for."

"Mareenians are born and bred to serve the Republic." I mutter this automatically; it's what we're all indoctrinated to believe from the time we're born. What Grandfather was reared to believe. And yet, I can't ignore that it's a hollow excuse for his choices when it came to my mother, and I hate myself for seeing the other side. For *feeling* Maiika's plight and for the flicker of resentment, on my mother's behalf, toward the father that did not place her first after all.

"I think Maiika would've been better suited to life in Mareen if Verne had obtained his war house already," Tariyal says softly. "She could've settled into life as your people's equivalent of an aristocratic woman and been a Donya with no other cares except planning parties and making social calls and finding a match. But Verne needed another warrior to succeed him and that she was not. So she was never happy with him, and he was always trying to change her and push her to be fiercer." Tariyal pats my hand. "But I'm glad to hear that you and he enjoyed a more positive bond. I guess *you* passed his muster, earned his unconditional loyalty and love even above what he held for the Republic. I should congratulate you, dear, for achieving a feat with that man neither I nor your mother could." She doesn't say it with venom, like some ex-lovers might. Only wistfully, like she wishes things could've turned out otherwise.

Which makes two of us where Grandfather is concerned. The man was a fool twice over in his past. I wish a spirit version of him truly was around so, this time, *I* could berate *him*. The father the Queen-Sovereign paints Grandfather as rips him down off his pedestal. *You were better than that*, I snarl in my head. Grandfather prided himself on integrity, and yet how he behaved with my mother . . .

It's equally as shitty as how Sutton treats Selene.

Is that why he died for me? I wonder and feel no comfort about it. Was it some stupid, misguided atonement for his fuckup? If so, he's a fool in triplicate.

"I think I've learned enough about the past," I say to Tariyal stiffly. "Our concern should be the tyrant that's going to eventually move to crush all of us beneath his heel in the present and the terrifying, bleak future for not only one nation, but the planet, that comes if he succeeds. You hate Mareenians for being repugnant. Accacians seem no better if we compare their war crimes, perpetuated against your people, too, the last go-round."

Tariyal draws herself up, her thin shoulders pushing back. "I know what is at stake, and the nature of all sides." Her voice has turned back to chilly. "Since we've arrived at the matter, I will let you know that I more than loved Verne. I believed in him and in his vision for a better world, with mended relations between the powers of the Minor Continent. It is why I supported his agenda during the first war and after it. But his death has changed things. It's reshaped the game board—and I don't only mean the war board. The very fabric of Iludu is being restitched. My Celestial All-Mother recognizes it as so, and it is *she* who holds *my* devotion above all else. I am her servant and her will in this world she birthed. So I, regretfully, cannot offer the allyship you seek. My All-Mother has bid me to keep the people of Ska'kesh out of this war and unaccosted by pledging to the warlord Ajani that Ska'kesh will not take up arms against his Blood Emperor or lend aid to any party that may. My All-Mother has chosen tribute-state standing for us, as we've been promised the same deal which Khanai negotiated.

"I gave Accacia my pledge this morning.

"I only summoned you here to inform you as to remove the possible influence of your companions when I say something else. I hold a fondness for Verne *and* the little girl I witnessed grow into a young woman and came to love as a daughter. Maiika once asked for a place in my court when she came of age, but it wasn't in my power to give it to her if your grandfather forbade it. You should do what Maiika couldn't do, but was smart to yearn to do if she was given the freedom. Do what Verne was too blinded by his love of that ruinous place to do. Your answer about the religious beliefs you hold makes it clear that you see far more down to the core of the Republic's rot than he did. So, cut it loose. Let it burn in flames that it's long deserved to be consumed by. It's shed so much blood of others and its own, so it is fitting that it meets its end by toppling into a sea of crimson. The Blood Emperor wants to annihilate only Mareen this second time. He will show benevolence to the rest of us if we yield without struggle."

"Did your All-Mother tell you that too?" I spit out the words, radiating with disbelief, fury, and horror. I was beginning to admire the Queen-Sovereign. But now she is speaking like a fanatic and a zealot.

"She did," Tariyal returns without, apparently, being so much as unsettled about the choice to stand aside and let hundreds of thousands be massacred just because some higher power supposedly told her so.

"There are innocents in Mareen too," I grind out.

"The citizens in Mareen that may be worthy of saving are not my All-Mother's concern. And, as I said, I am her servant. I do as she bids."

I snort. Of course. If this All-Mother is real and Tariyal truly is communing with her, then she's no beneficent being. The bitch is as callous and heinous and cruel as the gods and goddesses who comprise the Pantheon.

Tariyal rises from the pew. "My guard, Syiti, will see you out."

The Queen-Sovereign strides away, and I'm left sitting in the sanctuary, numb. We've done more than fail to garner the aid of Ska'kesh. We've lost a key ally to Accacia.

Tariyal, Mustaph, the other powers of the Minor Continent who will likely follow now that two big players have chosen to cower rather than fight—they are all either infinitely stupid or choosing to be willfully blind. Because it is foolish to believe Accacia will be benevolent to any of us.

The Empire isn't even benevolent to its own people.

12

I KNOW SOMETHING IS UP as soon as I enter the transport. The color is leeched from Dannica's face, leaving her hue, that's bronzed similarly to Reed's, as ashen as an unpolished blade.

Can the cosmos let up for one fucking minute? Gods.

"What is it?" I'm certain I'm not going to like the answer.

She doesn't speak. She only touches the screen of her Comm Unit, and a planet-wide newsvid projects onto the front windshield.

A holograph of the middle-aged man who's the anchor speaks in Morian, the national language for many of the microstates.

"The Accacian Emperor, Nkosi Zahai, has initiated widespread bombings of Mareen's Southern Isles. It began earlier this morning and persists. It appears he is targeting the incorporated cities and villages where mass pockets of civilians reside. It is unclear, as of now, the number of survivors there may be, if any, once the bombings cease. If the Accacian emperor's treatment of the first isle he attacked, Cara, is any indication, there will not be. Drone-captured footage transmitted images of staggering and unbounded

death. This seems a chief objective Accacian forces mean to achieve with the bombings, as after the last missiles were dropped in Cara, the Red Legions marched in to kill any Carans left among the carnage."

The anchor stops for a moment, his voice wobbling at the end, to clear his throat. Movement along the bottom of the holograph projection shows him squeezing the mug on the desk in front of him. He closes his eyes for a second before peeling them back open. At least he isn't recounting the widespread loss of lives in a sterile, uncaring manner. There's little solace in the observation, though.

In the silence that pervades the transport, my chest spasms. I forget how to breathe. I always knew Nkosi was a monster. A hellserpent walking the planet. But what the reporter described is beyond that. It's sheer evil. Unfathomably cruel. Soulless. He wiped out civilians. Women. Elderly. Children. Intentionally. The bastard *targeted* them. And he continues to repeat the massacre with the other isles. Bile sears my throat, especially when I think the people we want to support us are his *allies* now.

"This went live about five minutes ago." Dannica's voice quivers. "There's . . . there's more when he continues."

About thirty seconds later, the anchor has mostly collected himself and starts speaking again. *"Accacian soldiers have been placed along any points of retreat for Mareenian soldiers and civilians. The Emperor's forces are swiftly and immediately executing any who attempt to flee."* The composure he formerly gained shatters again. His hand slams down on the anchor desk. *"The situation in Mareen is heinous! What's more atrocious is that none of the remaining powers of the Minor Continent have yet moved to martial resistance against a man capable of committing such vicious war crimes! With each hour, he gains more footing on our continent. I, we, can only pray that this latest travesty shakes them out of their wait-and-see stupor and incites them to act! Now is not the time for cowardice. Mareen is the focus of Accacia's attention at present, but who is next? We should be looking to history. We—"*

He leans forward, clearly reading something intently that's being displayed in front of him. He turns as pale as Dannica. "I—there's a new breaking report."

Where he'd increased his volume to near shouting before, his voice is now but a whisper. "In addition to Khanai, other powers on the Minor Continent have issued pledges of fealty to the Blood Emperor and Accacian flags fly along their borders beside their national flags."

I listen in horror as he names Ska'kesh, which I know; Braxxis—Reed's sure bet and where we were headed next; the remaining countries among the Eastern Microstates and all of the western ones too.

Lythe is the only name he doesn't recite.

The air is knocked out of my lungs entirely. My gut twists, and twists, and twists. I sit beside Dannica, trembling. I'm sure my color has fled me, too, now. My nails dig into the seat cushion as my pulse howls in my ears. I try to center myself. I try to slice through the spike of terror and anguish and hopelessness that hits me. It's impossible.

We've lost before we've even really, truly started to fight. It was one thing if they had stayed neutral—at least that gave us a chance. Now any hope of gathering allies is quashed. Today hasn't just resulted in a loss of Ska'kesh. It's a loss of everybody. There's only Lythe, which is holding out, and even if we did journey south to try and work with them, it wouldn't be enough. The Blood Emperor's might was immense to the point of almost insurmountable before, and now, with nearly the whole of the continents—which is all of fucking Iludu—at his back . . .

That fucker has evolved to no less than untouchable.

A thing Lythe must have gleaned too. From Grandfather and my academy studies, I'm knowledgeable enough about the federation of fierce warriors to guess with near total confidence at their next move: they've chosen not to yield, and to die independent and free when the time comes and the Emperor makes them pay for their pride rather than kneel to a despot. So my heart bleeds for them, too, and for the rest of the Minor Continent. Because, the stark truth is, I can't even call the countries that have chosen to kneel cowards, or fools, or disparage them in any manner after seeing the images of what Nkosi did in Cara and continues to do in the Isles. It's a clear message to the rest of the world that once held out against him, and that message worked.

If I helmed a country and was faced with the extermination of every one of my people or bowing to a tyrant . . . The ferocious part of me insists I'd choose the Lytheian answer and stand free, fighting and dying for the right rather than choosing to live chained to a brutal empire. However, the deaths of millions of people would be on my hands. And I don't know. *Is* it better to find a way to persist, to survive, to keep your people and legacy enduring so that, maybe one day, those who come after you might find a way to set things right?

"What about the liquid iridium?! What about iridium, period?!" I cry, trying to make sense of how Accacia is decimating the Isles so thoroughly. Mareen has an abundance of war tech; the military possesses dozens of different kinds of weapons to use against an empire that primarily relies on magic. That fact combined with iridium's ability to dampen magic—or completely sever it, in the liquid serum's case—should've caused the news reporter to relay Mareenian forces were ferociously fighting back! My metal pendant may have been slow-acting, but Selene had me incapacitated in seconds and for a long enough time that if Republic armies are using it en masse, the attack on Cara shouldn't have been a massacre.

"Accacia must have found some counteragent against it having a significant effect," Dannica says hoarsely. "They've known about it since the war summit, and three months is a considerable time."

I wince because I'm the reason Accacia has known about it for so long.

"I—we—have you talked to the others?" I ask about the rest of our team, pulling myself out of the horror of the unconscionable, devastating tragedy unfolding in real time. "They must have seen this too."

Reed, like Dannica, has been constantly monitoring the newsvids for war developments and the planet-wide responses to Nkosi's presence.

Dannica might as well be a statue in her seat. Tears prick her eyes. "I don't know. That's the third thing. I tried Reed first. Then Haynes. Then Greysen, Liim, and Dane. Nobody is answering my Comms."

I suck in a breath. "If all of them are unreachable, they're in trouble." Somebody would've answered Dannica otherwise, or contacted us before we could reach out to them after seeing the newsvid.

I think back to our former attack. What if Sutton's dispatched a fresh Praetorian-merc team that tracked us down? Or it could be an actual bounty hit this time. *Either way, the squad is missing two people without Dannica and me,* I think, spiraling with panic. *Perhaps Sutton instructed Selene to hire several hundred mercs, learning from last time.* Reed and the others could easily fight off a hundred. But an entire small legion by themselves? Even if I were there, I'm pretty sure our team isn't that good.

"We need to get back to them," I say, my heart thundering and my mind compartmentalizing out of necessity. The devastation in the Isles is gut-wrenching and the alliances Accacia is collecting are petrifying, but I can't get ripped apart by that right now. Later, I absolutely will. At *this* moment . . .

"We need to find the others, STAT," I tell Dannica again, snapping her out of her stupor before rushing out the name of Haynes's brothel to the transport and telling it to calculate the swiftest route that will get us there.

We're less than a kilometer away when a mass-carry transport rams into the side of us.

The impact sends our smaller transport spinning, and my head slams against the side glass with a force that makes my teeth shred my bottom lip. Wetness stings the side of my head where it's pulsing with pain. I touch the spot, and my hands come away coated with blood. There's a second brutal impact and then a third. Two mass-carry transports pin ours in place.

Dannica rubs her shoulder beside me.

"Are you all right?" she asks, jerking her chin at my bleeding head. Her blaster is already out and her finger's on the trigger.

"I am," I say as I yank one of my own off my hip.

What the fuck is going on?

I scan the scene outside the window I'm seated beside. Dannica does the same on her side. The transport pinning us on the left has windows tinted dark that I can't see through. The street beyond it is vacant.

I focus past the ringing in my ears and my altered vision, which slightly blurs. I take my eyes off the transport on my side for a few seconds to see what's going on with Dannica's. It sits immobile too.

"Do you want to get out and shoot them up or stay in and let whoever the fuck is in them come to us?" Dannica asks, pissed.

"Out," I growl. "Definitely fucking out."

"Great. That's exactly what I was thinking."

There's no doubt the dumb assholes inside the transports are bounty pricks looking for a payday. Praetorians, agents of their government, wouldn't operate so conspicuously in a foreign territory. And I'm betting this is the same crew tying Reed and the others up. They were smart about one thing: ramming our transport at its doors. We're not getting out the simpler way. But I'm in a mood to break some shit anyway.

I shoot out the back glass so Dannica and I can climb out through the opening.

We stand back to back, guns raised and pointed toward the suspiciously still vehicles. Nobody is filing out of them yet.

I brandish a second blaster. "Whatever this is," I say to Dannica, "whoever is in those transports, they die. We don't. We fight our way out of this."

"You're damn right," Dannica says over her shoulder.

I step forward and let out a spray of bullets at the front window of the transport in my sight. I hear constant fire from Dannica behind me.

Unlike our transport, the glass doesn't shatter. It's bulletproof. *Shit.* I fire three shots into the metal hood of the transport. They don't make a dent.

"They're armored," Dannica yells before I can yell the same thing at her.

Of course they are.

It's useless, but out of pure fury, I empty the clips of both blasters into the front of the transport. Then I reload them since whoever is in the transports is clearly toying with us.

"Come the fuck out!" I scream. Bodies *aren't* armored. Flesh, my bullets *can* rip through.

I yell again in frustration. But I conserve my ammo in case I need it because I don't have an unlimited supply on me, and I have no idea what we're up against.

Finally the side door of the transport swings up. I glance and see if its counterpart has done the same. Its door has raised too.

I swivel back to the one nearest me, knowing Dannica can take care of whatever comes out of hers, and I need to take care of whatever slithers out of mine.

I grip my blasters tighter, and my hands turn clammy around the gun when a familiar Accacian man with copper skin, dark hair worn short, and light ocher eyes steps out. I'm not sure if it's the last person I expect to see, but it's close.

It's Ajani, the Red Order warlord I crossed paths with in Khanai.

His uniform, which is entirely death-black save for the bloodred collar, is as unnerving and ominous as it was back in Mustaph's throne room. The man himself is more frightening. He stands staring at me, pitiless, with all the brutality the Blood Emperor's loyal, deadly generals are infamous for exercising. My blood turns to ice in my veins. I recall how he wielded compulsion against me so easily, with merely a thought, the last time we stood face-to-face. I recall how I was entirely under his command and at his mercy until he decided for me not to be.

It pisses me all the way off while simultaneously paralyzing me in place. I swore a vow in Khanai. I knew he'd come for me at some point after I broke it and fled. But I'd hoped he'd be too tied up with critical battles in the beginning to bother with me anytime soon. Clearly, I was wrong. I lock my knees and choose to let the fury lead our impending dance, not the fear. I aim both of my blasters at his fucking head and without any more hesitation empty their clips into his face.

At least, I try.

He moves quicker.

A shield, similar in appearance to Mareenian protective force fields except glowing red, not white, springs up around him before my UVs make contact. They ricochet off it.

I jam fresh clips into the blasters and shoot more. That color means it's a blood shield, and it must have a max hit capacity. It's how all left-behind Pantheon magic works. Every variety has a different limit, but no Pantheon blessing is boundless. A fail-safe the gods made sure of when they doled the powers out in the Pantheon Age so their flocks would have a harder time using their gifts against them.

The problem is, if Ajani is a warlord—one of the individuals of the Empire second in strength only to the Blood Emperor himself—I have no idea what it will take to shatter his shield. It very likely is a great deal more than whatever I can dish with the ammo I've got.

I keep firing, though, because I'll be damned if I stand around and go down without fighting.

The bastard stares at me from inside his impenetrable, translucent sphere with a slow, taunting smile.

I reload and empty UVs into the damn thing again. It's not the smartest move, but I'm pissed.

"How much ammo do you have to waste?" Ajani says smoothly.

"As much as I fucking need," I growl, having sped a dozen miles past rational. Seeing him again, after the newsvid of what he and his liege and fellow Red Order are doing in the Isles, makes something inside of me snap. Something rabid and vicious that carries blinding, unreasonable fury.

I latch on and ride it for all that it's worth because it's exactly what I need. Bloodlust erupts with a vengeance that knocks the breath out of me. It ignites beneath my skin and in my veins, setting my entire being to boiling. The flux of power comes at the perfect time. I drop the guns and jerk free a knife that I cut the palm of my left hand with.

Ajani's eyes track the movement; he shoots me a sabine's smile.

"Now we get to interact like civilized adults."

The blood shield around him vanishes. It turns to a red spray of mist that coats him and then seems to seep through his uniform and into his pores. If not for the situation, I'd marvel because how the hell does he have that level of control over his magic to make it do that?

But I have a more pressing aim to accomplish.

"Civilize this," I snarl and hurl three blood spikes at his neck lightning-quick. He had started laughing, unfazed, but then the first one grazes the right side of his throat. A thin line of red streaks his brown skin, and all mirth is gone. The next two don't come close to striking him. He snatches them out of the air, one swiftly after the other, and throws them aside. He touches two fingers to his nicked flesh. He looks at his own blood in amazement, as if he's never seen it be drawn before. As if he's completely thunderstruck that it has been spilled in a fight.

Mad with bloodlust, I toss my head back and laugh because oh, you've got to be kidding me? Is he really this gods-shitting arrogant?

He snaps his gaze to me, no longer even remotely amused. He stares me down with enough rage and insult to fill the cosmos. "I wasn't going to inflict any injury upon your person when I came to retrieve you, but you've gone and made me mad. What you just did, you have to answer for," he says as if I'm a child who has misbehaved and needs to be punished.

I shoot three more blood spikes at his neck as my reply.

He dodges them all and then a blood spike of his own buries itself in the center of my chest. I never see it coming. I swear I don't even see it fucking form in his hand. One minute he's standing there, not holding a thing. And the next, the blade-sharp spike is jutting out of the skin below my left collarbone. Pain erupts at the site. I grip it to yank it out, but it won't budge. It stays firmly rooted in place. Ajani strides to me with a smirk, every inch a predator with trapped prey. It's identical to the lethal swagger he moved with in Khanai. "That doesn't budge until I want it to budge," the bastard drawls as if giving me a lecture. "Another thing children in Accacia know."

Dannica appears behind him. Her gleaming blasters are leveled at Ajani's head.

"Fuck. You," I rasp. He's so focused on me, he won't sense them in time to shield against the UVs about to shred the back of his skull. Let's see if he has the juice to come back from *that*.

My cohort sister squeezes the shots off, but not before a scarlet uniform barrels into her from the side, knocking them askew. I watch the blood spike form in the legionnaire's hand. My stomach plunges as time slows, stretches. When it snaps back into place, Ajani's soldier, a dark-skinned woman with a tall, swanlike frame, only stands over Dannica with the weapon, shouting at her not to move.

"You pledged a vow," Ajani says and I barely register it until he takes a second step in my direction. It was dangerous and stupid to have taken my eyes off the threat in front of me; I force myself to turn away from Dannica (if the legionnaire didn't kill her, there's a reason and she'll be okay for now) and focus squarely on the warlord. "You swore a blood oath. Then you forsook it." Ajani levels the accusation at me, disgust flashing in his eyes. "But the world over is aware that Mareenians know nothing of fidelity. Why do you think the entirety of your continent, your allies, are turning against you?" He takes another step in my direction and grips the blood spike in the center of my chest. He leans in close and whispers, "I don't actually need to touch this to do what I'm about to do next, but it'll feel better to have my hand on the spike when it happens." That's all the warning I get before he pushes the blood spike deeper into my chest. Agony and white-hot fire rips me apart. "You're Accacian, girl, and you *will* learn our ways. You will *submit* to our ways. When we swear a blood oath, we don't give it lightly, with the intention of never fulfilling it, and we certainly don't run from it. Accacians don't run from anything. Blood oaths are not lies to be traded or tools for playing games of intrigue that you were over your head trying to do in the first place. They are sacred, enforced by Amaka, the goddess of blood rites herself, and they are binding for as long as both parties live." He pushes the blood spike deeper into my chest. I heave, choke, and cough up blood. "You want out of it, then you have to die. That's the only way. Would you like that end?"

A savage smile accompanies his words, as if he's said them in challenge. As if he knows I'll submit, that I'll collapse at his feet and choose otherwise.

He has no fucking idea who I am.

I cough up more blood then spit it in his face.

"Go to a hellpit. Feel free to kill me because I'm not serving you and the monster you call liege."

Something dark flashes in his eyes, and for a second, the mask of urbanity that he likes to wear drops. He becomes every bit the monster, the brutal bastard who revels in cruelty that I know he, his emperor, and all of his fellow warlords is. As if he catches the slip and doesn't wish for it to show just yet, he fixes his expression back into carefully cultivated refinement. I blink at the instantaneous shift. It's another thing that's terrifying about him.

"I don't intend to kill you," he says. "I said if *you* want out of it, you must die to attain it. I never said anything about *me*. Because what really matters is that I don't intend to let you out. So I guess what I really should've said is, if you want out, you must find a way to kill me, and," he shrugs, suffused with ego, "that is something that you will never be capable of doing. No matter how potent of a power you possess."

"Conceited much?" I bite off around the pain pulsating in the center of my chest.

"Very," he says. Then, casually, he notes, "The blood spike won't kill you where it's lodged." He adds with a smile that makes me want to rip his head off his neck, "It *will* leave you in excruciating torment for the duration that it's in."

I do not give him the satisfaction, or display the weakness, of asking how long that will be.

Instead, I promise him, "Before we're done with each other, you're dead. *That* is an oath I intend to and will keep."

"I'll put you out of your misery once we arrive where we're going," he says, dismissing the threat. "That should be punishment enough for the offense you committed against me. If you were still a Praetorian, and you assaulted a higher-up, whatever the sanction is in Mareen, the penalty is worse in the Red Legions. Don't do it again."

If I were in better shape, I'd snort. Then I'd lob several more blood spikes—and knives behind them—at his jugular for good measure.

But I'm not in better shape. In fact, I'm pretty bad off. So all I can do is watch as he turns to the transport behind him and inclines his head.

In response, men and women in scarlet uniforms—more blood legionnaires—pour out of the transport.

"I've got this one myself," Ajani says to his soldiers. "Bring the other one with us."

Dannica.

I try to twist around to see her fully, but it hurts too fucking bad to execute the movement. Black swims before my vision with the exertion, and I'm left sweating and panting.

"If she's hurt . . ."

Ajani waves me off. "Calm yourself. Her, I didn't need to take such

forceful measures with. She was easily neutralized by compulsion."
Two legionnaires—one of them the female that tackled her—march a
stiff, vacant-eyed Dannica by me.

Ajani, towering over me by a foot, stares down at me appraisingly. "I
tried the same compulsion on you when I exited the transport to make
your retrieval less messy. I could not take your mind. But it worked easily enough in Khanai. You've learned how to block my attempts." He
says it as if in commendation.

Again, if the situation weren't so fucked up and twisted at the moment, I'd laugh. I haven't actively attempted to do anything, and I don't
know what the hell he's talking about. *The flux.* It's the only thing I can
think of. *It has to be the cause.*

"I've learned a lot of things," I bluster.

Ajani's eyes rove over me covetously. "Your power . . . it's more ro-
bust than in Khanai. I didn't detect that when I first cornered you." He
brushes a hand down my right arm, and I stiffen.

Behind the reflexive response, I give my best *fuck you* smile and
plant a lie that might be useful later if he believes it. "You have no idea
what I'm capable of. And you never will—until I'm ready to carve out
your entrails and feed them to you."

He scoffs, but his eyes narrow, clearly trying to discern if that's
true. The heady lust lingers, too, for whatever level of power he can
sense in me. "So you evolved? That must be the reason you're different
from before. When?" he demands eagerly.

I give him another polite *fuck you* smile. And again, his urbane
mask slips. The pitiless monster he really is peeks through, and it almost makes me freeze up. But sheer stubborn refusal and pettiness
keep me full of bravado, and from giving the motherfucker the satisfaction of glimpsing the bowel-loosening fear he really induces.

I return Ajani not the smile of a sly sabine, but the smile of a cunning, ruthless she-wolf. "I did. Like I warned, watch your flank *and*
your front."

He says nothing. Simply grips my elbow and forces me, his blood spike still lodged in my chest, to the transport that his men marched a mindless Dannica to.

As he deposits me beside her, my mind is already spinning through possible ways to get us out of his clutches.

THE TRANSPORT TAKES US TO the same small, inconspicuous, private aerodrome that my squad and I used to fly into Ska'kesh. A pair of Ajani's soldiers lead Dannica out of the transport and walk her into an idling jet nearby. Ajani and his liege, the arrogant fuckers, don't even bother with the mode of transport being inconspicuous. It's as flashy and ostentatious as you can get, the same blinding, menacing crimson that colors the high neck of Ajani's Red Order uniform and those of his legionnaires.

Ajani grips my bicep, pulls me off the transport, and leads me to the jet.

"How nice to have my own personal escort," I say, words dripping with venom.

"To keep watch over you, I'm trusting nobody else," he croons back. "At least not until you come to heel." He jerks his head toward his unit of soldiers filing onto the jet. "Your power levels are above theirs. But not mine. Yet." I startle at the knowledge, and it seems ludicrous that he'd let such vital information slip. There's no way it's not intentional. So why hand me the hope that I can get out of his capture since he's the only person who might be able to stop me if I use my blood-gift?

His chuckle is low, dark, and menacing. "It's foolish. Don't try it," he says as if he knows what I was thinking. "My legionnaires were never who you needed to worry about. Only me."

An intense wave that feels like a battering gust of wind slams into me from the side. It knocks the breath from my lungs, damn near cutting off my oxygen supply completely. Then it lights up my entire skin, like a live wire rippling over my body. I grit my teeth against the new shock of pain, my eyes watering from its intensity. "What the fuck did you do?" I can only groan as he pulls me along.

"Let *my* power slip its leash. So you know the full extent of what you're facing if you try to run or squirm out of the blood oath you swore to me . . . again."

The battering gust and the feeling of electric currents lighting me up head to toe vanish as quickly as they began. I can't help it. This time, I visibly shudder and stare at him with all-out terror. The undiluted fear is mostly for the warlord walking beside me, but also for his emperor . . . because if Ajani is this strong, what kind of power does the man he calls liege possess? What the fuck can the Blood Emperor do? Moreover, how will I ever get near Nkosi if Ajani is an obstacle to go through?

As we reach the jet, my legs turn boneless. I wobble on my feet from realizing the sheer enormity, the stark impossibility, and the true peril of my task.

I'm suddenly glad that some external force did cut me off from the rest of my squad before Ajani's ambush. I actually thank the Pantheon that he's captured me. Because at least he's taking me away from them. At least they're no longer chained to my mad mission. Ajani has cut them loose of it, and for that, I am grateful. Because when I prayed to Amaka and she answered, I asked her for power to get my team out of

Khanai. I didn't ask the goddess for power enough to face down a Red Order warlord, then the Blood Emperor himself. And Ajani just made it blisteringly apparent that even when I flux, he's right. I'm operating at infant levels compared to him—and the Emperor.

I was so, so fucked from the beginning.

But they're out, and that's what . . .

Ajani leads me onto the jet, and though I didn't think I could experience any more horror, I do. The blood in my veins plunges to glacial. Every single droplet, every particle of plasma, every cell, ices over. Because Dannica isn't the only one from my squad that's perched vacant-eyed and corpse-stiff in a seat. Reed is there, looking the same way. So is Haynes, Caiman, Greysen, Liim, and Dane. They all occupy the same row near the middle of the passenger cabin.

"Why the godsdamn are they here?" I shout to Ajani, panic choking me. "Let them go!"

Ajani gives me an incredulous look. "Why do you think they're here?" He pulls me to a row at the front of the jet that's unoccupied. It's situated directly behind the cockpit. "Call them insurance that you behave well and submit to anything and everything I ask of you." He points to a seat. "Buckle up."

Shit. Shit. Shit. It's all I can think.

Shit!

If I were alone, things would go different from here. I'd lash out, evoking my normal, reckless default mode. I'd tell Ajani to go fuck himself—thrice. Then, seeing as how I've had an (infuriatingly) hard time maiming him, I could crash the plane once we're in the air. It's damn difficult to keep control over a captive while completing a rushed HALO jump. I mean, *I* could do it; any Praetorian could accomplish it. A decent number of upper-class cadets could too. However, Accacia isn't Mareen—the Empire's military training mainly focuses on honing magic to its deadliest capacity. Therefore, when Ajani tried to execute a jump with me in tow, I would likely be the one to control how the descent would go, slip him somehow during the landing . . .

I'm not alone, though. I went into this mission with a squad. With a team whose help I stupidly accepted on a fool's op. And because I'm not alone, I obediently plop into the seat Ajani points to, doing precisely as he commands. For now.

All the while, my mind screeches, *It's no longer only Dannica I need to extract from danger—it's* everybody.

WE'RE IN THE sky for only about half an hour's time. The jet lands in front of a polygonal fortress complete with drum towers, bastions projecting outward from each of the front-facing corners, triangular ravelins, a portcullis built into the outer stone wall, parapets, and numerous watchtowers. Compared to the sleek look of Krashen and the rest of Mareen, it's positively archaic. Yet, I know the power behind those walls is enough to make this place virtually impenetrable even with all the tech at the Praetorians' disposal. That power is surely why the Accacian flag, a swath of obsidian black, inky as the night sky and with three crimson Blood Moons blazing in its center, disturbingly flies above each of the watchtowers.

And they aren't the only flags present. Beside the Empire's banner are flags sporting the same lightless black with a powerfully built, three-horned mahogany bull in the middle. I stare at the bull and pull its meaning from my academy studies: it's the symbol of Accacia's Apis, the Red Order warlord who sits above the other six by might of bloodgift and serves as second-in-command for the Empire.

Alarm bells ring shrill in my head. Those bull flags beside the Empire's flag mean this stronghold is under the control of the Apis . . .

And to add to the hellishness of the situation is the very fact of *where* we are. I've seen this fortress's old-world architecture in academy history texts. It was built near the very beginning of civilization. A Wonder of Iludu, it's drenched in Pantheon magic that's keeping it in such pristine condition, able to weather time and the elements and natural catastrophes without requiring restoration. Krashna reigned from here, the god of war's old citadel, which he wedged between ancient Mareen's northern border and the stubborn nomadic lands, now the Free Microstates, which were once inhabited by Iludians who did not wish to belong under rule of any of the Pantheon and fled to the wilds of the uninhabited far north.

Even from inside the jet, the same sinister, preternatural feelings that skirted over me in Onei's Expanse and on Hasani's Wrath in the Ice Wastes wash over me again. I can't suppress the shudder when thinking about the nightmarish Pantheon-cursed places and their visited horrors. I don't care to *begin* to guess at what might be producing the malevolence wafting off the god of war's citadel and what that means is prowling inside.

Why would the Accacians, or anybody with an iota of self-preservation instincts, select this place as a stronghold? I spin it over, trying to see what I'm missing, the advantage it adds that they've decided trumps the danger. I can't arrive at one logical answer for the strategic necessity if they're currently winning, and have collected the rest of the Minor Continent as their tribute states. Their Apis could've and should've established his stronghold literally anywhere else. Especially when, as a people who prize Pantheon Blessings, Accacians have retained vast stores of knowledge of the gods, their blessings, and their curses. Even much more ignorant Mareenians, the Tribunal included, stay far, far, far away from Krashna's citadel. It's why the fortress and the land surrounding it have been vacant since Krashna's ousting thousands of years ago. Everyone and everything that attempted to tear it down or blow it to hell met heinous deaths before they could succeed.

And we're about to go inside the place.

I look at Ajani, who's seated beside me, like he's mad. He, and whoever Accacia's Apis is, has got to be insane to outfit this as one of their war camps. The sheer evil, the sheer violence, the sheer malignant glee sloughing off the citadel whispers promises of a torturous death.

I realize maybe that's the point. They didn't invite us here—under compulsion—for a picnic.

I twist in my seat to check on my team, dread and presage chaining me in a vise grip. The seven of them remain vacant-eyed and still as if their bodies are mere hollow shells, no life present inside them. Seeing them like that with the insidiousness of the citadel so cloying inside the jet rattles me. Before I can prevent my mind from going there, I think of Zayne and how I couldn't save him in the last death trap we got thrown into. I think of the twins, Dex and Bex, and how I failed them too. My pulse whooshes in my ears, the tide of panic swiftly overwhelming me with the portent that things will turn out the same once we're marched into the citadel, either at the hands of the oily magic I feel or the Accacians.

"When will you give them their minds back?" I snarl at Ajani. They need to be lucid. They need to be aware of their surroundings. They need to be able to think and see and brace for and fight whatever comes at us next.

The bastard shrugs. "When it suits me. It certainly will not be until *after* you and I have a chat. We must come to some understandings about the blood oath you swore, what I expect of you, and what you *will* submit to. If I'm happy with your response, I'll consider your request."

My hands curl into fists. I envision hacking away at his neck, severing his head from his shoulders like I did with the Accursed. He's as abominable and as sickening as one—perhaps more monstrous than one of those horrors. Which is saying a lot since they skin, roast, and eat people.

As his soldiers march my squad off the jet, Ajani sweeps to his feet. "Come," he bids in a tone that brooks no argument. "Let's go have that talk."

For a moment I sit, stubborn and prideful, planted where I am because I'm not his fucking dog he's bringing to heel. If I were alone in capture, I wouldn't budge a godsdamn inch. In fact, one—if not both of us—would already be dead. But I'm not, and he still has the others. So staring a hole in the center of Ajani's skull, which I vow to the Pantheon to place there soon, I rise and do as commanded.

14

INSIDE THE CITADEL, AJANI LEADS me to a dining room with a table set for two. The table itself is big enough to seat a small company and as lavish as the food laid atop it. The wood it's fashioned from is the wretched ash white of the trees found in Onei's Expanse. I shiver not just at this reminder of the Pantheon-cursed forest, but also at being inside this rumored horror raised by a god. The table is what has my attention, though; its unsettling nature is exacerbated by the fact that instead of standing on four legs, it's propped up in the center by an intricate tree trunk with roots that travel the length of the floor, brushing against each wall, as if they're embedded in the sleet-gray marble itself. The trunk stretches up to meet the tabletop in a twisting fashion, all of it that sickly white.

All along the trunk and roots are detailed carvings of fauna indigenous to both halves of Iludu: scarabs, crocodiles, cobras, desert worms, jackals, and winged bulls that roam the Principal Continent alongside water owls, sabines, night bears, redcap deer, and she-wolves of the Minor Continent. She-gorgons and serpent drakes, terrifying creatures that live among the depths of the Tumultuous Sea, are present too. I think the trunk is meant to depict a tree of life because it includes a naked tribe of humans encircling its base. But this is life engraved in a place of death, and so I feel unbalanced taking in all the pictographs.

Trying to shift my eyes' focus, I find myself staring at the ten thick branches that sprout from the trunk and connect with the flat tabletop. Embedded into the bark of the branches are each of the ten gods and goddesses that once walked Iludu and claimed dominion over our planet. My eyes land on Krashna's ivory figurine, which grips his signature shield and his sword that always struck true—both the indigo blue of Khanaian steel and gifted to him by his twin, Kissa. A thing Kissa, Khanai's patron goddess, later regretted after he used the weapons to slaughter millions. The goddess of arts, riches, and wisdom's figurine rests on a branch beside that of the brother she once adored; she's carved from solid gold and holds the jade horn myth says that she, the only truly benevolent one among the Pantheon, played to gift light, love, and song to the planet. I also see Onei, the bloodthirsty huntress, fashioned from stone and pulling taut her sacred bow.

Amaka, created from a crimson substance that glistens as bright as fresh-spilled blood, ensnares me next. I've seen that exact shade of red before. It's the color of Amaka's Crown, her constellation that blazes in the sky; it's the hue Blood Moons shine; it's the lush scarlet I've beheld of her actual crown the times I've communed with her. So I know for certain that Amaka's haunting, miniature form is a blood ruby—the name given to the "gems" she liked to forge through a ritual involving the spilled lifeblood and lifted souls of her enemies.

The queasiness that settled in my stomach upon entering the citadel intensifies.

Chills ripple endlessly across my skin as I gaze upon the remaining Pantheon, who were just as heinous as Amaka and Krashna. Va'ia, the supposed goddess of beauty and love, rests on a branch, chiseled from smooth obsidian with fine shimmers of gold; she was a being who used the most ardent desires of humans against them, trapping them into an eternal, hellish servitude she demanded as payment for any blessings she bequeathed. Nanwi's copper features are concealed behind an apt jackal mask; the god of trickery and illusions had a penchant for cruel games and crueler jokes. Beside him is Imu, a pearlescent goddess of chaos and crossroads, who'd litter plagues across the world for amusement. Hasani, the god of the After, is cast in bronze, his voracious hellserpents twined around his body. Daja, the sea god who raised Iludu's ocean, flooded it with the ghastly creatures that call it home, and then lured countless humans to their deaths in his waters, is made from a lapis lazuli that matches the exact color of the Tumultuous Sea. Maliya is cast from an amalgamation of golds and reds. The fire goddess's figurine glows and glimmers like living flame, and she rounds out the line that the Pantheon stand in as a punctuated reminder of the devastation the ten of them wrought; she herself was notorious for swallowing entire cities in flame when a people pissed her off.

I'm not surprised that the awful table is a furnishing of the citadel. All of the gods were vain, with Krashna being among the most narcissistic of his brethren. Of course an arrogant jackass would decorate his stronghold with odes to godly might over mere humans.

Speaking of egotistical pricks . . . I pull my stare away from the terrifying Pantheon because there are more immediate threats I need to focus on. For one, Ajani stands far too near, watching me like a predator while I look at the tree of life.

He motions to it. "Impressive, weren't they?"

He can't be talking about anything except the gods. I snort. "You would think that. Shitty begets shitty. No. They were not impressive. They were murderous and reprehensible and monsters that terrorized the planet."

"It's all relative. They possessed untold power. They were matchless. They had no equals save themselves. They held dominion over their own selves and allowed nobody else to claim it. Isn't that what we all covet? What we war and live for and work endlessly toward?"

If it wouldn't make me lose face, I'd gape. Is he really trying to get philosophical? And does he actually believe the words he's twisting beyond their limit?

"Is that the doctrine you and your Blood Emperor preach to your people to ensure they stay on board with your massacres? Is that how you've gotten the lands and the people you've bullied into submission to accept your bullshit and call it prudence? Is that how the whole of the Principal Continent has become okay with you perpetuating the exact sort of barbarity the Pantheon did, which we all rose up against and cast out? Is that how the Empire stomachs Hyacinth and the rest of the west?" I say, descending into fury. "Is that how it digests Rykos and the east? And now Cara and our other Southern Isles? You bastards are *brutalizing* and *butchering* hundreds of thousands. Not soldiers. Not combatants. You target civilians who can't begin to fight back. You did it the last time too. You lot are precisely as soulless as the gods were, and Iludu, all of it, needs to rise up and be rid of your stain too.

"We war and strive against you *because* you seek to emulate the Pantheon."

Ajani stiffens, and some perverse, petty part of me delights that I've finally unnerved *him*—regardless that it took ripping open my own self to accomplish it. And yet he somehow manages to spit out more drivel. "War is never pretty. It's ugly business, yet necessary, and we have to make sacrifices to achieve the greater good in the end."

"*Greater good!*" I cry, incredulous. "You invaded the Minor Continent *twice* because of greed and because your liege is an arrogant fuck who thinks he should rule the entire world and suffers delusions that the Pantheon has ordained it. Has anointed him. There is *nothing* noble or remotely akin to the *greater good* in that!"

"We keep our war during this second campaign to Mareen," Ajani says, as if this makes them righteous. "We have learned from our previous mistakes; we seek to seize power with a gentler hand."

"Yet you still use the word 'seize' as if it doesn't inherently connote violence." I shake my head, not wanting to get into a semantic argument with him—they never go anywhere with the righteous. "That's why you attack solely us," I say before he can drone on, wrapping my head around the full scope of their strategy. "You're using Mareen as the calf for slaughter. You're using our bloodletting to make the rest of the Minor Continent assimilate, eagerly, into the Empire."

I don't need to ask specifically *why* we're the key pawn in their abominable game. Like Lythe, there's no way in any hell that Mareen wouldn't fight back, tooth and nail. That's what Mareenians do. We go to battle. As long as there's blood in our body and breath in our lungs, we fight back. Always.

His response is a shrug. "That's not the thing of consequence here. The common goal we share is."

I was only guessing at him having lost his damn mind before. I'm sure of it now. "We don't have shit in common. And where's the Apis? Will he be honoring us with an appearance soon?" Part of me hopes so. Might as well get that terror over with up front so I'm glass clear about what flavor of son of a bitch I'm working with.

Ajani walks to the head of the table, pulls out the chair there, and plops down in it. "You're looking at him."

A self-satisfied grin curves his lips. "Sit," he orders me, pointing to the seat to the right of his.

I stare at him. *Gawk*—most un-badass-like. Astonishment drains all the bluster and bravado out of me. *He's Accacia's Apis?*

"How old are you?" I ask before I can curb the question—or the awe that suffuses it.

Ajani brushes an invisible speck of dust off the red collar of his crisp Red Order coat. He doesn't play cagey with an answer. Instead, he practically preens as he says, "Twenty-three turns around the Iludu sun."

How? I manage not to ask and embarrass myself, or help stroke his ego more than I already have. *But how in the godsdamn did he manage it?* The Blood Emperor himself is centuries old. From what I learned at the academy, the Red Order is comprised of powerful men who are similarly long-lived. I riffle through every academy lesson and each of Grandfather's lessons on Accacian history, its political structure, how Empire society is stratified, and how power is disseminated among the Red Legions, seeking an answer for how Ajani is as young as he claims to be yet holds so high a rank. Accacia isn't like Khanai, where twenty-year-old Enoch is Emrir and second-in-command by virtue of being the Grand Monarch's firstborn child. The Empire isn't like the Republic either, where legacy lines and blood ties between scions of war houses give people automatic standing. Accacians have always bowed to the might of the blood-gift, and nothing else.

"Amaka's gift is not stagnant," I recall Grandfather once telling me of the intel he'd collected on the Republic's enemy over the years. *"It's a living blessing that evolves and surges—and can even ebb in some cases. I've never unearthed how or why, but I do know that the strength of the blood-gift and the number of Blood Moons an individual has lived through display a positive correlation. It's why the Blood Emperor, the oldest living Accacian, possesses so much strength. It's also why his near-as-old Red Order can do what they can."*

During that particular lesson six years ago, Grandfather mentioned nothing of Ajani, a juvenile warlord who would've only lived under Iludu's moons for a meager seventeen years at the time. Grandfather wouldn't have left that exception out. He was too thorough in his lessons and the knowledge he imparted. It means Grandfather didn't know about Ajani. So Ajani wasn't a warlord or Apis yet. The deduction then leaves me with the question:

Where did Ajani come from and how has he risen to his position?

I scrutinize the man before me, my training and Grandfather's lessons kicking into hyperdrive.

Know your enemies, Kenna, I hear Grandfather say. *Know them better than you know yourself. It's impossible to predict their assaults, block them, and deliver a counterstrike when you do not.*

I eat my pride and ask Ajani how he's risen to Apis. I keep the awe from before in my voice, *wanting* to stroke his ego now if it'll help extract an answer I may somehow leverage to accomplish freeing my team from his clutches . . . and then killing the bastard.

Ajani's smug grin stays in place. He kicks the chair beside him out from the table. "If you really want that answer, sit your ass down like I said."

I imagine slicing out his tongue. The intent must show on my face because he bristles, and the damnable blood spike continuing to poke out of my chest lodges deeper.

I hiss.

"If you want to play this game, fine," Ajani drops with casual, quiet violence. "Know this, *Praetorian*, Accacia's torture methods far outstrip anything Mareen will ever invent. Magic lends itself to extremely creative ways of making you scream and grinding obedience into you. You test my patience while I'm trying to be courteous."

I wave to the blood spike, which fucking *hurts*. "You call this courtesy?" I laugh, shrill, and pay for how it jostles the blood spike in stars. Heaving around the pain, I grit out to Ajani, "Piss off. I'll stand."

The Apis shakes his head, sighs as if he's an exasperated parent and I'm an ungrateful child. The blood spike slides deeper, continued punishment. Waves of pain so great that I sway on my feet pulse around it. I clench my teeth, curl hands around the thing, attempt to pull it out, desperate to achieve what's been proven I can't.

Ajani slides hands into his pockets, flicks a pointed glance at the chair near me.

I *will not* drop into it. It's a point of pride, a point of strength, and a matter of survival: I can't display a capacity to be so easily broken.

The blood spike pierces tissue a few centimeters deeper. I feel the fire of it jerking upward. I bite my tongue hard enough to taste my own blood. I lose the battle and cry out. And. I. Keep. Standing.

Ajani rolls his eyes, but a gleam of respect glints in their brown depths.

Thank the fucking cosmos; we can be done with this.

After extracting what's necessary, then, and only then, do I sit (collapse, really)—*at the time of my own choosing*—while swiping an unimpressed look up the length of Ajani to communicate that.

The grating cocky amusement from before washes into his expression. "You would've made a greater point had you kept standing. Capitulation at your own behest is still capitulation. Here's another lesson you clearly need: impudence isn't strength; it's a revealing act of the desperate when they don't have any craftier options left." He flashes teeth in a manner that's pure dominance. I brace for the fresh assault, for him to push the blood spike all the way in, perhaps add a second one beside it, drag this torture session out. I blink, disoriented, when instead the spike slides out a fraction enough for me to breathe easier. "Really, you should be thanking me for all this knowledge and the demonstrations of what you should be able to do yourself," Ajani says coolly. "To begin answering your question, since we have little time to persist with useless posturing: Those of the blood can easily register the power within the blood. We can mark our own relative power levels as well as that of others. It's another one of those first things Acaccian children are taught to do that you're woefully ignorant of," the bastard says, digging in.

I gnash my teeth, deciding I won't stop at hacking out his tongue. I'm going to shove it down his throat and make him asphyxiate on it. At some point. For now, I purse my lips and let him keep talking.

"The ability is what keeps an empire of numerous people with staggering might from collapsing from within, or falling to civil war, like Mareen once did," he continues, once again unable to help leveling another insult. Before we're finished with each other, he's going to pay for each one in stars, and his ass is racking up quite the debt. "We Acaccians, we know the pecking order within the Empire and there's no getting around it. It's set when we're born. There's no eventual rank to declare or trials to survive." He motions down the length of himself, haughty. There's a humorous, arrogant gleam to his eyes like he's privy to a joke that I'm not, but he's about to detonate the grenade on me in a second. I narrow my eyes, suspicious, and brace for whatever the bastard is about to reveal. "Take me, for example. I'm purportedly the most powerful blood-gifted to have been born in a century. Empire haruspices divined it from the entrails of the winged bull that was sacrificed when my mother conceived me. On my born day, Empire augurs confirmed what their counterparts foretold as they measured the power in my blood as a newborn, which was quadruple what some fully evolved adults possess, and gauged how that power would likely magnify each year I aged under Amaka's moons. In a few centuries, the augurs believe I'll eclipse my liege. Iludu and the Empire will see an individual gifted with more power than he who has held the most for two hundred years."

When Ajani divulges the last bit, the covetous gleam his ocher eyes like to take on radiates at max wattage. And it alerts me to the fact that I've gotten an important answer to my question while also learning a second, equally critical thing about Accacia's young Apis: He doesn't simply lust after my power.

He lusts after *absolute* power—his liege's included.

Oh, he may be of the Blood Emperor's innermost circle, and he may even be loyal, but I have no doubt that he is loyal primarily because he is forced to be. He has no other choice as the Emperor outstrips him in might, at least for the time. But if and when what Ajani and Accacia's sect of blood seers says comes true, Ajani *will* challenge Nkosi for his throne—or murder him and take it by usurpation. The man serves His Imperial Majesty of Acaccia, all while wanting to be it himself.

I file away what I've gleaned about this enemy. That kind of voracious hunger for power is usually insatiable, and it always creates weak spots in those who harbor it. Usually they're vulnerabilities born of hubris. So I just have to figure out what the particular gaps in Ajani's armor are that'll allow me to strike at him with deadly and unerring efficiency.

Ajani steeples his fingers below his chin, looking at me with an intense expression. It's the same laserlike focus he had when he captured me in Ska'kesh, and I realize he's reading my power levels like before.

I stiffen, because . . . shit. I'm not in the midst of a surge anymore. Whatever he sensed in Ska'kesh that made him conclude I'd evolved and helped me seem even mildly formidable is gone. Keeping a cool disposition on the outside, I frantically scramble to tug on my blood-gift and try to force the flux. Since my power likes to wretchedly do what the fuck it wants, when the fuck it wants, nothing happens. Beyond that, there's the blood spike. The wound it inflicted can't heal, while my blood-gift has been working an extended time to do exactly that. The overexertion has caused a drop in my normal levels of power, acting as a handcuff itself.

I switch to a backup plan. I bluff my ass off and pray I'm convincing. "Don't bother trying to read me." I smile my psycho smile at Ajani and throw in a dash of Dannica's venomously sweet one. "You'll only ever detect what I want you to, when I want you to. A boon from Amaka when I communed with her in Khanai to get my team out of the keep, in addition to *our* goddess guiding me through evolving. Thank you for snatching that nasty iridium pendant off my neck, by the way. It opened the path."

My heart slams against my chest as I lie. If I can't sell it and if I'm no longer of interest to Ajani's schemes, then my team will assuredly die. He's stated that up front. They've been captured alive to make me behave and do what he desires. Which . . . we still haven't arrived at what that is.

What the hell does he want from me in the first place? Why let me escape in Khanai and come after me now when he clearly could've stopped me then if he's taken me captive so easily? Why are we in this damn citadel?

Why not take me straight to his liege, if the blood oath he had me swear to him was in service to his emperor?

The barrage of questions spawns a plan to accomplish a dual aim: I derail Ajani from continuing to consider my power too closely by diving into asking every single thing that's come into my head. If he was exhaustive in explaining how he's become Apis, maybe he'll launch into more detailed answers that are necessary to have.

The cosmos smiles on me for once because he does. And what he says is something I certainly wouldn't have guessed.

"You want to kill his Imperial Majesty. So do I," he says in the perfectly, and wholly deceptive, urbane manner he likes to project. But then the mask shreds. The ruthless, savage truth of who he really is shows itself. "Which is why I was very precise when I had you swear the blood oath. You swore one to *me*. Not to Nkosi. And if you hear me out, I think we may work together well, given your level of power and mine, to accomplish our common end. Alone, I cannot take him on yet. With you, I'm confident I can kill him and forego waiting centuries."

While his brutal frankness is surprising, this time, I don't gawk in sheer disbelief since I've already ascertained he desires to wear the mantle of emperor.

"My six fellow warlords are the only ones, before I discovered you, who possess a potent enough gift to potentially aid me," he continues. "And each of them is either too loyal or too cowed. But you, Ikenna . . . you already want Nkosi's head."

"Yes. But why do you?" I ask suspiciously, trying to discern if this is a game. Some sort of trap he's walking me into, and by extension my team, like what the bastard orchestrated when we were in Khanai. However, why would he bother to set a trap at all? He's Accacia's Apis, for cosmos's sake, while we're fugitives of a Republic that wants us dead—and already under his thrall. Plus, even if we were to escape, all of Grandfather's old allies have chosen his side already. Any way you dice it, we have no political power. There's also the matter of his blood-gift. I've seen its strength. I've *felt* its harrowing levels. He could likely kill us all with a thought. What need does he have of subterfuge when all of that is the case?

As I mull it over, there's a long pause on Ajani's part. During it, he leans forward and plucks a bright pink blushing apple from a fruit arrangement on the table. A knife appears in his free hand, formed from his blood. Just like when we faced off in Ska'kesh, he produces the damn thing without having to bleed himself. That little act alone proves the staggering command he has over his gift, and how immense it is. He slices into the skin of the apple and cuts it away methodically in the endless, discomfiting silence. He tosses the peel on the table and sets the apple on the ivory plate in front of him. He reaches toward a platter of smoked meats and baked bread next.

"You should eat," he says as he fills his plate with food. "After *stupidly* attempting to fight me earlier and getting yourself hurt, I'm sure your energy levels need considerable replenishment. Nourishment helps restore us to full strength quicker."

I control my face and do not give away the fact that I didn't know that and am gobsmacked to find out. I've always used sleep as my restorative method, and for some reason, never thought about food getting the job done. Grandfather didn't either. Maybe it's because of how little stock we Mareenians place in food. Nevertheless, it's such a simple solution, a much more efficient, pragmatic solution than falling comatose, that I want to laugh and be disgruntled at the same time that I've lived a whole nineteen years of life without it.

Ajani raises an eyebrow. He tips the crimson knife at me. "I gather you didn't know that," the Apis drawls as if he's plucked my thoughts out of my mind. "Verne was sorely lacking in his supposed training. He should've—"

"This isn't about Grandfather, and I'd thank you to stop speaking of him," I cut in. "Why do you want your liege dead? Let's stick to that."

The bastard chuckles, pitching me a sneer that emphasizes I am nothing and nobody to order him around. Yet, when his laughter dies, he obliges.

"The blood-gifted of the Empire live like kings and queens," he says in a conversational tone. "But we're chained to His Imperial Majesty's will, nonetheless. I am a warlord, the equivalent of a prince among the Principal Continent, and I am *still* merely one more conscript in Nkosi's Red Legions. Every person who carries Amaka's blessing knows the same fate." Indignation radiates off him when he finishes. So does quiet fury.

"So you want the Blood Emperor dead so you can be free?" It's what his words hint at.

For a second, all of the suave arrogance deflates, and Ajani gravely dips his head. "We are not so different, you and I. You seek a new world order for your Republic. I seek a new world order for my Empire. I seek an Acaccia where conscription is eliminated, and those who serve in the Red Legions do so because they elect to serve. Yes, I desire liberation for myself, but I also desire it for every individual who is blood-gifted *and* the wider Empire. If you are a citizen of the Empire and you are born blood-gifted, yes, you are allowed your youth, but as soon as you reach the age of evolution, you are ripped away from any attachments to your former life and become the property of His Imperial Majesty. Your blood becomes his blood. And it is all used for one, narrow-sighted focus—Nkosi's never-ending divine expansion campaigns. It is all he aspires to. The thing he puts all his energies and all of Acaccia's greatest resources behind. It hobbles my people and, in turn, the Empire as a whole. My home, my fellow Acaccians, we could be so much more, soar to much greater heights, if every individual with a drop of power His Imperial Majesty can get his hands on wasn't conscripted and used for nothing except war efforts. My people deserve more. We *are* more. We are not slaves and Nkosi treats us as such. It is time for a new way in Acaccia. Since our liege will not permit us liberation, someone else must force it."

He's saying he wants to become emperor to abolish conscription. It's a rational explanation; one that might be admirable—and believable—if he were anybody else. He's played me for a fool once before, though, and I will not let it occur a second time. Learning from Khanai, I comb back over everything Ajani claims, everything I've learned about the Apis, and everything I know of the Blood Emperor himself and of Accacia's workings, for the manipulation.

However, I can't readily see the game board Accacia is arranging or how or why my team and I function as pawns. I shout in frustration inside my head, berating myself for the shortcoming. The failure also means I need to buy some time, string Ajani along, until I figure it out.

"Before this goes any further, I want my team beside me." I demand from Ajani what I'd actually negotiate if I did believe him. "If you're serious about not being my adversary, prove it with something more tangible. Free my team from compulsion this instant and have them brought to me. Then I'll talk it over with them. Together, we'll decide if our goals and yours really do align and if it's in our best interest to *possibly* work with you. That's how our squad operates, and I won't depart from it."

"And you truly believe you are in a position to demand of me these things?"

I say nothing.

He smiles.

His blood spike, mercifully, slips free of my chest. It clatters to the floor while he's twirling the blood knife in his fingers. He stabs it into another apple, cool gaze locked with mine.

Should I wish it, I could skewer you all over again, that gaze says.

15

FOR ALL HIS THEATRICS, AJANI does as I ask.

Reed and the others are walked into the room by a contingent of legionnaires with their eyes clear of that godsforsaken vacant look. Ajani's soldiers flank them. However, the close guard does not seem all that worried—the fact that the Accacians accompany a crop of the most lethal, elite soldiers on the planet and do so without blasters drawn is a thing that punctuates how little of a threat they view the Mareenians to be. But I guess they should be hyperconfident if they can fling a blood spike with even half as much speed and deadly accuracy as their Apis. It's a rather alarming thing to consider—a glaring reminder that the legionnaires, even those who aren't warlords, can wield the blood-gift with devastating capacity.

For my team's part, the Mareenians alternate between anxiously, and smartly, cataloging their surroundings and slicing death glares at the Acaccians.

"I won't negotiate if they continue to be treated like prisoners of war," I growl at Ajani. "Tell your people to back the hell off." I shove away from the table and push to my feet. I cross to my team, somehow preparing to make the legionnaires do what the fuck I said.

"I don't believe we *are* negotiating, Ikenna. And I know for a fact that there is nothing you can do should I decide to ignore your *tawdry, immature threat*." I am about to retort when he holds up his hand. "Give the Mareenians space. Treat them as friends of your Apis for the duration of our talks." I stare at Ajani, wondering what game he's playing.

"It doesn't take much civilized," Ajani continues. "I've already said we are on the same side." Reed raises an eyebrow at that, and I shoot him a subtle *he's insane* look. "But don't mistake my generosity for weakness. If you continue to act like a child, I will show you how Accacians deal with tantrums."

As he's saying all this, his soldiers have already heeded the directive and peel away, taking up position around the perimeter of the room. Two—a man with porcelain skin and bulging muscles who's built like an ox and the dark-skinned woman from Ska'kesh—stand at Ajani's back. From their position, I guess they're either his second and third or his personal bodyguards. Regardless of which, they don't cast repugnant looks our way like their counterparts. Instead, their expressions are scrubbed. I commit their faces to memory. Whoever they are, this man and woman standing behind Ajani's seat at the head of the table know of their Apis's larger schemes. I'd bet my life on it being the reason their demeanors are so carefully blank.

"What talks?" Reed, standing a few inches from me, clenches and unclenches his hands at his sides. He looks between Ajani and me. I internally wince and brace to see the condemnation. The distrust. The suspicion. Because for the second time, they've been detained, *stripped of their will*, and I've appeared by the enemy's side unharmed. Guilt pummels me. *People keep suffering* because *of me. My friends keep suffering because of me.*

Reed's gaze bores into me, and I must be doing a shit job of keeping my thoughts off my face because his eyes soften and he dips his head toward me as if to say, *Whatever this is, I trust you. This isn't like Khanai. And we'll get out of this too.*

I clutch on to the faith he displays in me, more grateful to him for pitching the sentiment than I might ever be able to put into words.

I scan the others, making sure everybody is whole and okay. "Dannica and I were ambushed on our way to the brothel," I say. "I'm assuming you all were, too, and that's why things went dead on your end."

"You'd be right." Caiman cuts a glare at the legionnaires nearest him before settling a chilled stare on Ajani that communicates he'd very much relish tearing the Apis in two with his bare hands. "What do you intend to do with us, you fuck?"

Ajani bristles, and I step between his line of sight and Caiman, just in case. "He claims he wants to help us kill his liege so he can rule the Empire in Nkosi's place. He's also not only a warlord. He's Accacia's Apis," I say, catching them up to speed. We'll have to discuss the fact that I don't believe any of the shit he's said later—I can't risk attempting to communicate it to them, even nonverbally, until we're away from the Accacians. For now, I need Ajani to continue thinking he's leading the dance.

As if on cue, the scheming Apis appears at my side, the swanlike woman and oxlike man in step with him. Ajani sweeps his hand to the table. "Take a seat. You may enjoy the hospitality of my stronghold and eat your fill. You're surely ravished. Compulsion drains the energy of the practitioner and of those it's wielded against." He says it like what's been done to my team is no big deal. Like it's not a complete violation and form of debasement. Like everyone is just supposed to be grateful that they have their minds back, thank him for the favor, and have snack time.

"We'll stand. Also, fuck you," Reed snarls before I can forget that I'm supposed to be feigning capitulation and deliver a similar response. Impressively, he stares the Apis down, fearless, with a death promise laced through his glacial eyes that says he will kill him, regardless of who and what Ajani is.

And okay, it's hot.

Albeit, it's not the time to be horny.

And also—I don't want Reed to be killed.

Not that I don't think Reed could fight Ajani and even hurt him. But I hate the idea of the risk. Of Reed covered in blood—his own and Ajani's gift.

Ajani chuckles darkly. He delivers his own smooth threat back at Reed. "You're the one that's half Khanaian, are you not? I'd expect you to have better sense and better preservation instincts, as your countrymen display in this new age."

"What I am and what I am not is none of your business," Reed grits out.

"Everything about everyone who is anybody on the Principal *and* Minor Continents is my business," Ajani says. "As it should be for any general worth his blood—or training, as you Mareenians say. Which is why I know Verne Amari took you, Darius Reed, under his wing and acted as your hensei. You were also the leader of Mareen's Praetorian Gamma Cohort before fleeing with Ikenna from the Republic. The old Legatus appointed you personally to the position." Ajani relays what he knows about Reed casually enough. But he looks at him with a dagger-sharp gaze, clearly assessing how much of a threat being Grandfather's protégé makes Reed. The warlord would be an idiot not to, given the combat brilliance of the mind and hand that shaped Reed as a warrior and what Grandfather is legendary for being capable of. Even when things seemed impossible and assured loss imminent, Grandfather was heralded for finding a path to victory. Always.

Reed, for his part, falls silent. He lets the ruthless, ferocious edge now stamped into every inch of his bearing speak for itself. The savage, lethal Reed from SSEE, who was pitiless about dragging a knife across

Enzo's neck up on the mountain, has taken up residence in Reed's skin. It's the same Reed who fought fiercely against Enoch in the Jade Palace's keep, a side of him he doesn't show until it's needed.

In answer, a whip of power arcs out of Ajani, aimed at Reed. It's not a compulsion attempt. If it were, I'd already be leaping between them and trying to bury a spike in the fucker's chest. Rather, it's the battering, near-overwhelming gust that almost feels like a wind current suffused with a high-voltage spark that Ajani pitched at me when he took us captive. I assume it to be a manifestation of the Pantheon magic that powers his blood-gift being allowed to spill out of the vessel containing it, like how the magic of Krashna's Citadel, Hasani's Wrath, and Onei's Expanse seems to ooze into the air, tainting it, when you trek into the Pantheon-cursed places.

I eye Reed and wonder if he can sense it as intensely as I can. He must be able to detect it in some way, otherwise it'd be pointless and a waste of time for Ajani to exercise his cute little intimidation tactic. I see Reed stiffen, so he definitely feels something. Instead of cowering as Ajani aims for him to do, Reed's lips peel back from his teeth. "Nice magic trick. I don't need a blessing from a god to end you," he lets Ajani know. He's turned back as cool as ever. "You've obviously gathered copious intel on me. Since you know who trained me and whose protégé I was, you'll recall that Verne kicked your emperor's ass once. I imagine I can easily kick *your* ass now."

A juvenile, petty-as-shit grin spreads on my face. Much of my worry for Reed fades at that, the vicious side of me almost wishing they'd go at it.

The two legionnaires at Ajani's side finally shed their unreadable expressions. They exchange cautious looks and step forward in sync in Reed's direction. "Try something. Anything," I tell them. "Please." Ajani might be out of my class currently—and now that I know I can eat my way back to full capacity, I'm guessing that won't be the case when I am ready to fight him—but these two.

I could do some bad things to these two.

"I got it, Amari," Reed says. Then he gives the pair the exact merciless, *I will end you* look he gifted their Apis.

"He is nothing."

The three curt words from their Apis leash them, and they fall back in line. Ajani rakes Reed with the look you give stubborn scum that won't scrub from the bottom of your boots. "The only reason you're free of compulsion, or actually the only reason you're not dead already, is that you are of use to me as a bargaining instrument. I'm refraining from ripping your throat out so you can be a good tool and do your job . . . for now." As he speaks, the air of an emperor lording over his inferiors already clings to him and he hasn't even killed his liege yet. I thought I'd met haughty fuckers before. The Tribunal and all of the Praetorian rank are stuffed with them. Hell, I'm damn arrogant. Ajani, he takes ego to soaring, impressive, eye-rolling heights.

"Say we believe your ambitions for *your* empire." Dannica speaks up, presenting as murderously now that she has her mind back as she did when our transport got pinned. "The real question is, what do you intend for *our* Republic? For the whole of the Minor Continent, for that matter, after you become Blood Emperor?" Her violet, no-bullshit stare narrows on Ajani, spearing him. "Because it is you, not the bastard above you, who has been going from state to state collecting pledges of fealty to Accacia. Yet, if what you say is true, I'm guessing those pledges aren't really meant to be to the benefit of the *sitting* Blood Emperor but for the successor." Dannica worked closely with Grandfather as Reed's and Gamma's third. The questions she skewers Ajani to the wall with are shrewd and emphasize the fact that she possesses an exceptional strategic mind, which the great Verne Amari had a hand in shaping too.

Ajani folds his hands behind him, unaffected. "I don't intend anything. I have merely been fighting my liege's war on the front he's assigned me to fight." He shrugs. "I possess a certain charm and ability to coax what I want out of others with minimal messiness. Nkosi recognizes the strength in such tactics in this war and has been using me, who am but a humble servant of His Imperial Majesty, to his advantage. To answer your question, KaDiya Dannica, when I am emperor, my concerns will remain what they are presently: my people and my lands. To further place you at ease, I've always been of the opinion that your corner of Iludu leaves a starsload to be desired in its caliber of inhabitants, worth of its resources, and the blessings left behind by the Pantheon members who held dominion over your continent. Your pathetic, *meager* sliver of the planet should be below the concerns of the mighty Accacian Empire and considered an addition that will be a blot rather than a true conquest. Aside from conscription, it's one more ideology where my liege and I differ. The lands and peoples of the Principal Continent that we've previously engulfed, we've spent centuries assimilating them into the Empire. They *are* the Empire now, truly, with everything that means. But the territories and undesirables of the Minor Continent will not be that immediately. It will take generations, and Accacia's brightest future and most prosperous gilded age lie in turning our focus inward to polish the pearl that we already are and make us a true, shining gem. At that point, I wouldn't be surprised if those disparate lands come to *us*."

The Apis's speech is pretty. Haynes hawks up a wad of spit and lets it fly at the floor, punctuating it with an emphatic, "Bullshit!" He does and says exactly what I'm thinking. "You must mark us idiots if you think we'll believe for a second that if we kill the current Blood Emperor together as allies and help you become Acaccia's new ruler, you'll simply stay on your side of the ocean. Your people never have. If we work with you, we'll only be cutting off one hellserpent's head so another can rise in its place—a successor that will then have intimate knowledge of Ikenna, who I'm betting is the only blood-gifted person outside of the Empire's fiercely loyal citizens who might be able to mount a successful strike against you and take you out." Haynes folds his arms over his massive chest. "Which means us saying yes lets you kill two doves with one UV. You get to use Ikenna to take out the competition that your *pathetic* ass can't do by yourself *and* you have extensive knowledge of the strengths and weaknesses of the adversary that's left when the smoke clears and you're perched on Accacia's throne, perpetuating the exact same expansion campaigns, drunk off your own power, with wet dreams of planet-wide rule like that psychotic fucker Nkosi."

Ajani claps dramatically when Haynes is finished. "Interesting to see Praetorians aren't complete mindless imbeciles made of all brawn and shit for brains," Ajani says. "Your sloppy fuckup in Khanai suggested otherwise. Had me worried about this working partnership."

"There is no working partnership yet," I snap. "We haven't agreed to anything. Khanai also wasn't a fuckup." My pride in myself and my team won't let me not point it out. "We acted on confirmed intel that proved true in the end." It doesn't matter if it was in a different manner than we'd surmised. The treachery was the same. Mustaph did betray the Republic, and the war summit was a ploy. And since Khanai and Mustaph have made their decision, that kingdom can't be counted on anymore. Neither can Ska'kesh or anybody else. Which means my rogue cohort and I are all that's left to stand against Accacia.

"This duplicitous bastard may be the best shot we've got," I say to my team, and I'm no longer feigning consideration of Ajani's proposal. Deploying strategy—which I was never exceptional at, but am learning fast since Grandfather's death, then the clusterfuck in Khanai—I begin moving war pieces around in my head better than I've been managing since these talks with Ajani began. "We need allies," I say to my team as I walk myself through it too. "We have a small city-state full of criminals, and that's it. The west and the east have already fallen. The Southern Isles are falling as we speak. The Republic drowns in blood just as last time. Krashen City and the north are all that's left standing. And it's only a matter of time before Nkosi directs his slaughter north. Whatever advantage the Tribunal thought it'd have with iridium clearly isn't working."

"Mareen may have scientists, but Accacia has something better: *scholars*." Ajani inserts his two credits where nobody asked him. "And when your scholars possess old and infinite knowledge of magical rites and claim Pantheon Blessings themselves . . . let's just say we quickly found a way to neutralize the effects of your iridium. Second, there's the simple numbers game we're winning at too. Mareen has none of the allies that added to its fighting forces as last time, while a breeding campaign over the last thirty years has swelled Accacia's Red Legions exponentially. Third, the Republic can develop all the war tech under the stars, but magic trumps technology every time, when the magic wielder is as exceptionally skilled in its usage as we Accacians teach our children to be from *their* youth." Regardless of how I feel about iridium personally, after being slowly poisoned over weeks by it, the asshole's smugness is grating. Though I do turn thankful for his incessant need to hear himself speak and preen about the unparalleled greatness of the oh so glorious Empire of Accacia. It's caused him to give up useful intel about how in the gods-created-hell Accacia's nightmarish legions have been fighting this campaign as if Rhysien War House never discovered the high toxicity of iridium's vapors and the Republic didn't gear up mass production of the metal to shore up its weaponry at the start of the war.

I file the info away and ignore the fact that I want to carve out Ajani's lungs every time he crows.

"As long as Krashen stands, the Republic stands," I impress upon my team. "Once it falls, Mareen crumbles. The Republic is gone. There will be no rebuilding to what we dream for it to be from such absolute and catastrophic obliteration. The Pinnacle is in the north. Krashen Base is in the north. Krashen Academy is in the north. The best bio-scientists, the major armories, the treasury with the notes and rough onyx that back Mareenian-issued credits as currency, the companies that lead the race in war tech . . . it is all housed in precious Krashen City and the Blood Emperor knows it. He's executing the same strategy he did during the former war; he's terrorizing and tormenting us with the knowledge that Krashen is a sitting dove whose wings have been clipped, the Empire has it sighted dead center in its scope, and there's not a damn thing anyone can do to stop the tide of death and annihilation about to rain down on its head. We have to stop Nkosi before he reaches Krashen City. Which means we're out of time, we're desperate, and we've got to act immediately." I cut a meaningful look to Ajani. "And deal with whatever shitstorm follows from making this decision when and if we and Mareen survive."

Reed curses. So does everybody else. But we don't need to take a vote. I see the bleak understanding and acceptance that there's no other course in the grim gazes of the entire team. They mirror my own gut-twisting feelings.

This is the first time I've gotten a moment to think, *really think*, about what losing the Isles, in addition to the west and the east at the start of the war, actually means. The impending doomed fate of the Republic wells up inside my chest. I ball my hands into fists and try to breathe, try not to let Ajani and the other Accacians glimpse my weakness of being petrified of the utter destruction that's coming for my home and how viciously it shreds me. The Tribunes, Selene, and folks like Chance are one thing; I wouldn't lose an iota of sleep over their demises. Nevertheless, there are citizens beyond them whose living or dying I actually give a shit about. Like Enzo, who flew back home injured after Khanai, and his younger siblings, whom he talked so lovingly about throughout our years in the academy and during the trials. There's also Zayne's parents, whom I owe *everything*, including fighting like hell to preserve their lives, for letting their son die during the trials on the mountain path *I chose* to climb. They're in Krashen now. Moved there by me to cushy quarters via Enzo's quiet help during the months we've been fugitives. I owe the parents of Dex and Bex, too, the siblings I failed to keep alive during the trials and whom Enzo also helped relocate to a less brutal life in Krashen.

And it's not just them. Grandfather's life's work, *our* dream for Mareen, and carrying the Amari name have left me a duty to safeguard so many more. I must protect the most downtrodden of peoples, the masses of labourii and all the akulu among the Republic who looked to Grandfather to make change and found hope in the promise he built, then left to me, that their condition would one day improve. I've failed those people by not stopping the Blood Emperor's war campaign yet. And I'll always carry that weight with me, the same as all the deaths that are on my head from the trials. I can't change the fate of the dead, or let the grief over those I didn't save *break me*—it's something else I've had to learn and continue to learn. But what I can do as long as I've got breath left to breathe and blood in my body is what I've always done best: *fight*. I can still fight to save the people who are *good*, who do not reflect the Republic's corruption, who are innocent in this war, and who deserve to be saved.

"So, it's a yes?" Ajani says silkily, and *gods*, I'm as sure as I know my name that it's hazardous to be working with the merciless, duplicitous Apis. This is all falling together too neatly. That tidiness makes my gut instincts, which Grandfather impressed upon me to *always* heed, whisper that we need to proceed with extreme caution and hypervigilance.

Us saying yes lets you kill two doves with one UV. You get to use Ikenna to take the competition out and you have extensive knowledge of the strengths and weaknesses of the adversary that's left when the smoke clears.

Haynes's earlier accusations come back to me, and I realize that Ajani never denied them.

I'm arranging my own strategy board, but Ajani is, too, and I'm pretty sure I see his endgame now. He may want power. He may want to usurp Nkosi. He may want dominion over the Empire. But he absolutely will see us dead after he gets them. It's the shrewdest course. It's what *I* would do. It's what Grandfather had counseled me many times to do when climbing in bed with one enemy to strike down another. Because just like he'll know our team's strengths and weaknesses after the smoke clears, we'll have hefty knowledge of his—and more important, we will have had an inside view of the inner workings of the Red

Legions, perhaps the Red Order, and how Accacian forces wield the blood-gift so skillfully. So, yes, the fucker will at some point move to embed a sundisk in our backs then watch it detonate. Which means we need to strike first; no matter how we go up against Nkosi, my team and I will need to have a plan in place to immediately take out Ajani too.

"Fucking cosmos. I can't believe we're really doing this shit," says Greysen in an echo of my own thoughts. My comrade scrubs a hand down his face. In his haggard expression, his thoughts are clear. *I hope to the Republic, for its sake and ours, we know what we're doing.*

I internally wince and hope—*pray*—to every and any higher god that might exist and be benevolent, or simply wishes to aid us to advance their own machinations—that we can manage to work with Ajani to kill the Blood Emperor, not die in the process, save what's left of the Republic, and be able to quash the foul aftermath that's sure to come once the scheming Apis gets what he wants.

Instead of descending into fear or dread or anxiety, because none of those things will do me any good or keep us alive, I lean on what I always have to summon strength. To summon conviction. To summon courage and hope and faith. To summon resolve and sheer stubbornness that I *will* succeed.

We are forged by adversity.

I say my mantra and Grandfather's mantra—our *family* mantra—in my head and let it fortify me.

We are tempered in perseverance. We are Amaris. We are as strong as Khanaian steel. We do not bend. We do not break. We do not bow. We do not yield.

We really, really can't, I add.

SEVEN DAYS.

That's how long we're to remain in the citadel while Ajani carries out his liege's orders to solidify the fealty pledges of the microstates before we travel to Nkosi's war camp among the Southern Isles.

It's an amount of time that feels perilously long while the Blood Emperor continues to sack the cities and villages of the Isles; yet it also feels too damn short because when the week is up, I'm going after the Blood Emperor on an expedited schedule *and* under the bluff I sold Ajani.

The ironic part, which is a cosmic joke, is that if I did have control over the full brunt of my power whenever I needed it, Ajani's plan for us to murder the Blood Emperor would be a damn solid one. We go to the war camp and there the Apis presents me, the powerfully blood-gifted and beloved granddaughter of Nkosi's greatest enemy, as a captured war prize that Nkosi can enslave, force into conscription, add to his harem—do whatever he likes with. And while His Imperial Majesty's guard is lowered, thinking the Apis has delivered me to him already shattered, and his hubris and glee in besting Grandfather one last time make him sloppy, I go for the kill.

It all sounds good until you actually listen to it.

Because without control, there are too many variables where things can go wrong. I wouldn't be half as concerned, I'd just say fuck it and try to take Nkosi's head or die trying without a tenth as much worry, if I were the only person in chains going into the war camp alongside Ajani. My team, as it turns out, is comprised of insufferable, stubborn, thickheaded pains in my ass, so I won't be. Reed, Caiman, and Dannica will go with me, under the guise of more delicious presents for Nkosi. Reed, the Legatus's half-Khanaian protégé, is yet another person of obvious importance to Grandfather, after all. Caiman is the heir to the Republic's most precious, venerated, and decorated war house; the fact that Caiman's a current fugitive won't change the statement Nkosi could make by turning Caiman's gruesome death at Accacia's hands on Republic soil into a full-on spectacle. And Dannica served as third in the cohort Grandfather left his legacy's stamp on; she's also beautiful and, according to Ajani, the Blood Emperor likes to collect lovely toys as much as he likes to collect powerful tools. Pawns for Ajani. Playthings for Nkosi. My friends—no, my *family*—merely tokens in this horrifying game.

But not to me. If any of them die, if I get any of them killed, like I did with people in the Expanse and then again in the Ice Wastes . . . I will never forgive myself. Their blood will be on me, and it will haunt me until the end of my days.

In the privacy of the sleeping quarters I was given, I allow myself to massage my eyes, anxious and so afraid for my friends that I don't know if I want to shriek, rage, or cry. I drop onto the bed I'm leaning against and mutter a curse. Then I slam my fist into the brass headboard. It dents, and my knuckles rip. Air stings my wounds, and I do it again because I'm me and hitting things feels good. I stop punching when, appalled, tears prick my eyes.

"*Get it the fuck together,*" I growl at the moisture then blink it away. "*You will not cry, Kenna. Not here. Not anywhere. You aren't that pathetic.*" Plus, tears won't help shit. What I need to do is be more effective. I need to master the surges and learn to control when and where I flux. I need to be able to toss around enormous levels of power all the time, and I need to learn how to do it quickly.

Seven days, I think again. *Seven cosmos-damned days.*

Then, I'm out of time.

A low, amused, male chuckle echoes around the room. I spring off the bed, yanking my Khanaian dagger from my belt, teeth bared and feeling feral from my state of rawness. I'm eager to slash *something* with a blade. A good fight always takes the edge off. I scan every inch of the room, lit up by bright overhead lights, for the intruder who's about to regret being an idiot. But my quarters appear empty. I stalk to the glass doors that lead out to the balcony—the only way into or out of the room other than the sliding palladium door off an attached great room. I palm a second blade—a push dagger—then shove the glass doors open and step outside.

The balcony is completely ensconced in night. My sight takes less than half a breath to adjust and cut through the shroud of black. I don't glimpse anyone on the outside landing either. I step to its balustrade and look over the granite columns to the balconies below and around mine. I see nothing among the darkness, shadows, and clouds that cling to the citadel.

The wind stirs, and oddly, it's many degrees warmer and stickier than it should be under Clement Season moons. A second chuckle floats on the breeze. Despite the unusual heat, ice trickles down the back of my neck, given that I'm in a god-cursed citadel where quiet laughs drift from everywhere and nowhere. My mind dredges up the horrors I suffered in Onei's Expanse and the Ice Wastes. I slam a mental door shut on those traumas, wrap them in chains, and toss them into a black hole. If I plunge into them now, I might run screaming from the landing, and I've got too much self-respect for that. I trained to be a Praetorian. The fiercest of soldiers, for Republic's sake.

The third time I hear the menacing chuckle, it's so damn real and solid I almost say fuck it and do flee. But I stand my ground. Scissoring my feet apart, crouching into a Xzana offensive stance, I grip my daggers so hard my knuckles crack. I drag in a breath, ignoring the hairs standing up along every inch of my skin. Then I expel the breath, staying calm. Staying centered. Keeping the head of a soldier.

The muggy wind stirs again; I swear I hear my name among its latest susurration. And it's not in any pitch of a voice that I know. *Or in a cadence that sounds even vaguely of modernity, or of this world.* It's the last thought you'd want to have while standing in a place that was built by a war god as his sacred fortress and continues to be cocooned in his magic. Once I think the harrowing thought, I can't unthink it. It morphs into a first rate mindfuck.

It takes me an embarrassing number of minutes to successfully compartmentalize. To shove aside whatever is going on with the wind, and the strange laughs, and the eerie sound of my name. The sinister, taunting magic left behind by a long-departed god isn't the chief thing of concern at present. Figuring out how to surge in power at will so my odds of assassinating Nkosi increase from slim to an actual fighting chance is the only thing that can matter right now. Because I'm working on *severely* borrowed time to figure my shit out.

I stand on the balcony, under the watchful moons and the hundreds of twinkling stars that make the pitch-dark cosmos explode with color, turning the problem over and over and over. I frantically try to see a surefire way of either killing the Blood Emperor with diminished power when I walk into the he-wolf's den or learning in a matter of days how to succeed in what I've been failing at for months.

Have you tried praying? Communing? It is what your ancestors did to amplify the blessings, and curses, of the gods they were gifted.

I hear the same unnerving male voice that spoke my name. Like the laughs, it, too, seems to come from somewhere specific yet nowhere. The silvery moonlight streaming onto the balcony dims, swathing me and it in heavier darkness. I look up to see thick, smoke-gray clouds have covered each of the moons. And I blink because where the glittering, colorful constellations of all the gods were present in the sky before, now there are none. Where the hell did they go? Whole stars don't simply wink out of existence—do they? But they are gone from the sky, lending a malefic quality to the chasm of black above me, turning it a hue it's never been before. Normally, Iludu's night sky is a lush, silky, gorgeous, luminous black. Tonight, it's a black that's joyless and soulless—*it's the flat, dead color of an Accursed's eyes.*

I jump at the revelation.

The uneasiness churning my stomach intensifies. Shards of ice stab deeper into my skin. I grip my Comm Unit strapped to my wrist with a mind to ping Reed or Dannica or one of the others in their rooms and ask if they're viewing the same thing. Or maybe the citadel and that voice have chosen to specifically fuck with me? I close my eyes for a second, rub them vigorously, look back up. The stars in their kaleidoscope of colors that usually dot the sky are still missing, and the blackness still puts me in mind of gazing into the eyes of one of the nightmarish, terrifying once-men who prowl Onei's cursed forest.

I hear my name again in the unnatural, Old World cadence. This time, there's no mistaking or questioning it because my whole name is whispered. *Ikenna. Amari.*

More disembodied, creepy words come behind it. *You, pet, should pray. You should commune. Frequently.*

I tighten my grip on my daggers. "Why the hell would I do that?" I shout and think maybe I'm losing it because what or who am I even talking to?

You know what you're talking to, the voice says, smooth as Mareenian silk and cutting as the knife point of my daggers. Bewildered, I realize it has responded to my thoughts and not the words I spoke aloud. I spin in a circle. There must be something or someone around? I only gaze at darkness. Nothing else. *What in the gods' hell is going on? What am I hearing?*

You're sharper than that question. The voice rumbles like thunder in the distance that's moving in swiftly. *You may be a Blood Daughter of Amaka, but you are also a warrior of Mareen. Mareenians have fighting spirits* and *exceptional combat minds. Use yours. It's already worked out half the puzzle, after all. You did deduce that magic signatures of the Pantheon left behind in the places we touched can be perceived among those places, did you not? So who do you think the voice you hear belongs to?*

Panic and fear make my lungs constrict. Though I'm outdoors under a wide-open sky, all of the oxygen evanesces around me. I lock my knees to keep my legs from trembling. I force the fear out. I force the panic out. I can't display either if I'm talking, or some way communing, with the vicious god of war. He will scent it, and Krashna was the same sort of sick, sadistic fuck as Chance proved to be during the trials. If he can somehow reach into this world from wherever he is, he *will* take me apart piece by piece. If not in body, then in mind.

"Krashna?" Despite arduous attempts to crush the fear, I croak out the name of the god that Mareenians once worshipped and who once hammered us into his ultimate tools of war. Terror drenches me in a cold sweat. *It can't be the actual god of war—*

But the innate, wiser, knowing part of my mind is screeching at me not to be an idiot. Or willfully blind. Of *course* it can be Krashna himself I'm talking to. If Amaka can reach into this world and commune with me, why not another? So I accept it quickly, no matter how bowel-loosening acknowledging it is, and shift to asking much more critical questions. Why either of them? Why both of them? Why are two gods meddling with me? And even more important, *how am I talking to any of the Pantheon in such real and solid conversations when they were cast out of Iludu centuries ago?* Communing with the gods on some mystical level to harness their gifts, like the blood-gifted are said to do, is one thing. Standing in this world, on the planet of Iludu, and having a conversation with one . . .

That's another thing entirely.

The god of war chuckles in a pitch that's approving and sensual, yet also somehow cruel, and slides along all of my senses. I feel the barest of touches that's almost like a lover's caress down the side of my neck. The wind lifts the single braid my hair is plaited into off my shoulders. I jump a mile in the air then bare my teeth in a growl. "Get the fuck away from me!" I snarl at the darkness.

Another skin-crawling touch trails down the other side of my neck, from earlobe to collarbone. I recoil and shudder, yet my body horrifically leans into the violation, an invisible force tugging it forward that's discordant with the snarling in my mind.

"You should show greater supplication," Krashna snaps, his voice and otherworldly presence become so nearly substantial that I almost expect him to materialize in front of me.

"I'm also awaiting gratitude for the boon I've gifted you in handing you the answer to your woes," Krashna adds. "My sister is not the only among the Pantheon who has a claim on you, girl. Regardless of what you've pledged to her, you still bear the blood and spirit of my flock too." His voice bleeds envy and enmity when referring to Amaka and the vow I made to her out of desperation.

I draw strength from the daggers I hold. I raise them, slashing through the air when I feel another unwanted touch. If this asshole, by some impossible way, turns corporeal, I will fight with all the breath in my body. "I said get the hell away. Keep your hand, or power, or whatever, to your damn self or I swear to the cosmos—I don't give a shit who you are—I will find a way to yank you into this world or smoke you out in another and carve you up. Do gods have dicks? Perhaps I'll start with your precious parts that you obviously desire to be relieved of."

Lightning cracks above the balcony, a storm roiling in when the weather was clear before. A long, thunderous roar of thunder rattles the balcony. I wait for it to cease, then ask the bitchass god of war, "Are you done throwing your tantrum?"

"Hardly." There's a miffed beat, then the grating chuckle slides along my senses again. This time, the bastard uses it instead of his phantom touch to visit a violence. The silky, throaty laughter slides down the column of my neck and between my breasts. Like before, my body tips forward, like I'm attached to strings and the god of war holds the reins.

"You're dead," I promise him. "It is now my mission to find a way to slaughter prick gods."

"I look forward to that clash in the flesh. I recognize and have always respected ferocity and a warrior woman's spirit. You have both in stars. If you were on my plane . . . or I was on yours . . . oh, how I'd enjoy breaking you, Ikenna Amari. I'd make you scream my name in the end, you know—from terror, pain, and my particular brand of pleasure. I'd eviscerate you as you begged to be broken. That was always better than the screams when I walked among humans. When my pets pleaded and didn't know if it was for deliverance or more of my attentions."

"It was music."

"You're disgusting." My heart slams against my chest. The perverse things he says . . . what he threatens . . . what he brags about . . . there are stories . . . accounts. . . . old records . . .

Krashna had a harem in this very citadel. He collected the fiercest female warriors he could find among his flock and, as he says, he broke them. Not enough to make them useless in combat when the need arose, but enough to be the cruelest, most barbaric sort of bastard.

The nerve leaks out of me. I lose the battle to appear fearless. I tremble violently, no longer able to pretend. I spin toward the door to tear from the balcony. Run. Find security in numbers. Find my people. Find a semblance of safety.

I reach the doors and yank on the archaic handles. Neither of them budges.

"You don't get to run." Krashna's voice booms behind me. "Nor is it becoming of one of my warriors, so you've double insulted me. No worries. You'll pay penance—for everything." My heart climbs into my throat. My hands, still gripping and tugging at the door handles, shake. I turn around, slowly, and know what I'll see before I complete the about-face. Krashna stands against the balustrade, every inch a deadly, brutal, *living* god. Cosmos, his form is tall. Over seven feet from a quick estimation. And he looks the epitome of everything Mareen worships as pure: painfully porcelain skin, the muscled build of a capable fighter, golden blond hair, and ice-blue eyes. I swallow. It does shit to lessen the lump in my throat. I scream inside my head. Perhaps I scream out loud. I'm not sure. All I know is that I'm drowning in suffocating terror.

The god of war wears a dashing smile that promises everything but charm. He pushes off the railing he's leaning against, outfitted in plates of shining, golden armor. A maroon cape billowing in the breeze behind him. His legs and arms are bare, with delts and biceps and quads quadruple the size of my head. There is nothing about the god that doesn't shriek *power*.

Frost-blue eyes sweep down the length of me, predatory and lust-filled. "Now we're having real fun and get to play my favorite game," he says, taking one step and then another in my direction, making it clear he is toying with me. Letting me linger in my terror. Letting me see the he-wolf coming while knowing I'm caught before he ever gets to me and there's no hope of escape.

He takes a third step, and in the next half of a heartbeat, he flashes to my side. Literally flashes—one second he's standing a handful of feet away and the next he is inches close. His right hand curls around my throat, the pad of his thumb caressing the flesh before he tightens his grip, choking me. I gasp for air and claw at his hands; fire roils across the spots where his fingers dig into my skin. He dangles me above the ground so we're eye level; his massive body pushes into my space, crushing me. "Did you really believe you'd get away with insulting me in *my* house? In my own war fortress, bitch?" He hisses the words into my ear, then slams me so hard against the glass at my back that it rattles. I'm surprised it doesn't shatter. Splitting pain cracks through my skull. Black dots swim in front of my eyes. I blink, grit my teeth, and will them away because I cannot pass out in his hold. If I lose consciousness, who knows what he'll do to me.

Although maybe unconsciousness would be a blessing.

But I'm not going to just give up, soul-crushing terror or no. I swing my Khanaian blade upward, aiming for his neck. He catches my wrist as if it's of no moment, shattering the bones, the blinding agony forcing my hand open. The knife clatters to the floor. Before I can attempt to use the second knife against him, he likewise breaks my other wrist and rids me of that knife too.

His cool, thin lips brush the side of my cheek. His nose nestles my neck. Everything inside of me retches and screams. When either of the actual sounds try to escape, they're stolen away by his grip, which has never ceased crushing my windpipe. Spots are starting to dance in front of my eyes again.

"The thing about this citadel . . ." he murmurs, placing his lips back to my ear. "While I cannot manifest in this form in other places across Iludu, you are Pantheon-blessed and thus much closer to our reach. And in my house, as in all Pantheon-cursed and -blessed places, the barrier between my world and yours is flimsy. Both of those things are why I can do this." He presses another kiss to my earlobe . . . then rams a fist into my stomach. Behind it, a dagger appears in his hand and he thrusts it into the spot he punched. He loosens his grip on my throat, just slightly, enough so this scream of agony can tear free. His frigid eyes glisten, heady, when I do.

"Ah, how I love that sound. I've missed hearing it from human pets. I told you you'd scream. Though it wasn't in the form I promised yet. Don't be disappointed. I'll reward you soon."

The dagger gets thrust into my chest, igniting a new wave of white-hot pain. I cough and gurgle blood.

Dimly, I wonder where the hell is my blood-gift. Where is the flare of warmth at any of the wound sites that should be kicking in to help heal me? And my biochip? Why hasn't the cool tingling of the healing nanos merged with my cells kicked in, for that matter? Though, under the circumstances, I'm not sure I actually want my body to repair itself. It'll slow my death. It'll drag this out.

As Krashna gleefully watches me bleed from multiple wounds, he shivers. "My sister wouldn't hear of me playing with one of hers when we walked Iludu. But you're one of mine too," he says heinously and possessively. "Amaka's non-touching rules can't apply."

I squeeze my eyes shut. Then I open them because that's unwise. I need to see his next attack. I need to keep him in my sight. I want to die, yet I also want to live—the Praetorian in me refuses to stop analyzing; the Amari in me refuses to give up. My mind scrambles for a way to extricate myself. With the tiny amount of air I'm able to wheeze out, I say, "You're not really here. You can't be. It isn't possible. This is a trick of the citadel's magic. It must be." I'm rambling and sputtering, trying to make sense of what is happening and *how* it's happening, all the while buying time.

"I'm present," Krashna assures me. But then he shrugs. "Admittedly, though, not in the flesh. This is a communing. So it's playing out in a meeting of the minds, rather than my actually having crossed into your world. Nevertheless, the damage you take and the fun I have will be no less authentic. The mind, after all, is in many ways far more fragile and more vulnerable to shattering than the body."

Okay, so he's not really on the balcony in the flesh. He's no less scary and I take no solace in the fact, but at least the realization allows me to seize on to something and helps me not unravel all the way.

He finally lets go of my throat completely. The oxygen that floods my lungs after being deprived of it feels like swallowing ice water. I gulp down air in case he decides he wants to choke me again.

But his next assault doesn't get aimed at my throat. Instead, he wraps his left hand around my braid and jerks my head back, keeping hold of my hair. He presses the center of his body against me and at that point I do retch. His right hand slides light and soft down my hip. "This would be much sweeter if I were in the flesh, but you—and I—will still feel every sensation, so fucking you in this form will suffice. You know," he says, as if we are buddies reminiscing rather than he a god about to violate me, "in my age, humans scrambled for the honor, no matter how short their lives were either during or after it. It's a third thing you should thank me for. Ikenna. Amari."

No. No. No. No. No. NO! Tears stream down my face and I shriek. I claw at him. I kick. I hit. I punch him. None of it has any effect. It's like attacking a mountain.

Then, out of nowhere, he goes rigid. He growls, and a split second later he's flying away from me and smashing against the balustrade.

Close your mind. Kick him out. Now! The new disembodied voice is female. Yet it doesn't have the cleaving pitch of Amaka's. It's gentle and infinitely benevolent. And I immediately suspect which goddess it may belong to.

"How do I do that?" I cry out to Kissa, doubling over and crying harder, shaking uncontrollably.

Her voice comes to me grief-stricken and kind. *It works if you picture a passageway. A window. Or a door, for example. Then imagine tossing my despicable brother out of it. Mentally seal it behind him.*

"Okay. Okay. Okay," I rasp. It sounds simple enough. I gingerly straighten, hoping the attempt works because I don't want to even think about the unimaginable happening if it doesn't. I look at Krashna's form as he picks himself up. He stares back at me, furious, emits a war cry, and charges. I don't think; I just follow the orders I was given. I picture a window on the opposite side of the balcony. Then I picture the motherfucker flying back across the space without being touched, like he did when Kissa threw him. This form of him that's invading my mind lifts into the air and hurtles backward once more, then out the window. I blink, stealing a moment to finally breathe in crushing relief, then I finish my orders. Like I do when I'm sealing emotional baggage I don't want to deal with inside a black box in my head, I imagine a sheet of steel sliding over the window, walling it off. Finally, I imagine dropping it into a chasm as deep and dark and bottomless as the crevasse I fell into during the Ice Wastes exercise.

The window evanesces. I wait, holding my breath, dreading that something went wrong and the awful god of war will reappear. I'm not sure how much time passes. I lose track. But eventually I weep harder, because he doesn't return. I fall to my knees and start hyperventilating, a terror that won't leave rooting me to the balcony's floor. I don't have a physical mark on me, but I *feel every* violence he visited upon my body as if the strikes did happen, the trauma still lingering within my mind, which I don't think will ever fully clear.

Soothing, healing energy cocoons me, and it's like being ever so carefully wrapped in a mother's soft, protective hug; my tears increase, although I feel the shifts from fear to grief to equanimity.

My brother is repulsive. I am sorry you had to suffer his abuse. I've dealt with him on my plane, and he should stay away. He's been informed of the price should he attempt to commune with you again. You're a Blood Daughter of Amaka, and while you may be a warrior of Krashna, you are also a beloved of Kissa. My brother can slither around Amaka's rules for her people, but not mine. Be assured that while your time here passes, I will not allow harm to come to you via him.

As Kissa's voice flows around me like a beautiful song, the inky darkness and cloying shadows crawling over the balcony lift. Silvery moonlight splashes onto it and me. So do a cascade of colors. I lift my eyes to the sky—it's returned to its usual glittering, soft black. The stars have returned too. And though all the constellations of the Pantheon paint the sky, the six jade stars of Kissa's Horn appear to shine just a smidgen brighter than the rest. Or maybe the effect is due to my immense gratitude.

"Thank you," I whisper into the now breezeless, placid night. "Seriously. Thank you."

The healing energy that wraps me in a hug lets go. *You are welcome. Though it is I who should thank you, Ikenna Amari, who continues to fight for Iludu and for my people, even when Khanai has made a decision in fear that causes me heavy sorrow. I hate what you've endured here, but I am glad that events in your world carried you to the citadel. I came not just to run my brother off, but also to deliver an imperative message to you: Amaka's empire and her Blood Son cannot seize dominion over the world. I've seen the age of untold terrors it ushers forth. Iludu will suffer a future worse than when the Pantheon reigned. Because at least then my brothers and sisters were chained to needing humanity alive to worship and thus fuel us. Nkosi is human, needs no such things, and is a man who does not even value the lives of his own people. As he enslaves them and slaughters them, he will enslave and slaughter the world once he's eradicated anyone that might fight back.*

"Yes, I know this," I say, harsher than I intend, and thus rude. I grimace. Mutter a quick apology because my quarrel isn't with Kissa and I have no desire to turn my savior into a second godly enemy.

I take no offense; I know your nature, Kissa responds, serene. *Never apologize for the fire that will serve you well, always. In your arduous battles to come, be sure to keep it.*

The goddess of arts, riches, and wisdom pauses and the quiet anger suffusing her energy buzzes around me. The goddess may be marked by benevolence, but I also sense a ferocity about her, her own inner, fiery strength, that I have no doubt is incinerating. It's got to be if she forced Krashna's retreat and if she was the power that made the rest of her Pantheon brethren never dare look to Khanai or its people for subjects to torment.

The promises the Blood Emperor makes to those like my ill-advised Khanaians who bow to him without quibble will not keep, Kissa says. *An inevitability you've surmised, beloved. It is why you seek a way to end him. It is why I hope that you're successful, and why you'll need your fire burning bright and searing as ever. But to accomplish both, my disgusting brother was correct in one thing: If you want the depths of the power Amaka offered, you must commune regularly with the goddess of blood rites, the wellspring your gift flows from. A single time, like in the Prisoners' Keep, is never enough, as our blessings are living gifts that must be perpetually tended. Just as they evolve and can be bolstered if nourished properly at their wellspring, they can devolve and disappear entirely if you starve them and cut yourself off. Amaka is a bitch and has her own agenda for you, so also be careful, but no matter her motives, you need to call to her and commune. Once you start doing so, you should see greater command over your staggering gift.*

Only then will you have a chance against Nkosi.

Kissa's presence vanishes from the balcony after she imparts her wisdom. I don't get a chance to thank her for it, let alone ask questions about the horrific future the goddess who gave a powerful sight-gift to her people has foreseen.

After she departs, I can't muster the strength to take the advice she lends and commune with Amaka straightaway. *Soon. Tomorrow. I'll pull myself together tomorrow. Tonight . . .*

Tonight I've had too much of the gods.

Weary, raw, and still so, so brittle from Krashna's assault, I drag myself through the glass doors, which now open freely. Once inside, I close them and lock them—though I know it won't seal a god out. Still, the soft click helps the pressure in my chest ease slightly more. I cross the room and drop into a chair that's against the far wall opposite the balcony's doors. I turn the chair so it's facing the glass doors straight on. I don't sleep. I just sit under the harsh, bright lights of the room and watch the balcony.

I grip my Comm Unit several times. To ping Reed. To ping Dannica. To not be alone. But anybody I call will immediately see how shaken I am, and I'll have to rehash what happened. It's another thing I do not have the fortitude to do right away.

For this night, I have no one.

I am utterly alone.

17

FOUR DAYS PASS, AND I haven't mustered the courage to face one of the Pantheon again. I know it's precious time I'm losing, but the mere thought of communing with one of the gods that isn't Kissa makes me violently gag every time I consider it. With my team, I mostly manage a convincing act that everything is fine. That I haven't been trapped in an awful, very specific hell that makes my lungs constrict with panic and my stomach roil with nausea whenever I think about Krashna pseudo-manifesting on the balcony. Or at least, I think I've been doing a decent job of pretending. The illusion gets shattered to hell when Dannica, Reed, Haynes, Caiman, and Greysen turn up at my room wearing concerned expressions.

"Something's off with you," Dannica says, parked on the arm of a sofa. "It's been off since we arrived at this hellhole."

"We're in a hellhole? Isn't that enough?" I say with the usual arrogance and bravado I don't feel right now. "I'm fine," I continue. The pitch of my voice conveys what I want it to, but my body language is treacherous. As I stand before the others, I shift from one foot to the other before I can quash the nervous tell.

Dannica's violet eyes track the movement.

I wince as they do.

Haynes, Greysen, and Caiman sit on the sofa beside Dannica. Reed stands next to it. The guys glimpse too damn much as well. All of my comrades, all of my *friends*, sense something is seriously wrong.

It's almost as if they have the same training I do, Pantheon-damn them.

"Does it have to do with the Apis?" Caiman asks tightly. Then he clears his throat. "You were . . . you were captured and held separate from the rest of us for a time." The implicit question and concern in his statement veers gut-twistingly close to the truth.

"Ikenna," Reed says softly, hesitantly, and with so much support it damn near crushes me. "What's going on? Talk to us?"

I shake my head. I cannot display such a level of weakness. I'm already ashamed that I am not entirely able to hide things. We've got battles to deal with on all sides, so much peril looming ahead of us, and we, *they*, do not need to be saddled with my sudden bout of fresh personal shit. And even though I reason all of that out, even though I should keep that night to myself, what happened with Krashna spills out of me. One moment I'm preparing to say something wiseass and witty and then follow it up with informing them they can leave and don't need to worry about me, and the next it's filling the room.

Everybody is several shades paler when I'm done.

"So we've added to our list of ops: summon and kill a shithead god," Dannica says with quiet rage.

She hops to her feet and pulls me into a hug. At first, I stiffen.

"There is *nothing* to feel ashamed or weak about," she whispers into my ear, and it's as if she's read my mind. "I'm so sorry, Kenna. I'm so immensely sorry."

I sag into her hold and hug my cohort sister back. The simple action, the small, kind gesture and words from Dannica cut through the terror that's been holding me hostage.

"I needed that," I whisper back.

When we release each other, I see the guys have moved closer, but keep their distance.

Each one of them looks positively murderous.

"*Can* you kill a god during a communing?" Haynes asks. "If so, the god of war is definitely now on our kill list."

"You mean after we torture the fucker," Caiman says.

"I never thought I'd say this," Reed says, "but I mightily wish the gods still walked Iludu in the flesh. Immortality *can* be a vulnerability. When you're hard to kill, it means you can suffer *at length* through numerous bloody torments."

"I love the way this team thinks." I smile savagely and feel more and more like my normal self.

"You don't have to commune with Amaka," Reed says. "In fact, I imagine we'd all feel better if you didn't since we don't know if Krashna can or can't hijack any communing attempt initiated within the citadel. If you say his magic lingers here and it allows him influence from wherever he is, then we can't rule out the possibility."

"I have thought about that." I laugh, grimly. "Though I don't see a way around it. It's a risk I've got to take. Albeit one I still need to work up the nerve to take," I admit. "Besides," I add, to begin dredging up some of that nerve, "Kissa said she dealt with her brother and she encouraged a communing with Amaka. I think she would've warned me against one while here if Krashna's interference is a possibility."

Haynes scrubs his jaw. "Are we sure? The gods, including the purportedly kindhearted Kissa, were said to have been excessively prideful—*to the point of their vainglory becoming a vulnerability.* Kissa could be overestimating the extent to which her threats will hold her brother in check. Or maybe not? We can be certain of nothing."

"*Exactly*," growls Caiman, pushing off the wall he's been leaning against and looking every bit like a soldier shoring up for battle. "Either way, I don't like you taking the risk, Amari, and we're not standing back and letting you take it. We'll figure out something else."

"An alternative exists," Reed says, positively, before I can argue. "'There is always one,'" he stresses, locking gazes with me. "'There are a hundred routes to win a war. You've just got to be able to see the ones you don't immediately consider.'" He is quoting a lesson Grandfather imparted untold times.

Burgeoning curiosity halts further insistence that my communing with Amaka is all we've got. I cock my head. "All right. I'm listening, oh wise protégé. What do you have?" I pray it's something good, and that I actually don't need to commune with another god, ever fucking again.

"Think about it," Reed answers, eyes sharpening fiercely as I watch his giftedness at stratagem shine behind his blue gaze. "If Ajani plans to present you to Nkosi as a war prize, and you're to strike at him then, you shouldn't *need* the boost in blood-gift. The speed, strength, and impeccable training you're already working with should be enough when combined with the element of surprise. You don't need to *battle* the Blood Emperor. When you go into his war camp, it won't be for a face-off. It'll be to carry out a hit. Those are two different things, and you already possess the skills to do the latter. The academy and then the trials and also Verne trained you to be an assassin. Your grandfather might have failed to kill the bastard, but he did successfully land a debilitating blow against him without *any* Pantheon Blessing. I have every faith you can do the same with what you've currently got."

Could it really be that easy? Can the solution really be this simple? Or is Reed being too optimistic?

In the end, it doesn't matter. We've only got three days left before we depart for Nkosi's war camp anyway, and Krashna and Kissa made it seem like I would need to commune with Amaka and keep communing with her over a period of time to achieve the mastery over the surges

I'm looking for. There's no way I could do that now with three days left. There's no way that could've been accomplished if I'd started at the beginning with the full seven days spanning ahead of me. Now that I'm thinking more clearly, I see this.

The understanding brings relief and new fear. I don't need to commune with Amaka because it'll be pointless, but that means I'm headed into Nkosi's war camp to try and kill him without being able to count on wielding the power I blasted around in Khanai. Normal, regular Ikenna is going to have to be enough.

And despite Reed's faith in me, I'm not entirely confident that she is.

18

THE BASTARD ERECTED HIS WAR camp among the ruins of Cara. As Ajani's jet flies over what used to be Trys, the sparkling, seaside capital city that Grandfather grew up in, smoldering rage consumes me. The jet skims low enough below the clouds, already in mid-descent and preparing for landing, that a full view of the landscape below is clear. Or rather, what is left of it.

The Blood Emperor demolished it.

No, Nkosi *decimated* it. All of it. Massive craters left behind by the bombs litter the ground in place of what used to be lush greenery, rolling hills, and coral sunstone streets. What damage the bombs didn't do was accomplished by the flames he set upon the city—there's no mistaking where the scorched earth, zero foliage, and ash for miles and miles and miles originate from. My stomach drops out from under me. I lean closer to the window I'm seated beside, my hands splaying and curling into the glass.

"Is . . . is the whole island like this? Are all the Isles left like this?" My voice is hoarse. I barely hold back a sob. If Grandfather were alive to see the devastation, he'd be destroyed. *I'm* destroyed and Cara doesn't mean half as much to me as it did to him. Cara was his home. His mother and father's home; it's part of our family's legacy. The Amari legacy. And now . . . it's just gone.

"From the newsvids I'm pulling up, yes," Reed says quietly. He's from eastern Rykos instead of the Southern Isles. The grief and pain and cold rage in his voice on behalf of Mareen as a whole—on behalf of the Republic he's so fiercely loyal to and believes in enough to fight against to realize a better vision of it, as Grandfather did—is clear all the same.

I turn to him, seated beside me. His eyes aren't glued to the window like mine were. They're fixed on his Comm Unit as he scrolls through endless newsvids reporting widespread carnage across the Isles. My hand finds his without me consciously initiating the act. I lace my fingers through his, halting the scrolling. "Seeing it in front of us is terrible enough. Don't gut yourself more."

His fingers flex around mine. "We need to be well abreast of the situation."

"We already are." Dannica, alongside Caiman, peers out the window across the aisle. When she turns to us, her expression is the same mask of grief, pain, and rage. She whips to face Ajani, seated near the back of the jet, glaring daggers at the Apis. She rasps the question I haven't yet worked up the stomach to ask. "Does the whole of the west and the east look like this too?"

Ajani shrugs, barely sparing the window his shoulder brushes a glance. "Whenever my liege conquers new territories, he likes to send a firm, strong message to those he grants survival to ensure easy submission."

Caiman stabs a finger at the carnage below us. "This isn't a firm message. This isn't remotely within the normal bounds of warring and conquering. This was attempted genocide, plain and simple. War crimes by *your* liege and *your* people. Are there even any survivors on the ground?"

"Mareenians have attempted genocide of all who don't look like them or embody their same beliefs several times over throughout history and were planning to do so again in the present with their disgusting iridium," is Ajani's response. "And let's not forget what *your* people and government did to your own who had a Pantheon Blessing hardwired into their DNA. That wasn't *attempted* genocide. It was *successful* genocide. Further, there is your treatment of those with darker skin. You have very little room to judge me and mine here, *Scion*."

Caiman's hands curl into fists.

Ajani laughs, darkly and mockingly, at his ensuing silence.

"That doesn't make Nkosi and the legionnaires that follow him and helped carry this out—yourself included—any less vile bastards," I hiss. "At least acknowledge that fact and stop trying to excuse it with the little game of tit for tat you keep trying to play."

He shrugs again. "I never said I wasn't a vicious bastard. I am, and I accept what I am. I and all of the Red Order warlords are. But as for the legionnaires who serve under us . . . they're *only* conscripts, a lot of them conscripts *bred* for the position, and the penalty for soldiers not obeying orders in the Red Legions is the same for Mareenian soldiers not obeying orders."

Fine. I can accept that. But the rest? "So you admit you're a monster. At least there's that."

"I haven't always been," he says, voice low, "but I have always been devoted and unwavering in my aims. To rise to lead monsters, stand as the second hand of a monster, and have the wherewithal and gumption to depose a monster, you must become that very same thing yourself," he responds without remorse. "No, I was not a part of the Southern Isles' decimation. I was busy at the time hunting you all and procuring the fealty of the microstates. But I did lead Rykos's fall and the fall of the rest of the east, so there's that. And I was prepared to do the very same thing that's been done to Cara, to Khanai and the other nations on the Minor Continent that Nkosi extended offers of Acaccia's friendship to if they were stupid enough to decline. Just so happens, most everyone has wised up with Verne's death. The whole continent, save Mareen and Lythe, has realized it can't go to war against the might of the Empire and the Red Legions and win this time around." He speaks of commanding the slaughter of thousands when Rykos fell, and then potentially doing it again so casually. If I had any doubt in my mind that we'd agreed to an alliance with a soulless hellserpent before, I am glass clear the answer is a resounding yes now.

I glance at Reed, who sits stiff-backed, his skin having paled. No doubt, Ajani's mention of Rykos was like being rammed into by an armored truck. An armored truck he looks like he very much wants to rip apart, chunk by chunk, with his bare hands, as he sucks in a sharp breath. "You are the most repugnant creature I've ever met," he spits at Ajani. "And I do not believe you'll make a more beneficent, less warmongering emperor than the seated one. After this op to kill Nkosi is successful and we're done needing to work with you, you don't get to depart Mareen alive. I swear on everything good within the Republic I will personally see to your demise. I owe you for Mareen, for Rykos, for dragging Amari into Krashna's hellhole citadel, and I owe you for Khanai. I swear on my life you will answer for *your* war crimes instead of merely flying off into the sunset to go play emperor."

Ajani rolls his eyes. "Are you finished? Your hensei really taught you how to stand atop a pedestal when your own shit stinks, didn't he? You've served as Gamma's cohort leader for the past two years, have you not, Praetorian Reed? Do we need to sit here and enumerate the missions your Tribunal sent you on? The ops you've led against people the Tribunal considered enemies of the Republic or mere annoyances? You've spilled your fair share of blood and participated in your fair share of atrocities, too, cohort leader. And let's not forget the mass slaughter of how many Praetorian aspirants during the trials you recently led?"

A muscle in Reed's jaw ticks. I recall laying similar charges where the trials were concerned at his feet when they were going on. He'd looked mildly uncomfortable with the allegation then, while rigidly explaining it was for the good of the Republic. A necessity. To prepare for the very war we're now embroiled in. I wait to see how he'll respond to Ajani. If he'll lend him the same rigid explanation. But this time, Reed says nothing. Not that he needs to. The shame that flashes across his blue eyes is unbidden and brutal.

I squeeze Reed's hand, still threaded through mine. "You fled Khanai with me. You broke from the Tribunal's command and temporarily from the Republic to fight for change. To usher in a different way," I remind him. "That makes you different from the Apis. We will fix this," I tell Reed, Caiman, Dannica, and myself. "We will make things right. We will make *everything* right."

Caiman turns back to his window. He shakes his head. "How? How do we fix what I see if . . . if all of the Republic, save the north and Krashen City, looks like this? How do we make so much death and destruction right?"

That I don't have an answer to. I wish I did. But *shit*, he's right. How do we fix so much brutality and savagery and devastation on so many levels? It was easy to proclaim with conviction that we *can* and provide that necessary boost in morale when going into the most perilous op of our lives. But coming up with the *how* . . . that is a much more difficult thing.

Made even more so because, right now, the only solution seems to involve a deal with a demon.

The jet lands in the middle of a crater before I can arrive at an answer for us.

Ajani stands from his seat. Less than a second after he does, the porcelain-skinned man, Sol, and copper-skinned woman, Iyko, from the citadel rise from their seats located directly behind their Apis. I've learned the pair serve as Ajani's marshals, a rank equivalent to the position of second in the corps of legionnaires loyal only to him.

"Secure her Mareenian comrades in cuffs," Ajani orders his marshals.

Before Iyko and Sol have reached them, Dannica, Caiman, and Reed have already shirked the grief and slipped into op mode, like the highly trained, deadly efficient Praetorians they are. It's three against two, and they could probably take Iyko and Sol with no problem. Yet the three hold out their wrists and allow Ajani's people to touch a slim strip of silver metal to their skin. It elongates on contact and loops around their arms, shackling their hands together.

"Ow!" Caiman yells. "What the fuck are these things?"

"Alerting us to the workings of your cuffs might've been nice," Reed snarls at Ajani.

That's when I see the rivers of blood dripping from their wrists beneath the bands of silver.

"What the hell are those things doing to them?" I shout. "Take them off!"

"They're standard Acaccian cuffs," says Ajani, nonplussed. "What do you want me to do? I wouldn't march four *supposedly* very dangerous enemies in front of my liege unrestrained—and without having already initiated a small bloodletting for insurance."

"Your standard cuffs make people *bleed*? Gods, how fucked up are you Accacian pricks?" Dannica raises her wrists, inspecting the cuffs, looking for a way to slip them, I'm sure.

"Why does that even need to be a thing?" I ask, reaching for calm.

Ajani sighs, exasperated, regarding me once more like I'm woefully ignorant and my ignorance is a personal affront. "There's power in blood *and* in bloodletting. The latter provides *our* people ways of extremely weakening our enemies when we take them into custody. In the case of Praetorians, it's a convenient way to seize control of your blood, shut down the nanoagents in it, and thus nullify the majority of enhancements that your hellish, unnatural biochips equip you with. It also makes Praetorians less of a headache to compel in a situation where focuses might be split since . . ." He pauses as if weighing what he wants to relay.

I arch an expectant brow. "You claim good intent, right? Well, give it up. Call it more good faith," I press, in challenge. "I believe we deserve and have earned it, given my people have allowed you to shackle them and, apparently, their biochips."

Ajani flashes teeth. Sketches a mocking bow. "I suppose you make a case, and you used maturity this time, like a good girl. I was going to say: since none but the most powerful Accacians can establish a compulsion link, and biochips make it . . . an arduous task, even then, where Praetorians are concerned."

I carefully file that information away for safekeeping and retrieval later. I'm pretty sure it isn't knowledge the Tribunal or the Praetorian ranks hold. Acaccia has definitely kept those secrets guarded. There have never been any lessons we learned in the academy, or during our lecture domes from the trials, or during the war meeting when Acaccia first attacked, that relayed any of that.

So why the hell did Ajani so easily give in and apprise me—and the other Mareenian Praetorians within earshot—of it? There's no way in hell he's that sloppy, that generous, or made that stupid by overconfidence. Which means we're being given the knowledge to soothe our anger over the cuffs and keep us compliant *only* because he doesn't intend for us to live long after the coming ordeal. I cut a look at my team. Their returned stares communicate they've already discerned the same thing.

"Your turn," Ajani says. He walks to stand directly in front of me. He holds the same silver strip of metal in his hand that his marshals placed on Caiman, Reed, and Dannica.

I don't give him the satisfaction of seeing me tense up, or balk, or give off any sort of reaction. I stare at him stoically and hold out my wrists. Inwardly, I brace for the bite of pain and instinctive aversion that will come whenever the cuffs draw my blood.

He lays the silver strip against my skin. I expect the metal to be cool. But it radiates warmth as it elongates and binds my hands. The sting I anticipate doesn't come. Nor do I bleed. I glance up from my wrists, over to the guys and Dannica, who are still bleeding freely, then look at Ajani. "Why are mine different?"

"The blood-gifted don't bleed other blood-gifted. Especially not other powerful ones. Unless doling out punishment, it's uncouth. Besides being a blasphemy, unless under very specific circumstances, it's fucking stupid. Subjecting people like you and me to a bloodletting only makes us more powerful and gives us added ways to attack. Your blood is a weapon, you already know that. What you don't know are the many, many ways in which you can wield it as one. There's a dozen more ways to kill a man with it than forming blood spikes. Yes, that method is a quick, dirty way to kill, but it's also the most rudimentary and lacks any finesse."

Okay. Grandfather's lessons never covered any of that either. I admit I'm intrigued. I make a mental note to figure out how to murder people in myriad and cool ways with my blood after my squad and I survive assassinating a psychotic emperor and treacherous Apis.

THE FIRST THINGS that greet us are the decaying, mangled bodies hoisted onto pikes sticking out of the ground around the war camp's perimeter. The stench is unbearable and sears the inside of my nose. But I've seen death before. Tons of it. In many gruesome varieties, and the rotting corpses themselves aren't what's truly awful. Some of the dead wear the microprene combat suits of Praetorians. Some wear the green fatigues of common soldiers. Yet others, the majority of bodies, wear the clothes of civilians. Many of those common garments covering bodies so small they're unmistakably children. The tears that rush to the surface are hot and angry and gutted. I don't try to curtail them. I weep openly for the innocent. For such heinous mass casualty. I'd be as soulless as the monster I'm here to fight if I didn't. No. The Blood Emperor is worse than a monster. He's as vile and debased as a god. Like the world needed to be rid of the Pantheon, it needs to be rid of Nkosi too.

I knew this. I've always known it. History and the last war revealed that. But seeing what Accacia's Blood Emperor is capable of up close and intimate—to not just see it, but to smell it and *taste* it—I stumble as we pass by a fresh cluster of bodies, more young among them, and dry heave.

The grisly displays don't end once we clear the perimeter of the camp. More Mareenians, more bodies of men, women, and children, soldiers and civilians alike, are scattered among the camp's interior. "*Why?* What *is the reason for this?*" My throat spasms, my voice unable to produce a pitch louder than a whisper from the unending horror. "*Who* is he making a spectacle for when *everybody* of the Isles is dead?"

Ajani waves a hand to the sky. "The newsvids. The rest of the world. My continent and yours. So the entire planet is reminded what's at stake if it doesn't remain at heel."

The Apis's words cause me to look up for the first time since landing. Flying beneath Iludu's white sun and among the suffocating ash clogging the sky are several drones. It's then that the full brunt of what I surmised in Ska'kesh, plus what Kissa spoke of, hits me. Nkosi rules even on the Principal Continent, his home continent that comprises *his* people, through torment, fear, and wide-scale death. And it's how he *will* rule the Minor Continent now that he's gained a footing. The territories that have sworn fealty have only negotiated the illusion of safety. Nobody, anywhere, can truly be safe or free as long as Nkosi lives and holds power. The sort of man who displays bodies of children as cautionary tales and war trophies across his camp is the kind of unhinged animal that takes only the smallest perceived insult or disobedience to turn rabid.

With that in mind, I keep walking toward the fire, instead of running as fast as I can away from it.

REED, CAIMAN, AND I are marched through the war camp with Ajani and ten of his men surrounding us. I slip into the mode of a Praetorian and take vital inventory of everything and everyone I spy around the camp. It's crawling with legionnaires, hundreds, perhaps thousands. The scarlet uniforms are loaded down with visible weapons—blasters, knives, and nanogrenades; the enemy soldiers move about transient yet sturdy barracks erected from corrugated steel. There are several patrol groups out. I mark them because instead of moving as if they're going to a set destination, they stalk about the camp constantly scanning for threats and intrusions.

Regardless of their activity, every legionnaire that we pass halts to bow low to Ajani.

The Apis strides out directly in front of us, keeping himself positioned between Reed and me. The profile of his face I can glimpse is set into a deep scowl. At first, I assume His Warlordship, who likes to play at refinement, absurdly finds the soot and shoddy lodgings of the camp beneath him. Then we pass a pair of soldiers on patrol who both visibly stiffen and pale as Ajani nears them. As they bow to him like the others, I see his gaze soften with empathy and ignite with fury all in the same moment. It makes me wonder if the permanent scowl he wears is less about the coarse surroundings and more about the hundreds of conscripted legionnaires in the war camp. If the reasons he fed me for wanting to depose his liege are true.

We navigate past the pair of Accacian soldiers and I twist my head around to look back at them, curious. They stare after us, their eyes lingering upon their Apis in an awed, enraptured fashion. The way they look at him, you'd swear they'd just bowed to a god as opposed to a mere man. I snort; I can't help it. Then, I turn away and give the structure we're approaching my full attention. The building is much grander than the utilitarian barracks we've passed, an imposing, octagonal-shaped pavilion with crimson pillars rising high; the distinctive, plush blue-black pelts of Principal Continent night bears hang between the columns in place of walls and are draped over the top of them to form a ceiling. The pavilion is ostentatious and reeks of pretentiousness and showiness. It reeks of someone who relishes spectacle, which means it can't be anything other than the Blood Emperor's war tent.

I despise how hard my heart crashes against my chest as I gaze at it. I hate the Blood Emperor. I want to kill him. I'm planning to kill him. All that considered, I shouldn't feel anything except blistering, vengeful rage. But there's a huge part of me that also plunges into fear. Yes, it's about the bodies staked around his war camp. It's also about having lived my entire life studying a history of my people where the tyrant just inside massacred a third of the Republic and a quarter of the whole Minor Continent, with the abominable, staggering blood-gift he possesses. But more than any of that, Nkosi being the man who ordered my mother's butchering and who tried to murder me in her womb sends the detested, ingrained fear shooting to interstellar heights with each step I take to behold him face-to-face.

But I'm not a coward—I've never been that—so I tell every drop of the fear to fuck off as I'm led toward the Blood Emperor in cuffs. I stack my spine, and I push my shoulders back. I hold my head high and unafraid and *furious*, letting an old friend—unbidden rage—lend me all the strength that I need for the impending confrontation. The ruse is for Ajani to present me as a captured war prize, but nobody ever said war prizes have to be quivering upon deliverance to enemy hands. And I refuse to be so. I've never been built like that and I never will be. I chance taking my eyes off the looming pavilion that inches ever nearer for a few necessary seconds to check on Dannica, Reed, and Caiman. The fact that they're here alongside me is my one regret.

The trio don't have the exact history with the Blood Emperor as I have, but they were children who grew up in a postwar society being cautioned and conditioned to both hate and fear the monster with hideous gifts across the ocean the same as me. And Reed lost his parents to the Blood Emperor's crimes. All of that visibly culminates in the three of them appearing to be faring about as well (which isn't good at all) as I am, seeing the pavilion that can't house anybody other than Nkosi.

Caiman has lost all of his usual smug arrogance and casts me a nervous look that's a knot of anxiety. His body is rigid, and he swallows thickly before snapping his eyes away from me and pinning them back on the pavilion.

Your asses should've stayed behind, I hiss at them in my head, my heart slamming harder against my chest. *I can't lose them inside. Everything has to go smooth. I have to protect them. I have to see them through this safely.* My mind explodes with the harried thoughts and a thousand crushing worries that I can't. That I'm not good enough. That I'll fail. But I quash every last one of them, quickly, because being stricken with the lack of confidence while literally walking into the danger that we are *will* see them dead.

I look at Reed now. He holds his head high, his spine stiff, his entire body unbowed, refusing to be beaten. He holds himself like a proud Praetorian, a proud Mareenian, walking through the other side's war camp and still saying *fuck you* to the enemy. Dannica displays something near identical.

Seeing their nerves of steel and resolve bolsters my own and helps me seal the last vestiges of fear away in the black box, slap a padlock on it, and pitch it into a black hole so it can't resurface. Despite the grave situation at hand, my lips twist in a slight, admiring smile at my cohort brother and sister.

Then, we're standing upon the pavilion.

You will not tremble, even a bit, when you enter, Grandfather orders me.

I will not give any Accacian or their bastard of an emperor the satisfaction, I promise him.

We are Amaris, we say together.

I start repeating Grandfather's mantra in my head to help center myself. To keep my head on right and turn a laser focus on the task in front of me. I use the mantra to remember there's no room for anything other than a successful op. I *won't* fail. I *won't* get my people killed. I'll save Mareen. I'll spare the innocent among what's left of the Republic in the north and the rest of the Minor Continent the horrors that the Isles and the eastern and western cities have suffered.

Amaris are strong as Khanaian steel. We do not bend. We do not break. We do not yield.

Fucking ever. Especially to asshole, murderous emperors who feign godhood, I tack on, adding my own addition to the words Grandfather ground into me time and time again since I was little.

By the time we're standing at the opening to the pavilion, where two heavy night-bear pelts meet to form a flap, I fully embody the mantra and have utter faith and conviction that Nkosi will die today.

19

AS SOON AS I ENTER the war tent I see the man who's been the evil, the monster, the savage murderer in my life for the entire time I've been on the planet. Nkosi, His Imperial Majesty of the Principal Continent, the Blood Emperor of Acaccia, and the megalomaniac bastard who killed my mother, sits against the far wall of the space atop a freaking godsdamned ruby throne. Other rulers would have their throne perched on a dais. But Nkosi's rests directly on the plush, richly colored black rugs carpeting the ground. The fact that he doesn't feel the need to sit above his inferiors affords him a deadlier air.

If any of the intelligence Mareen has gathered on him is true, the Blood Emperor is a man around 250 years old, having been blessed with extreme longevity by his blood-gift. His skin is dark brown, a rich, haunting ebony that's near the same color as mine, and his features remain youthful, despite his two and a half centuries. In fact, he looks ageless. He could be a man of twenty, thirty, or a well-maintained fifty who's aged like fine whiskey. His eyes shine a brown that's nearly black and his dark skin gleams as smooth as silk. His cheekbones and jawline are pronounced, sharp as the Khanaian blade pressed against my hip and concealed beneath the black tactical pants and shirt Ajani first captured me in.

All of the Blood Emperor's attributes congeal to paint a devastatingly handsome picture. I suddenly see why across some regions, he's spoken of as having a lethal, dark beauty that rivals what the world remembers Hasani, the god of death and the After, to possess. And for all his vicious beauty, there's an undercurrent of a brutality, of a terrible, hideous ugliness cloaking him like a second skin. The Blood Emperor is nothing like his Apis; Ajani projects just as deadly and pitiless a mien, but he also presents as the picture of urbanity near all of the time. Conversely, the Blood Emperor allows his savagery, the utter barbarism that comprises him, to ooze from his skin like an open sore he doesn't bother to bandage. It washes over him and coats him like an exoskeleton he clings to and dons as an additional weapon to spread fear and terrorize all who have the misfortune of stumbling into his orbit.

Surrounding Nkosi are six additional men near the same level of imposing as their liege and Apis. Three of those bastards stand on each side of their emperor. Like Ajani is currently wearing, they're clothed in a uniform that's one chilling tide of black from the neck down, and from the neck up rests the scarlet collar that marks the vicious men that serve Nkosi unwaveringly as his Red Order. Though Ajani warned me they'd be here, and I prepared myself to come face-to-face with the terrors that have haunted my nightmares since I was a child, I still suck in a breath in their presence. My eyes dart from one to another, wildly looking over all of them.

Beside me, Reed, Caiman, and Dannica take in the same ominous cadre we're being delivered to like winter does trussed up for the solstice. Dannica is the one who almost succeeds at appearing unaffected.

But I know my cohort sister and see she holds herself too tensely, the usual relaxed swagger she wears having fled. Caiman, for all his arrogance, bravado, and projected fierceness, can't quite keep his gold gaze from clouding over with fear. There's evident fear in Reed's frigid blue stare too. Honestly, who the fuck that is sane wouldn't be about to shit themselves when standing in front of the warlords and the liege who've slaughtered hundreds of thousands the world over, callously and gleefully? But there's also a deep icy fury and hatred that hardens Reed's stare, in particular, as he takes in the man and his topmost generals responsible for the skirmish that killed his parents.

What if this is a trap?

The thought crashes into me as my palms turn slick with sweat. Fresh panic blooms, making my lungs burn and making me feel like I'm choking on the fires that burned Cara to ash. Now that my mind has latched on to the possibility of a setup, it won't let it go. *If this is a trap,* I think, frenzied, *we have no way out of this after letting Ajani cuff us and march us inside this war tent.* Even if we get free of the cuffs, there's no way the four of us can fight all eight of Accacia's leadership and survive. Likely, we wouldn't even fight just one of them and survive if the power Ajani has previously displayed is anything to go by.

Once I venture down the black hole, I can't shake the paranoia. What if Reed was right all along? What if we never, *I never*, should have trusted Ajani? What if I chose wrong? Gambled wrong? What if I made a terrible decision out of desperation after the microstates announced their alliances with Accacia that's about to get us executed on the spot?

I clench my bound hands into fists. I stare a hole into the back of Ajani's head as he stands silent for the moment in front of Nkosi and his fellow warlords. I try to pull the truth of the situation, I try to pry Ajani's real intentions, from his mind with sheer force of will. That's not a talent of the blood-gifted, though, so it's only a desperate, futile attempt.

I grit my teeth, my clenched hands trembling with fury at myself, terror for me and my squad, and paranoia that Ajani has played us.

Amaris are strong, I remind myself, trying to calm down. I'm unraveling; that will get me nowhere if things are about to go to shit. *We do not bend. We do not break. We do not* fucking *yield. Regardless of the monsters we stand face-to-face with.* If Ajani is a duplicitous snake and I'm about to die, the men standing before me will find they'll have one hell of a fight on their hands as they attempt to achieve it. I'm not the helpless, spineless, gentle creature my mother was. I have teeth, and claws, and Grandfather's combat training, and the same fucking scary-ass blood-gift as they do. *If I'm dying*, somebody *is going out with me.*

I make the vow and pick my target among the warlords. I choose which man Hasani's hellserpents are dragging into a hellpit with me when they come to claim me in death. He's standing directly to the right of Nkosi, and there's no mistaking who he is. I know the exact shade of his brown-black eyes, the exact, pronounced angles of his high cheekbones, and the exact curves and fullness of his lips—because I've seen all of those things every day for the past nineteen years in the mirror.

They each belong to *me*.

The man standing to the Blood Emperor's right in a menacing black uniform and that daunting red collar is my father. I know it as sure as I know triplet moons orbit Iludu and bleed red in the sky a handful of times a year.

Once I see him, once I recognize who he is, I can't look away. Agony and scolding anger and denial all twist in my chest, knocking further air from my lungs. My eyes lock on him, and I realize *his* eyes are locked on me in turn. He scans me head to toe with an expressionless, cold stare. And once he's completed his inspection, he doesn't look away. His penetrating stare settles on my face, and a hideous sneer curves his lips. It is an acknowledgment of who I am and the link between us. There's no doubt he's mocking me, daring me to voice what I've discerned, and trying to intimidate me into looking away.

The snarl rips from me without my thinking about it because I've never fucking liked bullies. I like parents who are bullies even less. *Fuck you to the depths of a hellpit!* I scream it loud and clear with my uncowed, steely glare.

His lips twitch a fraction as if amused, but trying to curb it. Then he speaks to me. "You are nothing like Maiika."

Hearing him utter my mother's name is like having a dagger thrust in my gut then twisted and yanked, spilling my entrails with its removal. I lock my muscles. I go rigid, so I don't give into the urge to clutch my stomach in an attempt to assuage the physical ache. I blink, nineteen years' worth of rage and sorrow and grief making my eyes sting.

No, the godsdamn he didn't. This motherfucker has some gall.

Nkosi slices his warlord a look of censure and annoyance. "Rigaud." The name, my father's name, apparently, a name I've never known, cracks out of the Blood Emperor like he's brandishing an actual whip.

My father, Rigaud, turns to his liege and bows at the waist. "Forgive me. I forgot myself."

Nkosi cuts him down with a look that's so cleaving I think it might actually slice him in two. Too bad it's only a look, not an actual blade, and it doesn't.

You bastard. You bastard. You bastard. It's all I can think as I stare Rigaud down, swept away by the avalanche of emotions that I can't find a way out of.

In a way, I appreciate this distraction, because it keeps me from dwelling on the real power in the room. That is until the Blood Emperor rises from his throne. I snap my eyes away from my father and look to Accacia's emperor, his rustle of movement a clear threat that I need to focus on. Nkosi's attention zeroes in on me in return like a heat-seeking missile. His eyes narrow sharply, pinching tight in distaste at the corners, as he completes his own examination of me. The hairs on the back of my neck stand up under the weight of his scrutiny. I shudder a second time as Nkosi clearly takes me apart piece by piece with his eyes, mincing me down to the most basic components that comprise who I am. "You are precisely what I've thought all of these years," he murmurs. "You are merely Mareenian filth. An abomination spawned by my nemesis's whore of a daughter and a disloyal warlord." Hatred for where I come from, for the individual halves that comprise me, and for all that I am blaze in his light amber stare.

And though I hate him just as much, perhaps more, having the undiluted loathing of the most frightening, most powerful man on the planet focused entirely on me like a honing beacon sends chills skittering down my spine.

Reed steps closer to my side, growling. It's a protective, animalistic sound I've never heard him make before. I'd be amused and give him shit mercilessly for it if we weren't in such a gravely serious predicament. I glance Dannica's and Caiman's way to check on them again. The former watches Nkosi unblinking, statue-still, and the latter looks like he's beholding a ghost. No, Caiman looks like he *is* the ghost.

Nkosi ignores all three, for the moment, like they're not even in the room. His attention remains unnervingly and unwaveringly on me as his pure disgust for me and how I came to be seeps from it and crashes into me like a tidal wave.

The smile that curves his face would be devastatingly handsome—if it wasn't downright cruel and homicidal. For the second time, I liken Nkosi to Hasani; this time, he looks like the god of death might've appeared right before he let loose his vengeance and buried a civilization of millions alive beneath ice and snow. Which . . . Nkosi is well on his way to actually accomplishing, I guess. He's already buried generations of innocents across Mareen under fire and ash and bombs and missiles and blood. Then there's the carnage he spread across the Minor Continent in the former war.

Nkosi casts a glance behind him, pointing his index finger at the throne he rose from. "It's not made from mined stones. It's fashioned from more-precious rubies." His eyes glint with a sadism that makes my stomach curdle because I know where he's going with this. "The throne you look upon is one made of *blood rubies*," he says and as I've guessed. He pauses to flick an invisible speck of lint from the collar of the crisp black military coat that he wears. His collar isn't red. Instead, it blazes a kingly gold, and fitted over the coat is an ancient, chain-mail-like armor that glitters a radiant red. The old-school armor makes him look even more like some archaic god. Like one of the Pantheon has returned to walk Iludu and terrorize us all. And what he says next makes him *sound* like one of the reprehensible motherfuckers. "I forge a throne to sit upon every time I conquer a new territory. The one here, I made from Mareenian blood. All Caran souls, as a tribute to your grandfather. Not soldiers. Cara's women and youth gifted me my latest throne. I think Verne would've liked that if he were still around. And by 'like,' I mean he'd be positively devastated and incensed—which is a hell of a good time in my opinion."

The depravity of his admission leaves me numb. My stomach squeezes into knots at the heinous act he's committed against the citizens of Cara who he bled and brutalized to construct a throne simply as another petty *fuck you* to the dead man he's still locked in a power struggle with. It's vile. *He's* vile.

Retching comes from my left. I turn, just the barest fraction, refusing to take my eyes off the monster in front of me, and spy Caiman doubled over.

Beside him, Dannica draws in a breath. Releases it slowly.

To my right, Reed holds himself rigid as steel after the revelation about the hellish throne. The same need to carve something apart that's been etched into his bearing from the beginning remains there.

I feel you. Me too, I silently tell him. *Me. Fucking. Too.*

The need to slit the Blood Emperor's throat is near unbearable. In the moment, if I could, I'd do exactly what Reed looks like he wants to do. I'd carve Nkosi apart piece by piece just to bleed *him* and repay the favor in kind he paid to the poor people of Cara. In fact, I'm so blinded with rage and bloodlust that, if I knew how and could manage it, I'd do to him what he did to the damned souls he bled to make that gruesome throne. I'd bleed him dry, tearing his soul and very essence from his body, and fashioning it into a kill prize, a blood ruby. I'd then toss the damn thing into the bottom of the fucking Tumultuous Sea, pitching what's left of this asshole who craves planet-wide worship into such obscurity as to be forgotten about entirely as history drags on.

He likes to play at being immortal. At being a god. The thing is: He's not. He's *only* Pantheon-blessed. He isn't *one of the Pantheon*. Grandfather proved how red he bleeds; not gold like the gods. Which means when I strike, all I have to do is strike true and he dies.

When the time comes, there's no room for fuckups, Kenna.

Ajani, who's remained silent while wearing an expression on the side of bored since we entered the pavilion, finally speaks.

"True to why I'm your Apis," he says, full of arrogance and addressing the Blood Emperor directly, "I present you with the war gifts I apprised you of, my liege." He sweeps into a bow—though not before cutting his fellow warlords down to size with one superior smirk. The projected smugness makes me almost overlook the barely perceptible tightening of Ajani's shoulders as he goes to his knees in front of the Blood Emperor. I see it nonetheless, and it's a grace I seize and thank the cosmos for providing me. It's a small thing, but I use it as proof that Ajani is nervous, too, and that means he hasn't walked us into a trap—that maybe his desire to end the despicable creature before us is as ardent and ferocious as my own.

Please be genuine, I silently beg him.

Alongside Ajani, his corps that came with us kneel reverently, too, save for his marshals and two others who dip their heads but remain standing and watching us Mareenians closely.

The men and women continue kneeling until Nkosi vocalizes they may stand.

Ajani rises swiftly, straightening out his black and red uniform coat that bears no wrinkles. The set of his jaw paints a picture of him being positively insulted that he was forced to kneel in the first place. The Blood Emperor doesn't miss it; he slides a knowing smirk Ajani's way like it's an old game that they've long played.

"Your gifts are well received, Apis," Nkosi says smoothly to Ajani. "Your liege thanks you." He walks a few measured steps forward, keeping his strides toward us lazy and relaxed, sending the signal that Reed, Caiman, Dannica, and I are very much caught prey and he's the predator that's about to delight in playing with its food.

I gnash my teeth. The anxiety I'm stricken with that turns my hands and forehead clammy isn't something I need to feign. Ajani, the squad, and I went over this in excruciating, careful detail. Reed insisted on it several times. And for all the times we've hashed things out and I know what comes next, dread clamps around me in a vise grip. We can't strike straightaway. Ajani impressed how stupid and deadly that would be for us all. We need to let the Blood Emperor play with his trapped prey first, have a bit of fun and truly relax his guard. But strategizing and actually bracing to bear the brunt of whatever tortures the Blood Emperor has in store for us as a greeting are two entirely different things.

Nkosi continues his slow advance forward. At first, I'm sure he's going to stop directly in front of me. But then he changes course and steps to Reed.

And that might be worse than when I assumed I'd stay the focus of his attentions.

20

LEAVE HIM THE FUCK ALONE, I want to snarl. But we played at this during SSEE, and I learned well from the consequences that resulted with Enzo up on the mountain. Instead of protecting Enzo and making Reed back off, I turned Enzo into a target—a particular person of interest. So even though it takes every drop of discipline that I only *sometimes* possess, I do not speak a word. I barely breathe. I should look away from Reed altogether. Focus solely on Nkosi like he's the only one in the room. But I don't have *that* much self-control, and I couldn't take my eyes off Reed in the moment if the planet were about to combust. It feels too much like abandoning him; the mere thought of it feels like having a sundisk slammed into my chest and explode on impact.

Though . . . whatever damage Nkosi may be about to deal Reed will surely result in the same thing.

The Blood Emperor reaches forward and grabs Reed's chin. Reed emits a low, violent growl. Nkosi smirks and digs his fingers harder into Reed's flesh until purplish bruises blossom on Reed's skin beneath Nkosi's punishing grip. "I expect all inferiors—which means everyone who stands before me—to bow unless they have a good reason to remain standing. *So kneel.*" Ruthlessness flashes in Nkosi's eyes, and I assume he's issued the order with a whip of compulsion. I can *feel* the sheer power wafting off him when he speaks. It dials up the mildly warm air that suffuses the war tent to the heat of an inferno. The blistering air turns suffocating. But as I stare at Reed, he doesn't go glassy-eyed. He retains all lucidity, and Nkosi gifts him a vicious smile even as Reed refuses to kneel.

"I could force you with compulsion," Nkosi says as if reading my mind, "but I enjoy asserting my will upon the wayward and stupid by more thrilling methods." A blood spike isn't what forms in his hands. Instead, a full replica of an actual dagger—scarlet and glistening and lethally sharp—congeals in his palm as easily and seamless as I can form my blood weapons. He drives the dagger into Reed's gut, and I scream loud enough that I almost drown out the wail of agony that comes from Reed as he falls to his knees. He hunches over and clutches the wound, immediately breaking out in a sweat, blood leaking out of him and saturating the floor.

"That's better." Nkosi, the bastard, looks down at Reed with a mildly disappointed expression. "Though I expected . . . I don't know . . . something *more* . . . *someone actually formidable* out of Verne's protégé he took such an interest in. What I've glimpsed from you is pitiful." Nkosi emits a short chuckle, like it couldn't elate him more.

Reed grunts from the ground. Glaring up at Nkosi, he yanks the blood dagger out of his stomach. I expect him to simply toss it aside to make a point. But Reed's *fuck you* to Nkosi ends up being so much pettier and much more spectacular. He moves with the same reflexes he displayed against me during the Combat Trial. Moving with perfect Xzana form, despite being injured, he possesses speed that reflects the biochip he bears but that I swear whispers at something *more*. One minute the blood dagger is in Reed's hand, and in less than half a breath, it's hurtling upward through the air, straight for Nkosi's throat.

As exciting as all his actions are, this isn't *any* of what we planned. Things have careened off orbit so quickly my head spins. Adrenaline surges through me and I suck in a breath, disbelief and elation flooding me for all of the millisecond that it seems like Reed's throw might actually slice through Nkosi's jugular.

It's a pity it doesn't.

Because blood-gifted or not, it'd be damn hard to heal from that quicker than it'd take Reed to sever Nkosi's head while he's down. We could get things over with sooner rather than later and avoid the rest of the torture Ajani insists needs to play out. His Imperial Majesty doesn't even end up needing to move or lift a finger to deflect the attack, however. He merely glances at the blood dagger, and it drops to the ground a centimeter away from nicking his skin. Then he tosses his head back and roars. His laughter is booming and holds no mirth. It suffuses the pavilion the same as his power flooding the space does.

He stops laughing long enough to say, "I would be insulted if that move wasn't indicative of the truth I just spoke. Are all Mareenians save Verne so fucking stupid? And he wasn't that smart to begin with. Or else he wouldn't have failed to kill me. Yet, he did." The Blood Emperor grimaces. "I suppose I've answered my own question."

I shake my head, my heart shooting into my throat, because although I didn't think of it before, I realize that Nkosi is so right. The blood dagger was made of *his* blood. Which means it's Nkosi who'd hold providence over it—who'd be able to command it regardless of whose hand it was flung from.

Shit. Shit. Shit. It's all I can think as Nkosi glowers down at Reed with a look that promises Reed a fate worse than death. The Blood Emperor has decided to no longer be amused, and the man who tried to draw his blood is wounded at his feet *and* in cuffs. It's a terrible, precarious position for Reed to be in—one that a man like Nkosi will take advantage of without killing him outright. Nkosi likes spectacle. He likes a show. He likes to make statements. He's also infamously petty and prideful. So I already have an inclination of what's to come when Nkosi stoops down in front of Reed. Without looking at the blood dagger laying between them, he commands it to rise into the air. As it does, he wraps his hand around Reed's throat, squeezing until Reed turns red then blue as he gasps for air. All the while, the dagger hovers menacingly between them—until it doesn't. While Nkosi chokes the life out of Reed, the blood dagger slams once again into his gut—into the same wound that it inflicted before. It slides in and out of his insides with sickening swishes until Reed stops struggling in Nkosi's hold and turns limp.

I cry out once more.

I barely notice my scream, and the others certainly don't. We all have our eyes on the pair, Dannica shrieking herself, even as Nkosi's stare locks on the wound. Reed's blood gushes out of his body more swiftly. It pools on the ground and inches toward Nkosi's feet. "I'm sure I can find a spot for one additional blood ruby in my throne," he intones.

The bluish hue from a lack of oxygen has long fled Reed's skin. He's the pale white of death now.

I stand paralyzed, rooted to the floor, my heart twisting in my chest as it feels like all the oxygen gets sucked from *my* lungs. I can't breathe straight. I can't think straight. I can't do *anything* except stare at Reed's ashen, limp form.

I blink.

I still see Reed crumpled on the floor. But I also see Zayne lying broken at the bottom of an ice crevasse. I see Grandfather, too—lying damnably still in his coffin. Then I see my mother mutilated exactly how the accounts of her attack describe.

I blink again, the wide space of the pavilion growing tinier and tinier, boxing me in. The cuffs on my wrist feel like they tighten. My chest feels like it's being cracked apart. I'm losing it. I'm unraveling. I know that, and yet I can't do a damn thing in the moment to reel it in.

Then . . . I see it. Something that crashes through my devastation and gives me a glimmer of hope. It's faint, only the barest of movements that I might have missed if I wasn't so intensely focused on Reed's bloodied form. But it *is* there. Reed's chest rises and falls with the shallowest of breaths. And it's all I need to spur me into action. The snarl that rips from me is foreign even to my own ears. My head snaps from Reed to Nkosi with a raw cry that's savage and angry and grief-filled and suffused with all the agony and torment and pain and trauma the Blood Emperor has caused. It wants blood. It wants vengeance. It wants Nkosi's fucking life force rushing out of his body as he's sprawled on the floor at my feet.

I see Ajani's eyes snap to me. *Not yet,* they say. *Hold your position.*

"Fuck the position!" I growl at him, and I see his eyes widen just a bit, yet he doesn't react. His bastard liege is *killing* Reed.

I dimly hear Caiman and Dannica shout my name, but I don't listen to what they have to say either.

Yes, I'm cuffed. And there isn't much I can really do while I am. But that doesn't stop me. I fling myself at Nkosi, hurtling my body into him.

I'm guessing he wasn't expecting that.

We crash to the ground.

Caiman yells my name again, and Ajani spits out a vicious curse. I expect the warlords still standing around the throne to all descend on me. Or the guards to rush into action. The only one who steps forward is Ajani. Everyone else holds their positions around the room. Ajani plucks me up off his liege as if I weigh nothing. Nkosi hops to his feet, as lithe and nimble as any well-conditioned soldier. Which verifies one key thing: the Blood Emperor isn't the sort of warmonger who harbors a gift and solely relies on that gift to address threats. He's in top physical fighting form too. *Well, shit. How many fucking strengths does the bastard have? Does he not have* one *limitation or weakness?*

The thing is, I was about to find out, except Ajani stopped me. *Why the hell did he stop me? Isn't this what he wants?* Yet here I am, one of his arms banded around my chest. The other crushes against my throat. Both trap me soundly. The Blood Emperor faces me, glaring like he's about to punch his hand into my chest and rip out my heart with his bare hands. At least his attention is off Reed. *For all the good that it'll do.* Reed might already be beyond saving.

I wail to the cosmos inside my head. I've lost Grandfather. I've lost Zayne. I've lost Brock and Selene. I cannot lose Reed too. I'm fucking sick of losing people. And Reed . . . Nkosi wasn't just killing him. He was wrenching him toward a fate worse than death.

Which might now be my fate.

For Nkosi steps toward me in smoldering rage. And yet, for all that enmity, I don't care about him. Only Reed. I stare at Reed, still limp and so white on the ground. All the warmth, all the light, all the color has fled from his complexion.

I choke on a sob. I'm still looking at Reed, still trapped in agony, which is why I never see Nkosi's counterstrikes coming. Not that I could do a damn thing about it while being cuffed *and* restrained by Ajani. And not that the first one is aimed at me. I whip to the left, confused at first, when a scarlet dagger streaks *past* my head. My pulse roars in my ears when I see Dannica has somehow slipped her cuffs and lifted a blaster, assumedly from the legionnaire crumpled on the floor. Caiman dives in front of the blade Nkosi aimed at her, and I immediately understand what Caiman intends to accomplish. The blade sinks into his stomach, providing Dannica a few precious additional moments to get the shot off.

My cohort sister does. Unerringly. Her aim dead center of Nkosi's head.

A blood shield springs up around him and the bullet ricochets off the damn thing.

Nkosi lets it drop right after. A third and fourth dagger fly into Dannica's middle before the shield vanishes completely.

I have no time to process, zero time to freak out, before a blood dagger sinks into the center of my chest. I rasp, pain exploding around the blade. As I cough up blood, I become certain it punctured my heart. I glance down at the hilt sticking from me. A dark spot spreads across the front of my tactical shirt. My skin turns feverish. Nkosi steps closer and twists the dagger lodged inside me. I scream and my knees buckle. Ajani lets me go, allowing me to fall to my knees.

I glance up into a face that doesn't try to feign an ounce of humanity. The Blood Emperor stares down at me like I'm mud that isn't even fit to be on the bottom of his boots. He raises one of those said boots and its heel comes down slowly on my right clavicle, splintering the bone. I scream again, blinding pain shooting into my shoulder and down my sternum that's almost as intense as what's ravaging the left side of my chest. I look, frenzied, at my impaled chest and see my blood gushing from around the dagger preternaturally fast. Nkosi watches the bloodletting he's performing on me with a gleeful, enraptured, sickening expression.

"This was always going to be your fate. And your comrades' fate. You and the protégé's idiotic actions merely sped up my plans and cut short the reception I had in store. I was always going to utterly annihilate everything Verne loved and all that loved him back. But now you've made it personal between you and me, *little girl*." He exerts more pressure on my shattered collarbone, then moves his foot lower and crushes the splayed fingers of my right hand, breaking those bones too.

I grit my teeth, blinking against the agony. I lie helpless on the floor, so much of my life force having fled me already, and my blood continues to stream out of me. My skin no longer feels feverish. Coldness pervades every inch of me, and I shiver.

I'm going to die. I'm currently dying. I'm sure of it. I've skirted death before, but certainly not this time. This is it. It's all over. I failed myself. I failed Reed. I failed Grandfather. I failed Caiman and Dannica—whose deaths are likely following soon, if they haven't come already.

I snarl up at Nkosi with the thought. "Fuck. You," I heave, refusing to die cowed.

"No," he says blandly. "You're the one who's fucked." A slight smile curls his lips, and, growing ever weaker, I feel something else attempting to separate itself from my body. Since Nkosi's aim is to create one more blood ruby, it must be my soul, or life force, or essence, or whatever you want to call the thing that makes me *me*. The spark that comprises *Ikenna*. At first it feels like a deeply rooted thing that jiggles in place. Then between one ragged breath and the next it feels like it's clinging on for dear life but being clawed out of me anyway, snapping thread by precious thread.

I thought I knew pain before. This is different. This is *hell*. I roar in agony; the room spins. I blink. Severe dizziness assaults me and consciousness starts to ebb. I know that once I tumble into darkness, I'm never emerging. I'm gone. Another thread of the thing that's trying to desperately cling on to *me* is wrenched free by whatever Nkosi is doing. More black washes into my vision. Like on the mountain when I was injured and losing waves of blood, I swear I see those glimmers of gold among all the crimson that's spilled out. This time I'm positive it's induced by some combo of delirium and shock—my brain beginning to shut down while I'm so close to death and making me see bizarre things that aren't there.

"My liege!" The urgent but cool voice has the pitch of Ajani's. I dimly remember we're supposed to be aligned on the same side. If I had more strength I'd laugh. That fucking duplicitous, treacherous bastard. He didn't even try to intervene or derail things.

If anything, he facilitated my current state when he pulled me off Nkosi.

"What?" Nkosi bites off the question.

"Look. Do you see what I can?" Ajani's voice is lustful and covetous like it was in the throne room in Khanai when he sensed the level of my power.

For a precious, merciful second, the agony stops. The most vital part of me stops being ripped out of my body. The bloodletting slows too. And with both things subsiding, I feel my blood-gift jump at the reprieve. It immediately kicks into hyperdrive and starts furiously trying to repair me.

I don't think it'll work. I'm sure it's definitely too late. If anything, this is just delaying the inevitable. Prolonging the torment. The self-healing aspect of my gift has its limits, and Nkosi has damn sure taxed it. Pushed it beyond what it is capable of. I know this because while I feel my gift trying its hardest to patch up the vessel it lives inside, I also feel that it isn't enough. My heartbeat remains faint and erratic. The dizziness stays. The black roiling across my vision magnifies twelvefold.

"What the *fuck* is she? *What* is going on with *your* abomination?" Nkosi's voice has faded to some place far away, but I'm still present on the side of the living enough to hear it and understand that this time he isn't speaking to Ajani. He says "*your* abomination," so he must be talking to the man who sired me. My supposed father.

Ajani comes into view, though he's hazy. He kneels, but he doesn't reach for me. He touches two fingers—almost tentatively—to my spilled blood. He rubs them back and forth then stares at them almost like he's *afraid* of what he sees. "You can't kill her. At least not yet. Not until we check this out. What if she's—"

"She isn't." The voice that cuts into whatever Ajani was about to say is Rigaud's. Yet for all his confidence, the warlord sounds nervous.

"You'd do well to be silent at the moment," Nkosi says, low and threatening.

Ajani lays a hand against my brow. I feebly flinch. "Let me reverse this, my liege," the Apis says in a perfectly subservient pitch. "I do not have the blessing of augury, but that gift isn't needed to surmise what *visible* gold in her blood signifies. If she is all that she appears to be, consider the enormous strength she can lend you if you let her live for

now. Her death can end in something more advantageous than a useless blood ruby. Take the time to prepare for a Stitching. Kill her in
that manner. Why pass up the chance to add this power she possesses
to your own? Especially when it won't violate any of Amaka's edicts and
anger the goddess. How could it? The girl isn't truly Accacian. She isn't
technically one of Amaka's flock. By every definition that matters, she's
Mareenian. So you won't suffer the goddess's displeasure."

A murky Nkosi comes into view when he stoops. The Blood Emperor peers down at me, and his amber gaze takes on a similar lustful
quality as what I heard in Ajani's voice. "Perhaps," he says. The heel of
his boot eases the pressure off my fingers.

"I'd counsel that you leave her companions alive too," Ajani says.
"They'll be useful to keep her under control, and she'll need to willingly
agree to the Stitching."

Leave them alive. He said *leave*. It shouldn't be the primary thing
I grasp on to, that I battle to wrap my mind around clearly, but it is. If
those were Ajani's words, Dannica and Caiman, and maybe Reed, too,
aren't dead and they might yet survive.

"Your *counsel* sounds more like an insistence," Nkosi snaps. "You
forget yourself, boy."

"Never, my liege," Ajani returns. "I am but your humble Apis. The
servant and sword at your side who ensures the longevity and persistence of your reign. I know you'll be loath to do what it'll take for her
and the other Mareenians to live. So allow me to bear the burden for
you."

The fog clouding my mind is so dense that I can barely make sense
of anything the Blood Emperor and Apis are saying. I keep fighting to
do so anyway because it's evident that how their convo plays out deter-
mines my fate and my friends' fates. Is any of the exchange even real?
Am I hallucinating? Am I already dead and trapped in some hellish
existence with the two men as my tormentors?

I'm so weak it's impossible to turn my head and see what else and who else may or may not be around me. The hard ground beneath me and the warm, humid air I can still feel on my face are the only two things that give indications that I might remain truly alive.

I drag in a hard-won breath. Fresh stabs of pain bloom in my chest. That pain confirms that yes, I am alive. I am still very much inside Nkosi's war tent. He and Ajani *are* having the discussion I'm hearing around me. But what the hell does it mean? I comb my mind, rifling through every scrap of knowledge I hold about being blood-gifted for what a Stitching is. Nothing jiggles free.

I'm sure, though, it's not something I want to experience.

"Do it," Nkosi tells Ajani tightly. "You're granted permission."

"My liege—" Riguad interjects with a note of concern.

"Are you questioning His Imperial Majesty?" Ajani cuts him off. The words have a barbed edge and are wrapped in intimidation, arrogance, and challenge.

"No. I am not. I question *you*. This doesn't feel right, *boy*. This feels too convenient," Rigaud tells Nkosi.

"*Apis*," Ajani snarls before Nkosi can respond. "That is the only title you're allowed to address me by. Slip again and I don't care if we are in the middle of a war, I will cut out your heart. We're winning it by leagues; the Empire and His Majesty can spare one *aging* warlord. You'll be easily replaced."

"You little upstart—"

"Rigaud." Nkosi utters my father's name with all the authority of Emperor. "To question my Apis now that it has been decided is to question me.

"Are you questioning *me*?"

"No, my liege." The response is dutiful and low.

Not waiting for Rigaud's answer, Ajani has already laid a splayed hand against my chest, covering the wound Nkosi made there. He brings my blood to heel with just a touch, and my life stops seeping out. His brows knit together in intense concentration as he murmurs words that I can't make out, though I do discern from the softer vowels and grandiose consonants that they're in one of the Acaccian tongues. I also discern that he means to heal me. And he may be my enemy, but I'm fucking grateful and I want to sob because I sure as shit didn't want to die on the ground via the fate Nkosi had planned.

I expect a warmth to flood my chest like when my own blood-gift heals me. Yet the exact opposite happens. An iciness cascades through the wound site and pervades my whole body. It's so glacial it feels like icicles punch through my insides while my heart and blood and muscle and tissue and sinew freeze over. My body violently shudders, my extremities immediately stinging from phantom frostbite.

"Be still," Ajani hisses. "It'll be easier if you don't fight it."

I gnash my teeth. *How the hell do I accomplish that?* But I'll do anything to lessen the agony, so I try by forcing my muscles rigid. I close my eyes for a second, almost wishing the darkness still hovering around the edges of my vision would claim me. Everything fucking hurts and I once again doubt all Ajani has told me. Gradually, though—*so slowly*—the pain dissipates until my insides start to warm tiny degree by tiny degree and the black crowding out most of my sight retreats. It's then that I feel the roots of me, my soul, I guess, which Nkosi tried to rip free, settling back deep into my chest. Into my *being*. I breath heavy yet much easier, and wetness slicks my cheeks.

Ajani lifts his hand from my chest and stands. "Stay where you are. Don't tax yourself," he says before walking to Dannica, stooping, and pressing a palm to the wounds in her abdomen.

Her healing and Caiman's go swifter. The knots inside me ease when the pair is sitting upright and blinking bewilderedly. I tense when Iyko marches to Caiman's and Dannica's side. I tense more when my friends go robotically stiff and vacant-eyed.

"It's for their protection." Iyko nods my way, her voice astonishingly gentle and reassuring. I understand, and honestly, I'm glad for the compulsion. In this situation, a mindless Caiman and Dannica make for a safe, silent Caiman and Dannica, who will hopefully skirt Nkosi's renewed interest.

I don't have time to really process that they're all right because then Ajani is moving to Reed and kneeling beside him. Watching the Apis, I'm sure it's too late—Reed's been down much longer than me and I'm certain he suffered as great, or greater, damage. Surely he's already gone from hovering near death as I was to actually stepping both feet into the After.

Even with so little to hope for I turn my head so I can fully watch Ajani try to save Reed and I can't look away—or stop the mad, desperate prayer to the cosmos that by some fucking outlandish miracle he'll end up all right.

Several seconds drag on. Then several excruciating minutes. Time stops when for all the strength that Ajani carries himself with, the Apis sways. He sits on the floor, but he doesn't lift his hand from Reed. He's chanting the low Accacian words again, but this time, he's clearly exerting a visible effort to accomplish the unfathomable. His dark brown skin has turned a grayish pallor and his black uniform coat is drenched with sweat. His muscles bunch and quiver beneath the fabric. The arm he has outstretched to Reed shakes arduously.

As my head increasingly clears, I realize what he's doing. He's exerting a power only the mightiest of blood-gifted have—one I have only heard hints of (and those fairy tales at best): the ability to reach into the After itself, defy Hasani and his hellserpents, and haul a newly dead soul firmly back into the world of the living. Watching him exercise the power makes new grief crack my heart wide open, that Reed *was* dead.

But there's no mistaking the flush of color that returns to Reed's face. Like with my chest, his gut wound has stopped leaking blood entirely. Watching it being done to another, slowly, I see what I missed before. A faint red glow pulses from Ajani's hand and into Reed's injury. I shiver, thinking about how the red glow looks scorching but how utterly frigid it felt when Ajani healed me.

"Do you want to have the Mareenians come along as POWs as we conclude our campaign or should I fly them back to Acaccia and jail them?" Ajani asks Nkosi, exhaustion in his voice.

Reed's chest starts to rise and fall with micromovements. His eyes have yet to peel open, though, so that's what I keep watching for. I *need* to see his blue gaze. Beholding the shallow breathing isn't enough. I need to see life and warmth and light behind his *open* eyes to assure myself Ajani succeeded. That Reed is really alive.

"I'm sure you have a suggestion for that, too, Apis?" Nkosi says smoothly. In fact, it's smooth enough that you'd be a fool not to automatically detect some kind of trap is being laid for Ajani. Or maybe some manner of test. But I have no idea what and I almost don't care about the internal politics of the Accacian high council at the moment. Something important is happening, though, and I pry my eyes away from Reed to look between the Blood Emperor and Apis. I attempt to puzzle out the dance the two of them clearly started doing the moment Ajani suggested Nkosi spare us. Ajani plays the role of faithful servant well in the presence of a man who demands nothing except absolute submission and obedience. Despite that, in the moment, Nkosi also seems like he very much is aware that Ajani's deliverance of those things is an act. Still, Nkosi installed Ajani as his Apis and keeps him in the position. And, more mystifying than the fact that Nkosi permits Ajani to retain the rank and power that he does is that the Blood Emperor allows him to live at all. No Tribune would suffer so much as a suspicion of disloyalty from a subordinate. Grandfather wouldn't either. The person would be dead as soon as doubt got cast, regardless of their innocence or guilt, as a necessary precaution.

Know your enemy better than yourself, I hear Grandfather's baritone voice in my head. *The knowledge will hand you their weakness.*

I scrutinize Ajani and Nkosi. Is the Apis, in some way, the Blood Emperor's vulnerability?

Before I can consider it thoroughly, Reed stirs. Finally, blessedly, mercifully, *thank the fucking cosmos*, his eyes lift open. Not all the way—his lids peel back maybe all of half an inch—but enough to make me shout and sob internally. He weakly turns his head and gazes directly at me. I dig my fingers into the floor and nod to him. It's all I can do to keep from breaking down outwardly. *I thought I lost you. But you're back. You're back, and I'm so glad for it*, I tell him with the intense look I pass him. He holds my stare as his eyes open all the way, and he nods in return. With a groan, he tries to push himself to a sitting position.

Ajani's hand comes to rest on Reed's shoulder. His arms bunch as if he's holding Reed in place. Reed's eyes flash a glacial blue.

"I just regifted you life. Do not undo all my hard work, Praetorian," Ajani says as if Reed is his soldier and he's the general issuing an iron-clad command.

Reed grits his teeth. He glares at Ajani with clear hostility in his eyes, which crackle with such ardent hatred they sizzle a dark, electric cobalt. Yet he doesn't lash out.

Ajani sneers then stands.

Reed doesn't attack, but he ignores the order he was given. He makes it to his knees, breaking out in a heavy sweat and with quivering legs by the time he does. He grunts, braces a hand against the floor, and makes an impressive, admirable effort to shove to his feet.

He doesn't ever get off the ground.

Ajani smirks down at him. "Use the wiser, actually intelligent Khanaian half of your brain."

Reed glowers.

"Do what he says," I rush to say, hating that I utter it, the plea tasting like corrosive acid in my mouth. *For now*, I say with my eyes.

Reed's attempt to stand makes me realize I'm still lying on the ground, and I probe inward and take stock of the strength that's returned to me. I *think* I can stand. Unlike Reed, I was only *near* dead. Not *dead* dead. All the same, I only haul myself to a sitting position. I'm not going to push to my feet and leave him in the dirt on his knees in the room full of Acaccians.

The Blood Emperor clears his throat, and it makes my attention snap back to the chief threat in the room. But he's lost interest for the moment in us Mareenians. He arches an eyebrow Ajani's way while settling his mouth into what might pass for a smile—if it didn't look like he was a sabine baring his teeth in preparation to rip Ajani's throat out.

Then why not simply do that? I wonder again about the relationship between the two of them. *If he outstrips Ajani in rank and power, why not just kill him like he obviously so greatly desires?*

"I asked if you had a suggestion, Apis?" Nkosi says.

Ajani bows to His Imperial Majesty. "You like a spectacle, my liege. So I imagine you'd want to chain them and drag them into the north with you as you march on Krashen City. You'd want them to watch as you decimated their home, their prestigious academy, and the supposed stronghold that is Krashen Base. If you can't make Verne Amari behold it because that triumph was lost to you with his death, forcing his beloved granddaughter, his protégé, Gamma's third-in-command, and a perfect scion of his Republic seems the next best thing. I also wouldn't let them far out of my sight. If three of the four were shaped by Verne Amari, I imagine they have some capacity to be resourceful. Maybe even threatening, given luck and the right alignment of opportunity."

An aggrieved muscle in Nkosi's jaw ticks. He strokes the trimmed left side of the ink-black beard cut short to his face while he pierces Ajani with a look I can't quite discern. "I do intend to take our prisoners north. You and your corps will come with us. You will personally see that the girl is prepared for the Stitching and compliant. And you will make sure affairs are in order for it to be executed immediately, via live vidfeed, at the onset of our attack. I want every news station across the planet transmitting both as they happen. Let's have what's left of *Verne's* Republic that's holed up in Krashen really quiver before the city falls, and let's have the planet witness that imbibing the girl's power into mine makes me truly unopposable, even among our own. It will make me truly a god. The achievement will add a nice symbolic touch to my wiping the Republic off the globe and ascending to Emperor of Iludu."

Ajani bows once more to his power-mad liege. "Your will is already done. I'll see to whatever you order."

"As is your duty and place, *my son*. You'll do well to remember."

His what?

My mind barely processes what Nkosi calls Ajani. I gape. Am I really looking at father and fucking godsdamn son?

I'm so stunned, so colossally blindsided, that a mad laugh bubbles up in my throat. Ajani is Nkosi's damn son. That bastard definitely withheld critical intel and made us walk into peril with half the information.

I'm going to gut him for it.

My head won't stop whipping between Blood Emperor and Apis. I shake it furiously, reeling from a revelation that goes too deep.

I snarl at Ajani—*the lying, cagey ass*. I'm not reckless enough to voice why in Nkosi's presence when Ajani's machinations are the only thing keeping my team and me alive, but he motherfucking knows why all the same.

I see the amusement in the slight upward curve of his lips.

I don't take too much time wondering how well he could smile if I ripped the lips off his face. Rather, I focus on this:

If Ajani has hatched a plot to not only kill his liege, but his father, what the hell is his real motivation? Clearly, the reason he fed us back in the citadel is a mountain of wolfshit.

Know your enemy. The knowledge will hand you their weakness.

When a child wants a parent dead, it is very, very personal. Which means Ajani and Nkosi may be each other's vulnerability, and perhaps that gives me an opening. Perhaps the two can be used to orchestrate each other's demise, and there is a way to end them both and keep my team and me clear of the blast zone so we take no additional hits.

What's happened in the war tent was brutal enough. We severely fucked up and paid for it. The moves we make next have to be smarter and ten steps ahead of what Nkosi has planned *and* whatever Ajani ultimately has planned too.

Which means I need to start coming up with some plans of my own.

21

AJANI AND TWO DOZEN LEGIONNAIRES escort us from the pavilion. As they do, the Apis marches at our side looking pitiless, and very much like we're actually hated captives and he's actually the enemy warlord who will relish cutting us down if we think to try anything. Not that we could. Whatever innate power I supposedly have, I damn well don't know how to properly harness it. I've been outmatched by Nkosi *and* Ajani now while possessing it. So it hasn't amounted to shit.

Because you *haven't communed with Amaka.*

The sharp, scourging voice is born of my guilt, and it is right. That's the precise reason I have no control after all—a reason that's *entirely* my fault. I can't help thinking things inside the war tent might've gone different if I'd already communed. Nkosi might already be dead. Reed, Caiman, and Dannica would've been spared harm. We wouldn't all still be playing captives in his accursed war camp. I wouldn't have given him days longer to continue his atrocities, and there'd be no preparations to topple Krashen.

Then there's the fact that Reed can't yet hold himself upright on his own. He's stubborn as all hell and sure tried to give it a good effort before we departed the pavilion, but he swayed as soon as he got to his feet. At least, he would have if I hadn't already flashed to his side and slung my arm around him. And Caiman and Dannica . . .

They remain under compulsion.

I glance at Iyko, who keeps stride with my friends' jerky steps. Her presence at their side makes it clear she continues to be the legionnaire who holds their minds. One thing I have learned about the abilities of the blood-gifted through Grandfather's endless training sessions is that prolonged compulsion is much easier to keep up and takes far less concentration if you maintain proximity to the target. Curiously, Iyko slips me the same nod that she did in the war tent as if to reaffirm *I've got them; I'll take care of them*. I have no idea if I'm reading her right—if that's what her head bobs really say. I could be delusional, grasping for boons and friends among enemies where there are none.

"When does she plan on giving their minds back?" I ask Ajani in an even voice. Even though I reasoned in the war tent that the hijacking was for their own good, I detest seeing my friends stripped of free will.

"When I decide it pleases me to have them returned," the Apis answers, haughty as ever.

"That's not an answer," I grind out.

He obliges me with nothing else in return, and I envision stabbing him in the throat and carving out the response he's withholding.

But despite my violent fantasies, I'm still cuffed, and I've already concluded how sorely outclassed I am against men who've had entire lifetimes—*several* lifetimes, in the Blood Emperor's case—to hone their blood-gift into weapons. I may have raw power, but Ajani and Nkosi have *mastery*. I *am* going to figure out how to close the chasm between both of them and myself, but that's not going to occur this instant.

So, for now, I exercise a shrewder strategy that doesn't rely on brute force to pry info about Caiman's and Dannica's welfare out of this bastard.

"You love doling out your little lectures to make a point about how ignorant and unworthy I am to bear Amaka's blessing," I say to Ajani. "So school me on one additional thing I'm woefully uninformed about but I imagine *infants* in Accacia know the answer to: if you keep someone under compulsion for an extended time, does it do permanent damage?" It's something I truly don't know the answer to yet should. Because I've never tested the bounds of chaining someone's mind to my own will for any real length of time, mostly because of the very unknown I'm asking Ajani about. The brain and perhaps more so the psyche are such delicate things that I have to imagine screwing with either over prolonged periods results in some sort of lasting consequences. And we were in that war tent for a damn long time—a time that's dragging on with our trek through the camp.

Of course Ajani decides in this moment *not* to be a condescending fucker. "Nice try," he says, chuckling. "I should withhold the answer out of pure insult that you believe I'm that pliable. But I'm feeling generous. Although I'm sure you won't like my filling *this* gap in your knowledge."

I stand corrected. He hasn't dropped the superior-asshole act.

"Enlighten me, regardless," I drawl.

He slides me a look that tells me he really can't believe how deep my idiocy runs. He can think what he wants, though; he continues speaking and that's all I give a shit about.

"It all depends on the strength and finesse of the blood-gifted who is wielding the compulsion," he says with a shrug. "It also hinges on the will of the person whose mind is being held."

I gnash my teeth. "You're right. I don't like that explanation." Mostly because it doesn't tell me if Dannica and Caiman will be all right. A confirmation that he doesn't intend to and won't permanently harm my people is what a true ally would hand over. Spitting that at Ajani is on the tip of my tongue, but I rein it in because making that accusation in the middle of a war camp would be moronic.

I remind myself that my cohort sister is fiercer than a solar storm. She's had the mettle and gall twice now to level blasters at powerful pricks; never mind the ferocity she displayed when she Crossed me. Dannica has *beyond* a strong will.

As for Caiman . . . Golden Boy has a steel core that's as stubborn as mine, I remind myself. And Caiman thinks way too highly of himself to let some Accacian asshole get the best of him. It's a bizarre feeling— being so concerned about a person you've spent the past eleven years despising and who's spent all of those same years detesting and hurling insults at you . . . and at one point, trying to kill you. But here we are, and I am concerned about Caiman Rossi as much as I'm concerned about Dannica—so I guess the planet is about to implode *and* the sun is about to drop out of its orbit.

Reed must feel how tense with anxiety I am because even though *I'm* holding *him* up, *he* squeezes *my* waist in support. "They're tough," he mutters. "He's a Rossi, and she's KaDiya. One is from a war house that doesn't produce anything but formidable bastards; the other . . . I know what KaDiya survived during her trials, so I know she's going to be all right."

I nod, glancing once more into their respective golden and violet eyes, which have zero signs of awareness behind them. Even seeing my frenemy and cohort sister like this, Reed is right: they can take care of themselves.

I hope.

I raise the hand that isn't wrapped around Reed's torso to my head and massage it as we walk. I don't care how vulnerable it makes me look. Right then, it's all I can do not to crack. *What in the godsfuck have we gotten ourselves into? And how do I get us out of it in one piece?* Reed's already died once for it. Hasani and his hellserpents will not be denied a second time. Ajani isn't *that* powerful. Nobody is, including the Blood Emperor. There are certain laws of the cosmos that even the most powerful of Pantheon-blessed and the gods themselves can't violate, and being unable to pull someone back from death more than once is probably the first.

"I'd counsel that you leave her companions alive too. They'll be useful *to keep her under control"*; recalling the Apis's words bestows the opposite of comfort. They punctuate that we're neck-deep in danger while in the clutches of the Blood Emperor and the Apis, who has his own, shadowy agenda.

Discerning that, the advice Ajani lent Nkosi back in the war tent whistles through my head, blade-sharp, a second time. I catch it by the hilt and pin it in place to a wall in my mind so I won't forget it and make the error of ever trusting Ajani.

She'll need to willingly agree to the Stitching.

The rest of what Ajani said rings behind his obvious maneuvering. With Reed and my friends more or less okay, distance between us and Nkosi, and me not bleeding out on the ground, I'm able to probe my cache of knowledge again for that unfamiliar word. Maybe a kernel of recognition will come to me while I'm not in the middle of panic and imminent death.

It doesn't.

I refrain from asking Ajani about it. If he needs to prepare me and ensure my compliance—whatever that means—then I'll find out soon enough. If I try to extract it from him now, I'll likely just get another infuriating, shifty answer because he's a cocky shithead who loves to be difficult.

I save my energy.

WE'RE TAKEN TO a cluster of barracks among the southern sector of the massive war camp. We halt and I assume one of the corrugated steel structures I'm facing will function as our prison. I quickly survey the exterior surroundings while I have time to, immediately looking for possible exits or weak spots in the Accacians' patrols in this portion of the camp. Smartly, double the number of legionnaires are on patrol—and those are only the ones that perform the duty conspicuously. We also remain more toward the interior of the camp, instead of having traveled near its perimeter. If one *was* to break free and make a run for it, they'd have to cross a considerable portion of space that's crawling with soldiers to get out. It's little surprise that there are no apparent security breaches when you're dealing with the most feared army on the planet. But I wouldn't be worth my training if I hadn't at least scanned for any.

We're prodded in the direction of a modest-size structure. From the outside, the unit looks spacious enough that I hope Ajani will deposit the four of us together inside it, all while knowing the Apis is light-years wiser than that. No general worth their rank would house a quadrumvirate of highly valuable, reasonably strong, *biochipped* prisoners of war together—no matter their supreme arrogance. It would just be supremely stupid.

Proving what I surmise, Ajani tugs me away from Reed's side without warning. Reed falls in the dirt. Before I can react or shout a curse, Sol moves to Reed and wrenches him upright. Reed jerks away. For the feeble attempt, Sol huffs a laugh that makes me want to sever his vocal cords, then behind it he utters a low, "Stand down."

Reed's blue eyes gloss over, as vacant as Caiman's and Dannica's gold and violet stares are.

I snarl the marshal's way, "If you hurt him—"

"You are in *no* position to issue threats," Ajani says as he pushes open the door of the unit and yanks me over the threshold.

He turns around to address his marshals once we're inside. "Escort the others to separate lodgings. Post two dozen guards on each around the clock. I want three dozen posted near her. Make it clear that if one of our guests escapes, or causes any trouble whatsoever, every soul on duty will hand over their life as penalty."

Iyko and Sol dip their heads. Then the pair pivot to carry out his orders, hauling my team away.

I spin to Ajani as soon as he closes the door behind us. He moves at the same time I do. His left hand closes around my throat before I can hiss venom. He doesn't try to choke the life out of me in earnest, but he exerts enough pressure that it's a task to breathe. He leans in close, radiating menace and pressing his lips to my ear. A vicious, pissed off snarl rips from him. His cloak of urbanity, of coolness, has slipped. "Don't you think you've embodied enough of this rash, stupid behavior for one day? Do not speak *any* of the words you were about to or I swear to Amaka you *will* find yourself asphyxiating on your own blood. Are we clear, Praetorian?"

I claw at his fingers, but I might as well be scratching at steel.

A blood shield springs up, encircling us both. Once it does, he releases me. I sway on my feet from the restricted oxygen, while glowering at Ajani. I seriously think about lunging at him regardless of the cuffs.

Fighters need to fight, you know.

His lips pull back from his teeth in that smug, dagger-sharp smile that, gods, I want to smash my fist into. He waves a hand at the shimmering crimson blood shield. "You may speak freely now."

I bristle. "Fuck you."

"Is that all you were in a rush to say? I didn't need to expend the effort to make the conversation soundproof, then."

I roll my eyes. "Do you ever stop being a dickhead?"

"I'm capable of charm, too, when it suits me."

"Has it ever suited you? You didn't need to choke me, asshole," I grumble, rubbing the sore skin of my throat. "You could've thrown up a blood shield just as quick and *forewent* that route."

"Yes, but you—and your man—pissed me off in the pavilion. Consider it the milder form of the ass-kicking you're due. Neither of you stuck to the plan or played the roles you were supposed to. Worse, the two of you pulled your people into your bullshit."

I. Do. Not. Flinch.

"That was your plan? For Reed to get *killed*? Do you think we would have agreed to any of this if we had known that was the case?"

"Do you think I cared if you knew the plan or not? You're all alive, so instead of whining, you should be groveling profusely. You're welcome for the save. I don't give a shit about your life, make no mistake. I do, however, very much care about my aims and you Mareenians almost fucked them up. I tried doing things the friendly way, but you all are impossible to reason with. I would've let you die in that war tent because you're no good to me if you can't stay on book. If it wasn't for that gold you bled all over the place, you'd all be dead and I'd be finding another way to reach my goals." He pauses and looks mildly astonished at my confusion. Then, there's a disparaging twist to his lips. "I'm not surprised you have no idea what I'm referring to." He shakes his head. "Why did the cosmos let someone like *you* be born outside the borders of Accacia? It's truly devastating, *maddening*, and enormously wasteful."

I'm quickly losing patience for how much Ajani likes to hear himself talk without saying what's pertinent. "I know what the fuck I am." It's a lie, of course. Admitting otherwise exposes too great a weakness. And for that precise reason, it's yet another thing that I need to unearth straightaway.

Ajani sweeps a look over me that says I'm full of shit.

I project enough smugness and arrogance to fill the cosmos and say nothing.

He buys my bluff; his gaze shifts into something assessing and a little bit wary.

I take infinite pleasure in that second reaction, and it's one small victory I can claim today.

"Then you should've informed me of it back in the citadel," he says, quickly recovering. "Yet another witless thing on your part."

"Like you informed me that Nkosi is your godshitting *father*?"

"Watch where you tread," he says blandly, but with violence lacing his voice all the same. "What matters here is your failure to be forthcoming with useful information, not mine. My relationship to Nkosi has no bearing on anything. But what you are, it's going to give me *everything* I desire; so you don't get to make another dumbass mistake that'll make Nkosi move to kill you prematurely. You should digest that well because one thing I spoke became true in that war tent: your people, your entire squad, those in this encampment, and those back in the citadel, their lives *are* now being held ransom against your much smarter behavior moving forward, since that's what it's going to take to get you there. Now, this is what's occurring next. First, I'm going to drop this blood shield, because I do not feel like expending the energy to hold it after dragging your sorry man's ass back from death *and* healing your extensive damage. Then, you are going to do what the fuck I say, when I say it, how I say it, from here on out, *to the letter.* That includes letting my legionnaires sequester you away with *no* fights or attempts to escape so you don't place me in an undesirable position where I have to kill my men for incompetence." He stabs a finger at a low-resting cot with a dark green bedroll against a wall. "My orders, Praetorian, also include resting and regaining your strength, since you—and more importantly, *I*—will soon damn need it. I'll have regular meals delivered," he adds in a calmer fashion. Though not by many degrees. He's clearly struggling to recalibrate to his usual poise. Which means the Apis is well and mightily enraged.

I almost give a shit.

"To the end that I need you at top strength, you will eat every meal I have sent. No contrary bullshit. I'll return tomorrow after you've recuperated some. That's when we'll talk more of the new course I've walked Nkosi into that we can bend to our advantage."

"I'd prefer to know what the hell your conversation in that tent meant now."

"And I'd prefer to talk to someone who's awake."

"I am—"

"You're going to crash at any moment. You're only still upright from pure adrenaline. Your blood-gift might not have been able to do much to keep you alive, but it *was* expending the extreme energy to try. Did you also miss that I'm no longer negotiating with you? My orders aren't open to amendment by suggestions or rebuttals."

He steps back toward the door, letting the secure blood shield drop before I can deliver a response—wiseass, spitting mad, or otherwise.

There's not a chance in all of the hellpits that I do what Ajani commands and rest. After he leaves, I've got more important tasks to do, starting with what I should've done all along: get over my fears and initiate a communing with Amaka. I don't know what in the cosmos Ajani and Nkosi have in store with a Stitching, but I can control one variable about this situation—how strong I am when I face either of them again. I wasn't anywhere near powerful enough when Dannica and I were captured, and I was incapable of fighting back in that war tent. Neither of those things will happen again. Ever. Ajani has his own agenda, and I have mine. It's time I start making sure my team's ass is covered better and we're operating in this battle from a position of optimal strength.

It's time for me to actually master my blood-gift.

22

GRANDFATHER'S LESSONS NEVER FOCUSED ON any Accacian religious rituals; it leaves me out of my depth when I go to commune with their goddess. So I do what I tend to do when I'm trying something new:

I wing it.

I lower myself to my knees beside the cot, the only fixture in the
space. It's the position I saw Tariyal assume at the altar of her All-
Mother. Amaka isn't the same goddess, but I assume every deity is a vain
bitch who demands ardent genuflecting as a part of proper supplication.

"Amaka, goddess of blood rites, mother of the blood-gifted, lady of
the Blood Moons . . ." I begin, using all of her titles I know. It seems a
good, ass-kissing place to start. "I submit to you in . . . ummm, prayer . . .
and ask for a communing?" I mutter a curse behind the absurd question
that rolls awkwardly off my tongue. I'm positive I sound and look as
moronic as I feel. I'm a *Mareenian*, for Republic's sake. A Mareenian on
her knees praying to the goddess revered by her enemy.

"Your sense of humor is fucked," I growl to the cosmos. "I don't know what to say," I cry in frustration to a goddess that's probably either irate and deeply insulted at my butchery of a communing or who is laughing her ass off. "I've never done this before. This isn't an aspect of *any* part of who I am."

But learning to be more Acaccian, learning to pray and commune with Amaka as other blood-gifted do is necessary to fight and survive. So I get over my aversion to religious faith, the feeling that's been ingrained in me—and imparted to me—by Grandfather, who was Mareenian through and through. "So sorry," I'm compelled to whisper to him, hoping he forgives me from the Light Fields of the After. Then I stop holding back. I stop making a half-hearted attempt to pray to Amaka. I bow my head and breathe the same words the goddess demanded back in Khanai.

"I accept you, Amaka. I accept you as my patron goddess. I accept your favor. I accept my place as your Chosen." I didn't know what the hell they meant then and I'm still not sure but I say them, fervently and ardently, and shove everything I've got into them because if submitting to these words again will give me the strength that I need, if it'll help me master the fluxes, then I mean them 100 fucking percent. "*Help me*," I beg Amaka. "Help me, and I'll do anything. *Please*."

As soon as I finish the genuine prayer, a wave of vertigo sweeps over me. The dirt floor I'm kneeling on tilts beneath me. I dig my fingers into the ground to stay upright. Then, the cot, the steel walls, and the soil beneath me vanish. My fingers curl around nothingness, and the only thing that stretches before me is gold—gold and more gold that's molten in appearance. I wildly look around and behind me, and I glimpse the same thing. The gold surrounding me vibrates with an audible hum, and then heat blasts from it. The pool of gold I'm kneeling in blisters my skin in every spot that it touches. My knees, my shins, my toes through my boots, *everything* feels like it's been doused in gasoline and a match has been struck. An agonized scream rips from me. I try to jump to my feet to minimize the parts the gold touches. I get halfway to my feet before an invisible force yanks me back to a kneeling position. I'd swear actual roiling flames licked along my legs. My mind spins, trying to grasp what's going on.

What the fuck did I do? What the fuck did I trigger with that stupid prayer?

I screwed it up. That has to be it. I did something wrong, pissed Amaka off immensely, and now she's sending this weird molten gold liquid to incinerate me on the spot. My heart speeds up until I'm positive it's about to explode out of my chest.

Godsdamned. How much catastrophe can one day bring?

This isn't right, I think madly, trying to calm down. Trying to anchor myself from going off the deep end. I can't actually be in danger. Can I? The war camp isn't the citadel. It's not a place suffused with lingering Pantheon magic. Krashna and Kissa might've been able to manipulate things there, but the Pantheon has no power on Iludu otherwise. Not anymore. We cast them off the planet. They're barred from returning. The gods like Amaka who retain worshippers may be able to commune on a metaphysical level with their flock, but that's it. It's impossible for her to reach across space and the cosmos to actually torch me for some fumble I made trying to pray to her.

I keep assuring myself of that over and over again even as I burn, using logic and what I've learned and always known to be true of the Pantheon's power over Iludu's people. But the gold *is* present. More alarmingly, it's thick and viscous and coppery-smelling like blood. *The gods bled vivid gold.* Recalling the fact I once learned in an academy lesson shakes me to the core.

I close my eyes for a moment and rub them vigorously. Maybe I'm imagining things? Maybe I'm so fatigued and my nerves are so frayed from the confrontation with Nkosi that delirium, exhaustion, and post-traumatic shock have all set in and are making me hallucinate bizarre shit?

"Is that the explanation you're truly going to settle on? Willful ignorance doesn't become you, daughter. You wanted a communing, did you not? It is granted." The alluring, feminine voice that I've heard before doesn't comfort me. Nor does it help knowing that I purposely reached out to Amaka. She's one of the nightmarish Pantheon, and that makes her appearance automatically spark an innate fear born out of self-preservation any human would wisely have.

Before I can choke out a response to the goddess, the gold surges upward and crashes over my legs and lower body. I cry out in an ear-shattering pitch. I scream and scream and scream—the ravishing pain never-ending as the gold washes up my stomach, then my chest, then my neck, and finally my screams are cut off when it surges over my head. I choke down the liquid, the stuff cutting off my air as it singes my trachea and throat and chest and lungs to ash.

Then, as quickly as it appeared, every trace of the gold mercifully vanishes. I slap my hands against my legs, heaving in relief. Once I catch my breath, my eyes snap up to take in my surroundings. I *know*, while dreading it, that I'll *see* Amaka as if she's standing before me in the flesh, like I saw Krashna in the citadel, because I've seen the goddess in that manner before. Twice, actually. During the trials. When I thought my unintentional communing with her was mere hallucination.

But I don't glimpse the goddess of blood rites at first. All I glimpse is the same wide-open field beneath Blood Moons that she stood in the past two times we've communed. I kneel now in its grass. When I try to stand once more, not wanting to remain in so vulnerable a position even if this is all happening in some mental space I don't quite understand, I'm able to this time. My eyes dart left then right, bracing for Amaka to make her appearance.

I wait, nervous, and fall back on my training to muster courage. I scan the vacant field around me, cataloging what's present and what isn't, as if it is a real place and it's critical to my survival to survey the unknown terrain. There are a few red-leafed trees with black trunks—

Niisa trees that are found only on the Principal Continent in the original lands that comprised Acaccia. I didn't notice them before when I was last in the field. I also didn't notice how the grass below my feet is a lush jewel green comprised of skinny dagger-sharp blades that have a reddish coloring at their base. The soil the grass sprouts out of has the same crimson tint. I can't decide if it's a color natural to the grass and the soil or if it's imparted upon them by the red glow of the full Blood Moons above.

Using senses beyond sight, I *listen* to my surroundings as well. And I don't hear a single stir that indicates any presence in the field other than mine. Strangely, there's no noise at all. No swish of wind nor any other natural sounds that you'd expect outdoors. No scurries of animals, no rustling of leaves, no buzzing of insects. It's an eerie sort of quiet, like the absolute, endless quiet of death.

"Where are you?" I ask Amaka with a shaky breath, trying to fill the void with any kind of noise. I suddenly don't want to be in this place at all even though I reached out to her. Apparently, I was successful in praying. Maybe too successful? *Is this what all blood-gifted experience during a communing?* I wonder and hope the smoldering gold isn't something I'll have to endure every time.

"Show yourself," I demand of Amaka this time. I know the goddess is somewhere since she's already spoken once. The fact that she remains out of sight is more unsettling than her making an appearance.

A sultry laugh swirls around me, coming from everywhere and nowhere. "You think to give *me* commands?" The voice is amused, but vicious, and yet still spoken in sultry tones.

I'm getting sick of everyone asking the same condescending questions. You're cosmos-damned right I'm commanding you, blood goddess.

I say none of that, though, as the same version of Amaka that I saw in this field during the trials and during my Crossing appears a few feet in front of me. She's so near that I take a reflexive, defensive step back.

She tracks it, like a she-wolf watching a meek doe preparing to skitter away. Standing before me, even though she wears a human-looking skin, there's no mistaking Amaka as anything but one of the Pantheon. Her dark brown skin glows a hauntingly beautiful, otherworldly shade of ebony that I'm sure can't be spied anywhere or on any other being on the planet. Her dark brown eyes are awash in an innate power and shine with a mesmerizing etherealness. They, too, are arrestingly, unnaturally beautiful. As is the rest of the goddess's features. Her cheekbones are pronounced and blade-sharp, her nose regal and wide and queenly. Her curves are ample, and there's no doubt she dons a form made to be used as a weapon and tempt mere mortals to their doom. I stand before her, enthralled, and can't look away, even as I spy the terrible crown with massive blood rubies that sits atop her night-black coils. More of the macabre blood rubies rest at her throat, running the length of a choker, and a pair hang from her ears, fashioned into heavy, teardrop earrings. The fact that she wears the stones, with the souls of her victims trapped in their hardened blood, as mere accoutrements is a thing more horrific, for some reason, than Nkosi sitting atop a throne made from the jewels.

"How real are you in this space?" I ask, somehow finding my voice. In the citadel, Krashna might as well have been actually standing on Iludu.

Amaka's full lips twist into a faint smile. "While communing with my flock, in this space between worlds where my Blood Daughters and Sons pay homage, I am as flesh and blood as you are. Faith and prayers have always carried a certain transcending, *liberating* power of their own. That goes doubly when the proper person exercises both."

"We're in a space between worlds?" I boggle at what she says, my mind unable to wrap around the concept. "How? *Where* exactly are we?"

"Among the cosmos," is all she says, and I catch it as the intentional nonanswer it is.

But extracting a more forthcoming response isn't why I initiated a communing—at least, not on that question. So I let it drop and pivot to what's more critical, especially given I have no idea how long this meeting will last. Ajani was right about one thing: my body and mind are going to give out at some point and drop me into a coma whether I like it or not.

"I need your help. Again," I say hurriedly. "Whatever I submitted to in Khanai gave me a boost of power, but not one that persists or allows me to control *when* it flares. That's what I want, and communing is supposed to be the way to hone blessings from one of you, right? So I've communed. What happens next?" It's not the most gracious way to phrase things, but I don't have time to figure out a more decorous appeal.

Amaka's responding smile is as sly as a sabine's, cunning and calculating. Beholding it makes shrill alarms blare a warning that I need more clarity about what, exactly, I'm entangling myself with. There's no time for that, however. Nor does the answer even matter. Predator or patron, I *need* a permanent boost in power, and according to Kissa, going through Amaka is the only way to get it.

"You don't have the time the usual route takes to gain the mastery you request," Amaka says as if she's read my mind. I almost laugh, realizing perhaps she did.

"It's a feat that takes decades. A lifetime, in some cases," the goddess continues, cutting into my inherent unease at the thought. "Those among my flock must usually *earn* so great a magnitude of a blessing from me. But, Blood Daughter, luckily for you, I'd like for you to rid my people of Nkosi too. My son has lost his way. He serves himself. Not his goddess. Therefore, kneel and you will get what you seek."

I blink at how easy this is turning out to be. "Just like that?" The cosmos makes *nothing* this simple for me. Surely there's neck-deep muck to wade through first.

I'm returned another sabinelike smile; I'd be an idiot if my hackles didn't raise. There's definitely a catch. Or some trap. When in my short life hasn't there been? Amaka *is* one of the Pantheon, after all. History never knew them as beneficent or helpful beings. Rather, they were unkind and scheming and self-serving. Always. And while knowing this, I soundly ignore the warning alarms because Nkosi has to die and I have no other way of ensuring I can kill him while operating with my current, fluctuating power.

I kneel once more.

Like in Khanai, power slams into me. My blood-gift thrums from its immensity. The red glow that sometimes spills out of me suffuses me from scalp to toes. But during the communing, it's not painless. It is scorching, worse than the gold, and feels like it melts the skin off my bones—then melts my bones themselves. The torment drags on until time ceases to have any meaning. It might drag on for an eternity. For several eternities.

When the pain stops, the red glow fades into my skin. Amaka gazes at me with a gleeful, elated expression like she's won the prize. I flinch away from that look and from the hand she reaches out. When she strokes my cheek, her touch is warm, full of life, and harrowingly *solid*.

"You have what you asked for," she says. She stops caressing my cheek to cup it, the motion almost tender, a perverted, warped facsimile of how an actual mother would affectionately embrace her child. Amaka leans forward and presses a kiss to my brow. My skin crawls beneath both types of touches. "Daughters are such a special gift. You're the first that I'll own in a new era, and you, Ikenna, because of the gold you bleed, have been precious to me for a long time. Since your birth under my Blood Moons. We shall meet again."

With those ominous, unnerving, wholly perplexing words, Amaka steps away, retreating until she's standing near the tree line of the field.

I stare after her, the words she spoke about me bleeding gold swirling in a cloud of confusion around my head. "Wait!" I call out to the goddess, scared she might slip between the trees and disappear too soon.

I do not have the blessing of augury, but the gift isn't needed to surmise what visible gold in her blood signifies about her raw power levels. Ajani said that to Nkosi in the war tent.

"What does it mean that there's gold in my blood?" I ask Amaka hurriedly.

She smiles at me knowingly and cunningly, like I've asked the exact question she's primed me to. "You'll owe me a future boon for the knowledge."

Of course I fucking will. And I'll no doubt pay in stars—or blood . . . or both. So be it.

"I accept," I tell Amaka.

The goddess of blood rites appears immeasurably pleased by my assent, and the fine hairs on my neck stand on end in a warning that this is definitely a terrible idea. Not that I can heed it—or that I'll take anything back.

Laughing, Amaka says, "The gods fucked, daughter. When your kind cast my kind out, the Pantheon-blessed weren't the only humans touched by my brethren and me. There were Zeniths, mortals hailing from bloodlines that carried traces of our essence and our very DNA."

"You're saying there were . . . progeny lines descending from the Pantheon? And that . . . I . . . somehow . . . belong to one of them?" Disbelief makes me stagger on my feet as if my brain refuses to fit itself around what she claims. I was expecting to hear something about the gold signifying the innate power thrumming through my blood. But what the goddess reveals is . . . *surreal* doesn't begin to describe it. If that's true, it upends, *uproots*, everything I thought I knew about myself.

I feel the spiral coming on, but I can't descend into an existential panic right now. So I compartmentalize and fall back on old methods of coping with severe shit—shoving it aside to examine later. Or never.

Amaka smirks at my unsettled look. "Truly, it can't be that hard to believe? Then again, perhaps it is. Iludu has wiped that particular mark my siblings and I left on the planet from current memory. Your Republic took its cue to cull its Pantheon-blessed from somewhere, however. The entire planet annihilated its Zeniths first. Though," she waves pointedly at me, "it obviously missed a few well-hidden ones in the slaughter. The gold you bleed means you come from one of those surviving lines that remained loyal when the humans started their war against us, and that we tucked away so they might take up their place of dutiful servitude when we return."

My mind clamps on to the fact that Amaka doesn't say *if*; she says *when*. The adamant way she says it causes my entire being to lock up with dread, even though I know it's impossible. If the Pantheon could walk Iludu once more, they would be doing so already.

Ramping up the foreboding more and sinking claws in my gut, Amaka radiates the rage when speaking of returning that I've always gathered the Pantheon would exude over their flocks revolting against them. It's a fury that says *there* will *be vengeance*.

I brace for the brunt of her temper to blow my way, since I'm one of those people's descendants—at least by way of my Mareenian and Khanaian heritage. However, Amaka abruptly directs her attention and anger upward to the cosmos. "Our time is up," she says disdainfully, giving the impression the vexing limitation is being imposed on her by some power among the cosmos that's greater than she.

Before I can probe her about it—or, really, anything else—the goddess turns from solid to incorporeal. She shimmers a translucent, shining, blinding gold. I throw my hands up to shield my eyes, an inner knowing telling me my irises will be seared if I look at her in the gold state full-on. The air around me turns sweltering for several, lingering moments. When it cools, I chance opening my eyes.

Amaka is no longer in the field.

Then the field itself disintegrates, vertigo washing over me. I sway, my surroundings tilting before I'm wrenched back through the gold space. The agony of being burned alive in an incinerator only lasts, thankfully, for a second. The corrugated steel walls and dirt floor of my temporary prison form around me in a flash.

I push to my feet and tug on my blood-gift. It answers the summons immediately and floods me in a tide of battering power that cascades out of me and lights up every dark corner of the barracks in a furious red glow.

"*Thank fuck*," I breathe to the cosmos. No matter what else, I've gained an enormous advantage.

My grin is savage—and bloodthirsty.

And then I pass out.

AS PROMISED, AJANI visits me the following day.

I begin wresting things into my control as soon as he crosses the threshold. I start by not standing by, meekly silent, while I wait for him to cast a blood shield. Instead I snap my own into place immediately— one that does more than encircle the two of us. The shroud of red clings to the walls like a Mareenian grade-one sound shield that seals noise inside an entire room. It's a small display of the power I can readily and easily draw on after the communing that makes the statement I want—*I am nobody's prisoner*—without giving too much away.

Ajani's eyes widen at the display before he quickly recovers and quashes his astonishment.

Can you accomplish that too, asshole? I want to ask in the worst way. He can't, of course. He's too much of a showy prick *not* to have made the room soundproof in the same way while choking me the previous day—which I owe him for and *will* repay him in stars.

For now, I lean against the wall like the Apis is no actual threat, ignoring the throbbing in my wrists over being cuffed for so long. I gift the bastard a she-wolf's smile. "You were wrong yesterday. I'm in a fantastic position to make threats. I know what you really intend for dear Dad. I know you seek to commit patricide, regicide, and treason. I'm sure he'd easily believe the accusation since it was made abundantly clear to anybody with eyes in the war tent that Nkosi distrusts you. Moreover, I know his type—it's the same as the Tribunes'. So I'm also confident that, son or no son, Apis or no Apis, your liege is a paranoid, shrewd enough fucker that my merely stoking an *ember* of possible treachery will be enough to incite him to kill you for it. With that said: yes, you have my people as hostages, but moving forward, I'm holding the knowledge I have about your real intentions hostage against *your* good behavior. You don't hold all the cards. Fuck me, or my people, and I will fuck you back. Got it?"

He remains silent and stoic at first, his expression stone. I wait for him to return several cool threats. Yet he simply strides farther into the room and says, "Duly noted, Praetorian." I swear I detect an admiring quality to his pitch. Or maybe that's my ego projecting. Either way, I'll take it.

"I'm not bluffing," I inform Ajani in case he mistakes that I am.

"I'm well aware of such. I know *your* type. You're exactly the sort to blow shit up with yourself standing at the epicenter. And that's not a compliment in case you mean to take it as one. There's a fine line between the courage you Mareenians *supposedly* prize so much and fucking idiocy."

I supply him the look that statement deserves. Then, I push off the wall. "What's a Stitching?" I ask, getting down to business. "Explain the whole of it. Don't be cute and feed me bullshit."

The Apis returns me a long-suffering stare that comically, and oddly, reminds me of Brock. It seems I've hit several nerves. Good.

"That's why I'm here anyway." He drops the remark with his trademark condescension. "To educate you about yet another thing you are woefully ignorant of. A Stitching is a ritual that involves a transference of power from one Pantheon-blessed to another. It dates back to the Pantheon Age, yet even during the time of the gods it was rarely performed and heavily regulated due to the risks it carries. One such risk is that when both parties possess exceedingly high levels of power, it can be catastrophic on the scale of disrupting the natural order of the cosmos. But that's not what you and I care about here."

"It sounds like something I should care about."

"That's because you're a child who knows nothing."

"I—"

"Just, for once, let me finish without your infernal questions about things that are going to be answered."

Can't. Kill. Him. Yet.

He takes my silence as acquiescence and goes on. "The most vital risk to our mutual aim is the much more personal one the ritual poses. When undergoing a Stitching, the two parties, the acceptor and the relinquisher, are rendered completely vulnerable while the latter is stripped of power—and thus their very soul that it's bound to—and the former imbibes both the magic of the other and their essence. During that attempted transference is when I'm going to kill my father. I made a mistake before. Striking at him directly, even with the element of surprise, isn't a surefire bet. But you playing the bait during a Stitching is. Nkosi will be unaware and too engrossed in the battle of wills he must engage you in to take that which he doesn't innately possess."

From Ajani's explanation, a Stitching is straightforward enough. I also easily read between the lines. If Nkosi and I will both be vulnerable, then the Blood Emperor isn't the only one Ajani can effortlessly kill during the ritual. It's something I'd take advantage of in his position if I were gunning for the two of us.

Which all leads to this truth: there's no fucking way I'm allowing things to play out how the Apis is assuredly setting them up. I've already pieced together one counterplan that'll derail his intentions. If all this Stitching involves is a clash of wills where one eclipses the other in the end, then it'll basically be a battle of brute force. *That* I can do. *That* I excel at. I'll make sure my will is stronger than Nkosi's when the time comes, and I won't merely be a dangling worm. I can turn the tables on the Blood Emperor and swallow *his* power into mine. If I accomplish it quick enough, I can then pivot and kill Ajani before he has the chance to kill me. With the permanent uptick Amaka gave me, it shouldn't be too difficult. I imagine it'll be similar to the clashing of powers I had with Ajani in Ska'kesh when he set his battering against mine, just more intense. If it is, I've got this. I can get the job done. Especially if Amaka spoke true and I'm not only human. If I have some lingering traces of the essence of the gods themselves, then that must make me inherently *more* than whatever Nkosi is. I can harness it to my advantage, and use it to beat him.

And if not . . . well then, I'll let my confidence be a shield until I'm surprised by my death.

For all of that, I'd rather not even need to go that far. I'd rather circumvent this Stitching altogether. Since if it does go to shit, handing Nkosi that much power is a sure way to bring about the future Kissa foretold. Which means I need a better plan.

"What does preparing me for this Stitching entail?" I ask, chewing on a Plan A. For certain, a Plan B too. Undergoing a Stitching should be like Plan . . . oh, I don't know . . . Z.

"Making sure you're willing and consenting, as both parties must be in order for the ritual to proceed at all."

I snort, already knowing what that really means: that the Apis is supposed to be here breaking me, or whatever. Still, I ask, for shits and giggles, "Enlighten me further? What does making sure I'm willing consist of?"

"You know the answer, Praetorian," Ajani returns blandly. "But since we're on the same side, nothing more than the conversation we've already had. Namely, that you want Nkosi dead, you want your people and what can be salvaged of your Republic spared. This Stitching—

and being bait—it is the most foolproof way to achieve these goals. I assume impressing upon you that fact is the only thing needed to convince you to go along with things."

"You assume right," I say, and leave off that all his other assumptions regarding the Stitching are very, very wrong.

But let him think of *me* as the ignorant one.

23

"**I'M NOT ABOUT TO FLY** into Krashen without some protection for myself. I want to know how you're neutralizing iridium," I demand from Ajani the second day he visits for preparations.

He's cagey, of course, about giving the knowledge up, yet eventually does: Accacian scholars unearthed an archaic rune. From there, one blood rite performed by Ajani in Krashna's Citadel—a place with lingering Pantheon magic—and Accacia had its counteragent.

A rune, which means the gods, which means it always comes back to them.

Even though I'm glad for protection against the iridium (and glad it wasn't actually invented by the Rhysiens, just something they're claiming as an innovation that has clearly been around since the forming of the world—yes, I'm a petty bitch like that), I have to wonder:

Will we ever be free of the Pantheon?

I don't linger too long on that, though. Because, by the end of our third visit—and it irks me to no end—*I have the same rune etched in my back that legionnaires do*, placed there with a mixture of ink and Ajani's damn blood, no less. It seems the life force of the one who performed the rite that powers the damn thing needs to be what the rune's drawn with.

Naturally, the cosmos really loves fucking with me.

The Apis was enormously smug about imparting that tidbit—smugger, even, than his usual asshole self—but I rolled with it and asked to be inked anyway with the marking that continuously purges any toxins in the blood and therefore keeps the connection open between Amaka and her flock.

After I get that, I play the good, non-pushy prisoner for the duration of time I'm detained in the war camp—my returned proof of good faith to Ajani.

My entire stay lasts for a fortnight, and I don't see Dannica, Caiman, or Reed during any of the days. And then, before the first rays of dawn at the start of the third week, Ajani collects me from my barracks. He escorts me to a stealth jet that, thank the cosmos, has my crew sitting alive, whole, and in possession of their minds aboard it. From the seats they're cuffed to near the center of the warcraft, they look back at me in what I can only assume is a mirror of my own relief. Reed and I exchange glances underscored by something heavier. More intense.

I'm glad you're alive. Stay that way, mine orders him. His demands the same of me back.

"At least sit me beside them." I lower myself to uttering the plea as I stand next to Ajani at the front of the jet in cuffs.

While he says nothing, he does walk me to the row my people occupy and deposits me into an empty seat next to Reed.

Why oblige me? I want to ask, growing suspicious. I'm not going to probe, though, in case he changes his mind.

"Are you all right?' I ask them, so grateful to see the three without a glassy-eyed look that I want to sob.

"I'm fine," Reed says. Caiman and Dannica express the same.

"How about you?" Reed asks.

I pass him a nod that I'm all right too. Simultaneously, I fight the urge to lean into him, brush against the body of the man at my side and reassure myself that he's warm with life, not the cooling corpse from Nkosi's war tent that hasn't stopped haunting me.

Our group exchanges weighty stares. I see clearly Reed's and everybody else's worry for me, and the fact that they distrust Ajani's plan, which I insisted he find a way to share with them. They say nothing, however. Neither do I for the same reason: the jet is in no way secure. I hate that they're in the dark about *my* real plans, but . . . *later.* I'll have to fill them in later.

We fly north toward the final bloodletting, the final massacre, alongside a fleet carrying the Blood Emperor, his warlords, and his legions. Except, we go as captives, not as rescuers, and certainly not as conquerors. It's the most harrowing, terrifying flight of my life. Because soon after we touch down, the Stitching will begin as Nkosi attempts to raze Krashen City and the rest of the north as thoroughly as the Isles. The entire Republic might become nothing except ash and smoke and corpses and sacked cities. In this final assault, Nkosi means to visit the total destruction that Grandfather prevented him from accomplishing before.

Why in the hell couldn't he be the type of asshole who wanted a Stitching before marching on the Republic's capital? I shriek in frustration to the cosmos. If that part were coordinated to go down back in Cara, Nkosi might already be dead. Killing him during this next attack will spare the rest of the continent and the Mareenians who survived the beginning, yes. But it'll still likely mean staggering, unacceptable deaths. And yet I don't see a way to reorder things while we're careening toward the Republic's seat of power. I curse the gods, the cosmos, Nkosi, and all of fucking existence for my not being able to confer with my team before we reach Krashen City. Perhaps Reed, or Caiman, or

Dannica, or the four of us together could figure out a way to stop the further slaughter that's coming.

That we're, in no small way, facilitating.

TOO SOON, I see the flat landscape unique to the northern territories and their lush greenery, which remains intact. It takes all my restraint not to lean forward as I did when we flew into a destroyed Cara and splay my fingers against the glass in panic. But I won't betray a drop of my intense fear to the legionnaires I'm seated among. I press my spine into my seat and momentarily close my eyes, thinking of . . . it's insane and the last thing I should be thinking of, but I think of *Selene*. She certainly returned to Krashen after the failed ambush, and I wonder if she's still in the city. By now, the war house heads would've evacuated all scions to preserve their lines. Her rank as Donya of Rhysien War House should've placed Selene among the evacuees—but she's also stubborn and prideful to her core. And as a Praetorian in wartime, she would've had a steelclad argument to be allowed to remain among combat troops that Sutton wouldn't have been able to deny without violating wartime laws. It's something else I shouldn't be thinking of, but I can't decide how I feel about it if Selene is in Krashen.

Only because she's your *kill,* I tell myself. *Only because you don't want this war to claim her before the reckoning with her you deserve.*

And thinking of evacuation logistics sparks a new barrage of harrowing worries. Where would the Tribunes possibly send scions in the first place with the north facing invasion, the rest of the Republic already fallen, and every other Minor Continent power save Lythe having already kneeled to Accacia—and outright declaring Mareen an enemy as well? Mareen has *no* allies to receive evacuees. Which means if not Krashen City itself, then an adjacent northern territory *is* the safest, and only, place for them . . . for Selene. She has to be in, or near, the city, trapped alongside everyone else.

I hate myself for my former, treacherous, murderous friend being the one thing, the one victim above everyone else who I can't bring myself to stop worrying about. But I keep coming back, no more able to dismiss Selene than to ignore the sun rising every morning. Not in the current circumstances, with things as bleak as they are. When Nkosi's legions descend on Krashen, they will storm the base, the Pinnacle, the Tribune Tower, and every Tribune General's stronghold in and around the city. Nkosi will likely instruct the Red Legions to target and wipe out the mighty war house bloodlines and every one of their scions first. It's what any half-decent strategist would do when capturing a hostile territory. It's a basic principle of war, Krashna's Fourth Principle. Which means Selene will be among the lives targeted first to bring Krashen to its knees. I assume Nkosi would save the actual Tribunes for last. If he's able to get to them, he is exactly the sort of bastard who would round the Republic's leaders up and make them watch as their blood, their legacies, and every last of their kin was snuffed out, and take immense joy in it.

My fingers dig into the leather of the seat beneath me.

Accacia's power isn't absolute. Mareen and its Praetorians can and will fight back. This isn't the Isles, or the west, or the east. This is Krashen, where every might the Republic wields, every significant weapon, every technological advantage is concentrated. We do have a chance to hold up against Accacia's forces until I can kill the man who commands them.

That means Selene has a chance. And if she dies regardless—*well, it doesn't matter how she dies if you want her dead anyway.* I try to sell myself the lie and fail because behind *it* I think about the Mareenians we saw on pikes, their corpses rotting and left exposed to the elements in the Caran war camp. I want Selene dead, I've vowed to kill her myself when we next cross orbits, but she doesn't deserve the death she'd find at the hands of the Red Legions. Nobody does. Well, the remaining Tribunes do. But those are my kills, too, so Nkosi *has* to be stopped in the least amount of time possible when Ajani presents me to him for the Stitching.

I spend the rest of our minutes in the air preparing mentally to do whatever it takes so that I'm *better* than good, and successful, at the two things I was reared to be: the assassin that the Republic shapes us all into and the victorious warrior that Grandfather forged.

I'M OUT OF time and pray my pep talks were enough when the jet starts to drop lower into the sky. My heart lurches into my throat when the suburban residences among the outer sectors of Krashen City come into view. Beyond the neat rows of homes, I glimpse the outline of the chic, silver flats of the inner sector, and beyond that . . . the cloud-piercing skytowers of Krashen Base that were erected as monuments to the Republic's military prowess loom in the distance.

I lose face. Damn who's around and how I look. Because, yes, I was trained up as a soldier, a warrior, a fighter, the bravest and most fearsome that the Republic and Grandfather had to offer, but at the end of the day I'm also human. And while flying among the enemy on its way to sack the Republic's capital—my truest home, where I grew up and attended school and have lived and loved and laughed and bled and trained my entire life—tears sting my eyes. Krashen City's potential fall rips through me like a blade in broad daylight that I see coming and can't avert all the same. And although I shouldn't give a shit about the academy, or the Praetorian Compound, or the Pinnacle Tower, or the Tribune Tower, or any other building on the northern base holding mostly individuals who despise me and Grandfather for not being pure enough—envisioning the destruction of each one, of it all, is like that blade slamming between my breasts to the hilt then angling sideways and tearing a jagged path that carves up my heart. Because while none of it loved and embraced me, *I loved it.*

The pieces left behind rattle anxiously when a vidfeed projects onto a wall of the stealth jet; it transmits footage of an incoming Mareenian fleet flying maroon and gold: wartime colors. The Mareenians form a wall of firepower between the Red Legions and Krashen Base that we're about a mile out from. A hope explodes inside my chest upon seeing Republic forces. And even as it does, I am ill. I don't need to be able to count the Mareenian jets to assess the odds of this first line of defense. I'm well versed in our number of aircrafts outfitted for war. Even if Mareen managed not to lose a single vessel when the west, east, and Southern Isles fell, the sheer number of Accacian jets I saw assembled and awaiting legionnaires to board when departing the Caran camp outnumbers anything Mareen's got by at least three to one. Plus, with Khanai on Accacia's side, the kingdom that rules the aerospace-engineering arena wasn't available to lend us additional crafts. Which means Mareen's odds in the skies are fucked. So fucked.

Reed, Caiman, Dannica, and I let out vicious curses when Ajani leaps from his seat and shouts firing orders into his Comm Unit.

The live transmission against the wall displays the Acaccian fleet we're among swarming the Mareenians. The Accacians damnably open fire. But regardless of how ardently Nkosi has been trying to make Mareen cower since the start, this moment proves the fucker failed. The entire Republic, the masses and all our troops—the mighty Tribunes, the deadly Praetorians, the fierce war house scions, the battle-hardened common soldiers—everyone might be terrified, but the one thing any Mareenian has is nerves of steel. And mettle. And an endless fighting spirit. So our paltry fleet holds the line and fires everything it's got back at the enemy. A fierce battle rages that sets the pink and rose-gold hues of the morning sky ablaze in fiery orange.

It's glorious to behold.

Numerous scarlet jets are either blown apart or plummet to the ground.

Maroon-and-gold crafts are obliterated too. Yet, if the numbers were more even, Mareen would win this clash. Our air-to-air missiles have longer range, each of our stealth jets are crammed with twice as many protruding from their undercarriage than the Accacians', and the blasts Republic missiles deliver are designed to destroy everything within a quarter-mile radius. Nonetheless, it comes back to the sheer volume of warcrafts flying Empire colors, and they deliver more wide-spread damage to us.

There's a moment where a red craft a few yards away from the one I ride aboard comes under heavy fire, and I'm unsure if I want to shout in elation or cry in alarm because my team and I will be within the blast zone of any hit.

A missile strikes the adjacent Accacian jet, fires engulf it, and my jet shudders violently. I lock eyes with my squad, all of us looking from the vidfeed to each other at the same time. Reed, Dannica, and Caiman wear expressions similar to mine: dueling relief that Mareen is landing strikes and tension that *we're* about to die.

"We should be on the other side of this," Caiman grits out. "We should be firing at these assholes, not about to be killed *by* Republic fire."

I have barely enough time to grimace in agreement before our jet shudders again.

I brace my back against my seat, gripping the armrests. But instead of my stomach shooting into my throat from an uncontrolled spiral downward, the tremors stop. I blink at the fact that it seems the jet flies steady. I look at the vidfeed for how we're still in the air. See our marked craft on it. Gape at the blood shield encircling it. Then I gape at Accacia's Apis. "Is that you?" The awe in my voice is beyond treasonous. But I can't help it.

What in the hell?

How in the hell?

How much power does this man command?

"Who else would it be on board?" Ajani clasps his hands behind his back, haughty as ever.

"How many of you can do that?" The question comes from Reed.

That, the Apis doesn't answer.

I scowl. Shake myself out of the semi-reverence because it is so, so wrong. I don't gaze at Ajani again. Too look upon him becomes too much. I just keep watching the battle storm on.

In the end, it's an annihilation: every last Mareenian jet that courageously engaged the Accacian fleet is blown out of the sky.

A second and a third aerial squadron battle the Accacians, trying desperately to protect the precious target that it's clear the Accacians intend to strike with maximum force. Missiles obliterate those replacement troops too. Then there's no barrier left between the Accacian fleet and Krashen Base. Missiles careen toward the great skytowers first. The titanic structures of glass and steel that have stood for centuries—nearly a millennium—as homage to Mareen's unparalleled war prowess shatter.

I watch their destruction with horror, stricken with denial—a devastating inability to acknowledge the reality of what I see. To acknowledge the truth that Mareen is no more. Our skytowers, our great city of Krashen, the venerated base, the strong, proud, powerful north is tumbling down around itself. Beside me, Reed, Caiman, and Dannica haven't stopped shouting and cursing. But I've barely heard them over the roaring in my ears. When we finally land in the center of the destroyed base, the only thought I have is to tear from the jet. Instinct and rage and grief have me shooting to my feet to muscle my way down the loading ramp and yank Nkosi off his imperial jet. Fuck letting the endgame play out the coordinated way. Fuck keeping the true depths of power I got from Amaka concealed until Nkosi initiates the Stitching. Fuck the delay pretending to be bait will cause. I can stop this shit right now. I can fight with what's left of Mareen against our enemy right now. I can do *something* right now. My fingertips tingle with the burning need. My blood-gift—and bloodlust along with it—flares. Fiercer roaring kicks up in my head. In my ears. In my blood.

The war tent! Did you forget it? Grandfather's steel hiss in my head in the commander's tone he used whenever I was fumbling a training exercise slices into the murderous haze and plants me back on the jet.

I gnash my teeth, curl my hands into fists. However, for all my frustration, the voice of Grandfather's teachings, which will always reside inside me, is right. I *cannot* go off book. I have a plan. I need to stick to it. Shirking it opens up too many new variables. Besides, the lives of the Mareenians who will die at Krashen aren't what's important, and I see that clearer. What is most important are the lives of the entire world if it remains under Nkosi. And I've already screwed up a chance at killing him once.

So, I breathe and only breathe, letting go completely of the urge to be rash.

I keep breathing when Ajani orders his marshals to secure Dannica, Caiman, and Reed additionally via compulsion and leave them with guards on the jet to triple lock them down until he returns. One: It's a part of the plan. Nkosi believes Ajani and I have struck a bargain. After I willingly undergo the Stitching, Ajani will be bound by a blood oath he's sworn that the Apis himself will be the only one to kill my team and he will make their deaths quick, without bleeding them to make blood rubies. That keeps Nkosi's particular brand of sadistic violence far away from people I care about. Two: Even if our alliance isn't real and Ajani's motives *are* duplicitous, Reed and the others are Praetorians, we're at war, and we all went into this knowing— and accepting—the risks. I understand that, and everything it means, much better after we lost sight of that in the war tent. And three: I've got to place the whole of Iludu above the fate of my lover, cohort sister, and comrade, too, another thing I failed at in Cara.

So I keep the brakes on and wait, hold firm to the end goal, pull my strength and blood-gift tighter to me, fall back on training, bolster my physical and mental fortitude, and stick to my face-off with Nkosi playing out the way I've strategized. As long as I can do that, former mistakes shouldn't be repeated, and I'll have a fighting chance to kill the Blood Emperor. Nkosi might be Pantheon-blessed, but so fucking am I.

I can best him.

I am able *to best him.*

24

THE BLOOD EMPEROR STANDS AMID a pile of common soldier and Praetorian corpses when Ajani and I approach his imperial jet. The academy burns behind him, chunks of it reduced to rubble by Accacian missiles, painting quite the sight for drones to capture.

What galls me so much is how unnecessary this all is. The Tribunal *should've* begun emergency evacuations of the whole city—not only scions—as soon as the Isles fell; Krashen was the sole stronghold left, and it became obvious Nkosi would march for it soon. But the war house heads that sit the Tribunal are prideful and pertinacious by their very nature. If our brass meant to make a stand at Krashen, then they may have chosen to forego evacuating the academy and the wider city. Even if it was just to move noncombatants to unincorporated areas farther north, that decision would've made them appear weak—which they'd fiercely resist.

They are damnable, self-serving, shortsighted fools!

A fault made clear with Accacia's Blood Emperor holding a daunting, enormous scarlet saber in one hand and a blaster in the other and slicing through Republic soldiers who've advanced on him as efficiently and methodically with the blood blade as he blows holes in people with the gun.

The wave of reinforcements that replace the dead all wear uniforms of maroon with wartime-gold collars and a gold Beta insignia stamped on their biceps. And all twenty-two Beta men fighting against Accacia's emperor as a unit go down. The fight is staggeringly nothing like the more even matches between legionnaire and Praetorian taking place on the true, established killing field nearby. Here, only *one* Nkosi and almost two dozen Praetorians are locked in a match, and he eviscerates an entire cohort of the Republic's elite in a handful of minutes. He cleaves through nine Praetorians with his blood saber, shoots seven with the blaster, and gets creative with the other six, turning their life force into a weapon against them by having their own blood betray them in gruesome ways.

As I watch a man gurgle on the blood that drowns him, one thing is evident: His Imperial Majesty could've remained sealed away in his jet awaiting the Stitching. Hell, he could do so for the entirety of the battle. Could've been doing so the whole war. Nkosi could easily use the jet's guns to obliterate any attackers. The fact that he doesn't, and met the unit dispatched to attempt his assassination at the base of the jet's ramp, reinforces what makes him so dangerous, which I realized in the war camp: This isn't some general who will ever sit back and let his men do all the dirty work. Nkosi leads from the front not only to ensure victory, but because he revels in it.

For an unsteady moment, the world lurches, yanking my former confidence out from under me; the planet might even stop spinning on its axis as I breathe heavily, taking in the sheer brutality, sheer skill, and sheer number of people Nkosi single-handedly dispatches to the After. Reading texts and studying vidfeeds on what the Blood Emperor is capable of in combat and *beholding* his prowess in person are two different things. The Emperor moves and fights like an unstoppable force—like he possesses the might of the true *living god* he's hellbent on the world calling him. My chest spasms as I recall Krashna's assault at the citadel and how I had no chance of fighting back against a different godly figure; I preemptively feel Nkosi's blood saber slice into me swifter than I can counter and shred me apart. I wheeze, then blink as if that can change the sight I'm witnessing of the titan force I'm about to go up against. A hoarse laugh escapes me, my mouth turning sandpaper dry. The deep-rooted, intrinsic part of me that's keyed toward survival yells at me:

RUN!

I don't listen to it. I've never been a fucking coward, the odds tipped toward my death have never stopped one course of action I've decided on, and neither of those things is about to happen now either. I plant myself firmly back into warrior mode, not flight mode, and flex my hands, wishing I already palmed a blaster in one and a blade in the other. Keeping my head, I consider Nkosi's vicious saber and gauge what sort of blood blade of my own would match its reach and ability to slice off body parts. The thing is about two feet from pummel to point, holding his enemies at a distance while he cuts them down. A short sword won't work against such reach. Neither will a scimitar, but I think I've got something. I flex my hands again, already feeling the weight of what I'm imagining and becoming more centered. Less uncertain that I can beat him.

Soon, I promise the itch to be holding a blade and have its buttressing. *Soon,* at least one imbalance between Nkosi and me will be wiped away.

I don't take my eyes off the Blood Emperor to look to the broadcasting drones overhead that I'll need to facilitate Nkosi's demise. Instead, I keep my eyes squarely on my enemy and hope that the viewing world sees me as a hero, not a replacement monster, when this is all over.

For a few necessary minutes more, I keep playing the willing doe that's been brought to slaughter so I can analyze and learn firsthand, a little longer, how my enemy battles. When a new Praetorian cohort surrounds him, Nkosi is *too* caught up in the killing rage he's succumbed to as Mareen tries to replicate what Grandfather achieved, and wound the Blood Emperor severely enough, if they can't kill him, to stop the war. I realize something else: I've never witnessed bloodlust from the other side. It's a quick education I become glad for, that helps me finetune a few things. I'm certain I now know how Grandfather wounded Nkosi the last go-round. If that all-consuming need to make the world bleed I see twisting his features has the same effect on all blood-gifted who succumb to it as it does on me, then the great and brilliant Verne Amari exploited it. He found an opening to use a strength *against* the Blood Emperor, turn it into an exposed weak spot where *he* could strike faster than Nkosi saw coming. That's how Grandfather yanked Nkosi's ass back down to mere man status. And that becomes a part of my war plan. It's how *I* might kill him this time. It likely won't play out the exact way as before, but still, I can definitely borrow the most important, wider element of Grandfather's strategy: *identify the presented strength that's also the weakness and make it my weapon.*

I forget I'm supposed to be prey. Or rather, I'm about done with caring what Ajani *wants* me to be. I smile savagely, keep tracking Nkosi as he surveys the battlefield like a hawk, scanning for new corpses to make that might be coming at him. Currently, there's nobody. The Mareenian forces around all clash with legionnaires, halting in what they've failed to do thrice.

Nkosi, the bastard, almost looks let down.

Truly, he needn't worry.

Because it is time for me to be rash, a stars-ton of reckless, and to go off book—of Ajani's plan anyway. My plan was always this: *Take this fucker's head off. No matter what blessing flows through one's veins, decapitation will leave anyone dead. But if I can't land it, Plan B is go for the heart. I strike fast and true, and I bury a blood weapon in Nkosi's chest. Then I carve the organ out to be sure there's no healing him.*

"Are you ready, my liege?" Ajani asks his father, bowing slightly.

When Nkosi says yes without sparing me a glance, Ajani speaks an order into his Comm Unit that has a double wall of legionnaires forming a circle around him, Nkosi, and me.

"Do you want her to remain on the ground or be taken aboard your craft?" Ajani asks. "A vidfeed can transmit from either place. If we stay here, I've performed the proper rites to maintain a blood shield for added protection as long as you may need it."

"The ground space," I say. "I choose my battleground to be Mareenian soil."

Ajani goes rigid. I can almost see the rage wafting off him because those words were never items he prepared me to speak. In fact, I'm not supposed to say anything. I believe the Apis also mentioned kneeling to add to this show.

He really should have come to know me better.

"What are you doing?" Ajani says to me tightly. "That isn't what happens next."

"It actually is," I tell him with all my usual arrogance because he's not going to expose his own treachery by saying more, and he's an opportunist. So he'll at least shut the fuck up after what I say next and not interfere to see if this might play out to his advantage, like he charmingly did in the war tent.

I step forward, meeting Nkosi's suspicious glare, which swipes between his son and me. "This has nothing to do with your Apis," I tell His Imperial Majesty. "This is about you and me, and only you and me. You need me willing to undergo the Stitching, right? Well, I'm not. There is nothing on this planet you could threaten to convince me to hand you greater power to terrorize the world with." I smile sweetly and let that sink in.

"Your people—" Nkosi starts to snarl.

"Are soldiers," I finish for him. "Who'd make the same decision *and* kick my ass if I chose anything different. Sparing their lives, even sparing them from becoming blood rubies, isn't what matters in the larger scheme, and you have no leverage to force a Stitching by using them. If you want me willing, the only way to get it is to agree to what *I* want, and win it," I make clear to Nkosi. "So, as I said: *I. Challenge. You.* Accacians are familiar with the term, yes? Because you look out of sorts, Your Royal Dickhead. I assumed your people have something similar. Your governing rules boil down to 'might makes right,' after all.

"I'll spell it out. A challenge match is the only way you will *ever* make me submit to a Stitching. Because if I kill you, as I plan to, it will never happen, as it shouldn't. But if you break me to the point that I yield, since you need me alive, then I am willing to agree to terms up front that my yielding in combat means I yield to the subsequent Stitching, and I'll turn over the payment of my life then." I've considered this from every angle, calculated the risks, and it's the most direct, surest, and immediate route to have a shot at Nkosi while possibly getting around the steep price the world will pay if the Stitching goes to shit. "What's your answer?" I prompt Nkosi, who has yet to say anything. "Defeating me on these terms is all you've got if you want my power, my magic, my gold blood—and yes, I *do* know what that means. A challenge is your only way you get your godhood.

"Besides," I tack on in case he needs a final push, "think about the *pageantry* of it all, and more importantly, there are drones recording this." I finally flick a glance upward, point to the damn things. Give them a little wave. "You're the oh-so-fearsome Blood Emperor of Accacia who's already crushed most of the world, and *did* basically kill me once, right? This should be easy. You've got nothing to lose—unless you *do* fear me when I'm uncuffed and armed? That'd be pretty badass for the world to know too."

A muscle in the Blood Emperor's jaw ticks.

When he finally says something, it's Ajani he speaks to. "You failed to deliver what you promised, boy," he bites off, and there's promised punishment in the statement, but also . . . something else. I'd call it amusement if I didn't know any better.

Ajani's face, which has locked itself down into stone, remains that way, and the Apis returns nothing.

There's a moment where Nkosi's irritation swells so great and gets directed so blisteringly at his son that I think he might exact punishment right then and kill Ajani where he stands. Sadly, the cosmos doesn't pitch me that boon. Nkosi snaps away from Ajani, turns his ire 100 percent on me—and smiles. "Of course we're going to fight. I never thought you'd just give me your power," he croons.

All right. I guess I did read humor.

Now it's my turn to be maneuvered into silence and a shit-ton of confusion.

I don't need to puzzle things out, though, because the Blood Emperor silkily imparts, "Although you are correct. That's what you're going to end up doing anyhow. I accept your challenge, Ikenna Amari, and *you* issuing one was exactly what I needed to make sure I *can* strip you of that which you are unworthy to bear—willing or not.

"I'm ready when you are, *child*," Nkosi tells me. The blaster he holds is tossed aside. "You have my blood oath: I won't draw another gun. I won't need it," he adds raising the massive saber in the air, a clear attempt to intimidate. "You, however, may select any and all of the weapons of your choosing. You *will* need every last one of them, and then they still won't do you any good. Did you learn nothing from Cara?" The extended barbed courtesies and subsequent question are further meant to intimidate.

I say nothing in return because the time has come to cut the blustering. Cut the bravado. Cut the shit-talking. A fight that an intrinsic knowing tells me Grandfather was preparing me for, without ever saying so, my entire life is finally happening, and it is happening now. The Blood Emperor came for me once. He tried to end me once. In Nkosi's warped, narcissistic mind this is likely a rematch. A rematch Grandfather always knew, or at least suspected, the Blood Emperor would seek.

"Can you lend me a blade? Actual metal," I ask Ajani, sinking steel into the request and letting Nkosi know I am not afraid of him.

The Apis could be petty and not oblige, but he isn't. He presses a dagger into my open hand and issues a blink that tells me if I can get it done, *kill Accacia's Emperor.*

I nick my palm, call my blood to the surface, will it to flow in greater volumes than the shallow cut would otherwise produce. I forge a weapon as formidable as Nkosi's saber—a combat axe whose blade end consists of four sharp crescents touching at their points. I test the weight, turning it over and examining my creation. There's nothing like it in Mareenian weaponry—which by far prefers blasters and micro explosives for combat—but Khanaian weaponry includes magnificent blade work, and the axe I've fashioned resembles the old-school war axe crafted by my metallurgy-gifted great-grandfather that Grandfather used to have displayed proudly on a wall in the Cara villa. I turn my blood axe over twice, running an index finger along the outside of one of its crescents. My touch is featherlight, but it slices the uppermost digit of my finger open from tip to joint. I smile at the wound, which quickly knits itself closed, then at the man whose neck will be next.

Yes, the blood axe should do quite nicely to slice off Nkosi's head.

Yet, I'm not an idiot; nor am I so arrogant that I believe it's the single weapon I'll need. I ask Ajani for a blaster, he hands over two, and I tuck them both away along with the steel dagger.

After I'm armed, Nkosi doesn't attack. Only smirks at me from his spot within the circle of legionnaires, gives an unconcerned wave of his hand, and drawls, "*Inferiors first.*"

The insult aside, beginning with an offensive strike seems like a fantastic idea, as I've been wanting to launch one since the jet.

So I do.

My war cry is a savage scream, and I let all of the fucking rage finally out as I run at the Blood Emperor with my arm raised high and my blood axe poised to sever his neck from his shoulders with one, downward arc.

I throw my entire body weight behind it, pouring all the strength and the muscle and the fury I've got into the swipe. The blood axe's crescents come a bare centimeter away from Nkosi's head, then he ducks under it.

Crouched, several emotions flicker over his face at once. First, surprise that I got that close, then outrage, then pure, undiluted murder.

I plant my feet in the grass, assuming a Xzana combat stance. I'm driven back several steps by the power Nkosi lets loose. The immensity of the currentlike sensation overwhelms and stuns me for precious seconds, which I pay for. Nkosi springs at me faster than I have time to recover, his saber aimed at the dead center of my chest.

I fling my body to the side, managing to avoid the worst of the attack. The blood blade slides into the spot between my shoulder and clavicle then punches out through my back. I yowl in pain. It *hurts*—so fucking bad. Nkosi gifts me a smile that says *quit now* while promising unending pain if I keep things going. I flash my teeth because I played that game in the trials before, and he can kiss my ass. Nkosi thrusts the saber in further. Stars cross in front of my eyes from the agony, but I bite my tongue against crying out. I won't give the fucker the satisfaction a second time. I focus past the torture, and *think. Nkosi has me impaled on the end of his sword and the shithead is confident I'm about to die. How do I use it to my advantage? How can I turn this situation around? What can I do different?*

Or maybe the answer is that I don't *do anything different.* Instead, I keep to the part of a skewered, helpless pig that he's clearly about to draw out the death of to make a point.

But even as I play the role, I gift Nkosi a smile as homicidal as the one he gave me because he's too cocky to take heed of it anyway. But he's about to learn that I excel at the homicidal, stab-happy bitch game. So if he wants to play it, bet; we can go.

I raise one of my blasters, making the movement purposely sluggish and pathetically easy to track. Nkosi grips the gun with his hand not holding the saber and wrenches it from my grip before I can squeeze off three rounds into his temple. It's exactly what I want him to do. As he sneers at the gun, I raise my blood axe—lightning fast—and bury it in Nkosi's back. I aim for his spine, but he jerks his body to the right on my upswing, and it bites into his shoulder blade. Nkosi heaves in a breath, the only reaction he lets show that I've wounded him and that it might not feel great.

My death a thousand times over plays out in his eyes. I see my eternal suffering, my infinite torment—I see myself on the receiving end of the most brutal, twisted, perverse punishment Nkosi can think up as my penance for daring to draw his blood and succeeding. I do not flinch. I grind the blood axe deeper into his godsdamned shoulder blade, repaying the kindness he bestowed me.

"Next it's your head," I snarl.

His gaze cuts into me, skinning and filleting me, flashing dark as lightless hellpits. "Not a chance," he says, finally and blessedly snatching the saber out of my body.

I have little time for relief. He swings the wretched saber at my torso. I arch backward and out of its range, dart forward, hammer a kick to the side of his head, then retreat. Any ordinary man would stagger. Nkosi only bares his teeth and advances. I shoot three blood daggers into his gut before he can reach me. None slow him down. I drop to the ground, dodging his saber, and sweep my blood axe upward as I straighten, aiming to rip him open from balls to jugular. He steps out of its reach, and his saber flies at me again. It bites into my side. I spin away just in time for it not to cleave me in two. I hurtle my axe at his head. It catches his cheek. I keep successfully drawing blood. *That* I am able to do. But it isn't enough; I can't manage a mortal blow. Nkosi is stronger, bulkier, and towers over me by a good foot, making my objective exceedingly difficult. I'm lighter, but that doesn't lend me the advantage of being quicker. The bastard moves just as fast. So how do I end this? How do I beat him instead of merely keeping up?

"You are sorely outmatched," Nkosi calls out, casually wiping the blood away from his face and not looking one damn bit of taxed. Which is more than I can say for me. *Thank the stars* Nkosi is a gloating bastard who has paused in this fight to taunt me because I seize the few precious moments it extends to catch my breath. The fucker isn't slowing down. He might *never* slow down. I will—too perilously soon. I'm already feeling it. Nkosi, clearly having glimpsed that, smacks his chest, already victorious. "You want one final try before you die, *little girl?*"

Perhaps it's the delirium that accompanies certain death. Or perhaps it's just ingrained in my nature to be a contrary asshole, even right up to my demise. Either way, I laugh, strident and unhinged, at Nkosi's tired dig. And I think maybe I've finally become completely insane, because at this moment, I can't help but note that misogyny is universal.

But with my life and everything I love on the line, rationality cracks through—*the refusal to give up and renewed determination to find a way to win cracks strong*. I return to a calmer head and forego a second forward rush, like Nkosi tries to bait me to do. Instead of striking fast and hard in a burst of bravado, arrogance, and fury, as is my first instinct, I gamble on the shrewder approach: I pitch my weight more toward my heels and bend my knees slightly, settling into a crouch—and wait for my enemy to come at me.

Nkosi doesn't disappoint. As soon as he sees my defensive stance, he assumes that I'm cowering and rakes me with a gloating sneer. Then his saber flies at my head, the razor-sharp outer curve tilted so it's perfectly in line with my neck. I don't duck or fling my body aside to dodge it. Instead, I swipe my blood axe up to meet the saber. The sound of blood weapon against blood weapon rings out shriller than clashing steel. The vibrations from the impact shoot up my arm from wrist to aching shoulder joint and I force my muscles to not quiver. I grip my blood axe with both hands, throw my weight behind it, and push against Nkosi's saber. My biceps and forearms groan. But my blood axe holds steady. I don't give up ground. The hellish saber doesn't advance a micrometer toward my neck, where it so badly itches to make contact. And it's because I'm locked on Nkosi trying to cleave off my head and the saber he'll do it with that I fall into the trap I previously maneuvered him into.

A dagger slides into my chest.

Nkosi drives it past my breastbone and into tissues right above my heart. Fire ignites at the spot, and the breath rushes out of me. I finally yowl. Nkosi tosses the saber and yanks the blood axe from my grasp. He throws it aside too. Then he leans into me, his lips parting as if in rapture. His tongue darts out as if to taste the air while his eyes drop to half-lidded, the brown of them shining with something unmistakably voracious. Of all the terrifying things I've beheld about the Blood Emperor since arriving at his war camp, this twisted, grotesque look on his face is the most petrifying. It transforms him into something more than a Pantheon-blessed man, or even a power-mad Emperor. He truly looks like the monstrous hellserpent of Mareen's nightmares that's infiltrated this world to devour me whole.

Marrow-deep terror causes me to lose all ability to think strategically. I revert to a thing that's a trapped, skittish animal, fighting tooth and nail even as it recognizes it is futile. Survival won't let me just give up, though, and I twist and writhe and claw and kick and punch.

It doesn't do one bit of good.

Nkosi's mouth upturns in an amused, gloating smile.

NO! I shriek. *NO! NO! NO!* This wasn't supposed to play out like this. I was supposed to be stronger than this. I was supposed to be *better* than this. Yet I'm more than failing; I'm wretchedly fumbling and floundering against an opponent who's outmaneuvering me.

"I've won; you've lost," the Blood Emperor says. "You only remain mostly intact instead of me dropping your exsanguinated, mangled body at my feet because you must draw breath, your heart must beat, and blood must pump through your veins for the Stitching. Your little challenge is finished, nonetheless. I. Beat. You. The gold you bleed has become mine by *every* right. So I'll have it, now, and rule Iludu as its new, and only god, in this age. *Submit. Yield.*"

When I refuse, something darkly vengeful flashes in Nkosi's eyes. He leans in close, says in my ear, "You say I can't hold your team hostage to force this, but what about your continent? You claimed the world was most important, did you not? *I* only care about what's across the ocean, and by no means the whole of it. I will decimate this continent so thoroughly that it plunges into the damn sea when I'm finished. I will kill every single soul if you do not yield this instant. Are those enough lives to hold hostage to make it *worth* it? I swear, as a blood oath, it will come to pass if you do not yield to me in the next five seconds."

I—I want to gape. I want to deny that he's serious. That he's bluffing. Yet, he wouldn't risk a blood oath on a bluff, and that hellish look in his eyes screams he is serious.

"I . . . yield," I choke out because what else is there to say.

I lost.

I lost, and the price of *not* going through with a Stitching has become higher than stubbornly holding out.

When Nkosi starts to chant foreign Accacian words, I repeat them and struggle to remember I'm not actually defeated yet. If I'm not dead, the end hasn't come. And I *am* alive, so that's something, and Nkosi hasn't stripped my essence yet. I haven't given that over, and I can still retain it. I yielded to permitting a Stitching, which means letting only an *attempt* proceed for Nkosi to engulf my power. Yielding doesn't mean I have to meekly hand it over. I can fight against something still. I can fight against the Blood Emperor still. I can keep my power and take his. Which means this battle isn't over.

But it sure feels like it when the warmth flooding my chest invades the rest of my body, and a splitting headache erupts, leaving me dizzy. The disorienting sensation hints at being hauled toward some mental precipice, some precarious ledge that looms nearer and nearer as we chant. Abruptly, it feels like the ground, like the world, is pulled out from under me. I plummet into vertigo. The pain rattling my brain kicks up, like twin hatchets have hacked through my skull. A similar feeling cracks my chest apart; then it's like clawed hands reach for my psyche and heart, slicing them into cross sections, exposing the sum and core of who and what I am for consumption. For *imbibing*.

It's a violation and a violence that's worse than anything I could have prepared for. There's a tug at everything about me that's vital, and in response the red light that's the visible manifestation of my power shoots out of me. It crashes against Nkosi's body and pours into him.

But I'm not the only one this is happening too. The same thing takes effect on Nkosi. The crimson wash of his power floods me.

My skin instinctively crawls and I shriek because under ordinary circumstances I wouldn't want to own any parts of that monster. But then, something happens that makes me truly understand what a Stitching is and what occurs during the ritual. Nkosi's power doesn't try to burrow into me, like I thought mine was doing with him. The reality is much more horrifying. Nkosi's power submerges me; it tries to down me in its force; it tries to snuff out everything about me and enfold me into it. It tries to eviscerate me. Erase me from existence.

But if Nkosi's power is doing this to me, then mine is attempting the same to him. So I don't concentrate on the Blood Emperor's power encasing me, I focus on mine surrounding the fucker.

And I concentrate all the strength of my will and all the power I've amassed, down to the crevasse-size depths inside me that both fill, on drowning Nkosi in them. On eviscerating *him*.

The Blood Emperor's eyes widen as if he's been impaled from behind. His muscles bunch with tension, and his face twists into a mask of intense concentration—and burgeoning fear. Then, he visibly doubles down in wild determination to power through and not be the one who loses this battle of wills. This battle of power that is a separate thing entirely from our battle of combat.

Tough shit for him because I'm not about to roll over and be that person either. He underestimated me, assumed wrongly that the score from our former fight would carry over to this one.

His.

Fucking.

Loss.

When I double down in my efforts, too, a piercing shriek of denial rips from Nkosi. And I pour more of my power, my strength, my determination, my will into beating this motherfucker. As I do, my power ensconcing him amplifies and ribbons of gold, not merely the small shimmers in my blood, appear among it. The red-and-gold ripples over him, like furious flames.

"I did promise to kill you," I growl, staring straight into deliciously astonished, disbelieving eyes. "This is for Reed, and my mother, and my grandfather, and my team, and the world, and my godsdamned self." I imagine my power burning through Nkosi and all that he is until there's nothing left except ash. The ground seems to shake beneath our feet, the cosmos itself seems to rattle, as the streamers of red-and-gold light intensify. And there at the site of a demolished Krashen Base, in the center of Krashen City—Mareen's seat of power, which has been wrecked—on a battlefield soaked with Mareenian blood, with hordes of fallen Republic soldiers around us, the Blood Emperor of Accacia, who's wrought so much destruction on my country, my continent, my people, and my family, finally falls when my power fully engulfs him and his.

The red-and-gold surrounds me and dissipates into my pores when it's over.

Nkosi's bulk thuds to the ground. The brown of his skin pales to ghostly white. His lips frost over blue and his open eyes stare up at the cosmos, vacant, soulless, and glassy.

Heaving and nowhere near done, I bend and pick up my blood axe.

I swing its crescents down on Nkosi's neck and make sure the heinous, gods-shitting bastard stays dead.

"I might be a girl," I tell his corpse, "but you were just a man. And I'm half god. And now you're nothing."

Then I spin to Ajani, ready to deal with the Apis too.

Another mere man.

25

AJANI HAS DROPPED THE WIDER blood shield. A slimmer one encircles only his body.

"It's our turn," I say to Nkosi's son, blood axe raised, stalking him.

But he doesn't try to defend himself. "I told you I have no quarrel with Mareen," he says, walking toward me. "Let this be your proof, and the vidfeed's proof . . ."

His personal shield disappears entirely.

It's the one thing, the only thing, that could grind my intentions to a halt and make me pause in attacking him.

"All I wanted was Nkosi dead," Ajani says when we meet in the center of the ring of legionnaires, who, despite their emperor's death, hold firm to their Apis's existing order to maintain an outward-facing barrier. "You've done it," speaks the Apis gravely. He appraises me as if he can't believe it. I'd be insulted if it hadn't been the hardest damn fight of my life.

"I did," I tell the man who I've placed in the position of Accacia's new emperor. I jerk my chin to his Comm Unit. "If you are truly unconcerned with Mareen, pull your Red Legions out. *Now.*"

"I was already going to do that," he returns without hesitation. "We're flying home and away from this hellhole, useless continent, immediately. *Thank the Pantheon.* You're coming with us, by the way."

My hackles raise. *What the fuck does he mean by that?* I grip the still-raised blood axe. "I'm not going anywhere. Nor will you take me captive again."

Ajani sweeps a look down the length of me; he takes in the threat in my stance, the hostility that coils my muscles tight, and the vow of a fight. Yet, he doesn't advance with the answering attack I expect.

"When you stop a foe, Praetorian," he says, exasperated and holding position a few feet away, "wars don't simply end. Didn't they teach you that in the academy? There are talks, and negotiations, and formal cease-fires that must be hashed out and executed."

"I know that," I snap. "But what does it have to do with me? I don't helm Mareen." And I don't have any influence with the leaders who do, as Grandfather did during the last war, which placed him in the position of peace delegate. "I'm technically not even a Praetorian anymore," I remind Ajani. "I'm a fugitive of the Republic with a colossal bounty on my head."

"None of that matters. Your killing Nkosi makes you the only person of consequence that I need to negotiate anything with, henceforth."

"Be clearer, asshole," I say, losing patience. "What in the gods-damned hell are you talking about?"

For once, to my infinite amazement, Ajani gives up information without being a prick about it. "You, Ikenna Amari, slew the Blood Emperor of Accacia on live broadcast," he says plainly. "Those of us who bear the blood-gift and were born on Accacian soil are tied to our ancestral land by the enduring Pantheon magic Amaka put in place there. That same magic ties the individual who rules over Accacia to the land and its people. Which means the land itself needs to recognize that person as emperor to cement and legitimize their rule over Accacia and its blood-gifted. But the magic that does this also flows in a very precise direction: from the one who formerly held it to the one they either willingly abdicate the throne to . . . or the one who forcibly takes it. When you imbibed Nkosi's power during the Stitching, you effectively did the latter. So you're—"

"You're saying *I'm* Accacia's Blood Emperor? Or at least the one recognized by some warped magic the land holds?" My legs turn unsteady. This is too much, and *nothing* that I want. *Hell no!* The cosmos is seriously fucking with me. And the not-funny bitch has a sick sense of humor. "I don't want to rule Accacia!"

"Good. Then we remain on the same page. You'll travel to Accacia and participate in the abdication ritual that'll formally transfer your claim to emperorship to me."

For cosmos's sake! Of course things involve another godsforsaken cursed ritual. Seriously, what is with Accacians and the damn things?

Then there's the way Ajani spoke what he did. He said it *too* coolly. So coolly that the unspoken threat *if you're cooperative, then I don't need to attempt to kill you* suspends between us.

The problem with that sentiment is it rests on the idea that he *could* kill me. "You can try," I tell the fucker. "We see how well that turned out for the last Accacian bastard that attempted it."

"Don't make the mistake of comparing me to my father," he counters. "I'm not Nkosi. I'm sharper, more discerning, and have strengths at my disposal that go beyond being blood-gifted."

I snort at whatever the hell that means. "Arrogant much? Why hadn't you already killed him, then, if you're so quick-witted and formidable?"

"It took waiting for the optimal time and opportunity, but I had maneuvered his demise into place, if you recall."

"And you *really* didn't intend to kill me behind it and raise yourself to Emperor of Iludu?" I'm still having a hard time believing either. I continue to look for the trap. The deception in what he says. The war pieces he's arranging.

"Everything I apprised you of about my desires in the citadel were truthful where the territory I wish to rule over is concerned. As for you, the moment the gold in your blood revealed you're a rare Zenith existing in the After Pantheon Age, I had no wish to take you on in a fight or make an enemy of you if it could be avoided. As I said, I don't have the narrow-focused lust for power of my father. I also have the good sense not to risk pissing off Amaka. Slaying one of her last remaining Zeniths on this planet is likely a thing that would tempt the goddess to strip one of her gift.

"You want me firmly seated as Blood Emperor. Nkosi's death doesn't remove the threat to what's left of your Republic or the Minor Continent. I'm young and have evolved beliefs, but the other warlords are as old as Nkosi was. They are his contemporaries and share his war-mongering ambition of an empire that spans the planet. If one of the Red Order manages usurpation, you'll see a third war. You can ensure you avoid it by making it that much harder for any of the warlords to succeed when they inevitably try to scheme their way onto the throne during the initial transfer of rulership."

Well, when he puts it like that, he has sort of a point. It's no use cutting off the head of a snake if you leave opportunity for it to simply sprout a new one.

"Why don't we just team up to murder the whole of them wherever they are on this battlefield?" I offer a second, much preferred option to dragging my ass to cursed Accacia.

Ajani gives me the look, *I guess*, that suggestion deserves. "They are influential men who've lived over a century and who've spent most of the time shoring up power bases and amassing loyalties. I'm not so altruistic or enlightened that I'd risk the Empire's stability by executing them to spare a continent—which I don't care about—from the *potential* risk they pose. *You* care about this corner of the world. So you're going to ensure they're neutralized by accompanying me to Accacia. Though one or two might continue to resist, the smart ones will see the tide coming in and adjust, as long as the land itself recognizes me as liege *and* I have the backing and adoration of Accacia's Red Legions, enormous common populace, revered holy augurs, and government chancellors. I've already fostered all of the latter for years. I just need the land's recognition. Until I have it, it leaves room for one of the Red Order to find a rite that aids them in bypassing *your* claim since you aren't pure-blooded Accacian, nor were you born on Accacian soil."

I narrow my eyes. "That last part sounds like bullshit to get what you want. 'Might makes right' has *nothing* to do with blood purity."

When I level the accusation, Ajani only shrugs. "Perhaps. Perhaps not. It doesn't matter. The real question of consequence is: With you lacking deeper knowledge of Accacian rituals, are you willing to take the risk of throwing away what I relay as untrue?"

I envision thrusting something sharp and pointy into his smug, sure-he's-won face. In fact, my hands itch to use the blood axe and indulge myself.

"I'll go," I bite off. "*If* my squad agrees after I confer with them." I'm agreeing to what he asks, but I'm not an idiot. So I further say: "I'm going to want something more out of this arrangement in return if I'm handing you an empire and helping cement your rule. As Accacia's Blood Emperor, you will not only withdraw your legionnaires from my continent, sign a new peace treaty, and stick to it—*without* the bullshit skirmishes that skirted the line of your predecessor—you will see that Accacia pays reparations in staggering, mammoth, enormous amounts of credits and resources that will go toward postwar rebuilding and delivering aid to Mareen's most vulnerable—the innocent, noncombatant, common ranks—who suffered your people's war crimes. Accacia will likewise offer the same reparations to the people of every other nation on the Minor Continent. It won't *begin* to atone for your atrocities during the first conflict, but it'll be a start that's long overdue." I almost explicitly exclude Khanai from my demand—since the kingdom is the one that paved the way for this second hellish war when it sided with Accacia in the first place. But I'm not that petty or that reprehensible. My qualms are with the Grand Monarch's, Crown Prince's, and Elders Senate's previous decisions, not the entire kingdom.

"Is there anything else you care to dictate?" Ajani says without intonation that betrays how he may really feel about my requests.

"Yeah . . . one more thing," I say calmly—and then smash my fist into his lovely face quicker than he can block it or toss up a blood shield. "Don't mistake me for the girl you think you knew," I warn. "You will do as I say or I *will* fuck you up, and I'll figure out the rest later. Your plan was terrible, and a lot of people got killed because you were too much of a coward to challenge dear Dad outright yourself. You want to play king? Fine. But you're playing by my rules until you can prove you're actually capable of being the man you say you are."

I finally lower my blood axe; I don't need it. I could turn Ajani's blood against him with a thought. "For now, that is all," I inform him. "But I might think of something additionally later. Consider my demands open-ended. It's the least the Empire owes this continent, and the least *you* owe *me*."

Ajani readily assents—to the Empire owing the Minor Continent. (To him owing me, the bastard scoffs.) And then I'm left with the only decision there is to make. While I hate the prospect of leaving Mareen and all the people among the common ranks whom this war has decimated and will need the most assistance, which the greedy war house heads and elitist scions won't make it a priority to deliver, Accacia has got to be my destination—for them. Moreover, even though I said I needed to confer with my team, I know my rogue cohort well enough that I'm certain they'll decide the same.

Then after our business in Accacia is finished, I *am* coming back home, now that our first op is fulfilled and Nkosi is dead. Fuck my fugitive status. Fuck the bounty.

I just killed the Blood Emperor, a tyrant who nearly subjugated the world, a despot who would've enslaved the world. More than that, he would've *terrorized* and *tortured* the world, according to Kissa's precognitions and Nkosi's existing crimes. The feat is gigantic. *Huge*. Yet . . .

It doesn't feel nearly big enough. Because, as I told Ajani, it is up to leaders to prove to the world what kind of individuals they are. And as I look around at the smoking rubble that's Krashen Base, as my throat closes at the sight of the demolished academy that houses lives so young, as I remember the desolation of Cara, the civilian bodies in the war camp . . .

There is *no* question that the Tribunes have proven that not only are they duplicitous assholes, they're callous, base, and self-serving in the vilest manner. Their actions—and inactions—are unforgivable. Nkosi murdered so many, and the Tribunal, which did *nothing* to protect those who they were pledged to protect, were his accomplices.

So yes, I'm going to Accacia to get things set straight, but after, the Tribunes will pay for the atrocities *they've* perpetuated on so, so many fronts. Those bastards do not get to keep breathing much longer. They always had a reckoning coming for what they schemed against Grandfather. Now, they've added to their debts for the ruin and waves of death they ushered onto innocent people by instigating this war.

They had better be ready when I return home.

And even then, *nothing* will save them.

26

IN STEP WITH REED, DANNICA, and Caiman, I shove open the doors of a small council room Ajani has walked us to in the Accacian palace. The rest of our team greets us on the other side. Haynes, Greysen, Liim, and Dane stand beside a conference table facing the entrance, appearing anxious and relieved all at once. There's no missing the multitude of questions in their gazes when they specifically land on me. I'm not surprised; they're the same questions I got from Caiman, Reed, and Danica. All three had broken Iyko's compulsion and had watched most of my fight with Nkosi play out. Turns out, it is exceedingly difficult to keep biochipped Praetorians compelled when they don't want to be, *and* when you've shifted them in and out of compulsion multiple times.

"*Why'd you stay aboard? Why didn't you force them to let you off?*" I'd asked them, seriously enjoying the astonishment on Ajani's face.

"*I was confident you'd kick his ass,*" Dannica had said with her usual flippancy. "*Especially after he tried to murder your man and was gonna do so again if you didn't.*"

"*You didn't need last-minute variables that were distractions,*" Caiman had said much more seriously, hitching a thumb at Reed and Dannica. "*Which means you really did not need these two popping up unplanned anywhere in the vicinity. You care about them too much.*"

Reed had looked grave, completely off-kilter, and nodded in the affirmative. "*You had a strategy,*" he'd added tensely. "*You needed to stick to it, as we should've done in Cara.*"

Like Reed and the others have been holding off on asking their questions until we're alone, the guys we've reunited with don't start in with them either while Ajani hangs near the door.

In the taut silence, I scan those who've passed the last two weeks in the palace at Zelas, Accacia's capital, from head to toe. For Ajani's sake, they had better be perfectly healthy and without a scratch. They seem so. However, I ask to be sure, "Were you harmed in any manner?"

"No," Liim replies, his blue-gray stare traveling suspiciously to Ajani, who leans against the closed door making no move to leave. "We were treated a little too well here. It was . . . unexpected."

"It was damn unsettling and brutal, given where you all were," Haynes rumbles. He inspects those of us who flew into the war camp, visibly taking stock of our welfare as I did to his group. He grunts once he's satisfied, mumbles a curse to himself, and his stare grows conflicted as if he's wrestling with something. A curious *fuck it* comes and then he crosses the room with quick steps, smothering Dannica in a hug when he reaches her.

She shrieks in surprise, elbows him in the stomach, and he lets her go with an *oomph*. "What the hell was that?" she chokes out.

The way Haynes gazes at her turns more peculiar. "I got a report you were stabbed," he says. "*Stabbed by the Blood Emperor.* I heard it took *magic* to heal you. I haven't been able to stop thinking about it, or—*shit*— you. So I hugged you because you're back in front of me and alive. And now I'm going to do it one more time. You're free to punch me again."

First, Dannica gawks. Next, she scrubs all expression whatsoever. "Whatever," she tosses out without inflection. "I guess that's fine."

As she allows Haynes to swallow her up in his massive arms again without assaulting him, and even squeezes him back, my lips quirk as I wonder at a thing that I've thought a few times before.

"I heard you were stabbed too," Greysen says to Caiman.

Caiman folds his arms over his chest, lifts a shoulder. "Yes, I was. No, we aren't hugging. Hazard of the occupation; I'm good."

"Thank you for healing this one too," Greysen says to Ajani before giving Caiman a clear scowl.

I'm rendered dumbstruck by how freely he offers up the earnest sentiment to an Accacian, and by another thing.

"You ordered that they be given status reports on us?" I ask Ajani, not wholly believing he showed that level of consideration and generosity.

He shrugs. "Some of us can think and behave maturely from the onset. I figured your people would keep to good behavior that way, and be less difficult to treat as guests instead of prisoners. I did promise to extend every courtesy I would to a real guest in exchange for your cooperation and I'm a man of my word." He sinks a ton of meaning into the last part before dipping his chin to Greysen. "You're welcome, by the way. At least *one* Mareenian has manners enough to express gratitude for that save."

I roll my eyes. "Are you serious? The fact that you live and get a crown is more than enough. Speaking of which . . ." I point to the door behind him. "Don't you have *crownly* things to go do now that you've returned as Accacia's new emperor?"

His eyebrows raise at the dismissal.

"Hold up," Haynes says, head swiveling between Ajani and me. "How is he emperor? Since you beheaded Nkosi the palace has been abuzz with whispers that *you're* Accacia's ruler according to its succession laws."

I shoot Ajani a winning smile. "Our host informed me." The look on Ajani's face is absolutely priceless every time this topic comes up.

Which is why I brought it up, *a lot*, on the flight from Mareen to Acacia. "*Your emperor* is saying good-bye because she'd like to speak with her team alone," I tell Ajani, phrasing the request for privacy like I do simply to further ruffle him.

Might as well exhaust the means to do so while I have it, right?

His glower would certainly cleave a lesser person in two. "You're insufferable, and as always: You. Are. A. Child."

I wave him off. "Feel free to bow before you depart."

His features hilariously pinch. "I *do* have ruling responsibilities to attend and absurd whispers to quash. I will take my leave, *on my own accord*."

"Can we back up?" Haynes says after Ajani is gone. "If you, Ikenna, are really the Emperor of Accacia, why are we just handing that over to him? Is the plan to make him a figurehead?"

"No," I answer. "He gets the emperorship in full as long as he plays nice and keeps to terms we've agreed upon."

"Seems like a smart route and the best path we can take," Greysen says after I bring everybody up to speed on one of the things I wanted us to discuss without an audience. "If Ikenna tried to retain rule of Accacia, she wouldn't have the military or numerical superiority needed to hold a territory after a hostile takeover, while Ajani has both."

"Does that actually matter, though?" Dannica asks. "Kenna doesn't need either. Our girl has tactical superiority via her crazy-ass magic. She killed freaking Nkosi *and* took his power. Nobody can actually oppose her in whatever she does, regardless of how they feel about it."

I shift on my feet, the conversation veering into a territory that, ego aside, makes me uneasy.

"That is precisely why Amari shouldn't rule *any* territory." Dane, who's been studying me in an aloof manner since I arrived, speaks up before I can. He regards Dannica and Haynes like they've lost their minds with the mere suggestion. "You two saw what she did to Nkosi, right? I mean, I'm grateful the war is over and that bastard is dead, but

Amari ruling anywhere would be as bad as the former Blood Emperor. It's something we should all be in agreement about. I saw the gold leak out of her on the broadcast. I heard what she called herself. We all did, and we need to address it."

"What is your *problem*, dude?" Dannica snaps. "Get your shit together. Ikenna isn't the bad guy here."

"I have mine together. I have *my* head on clearly. Do you? Are or you overlooking critical considerations because she's your friend?"

"I'm not sure how I personally feel about all this, but he makes a good point," Liim says, coming to Dane's defense.

"Amari. Saved. The. World," Reed says, jaw tightening. "First and foremost, that means more than what was witnessed or said. Before we get into anything else, let's start there and acknowledge it. Then we can talk, levelheadedly on all sides, about whatever everything else may mean."

Dane draws himself up.

Now, unavoidably, we've gotten to reason number two I wanted Ajani scarce. This is a conversation, and split feelings, I knew we'd need to get out in the open immediately if we have any hope of moving beyond it.

"Dane is right." I clear my throat. "I shouldn't rule anything or anyplace," I say, beginning there. "I don't belong in any position of rulership. I think we can all agree that Nkosi and the Tribunal have made it evident that their similar doctrine of 'might makes right' is not the way that is best or most kind to the people made to live under it. It paves the way for an inevitable corruption that comes with holding absolute power, I think, because it props up a ruling body that goes unchecked."

Dane, at least, pitches me a nod of respect when I say it.

The others all have varying expressions of agreement, too, when I phrase it like that, and they should.

I continue, explaining the part that has some of the group rightfully nervous. "As for the gold and me calling myself a half god, I swear

I didn't know any of it before the war camp. I communed with Amaka there to gain the power to beat Nkosi and she told me. I *was* going to tell everyone in this room about it. It's why I asked Ajani to leave, so we'd have the space to hash this out in private, without needing to worry about appearing united, or not united, or whatever we're going to be after this. I am this thing called a Zenith." I wince at speaking it out loud, don't curb the discomfort that sweeps over me, and hope my friends and comrades see it and understand I am highly disturbed about it myself. "Basically, the gods had offspring with humans," I say plainly. "Their existence was wiped from the planet during the uprising against the Pantheon, but the gods supposedly hid away some of those humans who were descended genetically from them. And . . . yeah. I guess, I mean I *am*, one of them."

There. It's out there. And I'm sure they don't have more questions . . .

I look anywhere except at them because I slip into being a total coward. I can fight the Blood Emperor, no problem, but opening myself up to anyone? Especially about this? The society that reared us hates anything to do with the gods, and while my squad may be accepting of me being blood-gifted, being a Zenith who is basically kin to the goddess of blood rites is potentially something wholly relationship-altering and trust-shattering different. Even if it doesn't happen up front in this instance, it could happen later after folks have had time to really chew on what I am.

I try to force numbness, and fail, while I wait for them to respond.

"This won't go like Khanai. You don't need to convince us of anything," Reed says, and the fear knotting my stomach eases. "Honestly, I only didn't express that sooner because I was letting you be the one to decide when and how to bring it up."

Dannica cuts a side-eye at Dane.

"I wasn't wrong," he maintains.

"He wasn't," I say. "I understand," I tell him and mean it. "You had every right to be frank."

Dannica pops her lips. "Well, my response is exactly what our boy said. I didn't give a shit when I saw what went down from the jet. I still don't give a shit."

"Does my hug say enough? Or do I need to offer up something else mushy like these other two?" Haynes says, then passes me a very much mushy nod of solidarity and unwavering friendship.

Grateful, I pass him one back. I pass one to Dannica and Reed, and the rest of my old Gamma brethren too.

Then there's the part of our squad who weren't Gamma, but were Praetorians in Alpha Cohort. And the division among the seven of us hasn't been so stark since we fled Khanai. I give them the time they need to digest what I confessed and arrive at how they feel about it.

"I decided on the jet." Caiman speaks up first. "I just wanted to see you squirm a bit because even though you don't want it and plan to throw it away, I *know* temporarily holding an emperorship *will* inflate your ego more. But if I must say this, fine." He sighs. "You saved our asses *again*, Amari. The whole Republic's ass this time. So I'm good with whatever you are because you're on our side. You keep unquestionably proving it." He passes me a tried-and-true Praetorian's salute.

I roll my eyes, but snap him off one back.

Greysen does the same immediately after. "The fact that you are giving away power says all I need it to say," he states.

Dane and Liim take a bit more time to offer up a final response. I grimace but tell them, "No hard feelings. Neither of you really knows me like the others do. We've bonded little, and fear and hatred for the Pantheon is a deep-seated thing for a thousand understandable reasons. They were awful. I'm not sure how that changes the way we'll need to function moving forward as a team, but as long as you're not actively being dickheads or gunning for me, we can figure it out."

Liim is the first to break out of a stoic expression. He appraises me, both stunned and with admiration. "I've got to say, you keep surprising me. That was big of you. It's a sentiment somebody who is none of the things the gods were would relay. I'm good with you, Amari. I don't understand what this means, but even if Caiman hadn't said it, it's what I believe—you're one of us, no matter what."

He impresses a look on his Alpha brother who broke rank with him in Khanai. "You know I'm right, man. Put your issue with the gods aside. They're not Ikenna, and Ikenna keeps proving she isn't them."

It takes Dane a bit more time to pass me an accepting, albeit reluctant, head bob. "Okay, Ikenna. I guess . . . I'm good as well," he says when he does.

I want to be joyful their acceptance was this easy, all things considered. Unfortunately, I am not done copping to things that might fracture us yet—because their pledged faith brings us to the third reason I kicked Ajani out. It's time to confess the lie I have been keeping. The extreme votes of confidence I was just handed means doing anything less will shatter, at the very least weaken, the support that I've built here if I don't finally relay what happened with Mareenian leadership in Khanai and it comes out later. That goes for Caiman especially. Moreover, it's become inexcusable, disgraceful, and deplorable to do otherwise with the threat of Nkosi behind us and our assassination of Mareen's remaining leadership in front of us.

I suppose.

"I appreciate everyone's trust, but wait on pledging that you're all the way behind me still. In Khanai, it wasn't Ajani or the Gyidis who killed Rossi, Brock, and Caan. It was me." I just spit it out and relay why I did it. "I know we already agreed we're returning home to kill what's left of the Tribunal, but I also know us doing it that way and what I formerly did is different," I add.

The Gammas grimace but don't necessarily reflect surprise; I didn't think they would. The four of us *were* already conspiring to kill Tribunes before the summit in Khanai once we confirmed who among them were guilty of Grandfather's death. Caiman, Greysen, Liim, and Dane, however . . .

It's the four of them that my admission visibly rocks.

"That isn't what you said in the keep," Dane says in consternation.

"That's not quite true," Caiman replies quietly, gold eyes hard on mine. "Amari didn't actually offer up the identity of *who* was responsible for the brass's deaths when I asked in the prisoner's keep. You told me my father and the others were dead. That was it." He hurls the recalling of events—and what was expressed and what wasn't—at me like a dagger used to pin me in place.

"*You* killed the last Legatus and Tribunes?" Greysen scrubs his head.

"I—"

Liim cuts me off. "Of course she did. That's what this is about, isn't it? The whole war. Mareen in ruins—it's because *they* never went to Khanai to do anything but start shit. Plus, we are going to murder the rest, like she said. We *had* our vote of confidence, and for me it stands. This changes nothing. Truthfully, I would've killed those three, too, if I were in her place. None of us can say that we wouldn't." How the Alpha responds is the last way I guessed he would. For a second, I just gawk at how ardently he's all right with it and defends it.

"We took oaths . . ." Dane says, somewhat lost.

"Yes. Well, so did our Tribunes," Greysen notes, although he casts an apologetic look at Caiman. "To protect Mareen. And maybe they thought they were doing what needed to be done, but they were wrong."

"And now they're hiding, according to our intel about where the hell they were during the Isles and the Krashen attack," Haynes says, a thing none of us who flew in from Krashen previously knew.

"Is my family included in those reports of them hiding?" asks Caiman about this new revelation.

"The Rossis are," Greysen answers him gently. "I'm sor—"

"Don't apologize," Caiman says, curt. "You either, Amari. At least not for the blood you spilled. Scion or no. War house or no. Tribunal or no: We're Praetorians. We're supposed to be protecting the people of Mareen. We're only special because we chose to fight for them. So we were trained and given the resources to *be* special. But birth doesn't mean shit if it's the only thing we hang our rank on."

"Wait . . . am I hearing a *Rossi*, Haymus's son, excuse his murderer and this other stuff?" says Dane.

Caiman stands up taller, looking every inch the war house head, and given his interesting speech, perhaps acting precisely like how a war house head should act. "No. You're hearing your squad mate say that."

"But your so-called squad mate killed your father," Dane protests.

"That she did." Caiman's eyes return to me, as hard as they were before. "And she kept it to herself because in war, we've got to make hard choices for the greater good and we were literally fighting for our lives and the lives of millions. So she judged we couldn't afford the drama. Is that about right, Amari?"

"I—yeah, it is," I say, not sure what more words to form because this is going nothing like how I imagined. Caiman is definitely not behaving in any way I imagined.

"Just that we're clear: I am pissed," Caiman lets me know. "Not for the reason you assumed I'd be," he snaps further. "In your position, as Liim said, I would've killed all three too." He rubs a hand along the back of his head. "Gods, my father was a fucking bastard. *I* thought about killing him after the mountain so he wouldn't target Greysen again. That's the funny part and the part you didn't get. I still would've ended up on this path, eventually, even if your hand hadn't been the one to kill Haymus and speed it up. You killing him is not why I'm majorly, gods-shitting furious with you, Amari. It's the you-not-telling-me part for this long that's fucked up and irksome. It's info you should've given me enough credit to hand me up front. We all made a pledge to protect the Republic. Did you think I'd just shirk it like some shortsighted, self-absorbed asshole? Right now, our Republic is sick. It's *dying*. And while it may be painful, and it may taste awful, and may be hard to swallow, I do believe in you still and share your vision and plan for the cure. I guess what I'm saying is I wish you would've had the same faith in me that I keep placing in you, Amari."

Okay. I deserved all of that.

I'm sorry.

It's on the tip of my tongue; however, it is infinitely hard to get it out. Honestly, it stings, feeling too much like offering him grace for a mere three-ish months of evolving beyond an asshole. All the same, this isn't about him. Or even me. If Caiman can look past that to the bigger picture, I guess so can I. "I did screw up," I admit. "I'm sorry. I should've had more confidence in you as my squad mate. Also, I'm highly offended that you think I taste awful," I tease to thaw some of the persisting tension and keep a portion of my pride.

Caiman blinks, looks like the ceiling has crashed on his head. "Did she just—"

Reed waves in my general direction. "Ikenna apologies are like rare celestial events that happen once in an eon. This is special. Enjoy it."

I snort. "He better, and I'll likely deny it later."

Caiman mutters something about the cosmos keeping him trapped in a hellpit to pay for past deeds by chaining him to my side—which is a cool notion I can't really argue with—and then he actually apologizes for past deeds, including the cliff. It becomes my turn to look like the imperial palace dropped on my head.

"The two of you are absurd," Liim says, and it's another thing our team expresses unanimous agreement on.

Maybe they have a point.

Regardless, the air has become as clear as it is going to get, and Caiman and I turn to doing what allies, or frenemies, or whatever we are, do after they patch up their shit: plan assassinations with their mutual squad.

Twelve assassinations to be exact—since, according to intel, every last living Tribune remains that way after going to ground like cowards and letting Mareen's soldiers and civilians be their body shields.

27

I STAND IN THE LAST place I ever thought I'd find myself the following morning—the Accacian throne room, at the side of its Blood Emperor, on a cosmos-damned dais.

My reunited squad forms a tight, protective semicircle at my back. It's a formation they stubbornly insisted on, knowing it makes them appear like they're my Praetorian Guard, to assert a statement to Accacia, the Tribunal back home, and the rest of the world that will be gazing upon us soon. Not that it matters—I no longer feel I have anything to fear from the people here. But it's nice to have them back with me, to know we remain a strong unit, united in our agenda and dreams for the future ahead.

Aside from us Mareenians, the throne room—whose walls and domed ceiling shimmer the gut-curdling red of blood rubies—is packed with Accacians important to the Empire's governing. Its warlords, royal augurs, advisory chancellors, and highest-ranking aristocrats are among those present.

The necessary Empire press have been permitted into the room as well, although no outside news orgs have been allowed. The commentariat group stands off to the left of the dais, clustered together with press badges pinned to their sleek suits, unconcealed nanomics in their ears, and Comm Units in hand that they are already furiously typing notes on. Official imperial palace media drones hover in each corner of the room, snapping pictures and transmitting live vidfeed of this moment both inside and outside the border.

Soon, the world is about to be formally handed its freedom.

My only regret is that all I've accomplished, this immense feat my team has helped me accomplish, is occurring while we're wearing wretched Accacian court robes and not the proud maroon dress coats that mark a Praetorian.

The warlords—who, Ajani has explained, didn't wish for this affair to be happening in the first place—sit in seats on the dais to the left of their new liege with relaxed, accepting postures. That's exactly what they are, though: poses for the world that conceal the truth. They wear court robes, too, though theirs reflect the same color scheme of their Red Order uniforms—an ominous tide of lightless black with scarlet collars. I take a moment to study the six bastards who pose a fresh threat and decide that if Ajani can't keep them in line, then they can die too. He may be scared about the power vacuum they'll leave, but I now know how to fill it if necessary.

I will allow *nothing* to reverse the lasting, true peace I've negotiated.

Impatient and anxious, I glance at my Comm Unit. The impending news conference is scheduled to start in a minute and a half. The ninety seconds crawl by unimaginably slow. But at last Ajani is rising from a gruesome blood ruby throne and the room is quieting.

The former Apis walks to the podium front and center of the dais. The robes trailing behind him bear geometrical panels of alternating obsidian and scarlet, and make him, gratingly, look every inch like a man born to hold the title of Imperial Majesty. When I stride forward to join Ajani at the podium, I school my features into not betraying how much being in Accacian lands, in the hellish palace, and standing, peacefully, beside a man whose future intentions I still don't trust—no matter what he claims—itches my ass.

"Iludu underwent a monumental shift a mere day ago," Ajani says without ceremony or opening preamble once we're in place at the podium. "Nkosi, the man who ruled Accacia for two centuries, died during the battle at Krashen." He motions to me. "The planet watched Ikenna Amari slay him. She stands beside me today, as a representative of the Minor Continent, to sign the peace treaty that she and I have negotiated. The points important to the whole of Iludu are as follows: Accacia has pulled the Red Legions from Mareen. The Empire will no longer encroach upon any territory of the Minor Continent; instigate, engage, or incite in any conflict or skirmish on the Minor Continent; or attempt further occupation of any land on the Minor Continent. Moreover, the Empire will pay reparations in the sum of three trillion credits to each state it caused harm during the recent war and the former war. Lastly, the states of the Minor Continent who swore fealty oaths to the Empire are released from their vows; they are no longer considered holdings of the Empire. Independent status is wholly and unequivocally returned to them."

I imagine applause and cheers must break out around the Minor Continent among those who view the broadcast. I, for my own part, expel what feels like a deep breath I've been holding since the news of the attacks in the west and east.

Actually, no.

I've been holding the breath since Grandfather died and the whole planet realized war loomed.

And very tellingly, the Accacians gathered in the room do not cheer. They've had unswerving loyalty ground into them by Ajani's predecessor, so they do not openly express any dissent or distaste for what their current Blood Emperor decrees. All the same, there's an undeniable undercurrent of contempt that ripples through the air.

Not that anyone is focusing on them. But I see it, even as I'm bombarded by rapid flashes of light from drones snapping endless pictures of Ajani and me standing beside each other. A royal chancellor approaches the dais with a letter-size, cream piece of parchment paper. The short woman with warm tan skin wears the same crimson court robes we Mareenians were lent. She is one of the few Accacians in the throne room whom subtle disdain doesn't continue to cling to after Ajani's pronouncement. The chancellor bows to Ajani, straightens, and genially places the parchment paper and an absurdly ornate, obsidian glass ink pen on the podium. Ajani picks up the pen and signs his name at the bottom of the document that lists everything he just proclaimed to the world. When he hands the ink pen to me, my fingers close around its slender, smooth body tightly. It feels so strange and bizarre to hold it. To be pressing its tip to the paper below where Ajani signed the peace treaty. Grandfather once stood in the exact same spot and accomplished the same thing. Except that the peace he handed our beloved corner of Iludu didn't hold. It proved nothing is assured, *ever*, and little is truly permanent. Despite that, I seize on to hope that the peace an Amari wins for the world sticks and can be lasting. That this ink means something.

And more than hoping, I vow to do what Grandfather failed at, what all his strength and prowess and formidableness didn't help him conquer: I will endure. I will survive so that I stay around to keep fighting and do all within my power to ensure that this time around, the Minor Continent isn't hit with a conquest campaign again.

I KNEEL NEXT to Ajani and in front of royal augurs, who remained in the throne room when Ajani dismissed the other Accacians. The group of three women and two men wear pristine silver robes with threading along their hems that are almost as splendid as what their emperor wears. I gaze up at the Empire's seers, unsteady and distrustful. The only reason I'm submitting to the bloodletting they're about to exact is because it's part of the terms of peace Ajani and I brokered. Apparently, Accacians cling tight to their damn divinations as much as they do to their godsforsaken rituals. And Ajani insists the rite that'll firmly seat him as emperor can't be performed without royal augurs advising the best time it should be performed.

To me, there's no better time than right away. The sooner I can be away from here and the sooner I can determine if the Tribunal is going to capitulate or need encouragement, the sooner I can maybe actually believe we've accomplished anything.

Instead, I'm here. With fortune tellers. I nearly roll my eyes in front of the respected men and women due to the extreme ludicrousness of it all. I glance behind me to my team, who have moved off the dais and remain guarding my back a few feet away. They look just as uncomfortable and weary as I feel, all while glaring daggers at the augurs in warning.

And, all right, I'm touched. They care. Reed, Dannica, Haynes, and even Caiman and Greysen, are no-brainers at this point on that front. But Liim and Dane, who remain more allies by way of their loyalty to Caiman and Mareen's people than actual friends, exhibit the same fiercely protective expressions. I don't know if it's our time together, the sacrifices we've all made, our recent sharing circle, or the fact that I finally killed the Republic's greatest outside threat, but we are more than simply comrades. And because of that, their presence helps the nerves seep out of me. Regardless of what happens during the divination, my squad has my back. They won't let any harm occur.

"Let's get this over with already," I say to Ajani. Might as well rip the medgauze off and be done with this shit sooner. "You don't need to cut me for your bloodletting," I then inform the augurs, assuming some control of the cursed ordeal. "I'll bleed myself."

At the insistence, Ajani turns an amused look my way.

"What?" I ask, immediately on guard

He shakes his head. "Nothing." Yet, the smug smile remains in place.

"Whatever it is, go to hell, asshole."

One of the augurs, a young female with violet eyes a shade darker than Dannica's, skin that's a deep brown, and who's pretty in a delicate way, coughs as if she's choked on something. Behind it, she full-on chortles. She looks me over appreciatively, dare I say, admiringly. Then she winks. "Speak to him like that more, please. He could use his ego kept in check. Now that he's emperor, he's bound to grow *more* insufferable."

Ajani slices her a look, but there's no heat or real insult behind his brown eyes. Instead, there's a humorous light as his mouth curls into a genuine grin.

There's definitely some sort of close relationship there. Interesting. All knowledge of an enemy is good, and Ajani, while perhaps not an enemy, is certainly not a friend. He isn't even an ally, and I will not start to treat him as one either. As far as I'm concerned, he remains a threat—just one that, maybe, doesn't pose a threat for the time.

A second augur, a broad-shouldered, ebony-skinned man who has a build that seems better suited for combat gear than holy robes, clears his throat. "Shall we begin?" It's phrased as a question to his Blood Emperor but carries the tone of an order.

To my infinite astonishment, arrogant ass Ajani bows his head in deference.

The young female augur squelches her playful demeanor and walks to stand directly in front of Ajani. The male augur who spoke takes up a position in front of me.

As Ajani's augur does the same, mine lays a firm hand against my brow. I tense, but stay kneeling, and mostly force myself to relax.

"My name is Odion, by the way," the male augur says. "To answer your question, no. You cannot bleed yourself for this rite."

My teeth clench. *Of course I shitting can't.* "It's fine," I say.

To my astonishment, his brown eyes cast me an apology. Then, he reaches into his robes, as his counterpart does the same, and draws out a sliver-thin stiletto. I eye it, surprised for a second by this. As the two augurs hold the blades, it's the first time I've beheld an Accacian *not* forging a blood blade to inflict a wound upon someone.

"Why didn't you both use your blood?" I have to ask, curious. "Is actual steel a part of the ritual of it all?" I've yet to encounter an Accacian who doesn't prefer blood blades—hell, even I do at this point—so I'm genuinely curious.

"You're correct," Odion says. "The Pantheon Blessing that gifts us the ability to perform divinations via blood readings requires delicate handling and preciseness. If we use blood weapons to draw the participant's life force, it'd mix the power in our blood with yours and contaminate the ritual. Thus, what the divining says will be inaccurate."

"Right," I respond. That explanation is easy to understand—*not a single fucking bit.*

"May I proceed?" Odion asks and doesn't move the stiletto toward me until my explicit consent is voiced.

The augur is quick and efficient with his cut. He swipes the steel across the exposed skin on the right side of my neck, not biting into it deeper than he needs to in order to draw a steady trickle of blood. The knife gets replaced with a glass vial that he holds to the nick. He allows the vial to fill halfway before removing it.

"I am finished, daughter of Amaka," Odion says gently and kindly. When his brown eyes meet mine, they're gentle as well, and they twinkle with mirth at the surprise I look him and his disarmingly nice demeanor over with. "The whole of us aren't bloodthirsty brutes. Simply because all blood-gifted can easily do it, it doesn't mean we all *enjoy* bleeding people."

Riiight . . .

I chew on his words, try to decide if I believe him.

He seems to acknowledge my unsaid doubt with a sad smile but doesn't say anything more.

Ajani's augur hands the vial of his blood she collected to Odion. Odion gazes at the two, and shock flickers in all of the augurs' eyes as they look on. They've clearly glimpsed the gold shimmers among mine—and it's evident Ajani didn't pass along that information beforehand.

"How soon can we perform the Claiming?" rings Ajani's eager voice.

Odion holds one full vial and one empty vial. Ajani's and my blood that the augur has mixed together twine around each other in a double-helical fashion, my strand glinting gold and Ajani's uninterrupted red.

"You won't love the answer," Odion responds as he pulls whatever he divines from our blood and the shape it takes. "I must press the importance, Your Imperial Majesty, of waiting until the next Blood Moons to transfer the claim that she, who is a Zenith of Amaka, holds over our lands. We predict they'll present during the next vanishing gibbouses."

Ajani sweeps to his feet. "We moved past that phase only a day ago. We won't see a trinity of new ones for another thirty-odd days. It could be perilous if I wait that long. There are already whisperings of the warlords taking stock of who among the aristo and Red Legions remain believers in Nkosi's agendas. A month leaves too much time for them to make a move against me—or Ikenna—so the legitimate claim of liegeship passes to one of the Red Order."

"I can take care of myself quite well," I assure him, standing too.

"*Nobody* is coming for Kenna," Dannica says.

"Nobody is getting *near* Ikenna," vows Reed.

"I'm not what you need to worry about," I let Ajani know. "My squad and I can take care of me. Worry about preserving yourself so I don't have to slaughter warlords and bring about the instability you don't wish for your precious Empire."

A snort sounds behind me. "I told you Amari's ego was going to be unbearable now," comes muttering in Caiman's distinct pitch. "Though I like how she's thinking."

"I'm not overly concerned about your safety, Ikenna," Ajani says, "as you'll be staying in the palace under heavy guard. I'm concerned about my people."

"Wow! That's very presumptuous of you," I inform Ajani. "One: no, the hell I will. Two: you *should* be somewhat concerned. Remember: if someone else kills me, then *they're* the emperor, right?" I ask Odion. He looks at me gravely, nodding.

"Fine—even more reason to want to get this done sooner. What's the consequence of performing a Claiming against your advice?" Ajani asks Odion.

The burly augur pins his liege with a scowl. "If you do it sooner, your and the Zenith's blood emit an entwined energy that portends ruin for the Empire."

"You're positive it must wait?" Ajani says. "Check again. Be certain."

Odion draws himself up to his full, considerably tall height. "No. My augury blessing and the thread lines of the future I discern with it are sound. I will not check again."

A muscle in Ajani's jaw ticks. It seems the Apis-turned-Blood-Emperor-in-waiting is highly irritated. The gravity of the situation notwithstanding, I chuckle and decide I adore Odion. Anybody who puts Ajani in his smug, superior place is a winning individual in my book.

"I don't suppose you've divined a cautionary reason *less* vague that you wish to share, then?"

The woman who drew Ajani's blood swats his shoulder. "Stop being grouchy and bullheaded. You, more than most, should know better than to question the divinity sciences merely because you don't like what was foretold. You sought guidance from us; you have it; don't ignore it. *Please.*"

Ajani grimaces, but collects the woman's hands and kisses her knuckles. "I trust you. Therefore, I'll trust the divination on this." The way he utters the words and his act of affection leave no doubt the augur is a lover, if not something more. "I'll wait out the month," a calmer Ajani informs the collective group who have offered counsel.

"We'll fly home and return then," I say to my team.

"Glad to hear we're not spending a month in Accacia dicking around," says Greysen, not caring about the Accacians who hear him. I don't care either.

Taking stock of the whole of our group, the tension among them communicates their worries clearly. We're all eager to get back to Mareen, fugitive status aside. We can lie low at first, if needed, but we have to somehow help the people whose lives the Tribunal's courted war left decimated. Because as sure as I know anything, the Tribunes won't be bothered when there are surviving war house scions and legacy lines that'll take priority.

"They can do what they like. You will remain here. It's nonnegotiable," Ajani says with an authority that chafes.

"You're right—we're not negotiating." Who the fuck does he think he is? There's no way I heard him right—or the command in his voice that's begging for me to carve out his windpipe and relieve him of the ability to utter bullshit statements. "But in case you were wondering, I wasn't aware I solicited your input," I say, managing to remain serene. "I think you're confused about me giving a fuck about your opinion. Let me correct the error: I give less than a *half* fuck. This was a discussion between me and my people, nobody else. Certainly not you."

Ajani bristles and, again, I could give two shits.

"I flew you into Accacia as a friend of the Empire. To continue to work together toward a mutually beneficial end. But I will not let you depart before the Claiming. I *will* detain you if I need to."

And with that, my hard-won détente goes to hell. Ajani gets my best smile. "Do you want to see if I can go two-for-two for Accacian royals that I decapitate? I do still owe you for Rykos, and I'd relish gutting you where you stand. You are seriously trying my patience and commitment to decorum here. My squad wants to go home. I want to go home—there's work there we need to do. Your augurs just told us there's no reason to hang around for literally weeks. If your warlords want to come after me, they're welcome to. Don't worry your pretty little head about it. I've communed with Amaka and Stitched with Nkosi; if the warlords start a fight, I'm confident I'll bury them. *I'm. Going. Home.* Get me a fucking jet to do it on. That's not a request. Nor," I say, pretending to come to the realization I've had since the moment it happened, "do I really need to *ask* anything of you. Technically, *you. Aren't. Emperor.* I am. If you don't procure me a craft, I'll command someone else to do it. You're worried about destabilization? Try to forcibly keep me here and I'll start wielding power that is rightfully mine. Bet that will destabilize things a lot quicker."

I'm gathering my power about me to punctuate everything I've threatened and stress that he *cannot* stop me when Odion lays a hand against Ajani's forearm. "Let her go," he says. "You two need to remain allies to skirt this ruin too. We will help you keep the warlords in line in the interim. We holy seers are not without our sway over the rest of you."

Ajani gnashes his teeth. "Give me three days," he grinds out. "I'd like to at least start to do what I can to bring the warlords in line without the Claiming."

"One day, and that's as generous as I'm going to get," I say.

"Can you give him two days, please?" Odion cuts off Ajani's protest. "You have little reason to care, and I understand your passion to return to Mareen and help its populace, but the populace here may suffer greatly, too, if we do not deal with the warlords delicately."

"We could use the time to get things in place," Reed says. "It'll be good to gather detailed and multiple reports on the Tribunes' actions since the press conference as well as the specific condition of citizens, call in the favor you didn't use from Lusian so we go back with an army at the ready, and see which Praetorians survived and are as unhappy with the Tribunes as we are to shore up some support from within our borders too. You know?"

"I can give you two days." I say it to Odion, who asked nicely, *not* Ajani.

Afterward, we go home and take out Tribunal trash.

Finally.

We go home and achieve, *quickly*, the second part of what it'll take to make killing the Blood Emperor actually seem like it means more than removing one monster only to leave behind a crop of others.

28

"I HAVE A THOUSAND LEGIONNAIRES at the ready to depart, should you want them."

Ajani offers it as we travel in an unmarked transport to a remote airfield on the outskirts of Zelas in the dead of night. His pitch is uncharacteristically amicable, unassuming, and non-dictatorial.

It's so odd, my hackles raise.

"Why would you do that?" Reed, to my right, says, as suspicious as I've become.

"Great question," I say to Ajani. I turn to where he's seated on my left atop the U-shaped cushion that spans the transport that holds the rest of my team plus his two marshals. I scrutinize his profile since he hasn't turned to face me after dropping that. His scrubbed expression and increased generosity reek of his usual modus operandi when he's scheming at something. "If you are planning anything to undermine our leaving or hold us back—"

"I'm not," he says, turning my way.

"Why don't I believe you?"

Maybe not the wittiest comeback. Just the same, it expresses I'm not swallowing his bullshit.

"They're merely bodyguards that'll protect my interests. Which is all this is about, no duplicity," he states plainly. "Sending you with an army that's a thousand strong secures *my* crown and sees that you, along with your claim on the Empire, returns to it alive, without that claim passing to anyone else. You are the most reckless individual I've ever met, after all. While you've grown from the girl I knew in Khanai, and you wield a lot of strength right now, you haven't grown that much—gods help us—and even said gods were defeated. Do not forget that and take the legionnaires for backup, *please*."

The needling insults wrapped up in compliments aside, I fight a chuckle. "Who coached you to phrase the desire to have some control in all of this so nicely?"

"She means as nice as it'd get for *you*," Dannica, across from us, says behind a cough.

"Was it Odion or your girlfriend augur?" I ask. "They're the ones who remained sensible in the throne room and weren't jerks."

"Nneka and the old man are wise beyond their years," Ajani says, smoothly avoiding one of the questions I asked. "I'm trying to do things their way and work out solutions you and I can both be comfortable with, and more importantly, that protect the citizens we're both worried about. You're going to stage a coup, are you not? Sizable armies help with that, and the one I'm handing you can't be bought or turned against you. You'll know their loyalty to you is ironclad because I've selected individuals who are loyal to me and share my vision of a better future under my eventual reign. They'll guard your flank at all times, should you need them with the Tribunal or should any of the warlords decide to cross the ocean. Can you meet me halfway, *please*, and accept them accompanying you so I'll rest easier about that future?"

"Oh, it is killing you to keep using that word, isn't it?" I enjoy one last chuckle before I stop being a juvenile ass. "I can't take a thousand legionnaires into Mareen, no matter how appealing of a case you make." I inwardly sigh, torn with regret. The infuriating nature of the person lending them aside, Ajani doesn't make a terrible case about the soldiers' handiness, if they can be trusted. Nonetheless . . . "There's no way I can sneak that many soldiers into the Republic, and I will lose the common support we're near sure we can get if I openly bring the enemy en masse." I pay Ajani the returned amicability and maturity, I suppose, of explaining.

"I never thought I'd say this, but it's a damn shame we can't," Haynes says, shaking his head. "He's right about a highly specialized, highly magical army being the perfect flex in a coup."

"Something like that, under different conditions, might even make us able to force a regime change and minimize additional bloodshed," Dane murmurs almost to himself. Honestly, how is he still imagining this can end any way other than with more blood? I let it go; he'll understand when we get back and he stands in the center of what the Tribunes let happen. He hasn't been on Mareenian soil since the war started. He didn't see Cara and Krashen in person and have it rip through him.

"I can do something with about one hundred and sneak those in," I tell Ajani, deciding to meet him halfway, if he is earnest, for two reasons. One: I'm not passing up additional muscle completely with the fight ahead. Two—which I voice to my squad: "If everyone is okay with it, at the very least, the hundred we take can help fortify and run patrols at our base camp."

After each one of them states they are, I manage a thank-you to Ajani and it's settled.

"I've also spoken with Mustaph Gyidi to begin arranging Khanai's reparations," he says offhandedly as the transport stops for a security check at gates encircling the airfield. "I thought you might be interested in the update, and the Grand Monarch asked that I pass the request along for you to call him, since I'm apparently playing messenger for your family squabbles."

The squabbles that you caused.

It's the truth, and not the truth. Which is why I bite my tongue.

"When you speak to him next, tell him I'll consider it." It's the farthest my anger and his betrayal will let me bend.

"Or you could do it yourself since I'll have higher-priority things, that you demanded, to discuss. You're a Zenith, you killed Nkosi, you've orchestrated a revolutionary peace treaty, and you're leading an insurrection; those make you a head of state in every way that counts despite not governing an actual territory. You're going to have to have chats with the Grand Monarch anyway, probably sooner versus later. Seems like you should air out the personal stuff on a personal call beforehand."

I sink ice into my glare—though I'm not sure if it's directed at him, the king across the ocean, or inward. Likely, it's all three. "This is another thing you don't get to offer an opinion on. Can we drop the Grand Monarch now?"

"No."

I look past Ajani to the transport's window. Where the hell is the hangar so I can get out of the cramped carrier and not have to strangle him?

We pass several that are open holding nondescript, slim gray jets that sit in stark contrast to the showy red ones. People in legionnaire uniforms file onto every last one.

"Why are so many still boarding crafts?" I ask Ajani.

"I have to continue with the topic of the Grand Monarch to give you that answer," he drawls.

My eyes narrow. "What do you mean?"

"During our call, he also asked what you were up to. I informed him, as one head of state would to another about what's brewing in their backyard. He offered *you* assistance that *I* took him up on to aid *our* mutual aims, because I figured you wouldn't and it's witless not to."

I grip the edge of the seat. "Be. More. Succinct. Immediately."

The transport stops in front of one of the hangars as he says, "I thought you'd turn down the entirety of the legionnaires. Since you've agreed to a hundred, the remaining nine hundred are flying into Khanai, *as guests of the Grand Monarch,*" he adds quickly. "I didn't ask. He proposed it. He wants you to have them close to Mareen's border should you find their backing of greater importance than political maneuvering at any point."

"You're shitting us?" It's Liim who says it because I'm still trying to process.

"Hold up. Ikenna tries to kill Mustaph, and he gifts her the same thing she tried to kill him for?" Haynes's face looks a lot like mine: dumbstruck.

"Cool family," Dannica says. "Twisted, but cool."

Beside me, Reed squeezes my hand. "I hate agreeing with him, but you should reach out to Mustaph if that's the case. If only from a strategic point, you two need to have a timely conversation. Legionnaires waiting in Khanai gives you one hell of an ace card and wipes us clean of it. If Mustaph's in cahoots with Ajani and his legionnaires anyway, we could easily spin it as the Grand Monarch letting a hostile army in to aid you if we do need them. There is a precedent."

I massage my eyes. There are so many things wrong, and baffling, and ironic, and ludicrous here on so many levels that it's hard to think straight. "I'll give him a call," I finally say.

I keep massaging my eyes because I'm positive it'll be a mess.

"Did you speak to the Crown Prince?" I ask Ajani. "What does the Emrir, who leads *Khanai*'s armies, think about legionnaires returning to his turf?" The prince wasn't all too happy with their previous presence.

Ajani's nostrils flare at the mention of my former friend Enoch

Gyidi. *Interesting.* "You mean the individual who's about as mature as you? He wasn't present on the call, thank the gods."

That answers things well enough. Enoch still loathes me for attempting regicide against his father.

And I still despise him for trying to kill all my friends, not to mention lying to me and letting me walk into a trap he and his father planned.

But yeah, calling Mustaph is a great idea.

"WHAT ELSE ARE you about to dump on me?" I ask Ajani, weary. He asked for a private word before I boarded the jet with the rest of my team, and I don't want to even guess at what it could be, given the huge shit he divulged with an audience. I'm not sure I can handle anything bigger.

He's doesn't answer straightaway as he watches the legionnaires that will fly to Mareen with us board a separate jet. One of his marshals, Iyko, is among them. I still don't know her well, but I'm glad she's the one who's coming along to help me coordinate things with them. She formerly showed my team more than one small kindness when our sides were at war, and she didn't have to; it makes me already trust her a decent bit.

"Send a Comm; I've got to go," I tell Ajani, growing antsy with the urge to be home now that everybody is on the craft waiting for me and then all that's left is to fly out.

I'm so impatient that I've already placed one foot forward when he says, "I'd like us to try at being true allies, as the augurs advised. And even if they hadn't, I was planning on us getting here eventually. My goals for my Empire and my people aren't so different from your goals for your Republic and your people."

Yup. He's definitely setting a record for how many times you can stun the shit out of a person in one day.

I don't try to curb the frown—although it's not because I'm repulsed by his offer or his comparison of us two. In many ways, he might be right. "That's not possible if I'm going to be a part of Mareen's regime change and fight *for* its people. Those same people, even with the Tribunal ousted, would never accept it. There's too much bloody history— all of it on your Empire's part." I don't deliver it as a scathing remark. Merely a truth.

Ajani shakes his head. "Does Mareen really not teach its youth the whole historical truth? Has it scrubbed it from memory and record?"

I frown again. "What do you mean?"

"Mareen once invaded *this* continent and attempted genocide. It occurred right at the end of the Pantheon Age. The Republic raised and led a militant order of planet-wide zealots who aimed to cull *all* Pantheon-blessed on Iludu. The Principal Continent has always borne the highest concentration of those like us, so the Republic's despicable order crossed the Tumultuous Sea and hunted blood-gifted Accacians and other Pantheon-blessed before Mareen ever turned its bigoted slaughter inward. Nkosi's predecessor was an empress who, fortunately, was successful in protecting this continent's people and forcing the zealots back across the sea. Nkosi was a warmongering, power-mad tyrant, but when he took the throne, he easily garnered support for his conquest campaigns because of the crimes Mareen led against us and that the majority of the Minor Continent either joined in on or stepped aside to allow."

I digest what he says, and don't need to question it. Amaka herself hinted at something similar during our last communing. Then there's the fact that the Republic's current rot had to have started somewhere. So I say to Ajani: "I . . . can believe that."

Ajani turns to me, astonished. But then he nods. "I suppose you readily could after the harm your Republic visited on you. Think about my offer, Ikenna. With the combined strength of our Pantheon Blessings and levels of influence, we can do more than liberate the world from Nkosi. We can work to make it better for everyone all-around.

You keep wondering at my true motive. I see it every time you look at me. Here it is: from one magically endowed to another, I am telling you that I'm not only concerned with the welfare of the blood-gifted, I want to see a world where every living and future Pantheon-blessed individual is free to live their life *anywhere* in the open and thrive without the stigma of our link to the gods making us hated and feared." His words burn with passion and fervor. So much so that I chew on what he's said and take my time with a response when I was in a hurry only moments ago to ascend the jet's ramp.

"Your pursuit is noble, and Iludu's definitely overdue for planet-wide change," I say after some time. "Your proposal *is* appealing. We have a shit-ton of too much bloody history—too many fears and distrust and old grudges between nations and peoples that sprang up during the Pantheon Age and after from the power vacuums that were left when the gods were kicked out." Honestly, more than Mareen needs a restart. *Iludu* needs a restart. It's what really gave me pause to slow down and see this conversation through. And I could help give this restart to the planet if I get behind Ajani's mission. I could help other people like me who've long been forced to hide who they are and live with the daily burdens of fear for their lives and fear of discovery. But . . .

That's an entirely new mission and I still have an equally necessary, equally huge, and equally challenging one to tackle presently.

"I can't say yes; I can't join your cause," I tell Ajani. "Mareen comes first for me. At least for now. The change it needs will take copious attention and time. It might take years. Likely decades to restructure *decades* of toxic indoctrination. And there are people, like me, in the Republic who need my specific help. Not the Pantheon-blessed, but the akulu. I must make a better way for them before I fight for anything else."

"I don't like the answer, but I understand it," says Ajani respectfully. Dare I say, *admiringly*.

I awkwardly finger the handle of my Khanaian blade, which is back where it belongs on my hip, giving myself something to do other than stay washed in the bizarre-as-shit discomfort the sentiments coming from him induce.

Ajani, Accacia's new Blood Emperor in duties and in the hearts of its people, if not by rites yet, who's just offered me earnest allyship, also tosses me a pseudo smile that I could mistake as an offer of friendship too.

This weirdness means it is right about time to throw out a quip, get my ass moving, and stride to the jet.

If circumstances were different, if prior events were different, I might accept Ajani's proposal to work toward something similar to what Grandfather and Mustaph once had. They aren't, and it's why I hang back to grind out a reminder Ajani—and I—need to hear: "Rykos. Even if I find myself free of duties in Mareen someday, no day will come where I forget that you led its siege."

To his credit, Ajani grimaces and looks sorrowful. But apologies won't do shit for all the people who were slaughtered, all the families torn apart, all the innocent, civilian lives snuffed out as it burned.

And, perhaps, he doesn't see them as innocent. Perhaps he believes the ends justified the means. That those people had to die so that he could, eventually, depose Nkosi and usher in peace.

But peace that requires that much blood . . . I can't accept such self-righteous rationale. I can't accept this man doesn't still have that ruthless monster lurking underneath.

But then he surprises me once more.

"I was ordered by Nkosi to raze Rykos and spare no Mareenian citizens," Ajani says, and I'm about to tell him I don't want to hear it when he holds up a hand, asking for some patience.

Fuck you and your god-shitting patience.

And yet I somehow hold my tongue.

"It was an order I made the decision to follow—for the greater outcome. I own and accept full responsibility for it. But, if it makes a difference, I tried to mitigate the casualties among the most vulnerable. I had my marshals and a team quietly shuttle what women, children, and elderly they could across the border to safety in Khanai."

I almost don't think I've heard him right. Yet, I did. "Why would you bother? Why would you take the risk?" Maybe I don't have him figured out.

Ajani slides his hands into pockets of his Emperor robes that I didn't notice were sewn into the fanciful material before. "I'm many things, including a ruthless bastard at times, but as I said before, I do have a code."

"I'm going to verify Rykos."

"Of course you are. And after?"

"Afterward, if it checks out, I still make no promises I'll like you," I say. "But it will help me trust you ruling Accacia better."

Seeing as how this is Ajani I'm dealing with, I'm sure that was the point of this sharing-is-caring exercise. Earnestness aside, the man will always have an agenda. I can't be mad when he hasn't lied yet and when his aims keep helping mine, though.

Our one-on-one ends up being good for another thing too.

When I finally march forward to the jet, and the battles waiting for me in Mareen, I do so while trusting that I can wage a rebellion without being attacked on my flank.

Which frees up all the more focus for me to burn the Tribunal down with.

29

I DO THREE THINGS AS soon as we're in the air. The first requires me to school my face into cool professionalism as I wait for the Grand Monarch of Khanai to pick up my call.

When he answers, a holograph of his form stands in the center aisle of the jet, donned in full court dress. The gold crown sparkling with purple amethi rulizi, black diamonds, and jade sits atop his long locs. The black sabine's pelt is draped across his wide shoulders. The gold herringbone chains crisscrossing his broad chest are present also. Mustaph appears exactly as the proud king I left in Khanai and have always known him to be, while looking nothing like the man I recall who was like an uncle to me my entire life. There are fresh lines wrinkling his dark skin, a dimness to his brown eyes that usually glint like precious obsidian, and a general heaviness about him that makes him seem as if he's aged decades in a handful of months. I keep the mask I've chosen to wear for this call erected; I don't dare drop the barrier. I *cannot*; the hurt remains too fresh. Mustaph's actions and choices that he kept from me will always remain the blade he slipped between my ribs in the dark, which I—*we*—can't recover from.

Likewise Enoch, who is at his side, glowers at me with clearly similar sentiments of permanent betrayal. I study him, if only to appraise the enemy I've made and will never be free of. The Crown Prince is different too. He's more hardened, gruffer than the boy-turned-man I'd first reunited with when Khanai hosted the war summit. I've played a role in the loss of some of that kind, easy merriment Enoch always exuded, and for it, I *am* sorry. But he played his own part in our schism, and what's done is done.

I become infinitely grateful that I opted not to make this call with my personal Comm Unit's vid interface. Had I done it, my holograph would be standing back inside the Jade Palace's throne room with the Grand Monarch I tried to kill there and the son who wants me dead for it in turn. It would've made things too personal, and I refuse to go there. I don't have the time or the head space for it. Instead, I dispatched the call with the jet's Comm system, and what Mustaph and Enoch see on their end is a vidfeed of me and my surroundings, Mareenian team included. Which helps to keep up the walls and not have this meeting end in a mess.

"We should discuss what will happen on my end and your end with the legionnaires you're allowing into Khanai," I say to Mustaph, getting straight to the point, the *only* point, of this call.

His eyes tighten at the corners in sadness, or dismay, or disappointment, I'm not sure. All of those emotions irk the hell out of me; however, outwardly, I keep the decorous mask in place.

I can get through this without drama.

Mustaph must decide on a similar sentiment because when he speaks it is only to say, "I am glad that you called so we can coordinate how I will facilitate movement of the Accacian unit to your side." I think that he's done until he adds, "*And* the Khanaian unit of three thousand more men that will travel with them if things devolve to such a state that you need an army."

I blink. Wait for Mustaph to say more. He doesn't.

I'm so rattled that whatever professionalism I've tried to maintain disintegrates. "If that is supposed to absolve you, it doesn't," I let Mustaph know. Yes, I realize how hypocritical that sounds, but I'm not the one ludicrously trying for absolution here. I know what I did, and I know there is no forgetting it.

"It's not an apology. You don't deserve or get one. I'm not even sure why my father believes you deserve to draw breath," Enoch cuts in. He's dressed in his Emrir uniform, purple coat with snowglory flowers curling over each of his shoulders and blue steel ceremonial sword buckled to his waist. During this face-off he doesn't grip the sword's pummel, a lion's head in mid-roar, in a clear indication that he intends to one day use the blade to cut me down. But he might as well. Because as he stands beside the Grand Monarch, feet planted inches apart in an attack stance, he is vibrating with violence—and a vow—all the same.

I flash him teeth, since this has already turned into a shitstorm, and sink a warning into my voice when I say, "You're the feared Lion of Khanai, and that is lovely. But don't let the honorific go to your head. I'm the Emperor of Accacia, for the time. A half god, too, it turns out. The former, I earned from going to war instead of craven capitulation. The other . . . apparently, I was born with the power to kick your ass. Today, tomorrow, decades from now—I can do so at any point. While you have every right to be furious with me, remember who and what I am and don't make me have to rob your parents of a son and your dear sister of a brother. I'm aware you're a threat, Enoch, and I won't come after you so long as you don't give me a reason. If your father is dangling soldiers as a show of some comity that might exist between us, let the fact that you remained breathing after the shit you pulled in the keep and that you'll *stay* breathing be mine."

"Peace, my child," Mustaph says when Enoch makes no move to

lessen his display of hostility. He declares it with a tone of authority and finality, and slowly, Enoch pulls his shit together.

My gods, is this what Ajani has to deal with from me when he's being the bigger person? I almost owe *him* an apology.

Almost.

I hang up with the Gyidis after basically discerning (and yes, it damn hurts) that Mustaph's peace offering is less about family and more about throwing support behind me as the blade he uses against the Tribunal that ordered his death.

The Grand Monarch might've expressed it could be both, but it doesn't make things any less fucked up.

With that taken care of, I make my second call. It is much more pleasant. Even entertaining,

For Edryssa Cyphir, I do call from my personal Comm Unit. The Lady of Lusian answers wearing a sheer, emerald-studded sheath that leaves zero to the imagination and a smirk that says even more. "Took you long enough," the syndicate boss snaps. "You didn't end up needing my mercs, but you did use my cargo jet and guns. That counts as me fulfilling my end of the bargain—do not think to renege."

I wave her off, half amused by her threats. "I was never gonna argue the point. I'm simply calling to tell you I'm ready for those mentioned mercs now after all." I can't show up in Mareen with visible legionnaires in tow without looking like a traitor. However, I can bring a private army with me that has no ties to a foreign government. It will matter little that they're criminals if the war house heads have shown themselves to be criminals, and I set *my* criminals to helping the people as soon as I touch down.

"I thought I was getting off too easy. Fine, I get it: Nkosi's dead, and you're going after Mareen's Tribunal, which killed Verne," she says, not missing a beat. She inclines her head. "You slew the planet's monster, and you're about to go behead all the heads of its snake. Just don't forget your promise, girl." This time it doesn't sound like a threat, but more a plea from one ally to another. I appreciate it even as she appraises me, much like I did Enoch on my last call. Admiration and schemes glint in her gray stare. "At the end of this, your voice might hold *too* much weight in the world. It's a good thing we're allies, and we'll stay that way. Whatever you need, Ikenna Amari, you will have it, and remember my friendship later."

Reed is of course rubbing his eyes by the time the call disconnects. Impressively, he holds his peace. "Edryssa and Mustaph are the last of them," is what he says instead. "Lusian, Khanai, Ska'kesh, Braxxis, every other microstate in the east, the entirety of the ones in the west, *and* Lythe have all extended sentiments in some manner that they aren't your enemy, they want the Tribunal gone, and they'll let your actions speak for what you being a Zenith might mean." He's gone from rubbing his eyes to grinning triumphantly by the time he finishes. The last part, about the world's response to me being a half god, is one of the key pieces of information he passed the extra days we remained in Accacia ascertaining, while vouching for me or negotiating where he needed to.

Everyone else is grinning too. We're not going into this next fight with the odds stacked against us—for once.

Naturally, that means the cosmos decides to enjoy a laugh and fuck with me.

"Not to be a buzzkill," comes Dannica's terse voice, "but a friend just sent a message that the Tribunal is about to hold a postwar briefing that will stream to the wider Republic, but not beyond its borders, and what they'll announce isn't good." Her violet stare is grave and fixed on her Comm Unit; her eyes move left to right as she further reads what's on the screen. Along with Dane and Caiman, she's been quietly identifying Praetorians and scions who aren't so happy with the Tribunes' handling of the war, want them to answer for it, and are willing to pass along pertinent information about what the Tribunal is currently doing.

Dannica's head snaps to Caiman mid-read. She visibly winces. "I . . .

ummm . . . I need to tell you something before the briefing starts . . . about Rossi War House."

"What?" Caiman grits out. "Just tell me what bullshit those who survived are shoveling."

Dannica shakes her head. "It's not that. After a Tribunal Council vote this morning, there *is* no more Rossi War House. At least, not as a formal entity. With Haymus dead, you labeled as an enemy of the Republic and a deserter, and all but a few adult male scions dead since the Rossis were among the upper crust who fought on the front lines, the Tribunal has dissolved Rossi War House, seized its accounts, and turned all assets and holdings under its name over for redistribution to strengthen the remaining houses postwar."

"They fucking *what*?" Caiman explodes. "*We* didn't go to ground! *We* fought and sacrificed our lives in defense of the Republic and that's how we're repaid?" Yet, for all the bluster, behind the outburst, Caiman Rossi slips into the devastated skin of a man who has lost *everything* in a blink. The grief and misery that crumple his face are gut-wrenching and worse than when he learned that most of the Rossis lost their lives fighting one of the Red Order. Before—while a severe wound in itself— he'd only lost individuals among his war house. But now he's lost the institution he loves and that reared him, which he's always intended to return to the Republic and helm. It has to be like losing his entire identity. Like having his heart, or both lungs, or some other vital organ he can't live without hacked away.

Greysen, seated beside him, reaches out and grips Caiman's hand, and Caiman does nothing to shake free. Greysen scrubs his other hand down the front of his face. "I—I don't know what to say. This is so messed up."

I'm not sure if I should speak up and say something in support—or that I *can*. Chiefly because the Rossis were part of what we're trying to overturn. War houses that exist as an aristocratic class with oligarchical powers really should be obsolete in a true republic. However, politics isn't *all* this is about. This is about the various elements that we think of as family and kin and roots and binding ties and reciprocal loyalty. Caiman is my squad mate, he's suffered a heavy wound, and I decide I'd like to—and need to—hand him empathy for the loss of so much. Yet, I'm also aware he might not welcome it; he might detest me for it. It may deliver a subsequent blow he can't take after my confession in Accacia. I consider saying nothing. But that doesn't feel right either. Not after we've been comrades fighting on the same side for as much time as we have been and not after the accords we did come to. So I risk his wrath being tossed my way, while phrasing things carefully, to promise him something I never thought I would to a Rossi.

"I'm with you. We all are. We'll get your house back in some form."

His gold eyes startle, widening at me seated across from him as if he can't believe the promise comes from me.

"I can't give you your father back," I say, laying it out in the open. "And I am sorry about that. I'm sorry about how it hurts you, even if I can't be sorry for what I did. You don't deserve to lose everything. I will help you get back what I can: the holdings that were stripped from you."

For several seconds, Caiman regards me with steel. But then, he nods. "Thank you, Amari, for saying that. I—you didn't have to. I appreciate it."

"Do we have a transmission of the stream incoming too?" asks Haynes after clearing his throat. "Not to take away from this moment, or ignore your grief, man," Haynes says to Caiman with surprising sympathy, "but we should see the lay of things for ourselves if we can."

"Am I good at what I do, or am I good?" Dannica winks, her cheekiness always lightening the mood when the team needs it. "Give me a second; it'll be here."

A few moments later, a grand hall inside Rhysien Manor, the family home large enough to house every relative that the war house maintains, appears on the back wall of the jet. Before today, according to former intel, the estate has been vacant since Accacia attacked the Isles and the war house heads took themselves and their relatives into hiding. Now the mansion swarms with scions from all fifteen—fourteen minus the Rossis—of the war house lines, the remaining Tribunes (who decided Brock's, Caan's, and Haymus's seats were better left vacant during wartime than to elevate untested successors—a clear power grab that intel turned up), and the Republic's surviving Praetorians.

I grimace when doing a quick count of the third, as I know everybody aboard the jet does. I also know the instinctive cataloging isn't merely because we'll likely be fighting against some of them soon. It's because they are us, and we are them. That is our rank. Our brethren. Our comrades. Our *people*. In the moment, it goes for even the ones among them we don't like because I count perhaps half of the sizable number of Praetorians that held the rank before the war. I clench my jaw when I note something else.

"Mostly Praetorian scions survived." Dane, a legacy who is not a war house scion, beats me to sharing that discovery. "Yeah, that's what our eyes on things back home told us, but *seeing* it for myself . . ."

Greysen's laugh is bitter. "It is *no* coincidence."

Liim, a non-scion legacy like Dane, curses in a manner that's somewhere between a ragged breath and a vicious hiss.

Caiman is—*was*—the sole scion on the jet. Greysen occupies the same position as his other former Alpha brothers aboard. Haynes, Dannica, and Reed were born labourii.

Me . . . I'm a legacy with a labourii great-grandfather whose grandfather's Legatus achievement placed her on a similar playing field as a scion—or would have if I wasn't an akulu. Obviously, I'm straddling multiple crisscrossing lines; but the straddling makes the stark nepotism that's resulted in so many of our brethren's deaths shred through me in triplicate.

"*Gods, I hate them,*" Haynes says.

At the same time Dannica asks, "How are they this awful? Seriously, I want to know. How do you get here from the rebellion against a tyrannical war god for freedom, which founded our country?"

"You lose sight of the who and the what and the why. Lose sight of the principles that really matter," answers Reed tightly.

"It's not that hard when elitism and classism are upheld and fear-mongering is used for the rationale of too much," supplies Caiman, voice low.

"Do not put this on yourself," I growl, trying to assuage the guilt that's plainly riddling him. "You're not them."

"I was for a long time."

"You were as a child and then for like the six weeks after we graduated during the trials. By the end of them, you started seeing some truths and the stars-ton of bullshit they perpetuate. That counts for a lot."

I hold his gaze, don't let him look away until some of the self-recrimination bleeds from his demeanor.

We turn our attention back to the feed and watch as the treacherous Tribunes move from among their respective clusters of war house relatives to the high-back chairs behind the podium at the front of the hall. The eight of us witness this in utter silence and cold fury.

My eyes pop wide at the person I watch move among the Tribunes and drop into Rhysien War House's Council seat. *Selene*, not Sutton, occupies the chair.

"What. The. Shit?" Dannica gapes, seeing the same thing. "I did *not* have that info beforehand, Kenna," she says hurriedly. "I would've told you."

"I know," I say, head spinning and not really believing the sight. "Sutton is in that room. So why is her ass in his Tribunal spot? Furthermore . . ." I start pulling it together, pulling *myself* together, and thinking. "There is no game Sutton would be playing at where he'd let her occupy it in his place. Not even if she was acting out his will that he, for some reason, could not. Her brothers survived the war." Most of Epsilon did because they were nowhere near the front lines. "One of them would've been chosen to represent Sutton if he needed someone to do it."

"Since none of Rhysien's sons are up there, that has to leave Selene *as* Rhysien War House's head." Reed draws in a sharp breath after voicing what I cannot because I will lose my shit if I speak it out loud. The only reason I'm remaining somewhat calm is because the bitch I want to lose it on is across an ocean.

And that won't be the case soon.

"She isn't wearing a Tribune's coat," Caiman notes. "She remains in Praetorian battle dress."

He's right, and it's an oddity in a sea of oddities. "I need details," I say, fists clenched. "Fucking details on if she really is a Tribune and how she accomplished it, or what the hell else is going on and why she's sitting among them if she isn't? If you can dig them up before we get to Mareen, Dannica, that'd be fantastic." Selene doesn't get to keep it, whatever *it* is, because dead women can't retain shit. Beyond that, if she's now involved in steering Mareen in the direction it's been going, she's become more than a personal revenge target. She's an entity that's a part of the regime we're ousting, and presently, she's an unknown fucking factor that I do not like existing one bit.

I only pull out of the beginnings of a hazy rage because the briefing starts and—surprise, surprise—it is Selene who rises and struts to the podium. Old Ikenna would be fuming at this sight, but I want to be 100 percent clearheaded so I miss nothing when she says whatever she is going to . . . and shove it down her throat when I finally meet her.

It turns out to be a fight that I damn near lose when my former, traitorous friend stands at the podium with manicured nails a gleaming dark green, red hair in a braid, gray eyes superior, and mien gratingly presenting like she's the new fucking Legatus, postwar.

I brace for her to proclaim it. I'm shocked when she doesn't, and only marginally stay above a blood rage at that lack of revelation. Somehow, though, what she says is worse. First, she speaks of reconstruction mandates the Tribunal is putting into place, including curfew laws, bans against future protests and riots, and requirements that any and all food, shelter-related, and other essential resources be turned over to the Tribunal for redistribution among the populace.

"I can bet where those resources are actually being distributed," says Reed during a pause.

"The same lot that's inside Rhysien Manor with her and who is benefiting from pilfering Rossi War House's considerable assets," Greysen says darkly. He stabs a finger at the vidfeed. "They all look like they're sitting damn comfortable and pampered right now, and certainly weren't facing any privation wherever they hid during the war. I can bet the only thing trickling down to those who actually have need is piss in the face."

Caiman curses; fresh embarrassment and shame color his pale face as he knows his own house would be doing the same thing if they still existed. Before anyone else can comment, Selene continues, not lingering too long on the shitty way of life the mandates will usher forth. As appalled by these strictures as I am, it's nothing compared to how I feel about Selene. By the end of her recital of the extreme new classism she's codified into law, she's become a stranger. I've never met the girl who speaks in support of essentially subjugating the majority of the Republic to abject poverty for the foreseeable future. Who proudly proclaims the Tribunal's decision to lower the commencement age to fifteen (*which are children*), enforce that one-third of yearly graduates be assigned either common soldier or Praetorian rank to replenish their numbers, and reactivate service duty of recent military retirees for an undetermined time. Who, in her final act of betraying the person I called my sister, urges that while the rest of the world may accept me existing, Mareenians should not because they know better and they've always stood against anything having to do with the gods.

I study her, scrutinize the Tribunal behind her, and know for certain she includes the last part because *she* knows I am coming for her, and the Tribunal knows I am coming for it. Though barely noticeable, the slight tension most of them can't quite mask says it all.

The world knows they killed Grandfather.

I know they killed Grandfather.

And Selene knows me because *I* haven't changed on the most fundamental level. She knows that even if I let his murder stand while I dealt with Nkosi, once he died, Verne Amari's assassin—and the ones who sanctioned it—would be next. Furthermore, she knows that if I took on the Blood Emperor to spare Mareen's people, I am not about to let their own Tribunal get away with harming them.

"Ikenna Amari is not a friend of Mareen," Selene says in closing. "She remains a fugitive and enemy of your government. Do not mistake that she is anything else. If any citizen should encounter her, or the rogue Praetorians traveling with her, it should be reported immediately. She is dangerous, hostile, and unpredictable, and so are they. Their capture and executions are of the utmost security importance to the Republic."

I smile for the first time since the accursed briefing started. Selene's initial falsehood aside, everything else she said isn't a lie.

I'm glad she's aware and terrified enough to try to make *me* into the monster.

"Could you facilitate messages being transmitted from us to people in Mareen other than your contacts?" I ask Dannica.

"Yes," she says readily.

"Perfect." I smile bigger. "If everyone's all right with it I'd like two dispatched. One that's widespread to Mareen's people that states the Tribunes have no right to govern people they've chosen to sacrifice and tyrannize; and we are coming to Mareen with food, supplies, credits, clothing, *protection*, and whatever else the populace needs, which will be given generously and indiscriminately. I'd like the other one to go straight to the Tribunes and Selene Rhysien and apprise the fuckers

they don't need to renew a hunt. We're coming to them, we'll be aiding Mareen's people and proving why the Tribunal is unfit to lead, and
that they better enjoy the lush life now because it's going to be snatched
away from them as easily as I took away the Blood Emperor's power."
I intend to say everything level; simply make a reasonable case and not
seem like I'm being led by my temper and rage at Selene and the Tribunal.

That's what I *intend*.

And I do. I really try to hold the brunt of the bloodlust in, be the
cool-tempered general, the even-keeled leader. But it turns suffocating
and is a skin I know in my bones doesn't fit. So . . . I just stop pretending to be someone I'm not. The cabin gets doused with a red-and-gold
light as soon as I do, the air crackling with the electric current that's my
power I let arc out of me freely.

I don't rein it back in.

I am what I am.

"I vote fuck the circuitous games and guileful plans," I say to my
team while I'm being *me* and everything that means. "We've tried that
way a few times, and it went to shit. So let's skip it." I had to resort to
doing things *my* way those times anyhow. That is what worked, and I
understand now why it did. I'm a warrior first and foremost. We all are.
Always have been. Always will be.

So let's warrior the fuck out.

"When it comes to being the blade that hurtles directly at enemies
and cuts them down, I know what I'm doing, I know how to be it, and
I know how to win. All I am asking is you let me—let *us*—do what we
do best. We're killers. That's what they made us. Yes, we can reason.
Yes, we can find empathy and compassion. But those aren't the tools we
need right now. What we need is what kept the Blood Empire at bay.
What makes us *Praetorians*. That's the only way we strike at the Tribunes. And if the people are behind us from the time we touch down—
and a lot of them *are* going to side with us if for no other reason than

they saw I killed Nkosi and I'm promising to feed them—we don't have to go at them any other way because we'll look like heroes, a Zenith among us or no, not the traitors the Tribunal portrays."

"Of course Amari isn't satisfied with a mere change of guard," Caiman murmurs. "She wants to stir up mass rebellion alongside the bloodshed."

"Damn straight," I say, grinning.

He breaks into a grin himself. "Like it's been since Khanai: I'm on board to tear the whole shit down."

"Are you going to turn the glow off when you're kicking ass or leave it on and really put on a show?" asks Haynes. "It's scary—and sexy—as shit."

"Yes . . . she is," Reed says. He holds my gaze, an intensity in his stare that's so intimate it relays that as always, he's with me, but he'll leave what he specifically wants to say for later.

It's proven I've got the best squad possible beside me when none of the rest disagree either.

"By the way, I have a good cohort name for us," I say and execute a showy, wiseass bow, feeling fantastic, confident, and settling into the Ikenna I will be on this mission. It was the third item on my task list and got waylaid by the briefing.

"Finally," Haynes says.

"Sorry—been a little busy killing the Blood Emperor and all," I snap.

Haynes raises his hand in defense, while Dannica's eyebrows shoot up. "Do tell, wise one."

"You're going to be a smartass too?"

"Until I die." Dannica grins. Meanwhile, Liim leans forward in his seat with interest and Greysen turns slightly wary. So does Dane—my homicidal smile sliding back into place while I'm glowing probably has something to do with it.

Reed . . . Reed is still looking at me with that unnerving yet silent intensity.

Caiman snorts. "Took your sweet time with that one, huh? This better be good, Amari, if you needed *weeks* to deliver. Besides, I need *something* positive today."

"I got sidetracked saving the world, asshole," I shoot back with no real heat.

"Don't keep us waiting," Haynes says. "You already got the dramatic lights emanating from you . . . now let the words come forth!"

"*Invictus*," I tell them all, supplying what they asked of me in Lusian. "That's our name because the Blood Emperor didn't defeat us; neither will the Tribunes. They *won't* win this fight. They don't get to hold on to Mareen, they don't get what they are stealing from the people, and they certainly won't be executing a single one of us."

"Invictus," Liim says, like he's trying it on for size.

"Invictus," Dane says with conviction.

I look at the rest of them, and one by one—Dannica, Haynes, Caiman, Greysen, Reed—all say our name.

Invictus.

"They want to take us out," I say. "They think we're monsters that need to be hunted down. But we're not. We're a team. We're Invictus.

"And I'd like to see them try to stop us."

30

WE FLY INTO ELKSPUR, A farming village just south of Krashen that escaped the war.

Edryssa's mercs meet us in the rural area where the Tribunal has been herding *hundreds* of displaced survivors and then forgetting about those who aren't scions or high-standing legacies. We at once set the Cyphir Syndicate to passing out food, toiletries, clothing, and small toys for children, erecting tents so people no longer sleep on the ground of seized croplands, and securing the village's perimeter against any efforts by the Tribunal to send soldiers to halt things. Basically, we give people the governing their government denied them and turn Elkspur into our stronghold, which extends them protection too. It delivers necessary aid and makes a very public statement about what Invictus, the rogue Praetorians, have returned to the Republic to do.

Given the warning the Tribunal issued about us, I'd expected them to send Praetorians to arrest us soon after we landed on Mareenian soil. It's why we set up Invictus's personal camp in an unpopulated field three miles east of Elkspur, so the battle would claim no civilian casualties. However, five days pass without the clash and with my out-of-uniform legionnaires running patrols around our camp and turning up nothing. The passage of time makes everyone nervous; we know firsthand how the Tribunal operates. Their inaction up front means they have a precise reason for waiting, a precise strike they want to launch at a precise moment.

But *we* have a precise reason for the current calm before the storm, too, after all, and in many ways our training is their training. On our end, Invictus wants to take them out simultaneously, so they all die at once and no Tribune is left alive to drag this out.

The night of the fifth day is the eve of our attack. The eight of us stand in a war tent around a table that has a blueprint of Rhysien Manor marked up with Praetorian guard routes, the number of soldiers the latest reconnaissance relayed are stationed there, and the hall the Tribunal meets in. I've yet to unearth why Selene sat among the Tribunal and gave its most recent briefing, but maybe it's because her family home is the Tribunal's transient seat of government. We strike at that seat in the morning, and if everything goes right, this will all be over before the sun sets. Tomorrow, I am getting my revenge from all who will attend this Tribunal's last council session, and extracting Mareen from rotting hands.

I am also getting my answers from Selene—every last one of them.

"Is everyone good?" Reed asks. He's insisted—because he's Reed—that we comb over plans a final time. My grandfather's protégé stands beside me at the head of the war table and reflects every inch of the tempered, methodical co-general, the perfect counterpart to me, the brazen, charge-ahead blood blade. As the squad assures Reed they're fine to go, there are no gaps we've left exposed or variables we could foresee yet haven't considered, I gaze at Verne Amari's mentee and glimpse the future for the Republic that Grandfather intended when he became

Reed's hensei. If I was supposed to give Grandfather his war house, Reed was supposed to succeed him as Legatus. My lips curl slightly as bittersweetness washes over me; I experience a moment where I both mourn the loss of what could've been had Grandfather lived to usher in his vision, and look forward to what Invictus will help bring to the Republic, which is far different, far beyond, and far better than Grandfather's dreams.

"If Reed's done holding us hostage," I say, breaking out of my thoughts to do something important before the squad disbands, "I have a last order of business too." I can't stop grinning like a fool at everybody's puzzled looks.

This is going to be spectacular.

I stoop, haul a box from beneath the table, and place it in the center of the blueprint. "This should make up for me taking forever on a name," I say.

"Is it candy? I could go for some sweets right now," Haynes says.

"Like your ass needs more sweets," Dannica retorts. She smirks, peeks behind him, and pinches his hip. "On second thought, maybe you do. You're losing some thickness, my friend."

Haynes looks at his own backside in actual fear, despite the fact that his giant frame continues to sport a seriously shapely and luscious ass.

"I think she's messing with you," Liim says.

"You butt is fantastic," Dane adds.

Dannica's eyes twinkle before they roll back and she shakes her head.

"I'm going to start messing with all of you if you don't shut up," I grumble. "You're ruining the moment."

"What do you have for us?" Reed asks, his low, steady tone exuding all I could want from a voice. It takes me a second to remember what I was about to show them.

"Yes, right. I have something for all of us that will make a big difference tomorrow. Nkosi was a bastard, but I learned one thing from him: there's power in pageantry."

Haynes tilts his head to the side, eyeing the box. "I'm a little afraid of this box now."

"A little? I'm highly terrified. What's in there?" asks Greysen, sizing the box up too.

"You sure you didn't learn that pageantry lesson from the trials?" Caiman says, only half serious. He jabs a good-natured finger at Reed, Dannica, and Liim in turn. "Those three assholes had a Death Board going, remember?"

I laugh because the contrite look on their faces is just too good.

"Very true. Perhaps I did." I slide easily into the banter and realize how much it was also what's been missing for this team. We have a name, and we have the camaraderie, both essential weapons that need to be as sharp as any of the others for tomorrow.

This last piece will bring that—and us—all together irrevocably.

"Whatever," Dannica says, dramatically flicking the raven braid her hair is bound into over her shoulder. "That was *so* many months ago. What's in the box? Can we see already?"

Obliging and feeling particularly sentimental, I grab my Khanaian dagger—Grandfather's old dagger—and cut the tape running down the center. I open the flaps and step back. "We've now got badass combat suits with an Invictus cohort insignia. I—*we*—are not kicking the Tribunal's ass in plain tactical gear. We're Praetorians. In hearts, in minds, in souls, and in blood. They don't get the power to strip us of it, or to even *think* they've stripped us of it. Tomorrow, the people will see what true Praetorians are supposed to do and we'll look like true Praetorians while we set the standard."

Either my continued grin is contagious or everyone really misses a combat suit because the eight of us end up smiling like idiots after Dannica eagerly lays one of the suits out on the table for inspection. It's my first time seeing one, too, since I put in the order. I take in the design, the colors, the symbolism—and I congratulate myself because the suit is as fierce as our new cohort name and is worth every bit of the two unnamed future favors Edryssa charged me to procure and deliver. The microprene material (that will, on a more pragmatic level, provide us supple armor) bears black as the sole color of its pants portion, but the upper body is maroon with two vertical stripes (one a wartime gold and the other a peacetime white) slanting across the chest. An entwined *I* and *V* for Invictus, our cohort insignia, blazes gold high on the left bicep of the suit and over the spot that would cover one's heart.

"It's perfect," Reed says, standing behind me, his mouth close to my ear. He drops a kiss to the curve of my neck and hugs me like I've just given him the best present. Given all of the squad the best present.

It *is* perfect.

"We're ready," I declare.

"CAN YOU HANG back?" I say to Reed as the others are leaving.

He must hear the off note in my voice because his forehead creases. He doesn't say anything. Just does it and waits until we're alone to ask what's wrong.

I don't respond with words because the right ones to articulate the answer get stuck. With the rest of the world shut out, if only for a brief second, I do what I've been needing *so fucking bad* to do, what it's been *hell* not taking the time to do, since the Cara war camp. I wrap my arms around Reed, clutch him fiercely to me, and simply lay my head against his chest—I need to hear his pulse, especially tonight, feel his heartbeat and warmth beneath me, inhale the rich and present notes in his scent of Khanaian snowfalls, mountain storms, smoke, and steel, so I can obliterate the image that keeps haunting me: of seeing him stabbed and bleeding and dead in the pavilion. As I do it, I send up profuse thanks to the cosmos that he is standing in front of me alive and that I am alive to do so. And I ask the cosmos that things stay that way.

Reed clutches me, his arms shackling me to him, his hands tenderly stroking my spine. "Are you all right? What is it?" he asks with protective worry. His hold on me tightens, and it makes me press my body into his more. For a long time, I still can't manage words. I just keep being grateful that he didn't die in that pavilion.

"In the war camp . . ." I squeeze out once I'm less of an emotional mess and can speak. "I thought . . . I thought we'd never have a moment like this again. I thought Nkosi had taken this future from us when it had only started to form. But that bastard failed, and you're here. I'm just taking a moment to appreciate the hell out of being pitched that grace, all right? I didn't do it before because us, *being like this*, is a distraction. But tonight is different. Unforeseeable shit happens sometimes, and I don't want tomorrow's mission to get here without having done this."

"I get it," Reed says quietly. He presses a kiss to my temple, breathes in my scent, just as I haven't stopped breathing him in. "I get it too well because . . . because I love you, Ikenna," he says after an exhale that is ragged and tortured. "I love you, and if we're laying it bare, I am having an extremely difficult time being okay with tomorrow, regardless that it must get done. Unforeseen shit does happen, and the Tribunal feels more dangerous *for you*—and for all of us—than Nkosi. I've been thinking about this, and I can't stop. It's why I keep having us go over the details. Nkosi was the enemy that didn't know us. Mareen's Tribunal Council is the enemy that knows us, extensively, and trained and forged the weapons that have turned against them. They have in-depth knowledge of our strengths, our weakness, everything. They've profiled us every year as cadets and Praetorians, have been conducting psych evals since we were children. They've been the hands to literally shape us. I didn't say this in front of the others, but it makes me nervous. This enemy knows us better than we know them because they made us. It leaves me terrified. Not of them, though. I haven't allowed myself to feel like this for anyone in a long time—since my parents; I *cannot* lose you."

Reed doesn't add *like I lost them*. But it rings inside the tent, shrilly.

My heart squeezes in empathy, while crashing against my chest and coming perilously close to bursting right out at his declaration—and admissions.

I kiss his strong jaw, along the smooth, sun-kissed skin that he freshly shaved this morning, offering comfort and hopefully easing some of the strain. I nip his full bottom lip, languishing in its lushness and softness. *In case I don't*—I abruptly cut off the thought.

I cup Reed's face how he's been cupping mine. "I love you too, Darius Reed. It's a first for me as well. It's terrain I have no clue how to navigate, but it's nice to discover I'm not the only one struggling with what it means to be in love with the person I go to battle beside and how to function without losing my mind over worry. It makes it feel more normal and like something we can figure out together. Which . . . I think maybe I have an inkling of how to deal. The fact that I love you, and that it means I'll always be frantic about your welfare in a fight, has stood out knife-sharp for me since Khanai. When you were fighting Enoch and a slew of our people were falling and dying around us, I kept thinking, kept being terrified, that you'd be next. That's what made me blindly pray—I reached out to whoever and whatever might listen because I couldn't watch you die. Amaka could've made a bargain with me that imploded the planet that day, and my answer would've been a swift yes as long as you got out and home. It's a decision I'd make without remorse every time in the future if you're at risk. I think there's something to be learned there.

"Damn what the Tribunes know about us. I guarantee what they *don't* know is much greater. Specifically, where you and I are concerned because those assholes didn't shape us. Not truly. Verne Amari did, and I guarantee he *never* let them glimpse all he was comprised and capable of. And how we feel about each other, that fear of losing each other, could be a strength if you're worried about them knowing us too well. I did what I did to get us out of Khanai because of my feelings for you, and it's something nobody, myself included, would've predicted beforehand."

Reed nods, seeming to internalize it. He turns his face into my touch at his cheek. He clasps my hand, squeezing it, and lays a kiss to my palm. "Thank you for helping me place things into a different perspective. I needed to hear that." He kisses the bridge of my nose, featherlight and disarmingly reverential, pouring the gratitude he's expressed into the loving gesture. "You'd never allow me to, because you're too much the fierce and stubborn warrior yourself, but know the feeling is the godsdamned same and if I could, I'd fight all your battles for you—if only to just hand you the peace and solace you never seem to have but keep seeking and absolutely deserve. I know you can handle it all yourself, but I don't want you to. One day, I want you to not *need* to be anybody's blade. I want you to no longer have to accrue blood on your ledger. To have to let death and war and endless battles and anger and strife consume your existence.

"I'd go to war with the very cosmos to hand you that."

His vow leaves me breathless. Makes my heart somersault in my chest.

Reed's fingers cradle my chin and tip my head upward because, apparently, he isn't done sending me into cardiac arrest yet. "You may be our blade, Kenna, but I am *your* sword, your blaster, your shield, *permanently*. It'd take the planet cleaving in two with you on one side of the chasm and me on the other to tear me away from your side. And even then, I'd battle my way back to you. You aren't dying tomorrow." He says it as if he's commanded it and his will alone makes it fact. Just like that, Reed's trademark hyperconfidence snaps back into place, and I worry less in turn, having faith that as long as Reed goes into things as Reed, and I go into them as Ikenna, we make a damn durable, hard-to-kill pair.

"You aren't dying tomorrow either, Darius," I let him know. "I want to share that future you paint with you when this is over."

He kisses me then. And I kiss him back, my throat and chest, and perhaps even my soul, spasming at the enormity of everything we've just promised each other.

When he deepens the kiss, shifting from tenderness to hunger, I give as good as I get. A tide of something molten, all-consuming, and all-powerful, something that feels akin to lust but more potent and too intense to be simply labeled lust, sweeps me away.

He says he isn't going anywhere,

Neither am I.

I still want this night.

In fact, I need it more than ever.

Not caring where we are, I make it so we're fitting together as compactly and connected as two beings can get. I drag my hands down the length of the rigid planes of his torso, stuff them under his shirt, and move around to his delicious, corded back. I revel in the feel of his muscles strengthened, hardened, and honed by eleven years of brutal academy training and three solid years of Praetorian-level conditioning.

Reed shudders, kisses me more urgently. I shudder too. At once I know the name for the sweeping cascade of things I'm feeling that isn't merely lust: *desire*. That's what this is, and the distinction is crucial. Desire is more than just wanting to fuck Reed senseless and wanting him to fuck me senseless back. Make no mistake, I do want that. But I also burn with the compulsion to crawl inside Reed's skin and wanting him to crawl inside *my* skin. I want to tangle and tussle with him always. I want us to be in each other's orbit, each other's gravitational pull, always. I want to claim him. Own him. Possess him in the most carnal, intimate of ways, so the After is aware Reed is mine and there is no way in hell it gets to reclaim him. Hellbent on diving headfirst into that desire and my claiming, I reach up, skimming my fingers along the silken column of Reed's throat, breaking our kiss momentarily to lick and suck and nip at the tattoo on his neck—the stoic, black, bold, four-pointed star of the Republic that stands at fierce attention and proclaims to the world that this man is a soldier. A warrior. That like me, he's a fighter. That combat is in his blood. It's not a bad thing. It will *never* be a bad thing. It's a heady thing that induces shivers and makes him a wicked temptation.

Makes him mine.

His next breath escapes him raggedly. "*Ikenna.*" My name is a plea and a caution. "We can't go this far. Not here. Later . . . after tomorrow . . . we need a more secure place . . ." He says this, but his gaze is half-lidded, his blue eyes have darkened to the cobalt hue that means he wants things to proceed as badly as I do, and his low voice comes out sluggish and husky.

So I take that as my cue to press on. I circle my hands around the back of his neck, trapping him in a vise grip. Crushing our mouths and every place on our bodies together. "Please," I whisper against his mouth. "I want you. Not later. This moment."

He groans and the tension riding his shoulders tells me I'm about to get another round of an argument. Of him trying to exercise control and be sensible and make all of the supposed *smart* and *appropriate* decisions.

"I know this is a terrible place to do this," I say, expressing what he'll say before he can. "It's reckless, and we shouldn't drop our guard so utterly, but we've secured the camp several times over. We're running air and ground surveillance. Dannica's personally overseeing the current shift as we speak. We're surrounded by legionnaires that are on our side, patrolling for us. We'll be alerted if a threat arises. We can snatch tonight, Reed. Give me this." I should leave it at that as to why I'm pushing. I should let the reason simply be that I'm a selfish, greedy bitch and "reckless" has been my first name *and* my surname since I was born. But I let myself be more vulnerable with Reed and admit the whole of the truth. "When you died, I felt like I died too. It shredded me apart. Then scattered those bloody pieces across the stars. I don't just want you inside of me. I *need* you inside of me, filling me, to restitch those pieces together and make it all right. I want to fuck you until I can't think straight; and afterward, I want to sleep by your side; and in the morning, I want to set the world right so I can spend many, many, many days repeating that sequence."

The cobalt of Reed's eyes darkens even more to the deep, preternatural shade of Khanaian blue steel. "This is an awful idea," he murmurs, already backing me up until I bump against the table. He plants his large hands on the surface, the muscles traversing his arms flexing and standing out sharply as he leans into me and cages me between the table and his body. Those same hands, finally, mercifully, slide under my clothes. One cradles my hip, the other palms my breast, both touches searing, possessive brands as he kisses me until every bit of oxygen gets sucked out of the tent. And it's of zero consequence. I don't even think of breaking for air, because I find I don't really need it all that much. Reed is breath enough. *Gods*, we fit right in every position and in every way. It's like the cosmos made Reed exactly for me, and I for him.

"I'd be lying if I claimed I didn't need, viscerally, the same thing you do," Reed says, low and roughly, no longer bothering at restraint. "Have needed it since Cara. So tell me, precisely, what you want tonight to be and we can have it." As if in demonstration of the options, he rolls my braid around his fist, tugs my head back harshly, but kisses the column of my throat so damn carefully and tenderly. The two gestures sit in stark, intoxicating contrast and make me throb, *ache*, for Reed to be inside me.

I know what he's asking with his actions and words. Do I actually want a hard, intense fuck, or do I want him to make love to me?

Heat coils in my belly and lower, spills between my legs.

While waiting for my decision, Reed continues to exhibit how good either will be. His hand not gripping my hair skims between my breasts, down my stomach, and slips beneath my waistband. His thumb works gentle, slow circles over my clit, applying just the right pressure, while he spears me with three fingers, pumping brutally in and out of me.

I moan and arch into him, riding his hand. Riding the utterly bliss-ful twin sensations of Reed handling me like precious glass *and* like I'm unbreakable.

"The answer is both," I say to the man who started off as my kill target, became my ally, and is now my co-general and entire heart.

"Thank fuck," he breathes and captures my mouth.

Keeping us sealed together, Darius lifts me onto the war table and makes sure I get all that I want and more.

31

THE ATTACK COMES IN THE middle of the night. The siren's pitch alerts which enemy it is. Reed and I are clothed, well enough, and armed in an instant. I'm thankful for the warning because I step from my sleeping tent and my blood axe bites into the chest of an attacker who was on his way inside. He's down before I'm able to mark his face well. I glimpse the solid red uniform, have a moment where I believe Ajani's legionnaires have turned on us. That can't be it, though. Our legionnaires wear black and green, Cyphir Syndicate colors.

"*The warlords,*" Reed and I growl at nearly the same time. He shoots a hole into the skull of a man who rushes at us, snaps the neck of another, sinks a dagger into the gut of a third. It's the first time I've seen him fight against legionnaires, and I'm thunderstruck as I swivel between Reed's deadly movements and cutting down three more intruders. He more than holds his own. Like with the Praetorian-merc team that came after us, Reed's speed is staggering, and he's always one step ahead of his opponents. The effect is nothing short of a storm of death.

The rest of Invictus are out of their tents and embroiled in combat too. Caiman and Greysen fight back to back, the former proving why he graduated top of our class and the latter exhibiting the true extent to which he *let* Caiman have the spotlight all those years. It's a little beautiful to watch them slash, shoot, and kill perfectly in sync. Liim and Dannica have paired off similarly and found a good working groove. Haynes and Dane fight independently and fiercely. Seeing Invictus hold up against the legionnaires, it's clear why Nkosi used the fearmongering and mass-bombing tactics that he did. The war would've been more even otherwise, Accacia's larger numbers of lesser consequence. The biochipped Praetorians kick the magically gifted legionnaires' asses that they square off with.

I swell with pride.

We're incredible together.

But whatever warlords lead the raid must have known the number of Ajani's legionnaires with us because there's approximately three times as many in red uniforms swarming the camp. Ajani's soldiers fight alongside us; however, there are *a lot* of the others. I'd laugh if not for the situation. I guess Ajani and his augurs failed at being as convincing as they thought they might be as a unit.

They did warn me.

Keeping my back to the tent, which I know nothing is coming out of, I let the legionnaires come to me and pick them off as they do. Reed mirrors me, silently understanding. As we collect corpses around us, I scan the fighting for which Red Order bastards are making a play for the emperorship. I spot one warlord advancing my way from the western side of the field, clad in the scarlet-collared, black uniform that immediately makes him stand out. I keep Rigaud, *my father*, in my periphery as I hurl blood spikes at a woman on my left after ducking beneath blaster discharges. I pivot to slice through the torso of a man who swings a blood sword at my head, then take advantage of a brief lull to scan the fray for other warlords. I sight all gods-shitting six of them. They each prowl forward from a different area of the camp, blood weapons in hand. They don't use them, however; they let their soldiers engage Ajani's legionnaires, solely focused on one priority.

Rigaud sneers my way when I catch his gaze, as if I'll cower. I cut him down with a glare that promises he dies today. The entire Red Order does. They don't get to come for me and mine and not pay for that.

Reed rasps my name. Dannica and Greysen shout it. All of my squad has noticed the exact thing I did. The warlords move concertedly toward the same target: *me*.

I do laugh then—shrill and bitter and disbelieving. The cosmos really does have a sick sense of humor because shit has come full circle. The warlords came at my mother in a similar fashion. The whole of the Red Order feeling like it took multiple men to slaughter one woman. In her case, it didn't; it was bitch-made and pathetic. In my case . . .

Six assholes won't be nearly enough.

"I'm not Maiika!" I yell to the warlords and send a blistering wave of my power roaring at them. "If you want to die, fine! I killed your emperor; I'll kill you!" Ajani will have to understand and just figure out how to fill the power vacuum.

There's a moment where glances get exchanged among Invictus as we continue to clash with legionnaires. My team's hard gazes are clear in their resolve: *we fight them with you.*

No! I want to shout when I recall Nkosi and the war tent. The Red Order aren't him, but they're close to it. Damnably, I know my squad; I'm positive any such urging won't matter. I hurtle toward the warlords intent on putting them down and quickly so my worries are moot.

I should've gone for Rigaud first. As my axe slams against the scarlet hammer of a warlord that was closer, Dannica and Haynes go for my father. The pair shoot a barrage of UV bullets at their target. A blood shield appears around Rigaud. Dannica dodges the blood dagger that rushes her way. Haynes . . . my cohort brother . . . *my friend* . . . staggers backward. I blink, crouching under a swing of the blood hammer. My heart races, my mind shrieks, as I spring upward and my axe opens up a femoral artery in my warlord's left thigh, exposes his intestines on the second swipe, and buries into his heart on the third. I yank it out, to take his head, and make sure he dies. Reed beats me to it. The sundisk he throws embeds in the side of the warlord's head. I dance back as it explodes.

That's one interesting way to get it done.

I am heaving, trying not to shake, and my pulse whooshes in my ears by the time the body drops at my feet. None of those reactions are about the corpse with its head blown apart. They're about Haynes, who is slumped to the side on his knees—blood spikes jutting out of multiple places the length of his torso that never flew from Rigaud's hand. They were formed from Hayne's own blood, a hellish thing I watched Nkosi do at Krashen.

I send my power blasting into Rigaud, whom Dannica's shooting at wildly. Reed joins her, body rigid and face ashen. The warlord's blood shield has cracks, and Rigaud's features—that are *knifingly* too much like mine in the moment—are twisted in intense concentration behind the faltering shield. *Thank the stars*, I was right about a max hit capacity when I encountered Ajani's because Rigaud needing to focus on keeping his barrier in place is likely the only reason the same accursed use of his blood-gift hasn't been turned on Dannica and Reed yet.

I hate doing it, but it's imperative. I take my eyes off them to sweep the field. I brace to see somebody else from my squad dead. I exhale in relief that the rest are alive. They fight in units with a number of Ajani's legionnaires against the remaining four warlords. I spin back to Dannica and Reed. A legionnaire has joined them. Iyko, Ajani's marshal, has a blood shield encompassing the three of them, while Rigaud's shield has dropped and the motherfucker tries his level best to shatter hers with blood blade after blood blade.

I run at them before he can be successful. I snap a blood shield of my own around me in place before I reach Riguad. At least, I manage something similar. I envision the red-and-gold light from when my power manifests outwardly not only limning me like it does in a glow but being an impenetrable barrier. It's a gamble on a hunch that works. When I stand between Rigaud's and Iyko's blood shields, the daggers that smash against them vaporize, turning to red gas.

I'll give him credit: Rigaud isn't much fazed. He sends blast after blast of his own power at me, sneering as if *I* should cower. "This will not end how you imagine," he says plainly as if we're chatting about the weather. "You are young, with power you can't possibly have learned how to manage in so short a time. You killed *one* of Nkosi, girl, and there are *five* of us left here. There are ways magic can be amplified across wielders to take down even a god."

I have no wiseass comebacks. Don't have the time or the emotional capacity or the presence of mind to issue cool or heated threats. Haynes is dead. My squad mate and friend *is dead*. Reed and Dannica just saw their longtime brother die. My stomach churns, the reality ripping through my chest. I snarl at Rigaud, devastation giving way to blood-lust and the need to *destroy* the cause of it. "Do me a favor, will you?" I spit out with cold rage. "KNEEL!" I draw on the depths of my blood-gift, on the power that's threaded with gold that makes me a Zenith, and on the additional load I stripped from Nkosi when I say it. I don't only direct the command that I thread compulsion into at Rigaud. I order every warlord and red-uniformed Accacian to do so, asserting my will over all of them.

The enemy Accacians fall to their knees a nanosecond later. Like in Khanai with Enoch and his guards, the wide-scale thrall is absolute and unbreakable. I see the same filaments in my mind that resemble steel cables running from me to each of the minds I hold firmly. Unlike in Khanai, the filaments blaze an entwined red-and-gold, the same colors forming the light that now flows around my shield. If I had time to dick around, I'd stop and marvel at the effect. It's seriously cool—and probably makes me a scary bitch. But I place the awe aside because there's no room for it in the current circumstances.

Bloodthirsty for vengeance, raw over Haynes's death, I turn in a circle around me, gazing at the Accacians in the dirt, and consider shooting them all. For the time being, I place the legionnaires who turned up with the warlords aside to deal first with the men who brought them here—and I have the perfect way to do it.

I'm not entirely sure how to execute things, but with the levels of power I possess, I gander I should be able to achieve the feat. So I do what I do best: I wing it. I curl a mental grip around the red-and-gold filaments I see in my mind's eye that travel from me to each of the warlords and imagine numerous blood spikes punching out of their chests. The blood of the Red Order obeys without resistance, delivering the damage that I will. I direct blood spikes to jut out of their necks, torsos, and skulls next, visiting enough damage that their bodies won't have a chance in a hellpit of repairing themselves. No matter *their* power, four Accacian warlords die on their knees.

One particular bastard got spared for special treatment. I step closer to the man who lives and release my asshole sperm donor from compulsion. I give him a moment to gaze upon his fellow dead warlords. To see that they've died and to understand that his long-lived existence is coming to an end too. But before it does, I have questions. I shouldn't because it makes me absurd and makes him mean something when he should mean *nothing*. Yet, I can't bring myself to kill the man who is my biological father without discovering things I've long wondered about my mother. "Maiika," I say, and keep a steel grip on my outward calm as a storm of emotions and fury rage inside me that's brought on by my utterance of the name. "What was the real nature of your relationship with her?" It's a question I've lived with my entire life, since I've known I was blood-gifted with an Accacian father. "Did you manipulate her? Did you force her? Or was it something else? Did she—"

Cosmos, I can barely say it.

"Did she, somehow, have a fondness for you?" Nausea roils through my stomach at the last question more than it does with the rest. Because how the hell could she? How could she feel anything close to tenderness, or love, or desire for a man of Rigaud's caliber? The bastard flew across a sea, for godsdamned sake, and arrived on Grandfather's doorstep with six other men to murder a vulnerable woman and *his* unborn child.

The sneer Riguad doesn't ever seem to drop when regarding me crawls back onto his face. He purses his lips, making it clear he intends to remain silent.

I have a cure for that.

I shove my blood axe through the center of his stomach. He gurgles blood. I twist the blood blade and his scream shatters the air. When it dies, I give him two options. "You can answer my questions and die as quick as your counterparts. Or you can be an ass, stay quiet, and die much slower. Which one will it be?" All right, maybe I have slipped a teensy bit *too far* into bloodlust with this son of a bitch? But he's the only remaining pseudo-threat alive; I can indulge. Which I do. I withdraw my blood axe and bury it in his side. "Next, I stop fucking around and start removing limbs."

"Maiika knew the risk we took with being together," he spits out with venom. "We both knew it. We also went into it with rules. An infant, *you*, a child of mixed Mareenian and Accacian blood, could not come of things. But Maiika unwittingly took measures for her belly to swell with child, and she paid the price I was always clear would be paid if it happened." He says this bullshit explanation like it absolves him from any blame.

It fucking doesn't. And I've heard enough. I leave him lucid and aware that he's kneeling before the daughter whom he tried and failed to snuff from existence as she's about to kill him. I turn his life force against him. He clutches at his throat, eyes bulging. His brown skin turns a ghastly purplish blue as he struggles for the breath I'm stealing by directing his blood to begin to drown him. As it does, I have more of it rush out of his mouth, his eyes, his nose, his ears—every orifice *and* the new holes I create as more blood spikes jut from his torso. Rigaud slumps in the grass at my feet, the pale hue of death. But the bastard's chest visibly rises and falls with the tiniest of movements. So I continue to enact my first bloodletting, and command every drop of Rigaud's repugnant blood out of his body. And then, the man who helped conceive me, whose DNA I half carry, who *surely* had to have manipulated my mother in some way, and who tried to kill his own daughter not once, but twice, is dead.

It doesn't end up being one of those times where you hurtle toward doing something and feel much less vindication once it's done than you thought you would. *No.* I feel exactly the level of furious, petty, vicious pleasure that I was certain I would, if I ever got this chance, the moment I learned who my father was and what that meant in the Caran war camp.

Next are the men who came with him. The bloodlust croons it, rages further when I look down at Haynes, at Dannica in the grass hugging him, at Reed still standing, ardently trying to hold it together with naked anguish apparent, nonetheless. I'm about to give in to the impulse to spill more blood. The temptation to make the horror that is tonight better with more deaths. A different facet of me—perhaps my conscience—reminds me that my own people were in a similar position not long ago and I pleaded for their lives, claiming they were only soldiers acting under orders. It is what halts me, because if I kill the legionnaires in my thrall, then I become a monster extremely similar to Nkosi and the Tribunes. Maybe more so since Accacians are conscripted rather than soldiers who chose their professions.

They had somewhat of a choice. They followed the Red Order to move against you, broke from Ajani.

While that's true, it's the bloodlust talking, and I can't let it rule me. If I am to lead, that is not how I want to do it.

"Iyko, if I release them from compulsion and the warlords are dead, will the legionnaires obey you and stand down?" I ask Ajani's marshal.

When the woman says yes, I do it, handing off the Accacians to her and letting their superior decide their fates. As she has her team round up the legionnaires I released, cuff them, and strip them of weapons, I can finally stop being the general that was needed to remain on the field. Letting the grief finally wash fully and freely over me, I move to stand with Invictus in the tight mournful circle they've formed around our fallen brother.

Staring down at Haynes's lifeless body turns as hard as it was to stare down at Zayne's. What's harder is witnessing Reed and Dannica so utterly wrecked that they openly weep. Needing to do something, *anything*, to make it all right for everyone, I sink beside Haynes and desperately try to figure out how to do for him what Ajani did for Reed in the war camp. I should've thought of it before. Should've killed Rigaud quicker. Recalled Cara and tried to help Haynes sooner. I do it. Pray it works. I cover Hayne's heart, where it seems I should start first, the organ most vital. But I don't see a wretched gold-and-red filament running between him and me like I can when wielding compulsion, or like I did when turning the Accacians' blood against them. Without it, I can't begin to intuit what to do.

Still, I stubbornly focus my will on making Haynes's heart knit itself back together and beat—all while knowing that can't possibly be the whole of bringing him back. Because life isn't mere body tissues and blood and muscles and bone and skin. It's comprised of a person's essence, their soul. And how the hell do you wing reaching into the After to restore that part of somebody? I frantically think of the way Ajani chanted in an Accacian tongue when he did it for Reed, and the way Nkosi instructed me to do the same alongside him for the Stitching. So I know that's part of the Accacian rite that defies death. I scrabble through my mind to dredge up the exact words I heard Ajani recite. Only snatches of syllables and phrases in the foreign language I don't speak come to me. I sputter everything I can remember. It doesn't work.

"No! No! No! No! No! Shit!" I scream, crying, keeping my hands to Haynes's heart and refusing to stop yanking on my power and attempting to pour it into him and give back the big westerner the full life he deserves to live out. I can't give up. I won't give up. We can't lose him. *Reed* and *Dannica* can't lose him.

I flinch at the two different hands I feel on my shoulders. The left touch is Reed's. The right touch is Dannica's.

"I'm sorry," I croak. "I'm sorry. I'm trying. I won't stop trying. I'll figure it out. I'll get him back."

"Ikenna," Reed says in a soft, hoarse voice that bleeds pain. "It's all right. I don't think you can."

I shake my head. "No. I *can*. I *have* to." As I insist it, I'm pitched into the ice crevasse where Zayne died and I had to climb out of that hole in the planet and leave my friend's body behind because I couldn't do shit for him either.

This cannot be happening again. We're soldiers; I get that. I get death is a part of war too. But gods, *does it ever get any easier to gaze upon dead friends?*

As the seven of us who are left stand in the dark camp, not moving from Haynes, Iyko softly walks to our side. "We've detained the other legionnaires in the camp. Ajani is sending Sol and a unit to pick them up; it will be inconspicuous," she says to me respectfully.

I nod. Look back at Haynes. Then her. "Do you . . . can you—"

"No." Her eyes tighten in apology. "I am sorry for your comrade." She says it in the tone that only one soldier who knows what it's like to lose one of their team could utter to another experiencing the same.

"Ajani!" I say, trying desperately for another way. For any way. "Can you get him on a Comm?" I seize on to the last mad hope.

Iyko smiles tightly. Keeps the same apology about her. Appears like she wants to say something, but decides against it, and simply calls Ajani.

He answers straightaway, his holograph projecting in front of Iyko.

I never thought I'd be so happy to stand in the presence of the former Apis in my life.

I point at Haynes. "He needs help! Now! Can you instruct me how to bring him back? I need the right words and proper ritual."

Ajani looks upon Haynes grimly. I don't at all like his somber expression.

"How long has he been dead?" he asks.

I check my Comm Unit to gauge the time.

"It's been forty-two minutes since he went down," Dannica answers before I do. Her voice cracks near the end, and it reminds me of the clear feelings I've glimpsed many times between Dannica and Haynes.

I grip my cohort sister's hand and squeeze it. She squeezes mine back. Then I take Reed's hand into my other one and do the same. "What are you waiting for?" I growl at Ajani when he hasn't chided me that I should already have the knowledge and then started handing it to me, smug. "Do you want me to grovel? Beg? I'll do it. Just say you'll explain how to heal him."

"I am sorry," Ajani says. "I, regrettably, can't lend assistance. The time since he's passed into the After is too great. Hasani won't give him up." His answer is like an axe hacking into my chest. And fuck all among the cosmos for that bullshit statute.

Dannica's shoulders shake uncontrollably, and I cannot take it.

Reed emits a strangled noise that sounds nothing like the man I know. He lets my hand go to scrub his face, then spits out a string of curses. He gazes back at Haynes, blinking as if the corpse he's seeing isn't real. *Gods*, I wish that it wasn't.

Nobody was supposed to die.

I was supposed to pull us all through this.

If I failed Haynes, who else will I fail?

Who else will I lose in the coming battle?

32

THE MORNING COMES, AND WE don't adjust course or delay plans. I want to be able to give Reed and Dannica time to grieve, but they wouldn't have taken it even if I'd suggested it. We are soldiers first, with a duty first, and that duty to *the people*—who suffer—is what our whole mission has been about since the beginning.

So when our pickup team arrives at the camp on schedule, we're ready, in Invictus uniforms, on schedule as well. The armored transport rolls to a stop in front of our gathered rogue cohort. Four Gamma squad mates climb out of it.

"It's damn good to have you back, man," says one of the Gamma guys, Daiyhlan, whom Reed made contact with before we left Accacia. The twenty-five-year-old, brown-haired soldier embraces Reed in a hug. "It's good to have you both back," he says, hugging Dannica second. "I'm s—"

"Later," Reed stops him. "We'll do it later."

Daiyhlan nods in the affirmative, easily pivots to something else. "Enzo wanted to be here. He's upset that he isn't. Asked me to relay he should be here."

Reed's jaw ticks. "Enzo knows why he isn't. There's no way in hell he gets involved in this. I'm not putting Amari at that kind of risk."

"Is that dumbass really whining about it like it can be any other way when he has a history with Selene?" Caiman says with less chill than Reed.

Daiyhlan draws himself up tall at Caiman's words. "Since you *are* here, I have a question," he says angrily. "Tell me: Have you gotten word? Where were the scions hiding out? And how much persisting luxury are coddled, expectant fucks like you enjoying at the expense of the rest of the Republic?"

"I don't know what you're talking about," Caiman responds through clenched teeth. "I've been in exile, remember? So why would I, asshole?"

Daiyhlan bristles. He steps toward Caiman, clearly spoiling for a fight with anyone from the upper strata.

Reed and I plant ourselves in front of the Gamma Praetorian at the same time. Reed throws a hand against Daiyhlan's chest. "Cool it," Reed says. "If you're joining up with this team because you believe in what we aim to accomplish, Caiman Rossi is a part of the team. He's got nothing to do with the shitty treatment the common ranks are being subjected to. Not in this instance, at least. He's on our side and prepared to fight the necessary fight *for* the people we all want to safeguard. Every last one of us who stand in this spot do so under threat of our lives if we fail today because we all give a shit. We all hold the same vision and mission. The same conviction. We're willing to risk our asses because we understand change needs to come to Mareen. For the betterment of everyone. Sparking fights among ourselves achieves nothing and is counterproductive at best. It's detrimental to what we wish for the Republic and a quick way for us to lose somebody else at worst."

Reed clasps the Gamma's forearm in the way of respect between

Praetorians after the dress down. "You're right to be upset," he says earnestly. "Let's be pissed off, as a squad, at who deserves it. All right?"

Daiyhlan clasps Reed's forearm back. "All right."

The rest of the Gammas snap their former cohort leader a respectful, passionate salute behind the one Daiyhlan delivers.

Invictus does the same to Reed. And as I did during the trials—like I do whenever I witness it—I marvel at how extraordinary Reed really is when he wields his uncanny oratory skills. I don't think it's possible for the man to not give a speech that enthralls, ignites fervency, and unifies a squad behind a common, noble goal like Mareen's old wargifted, revered generals once did before we purged such strengths in our people.

"If we're done with the bullshit," he says to the Gammas, every inch the impressive co-general, "someone give me a sit-rep while we move out."

AS OUR TRANSPORT carries us through Krashen City, I take heart, *pride*, in seeing the flames of rebellion from Mareen's citizens already burning, and burning bright. Despite the Tribunal's protest bans, we pass several on our way to the western quadrant taking place in districts reduced to ruins and those that skirted the worst of the bombings. Angry, impassioned shouts for justice and equality reach us behind the one-way glass. It feels good, *hopeful*, to hear them—and it is more than bolstering to see that the vocal crowds are comprised of *all* Mareenians, across classes and complexion variations, united behind common wrongs. It helps me know with conviction that this path Invictus is on is right and the governing system we aim to give the people is right. Moreover, once we accomplish ousting the Tribunal Council, the people will do the rest. They won't let the surviving heirs, scions, and Praetorians who'll try to cling to the old status quo achieve it. They won't let any of the old guard retain the Republic, and it lays one concern to rest about civil war and deleterious in-fighting between the old guard.

When we near Rhysien Manor and the estate comes into sight, the inside of the transport crackles with energy and adrenaline. Nobody is nervous. We are all *ready* to fight. We lost our brother so we can fight. Caiman lost his war house so we can fight. I lost *Grandfather* to get us here at the end of this path, staring down this confrontation. And it is time.

Reed must mark the ferocity on my face because his eyes meet mine and the blue of his sizzle with a heated promise of later and a firm order to stay alive. Before I process what's happening well, his calloused hands are cupping my face and then he's kissing me. Thoroughly. "I know that look," he says against my lips. "Keep your ass intact, Kenna. Be our blade and let us be your shields."

I slap his chest, wedging some space between us so I can gather my bearings because *godsdamn!* "First, if that is your directive," I say when I won't sound pathetically breathy, "then you shouldn't have kissed me like that because now I need to make the world stop tilting around me. Two, same fucking order. Keep your pretty ass intact too, Darius."

His lips twitch. "Affirmative. Sorry," he says, turning slightly embarrassed to the squad. "I needed to do that."

Dannica snickers. "Shut the fuck up, *Darius.* It was sweet. Though if Haynes were here he'd give you endless shit," she says, her tone bittersweet.

"We get it, man," Greysen says. "Matter of fact . . ." He swivels to his left and kisses Caiman. Passionately. All-consumingly. Ardently. "You, Rossi, no heroics either without somebody else covering your ass. Got it?"

"Back at you," Caiman says, brushing fingers over Greysen's cheek.

The Praetorians on guard at the gate are on our side; they wave us through after Daiyhlan submits to a security scan.

The pair at the base of the steps outside the front doors—that we're storming right the fuck in through—haven't shifted their allegiance. "We're supposed to be here; let us pass," I tell them quickly, using compulsion, because surveillance vidcams will have already picked up our presence on the lawn.

The men in battle dress bearing Epsilon symbols step at once to opposite sides. Their faces contort. One levels his blaster at me. So does the other a second later.

I don't have the time to wonder why the compulsion didn't work because the guy on my right squeezes the trigger. The muscles in his forearm flex a nanosecond before. The tell leaves barely enough time to drop beneath the shot aimed at my head. Caiman is in his face by the time I'm back standing, wrenching the blaster away and shooting the Praetorian with his own gun. Reed shoots the guard on my left. Both Epsilon men crumple.

"I don't know why that didn't work!" I cry, bewildered, as more Praetorians pour out the doors atop the steps and stand shoulder to shoulder between us and the entrance. I reach for my blood-gift, frenziedly, to make sure it remains present and *strong*. I did kill five warlords with it while holding hundreds of legionnaires under a thrall mere hours ago. I tried to heal Haynes with it as well in the same time frame. Perhaps, I think, panicked, it's suffered a drain? But it thunders in my blood at the ready when I call it forth.

"It doesn't matter," says Caiman, gripping the two blasters. "This fight was happening at some point before we reached the council session."

"What about everything else?" asks Reed, sight trained on the Praetorians, about thirty in total, who've come to intercept us.

"Everything else is good," I assure him, probing my power a second time for confirmation.

"Glad to hear it. If it changes, we'll adjust strategy. Other than that, let's clear the path to the Tribunal," he says to the whole of Invictus. The seven of us stand shoulder to shoulder too. "We keep doing this exactly how you wanted to do it, Amari," Reed says to me.

Our squad echoes it.

"Affirmative," I say, because one thing is true: I've still got everything I need without compulsion.

I cut a look that could mow down an entire army across the soldiers who think they've come to stop us. "Who's the fucking op lead here?" I yell, my team training blasters on them as quickly as they turn them on us. "Whoever it is tell your squad to stand down! This is the only chance you get. Otherwise, you die on these steps." I'm aware whoever is in charge won't do it; we've already confirmed who's on our side and who isn't. I give the opportunity to clear my conscience and my squad mates' consciences.

"I am, you treacherous bitch," answers a grating voice that will never not itch my ass. Chance steps front and center in the line of Praetorians, hailing from various cohorts, facing us.

I pitch *this* motherfucker an unconcerned smile that's all venom. "I admit, I'm surprised. We kicked your ass once. The Tribunes gambled on *you* to keep them safe a second time? That was stupid." I rake Chance with an identical contemptible sneer as what he's giving me. "Works for me, though. Since they won't put their rabid, *incapable* dog down, I will. We've long had a score to settle."

He bristles with violence, then trains his blaster between my eyes like he loves to do. "We sure have, akulu. The Tribunal, and I, did learn from Lusian. It and the war brought knowledge and biochip innovations too." I do not like the slick, trademark sadistic glint in his eyes at all when he drops it on me. His gaze that blazes hatred and smugness slides from me to Caiman. "You, Rossi, and your war house are *nothing* in this Republic anymore," he spits out. "Perhaps if you hadn't decided to be a fucking, akulu-sympathizing traitor and you did what you were supposed to do—give the order for us to kill her in Khanai—that second fact might be different. The ruin of your war house is on you. Just wanted you to know that, bitch boy, before I kill you both."

I don't wait for Chance to play whatever trump he believes he's got. I lunge forward, snapping up a shield that his blaster's discharge cracks against. I drop it to swipe across his neck with a blood dagger. He steps back as quick as I move and my dagger opens up a gash across the length of his chest. His smile is savage when metal claws shoot out of his knuckles. It's even more savage when he slashes at my face. I dance to the side, mind racing to process and make adjustments for the fact that the Tribunal has apparently given fucking Chance, of all insane people, further augmentations to enhancements Praetorians already have.

Chance gives the order for his people to kill mine, thundering he'll take care of me. I track my team engaging in battle as I dodge another slash of Chance's metal claws, which attempt to expose my intestines.

I'm about sick of these accursed things.

I feint to the left with my blood dagger, jut blood claws from my right knuckles and shove them into Chance's side to make the fucking point that whatever he and the Tribunal's got, I can match. I jerk the blood claws out, drive a knee to his face as he's doubled over, and use the breathing room to see if the rest of the Praetorians display Chance's augmentation or other ones. None do, and if Chance is playing lead here, perhaps that means he's a test case before the Tribunal rolls the adjustments out in full.

I crouch beneath another attempt to claw off my face. I barrel a punch upward and bury the blood claws in Chance's gut. His counter-strike flies at me at the same time that I catch the blaster leveled at my head, held by a girl with red hair, at the top of the steps just inside Rhysien Manor's entrance. I toss a shield up. Reed is at my side, forcing Chance back with a blow to his temple and a knife slash that opens him up from ear to pectoral. Blood pours out of him. Chance thunders and turns his rage on Reed.

Selene's UVs continue spraying against my shield.

"That's gonna drop eventually," Reed growls, dodging a clawed fist Chance aims at his eye. He answers it with a jab of his elbow to Chance's nose. I hear the satisfying crunch of bone. Reed goes for Chance's heart, but his blade sinks into flesh a few inches to the left. "I've got him," grits Reed. "Go deal with her." I've seen Reed move. I've fought Reed myself. I know his strength and his speed. Chance is faster and stronger than he was when I fought *him* during the trials, but I can still keep up with him, which means Reed can too. Assured, I spin around, shield locked in place, and give my former friend my full attention.

If she wants it, she's got it.

Her laser-focused shooting at me isn't why my eyes are narrowed murderously on her, though. I see red because Selene Rhysien, the bitch who killed my grandfather, the former Legatus, stands inside the doors of her family home wearing the maroon-and-black ceremonial coat, medals, and fur pelt that is the garb of the office of Mareen's Legatus Commander.

She smirks down at me, taking it in. "Sorry," she yells. "I needed my freedom. I took it, and you're going to make sure I retain it *and* real power—one way or another."

I stalk straight for Selene, and there isn't a force in the world that could keep me from *not* getting to her. I drop the shield, dodging one of her bullets, and lob a blood spike at her head. She barely ducks under it. I pitch another, and another, and another, not giving any let-up and allowing her room to shoot again. All three land gratifyingly where I aim—dead center of her abdomen. They aren't lethal hits; I'm not ready for one yet. I was denied doing this up close and personal in Lusian because of iridium. It can't affect me anymore and iridium won't save her on the steps if she tries to use it. I send a blast of power hurtling at her, knocking her on her ass. A second blast tears the gun she's held onto out of her grasp.

I cut down three Praetorians that try to intercept me before I reach their new Legatus.

Dannica drops two more. Liim and Dane, Caiman and Greysen—the guys fight small groups of Praetorians a few yards away trying to get to me before I reach Selene. My team acts every bit as my backup to get me to my target—the first of Mareen's corrupt leadership who's kindly presented herself outside of Tribunal chambers—with expediency.

I snatch Selene up by the maroon-and-black coat when I reach her. I vibrate with pure wrath when I spy the familiar shade of brown leather that covers the handle of a knife sheathed at her waist. I yank Grandfather's missing dagger off her weapons belt; it takes all of a second to identify the intricate patterns etched into its blue metal that confirm she took it for herself when she murdered him. "This doesn't belong to you," I growl and smash its hilt into her face. Thrice.

It's even more satisfying than when I punched Ajani.

Arms wrap around me from behind, choking me in the muscled band they form around my neck. I'd recognize the stench anywhere. I twist out of Chance's sub hold, driving the blood claws I've kept into his knee. Reed is right there. Slams a boot into his torso with enough force that I hear ribs snap. Chance, who is bloody and sports about a dozen vicious bruises, doesn't fold. He keeps swinging. Keeps slashing at Reed. Reed, who doesn't bear near as many bruises, isn't letting him get in anymore hits.

Selene takes in Chance's state. She takes in me. There's a moment where she reaches for another gun.

I sink into a Xzana attack stance. Don't bother with a shield.

She takes two clipped steps backward toward Rhysien Manor.

I flash to where she is. "No, you don't get away this time," I tell her.

Dannica, Caiman, Greysen, Liim, and Dane appear behind her, forming a wall. They're covered in blood, but don't seem to have any major injuries. Dannica tips her head to me, signaling they're there because there's no other Praetorians left to fight. I nod back, look coolly at Selene. "Retreating inside wasn't going to save you. I was on my way in already, or did you forget?"

I hear Chance's roar behind me. Reed's growl.

Caiman's lips twitch. Dannica all-out beams. Curious, and feeling like I'm about to miss something good, I tell Invictus to keep Selene at gunpoint, throw up a shield for added protection, and swivel around right on time to witness something more than good. Reed hammers a kick to Chance's broken ribs. Snatches the blaster away Chance has re-armed himself with. Hits Chance in the temple with the butt of it. Then shoots him three times in the stomach. "That is for Ikenna during the trials," he bites off. He shoots Chance in each thigh. In each arm. Another in the gut. "All of that is for Dannica, and the shit you helped put her through during her trials." Reed tosses the blaster. Grabs Chance's head in the crook of his arm. For all the damage he's taken, Chance still tries to wrench free—no matter what, someone with Praetorian training isn't going to go down easy. But Reed's sub hold is just too strong, a vise grip with no release mechanism. "This is just because you're a general vile asshole that never deserved your rank or to call yourself a Praetorian to begin with." Reed twists, and Chance's neck snaps.

It is glorious—though I am a little disappointed I didn't get to do it.

Without a word, I turn back to Selene. I use the blood claws, since I sort of like them, to cut through that damn coat she's wearing, leaving a dozen deep, furious cuts across her upper body quicker than she can twist out of range.

She falls to the steps, hands braced against the marble, bleeding profusely. I kick her onto her back. Plant my boot on her sternum. Press down.

She grinds her teeth together. Tries her damnedest not to cry out.

"You killed him." I hurl the truth at her that I want stated, explicitly, between us in place of a dagger. The blade will come. But first . . . "You murdered him and you lied to me about it for months. How the fuck could you?" My fingers itch to reach across the space between us and strangle the life out of her for the deed. I decide that's how this ends, my vengeance and her retribution. I want my answers, though. And she doesn't get relief until I hear her try to rationalize her betrayals.

"*Why?*" I hate that my voice scales up reedily when she says noth-

ing. "Explain," I order more evenly. "About all of it. Grandfather. Me.
The iridium. You will die regardless, but you die quicker and less painfully if you tell me why the fuck you did it. You owe me that much. You
owe me the details." A part of me I can't excise, that is maddening and
infuriating, can't end her without the details. That part needs the reason for her betrayal when we were supposed to be sisters.

Selene's lips thin. She doesn't insult me by denying anything.

She doesn't start talking either.

I snarl. Press my foot down harder. "You're biochipped," I remind
her. "I can crush a lung, let it heal, do it again."

Pride and defiance flash in her gray eyes, the mini flames that spark
in them when she's pissed making an appearance. "You don't have the
time to draw out a torture session. More Praetorians will come."

I increase the pressure, watch her struggle to breathe as I call her
bluff.

"Bravado was always my department, not yours," I tell her. "And
I'm certain none will. Your Tribunal has displayed a habit of cutting
and running, and of throwing bodies in front of them to die while they
do it." I wave around at the steps holding the Praetorians that are already dead, with no new squads having replaced them. "Looks exactly
like that's what has happened here. Let me see if I've figured this right:
when we turned up here, they sent Chance and you with a unit to kill
us, and if you failed, it bought them time. Yes?"

When she says nothing, I look to Dannica, who has Comm eyes on
the Tribunal Council. "Have you confirmed that?"

She answers in the affirmative, and the whir of a jet taking off overhead sounds.

I smile down at Selene. "You should've learned. They don't give a
shit about their Legatus—especially one they just dressed up to play
the part—one another, or anybody else. The only thing an individual
Tribune cares about is preserving their own self. If you were truly a
Tribune, you'd have known that too. Now, I want answers. Real ones.

You murdered my grandfather, you lied to me about it for months, you let me spiral for months, and then you fucking played like we were family, *kin, sisters,* when you gave me that godsdamned pendant made of iridium and poisoned my blood. I know you ostensibly did it all so Sutton and the rest of the Tribunal could study its effects on me then eventually kill me when they had the data they needed and I'd outlived my usefulness. Before today, I also thought that you did it, pathetically and unforgivably, because you chose to just bow at Sutton's feet and do whatever he ordered you to do. No matter how sick or reprehensible or how viciously it would hurt me. I thought you didn't tell me, warn me about Grandfather so I could've warned him, or warned Grandfather directly yourself instead of killing him because you let Sutton finally break you. But the person who was supposed to be loyal to me, above anybody and everything else because they were supposed to be *my* family, my sister in every way that mattered, *my person,* didn't do what she did because of fearing repercussions from Sutton, did she?

"No. You didn't choose that scheming, greedy, bigoted, repugnant, bastard over me. That . . . I could reasonably get. I'd still be pissed and still need you to die, but I could understand why. You're a war house scion—it means you're expected to place your duty and oaths to your war house above anything else. It's the rules of the system you grew up in, and I can understand rules.

"This, though . . . the truth of why you did what you did goes beyond that, right? Was Legatus always your endgame? Or did you have something else in mind? Did Sutton promise you didn't ever need to play Donya? Did you bargain to be made his heir? Is that why you sat in his Tribunal seat during the postwar briefing—some demand of yours for good faith?"

The unapologetic look on her face says it all. Answers everything. She wheezes in a breath as I let her feel like she's drowning, feel like she's asphyxiating on her own blood. My rage howls at the depths to which my former friend so grossly betrayed me and slammed knives in my back, repeatedly, over many months. But then, I cut the attack on her blood because truly, I want to hear what she has to say, what she thinks she *can* say, in response.

"You've always had your freedom, Kenna," she rasps. "Always. Being the Legatus's kin is not the same as being a war house head's daughter. You can't possibly know what it feels like to not have any control over your life. You were free to do whatever you felt like, step onto whatever path *you* chose. I always had mine set for me from birth: Rhysien War House's breeder," she says bitterly.

I laugh, harsh and shrill. "Are you kidding me? You knew my grandfather. You knew his goals. You knew my goals. You knew the prejudice we faced daily in Mareen. How did that leave me with *more* freedom, or *any* freedom to walk anything other than the path I am walking right now to fight for that freedom?"

Her eyes flash with a resentment that she's so obviously harbored for a long while, and yet kept hidden very well. "It *is* different." Her hands wrap around my ankle. She tries to yank me off my feet. I do fall, but only so I can drop my knee into her solar plexus. I stay kneeling, pin her neck with the same knee. "Becoming Legatus was the only way," she says as she tries to dislodge me.

She won't. Hand-to-hand combat is another thing I was always better at.

"First, it was only about becoming Sutton's heir," Selene says, not giving up on throwing me off her. "Then he screwed up when he sent Praetorians after you when we were at war and got them killed when we needed those men. So I took advantage of that opportunity. Being heir still meant I had to play breeder, but deposing Sutton in a vote of no confidence and becoming a war house head meant I set the rules, nobody else. Legatus was icing on the cake. Verne showed that while Republic-wide change is slow-crawling, it *can* be forced. Which I plan to do for other women in the Republic as Legatus."

"Except they clearly left you to take the heat rather than protect their precious Legatus."

"They fled on *my* orders."

No the fuck she does not have the audacity. My hands clench into fists. My knee stays right where it belongs. "You are supporting and were the voice of their bullshit mandates that do the opposite of helping women or anybody else," I say. "More than that, how do you even pretend you have noble intentions toward anybody except yourself when you stabbed your own damn sister in the back so you could wear that coat and those medals? *Godsdamn, Selene* . . . I thought we were better than that. I thought we were forged of tougher shit than that. Because if our positions were reversed and I was faced with the same sort of choice, I would've found a way to duck beneath the barrel of the blaster and the wall it had me pressed against without betraying you. I would've found a way to spare you. To safeguard you amid my ambitions. Not throw you to the fucking wolves and leave you ignorant of it *and* therefore vulnerable as fuck."

When I've finished saying those last words to her, I'm *done* speaking. I let my actions bellow the rest of my fury. I shift to the side. My hands fist the front of her Legatus dress coat. I stand and snatch her up to me so we're standing eye level because I want her to be on her feet and looking directly in the face of the friend she betrayed so grossly when that *former* friend ends her miserable-ass life. Hellbent on that mission, I release her clothing and wrap a hand around her throat. My muscles bunch. I squeeze Selene's throat tighter until she starts to claw at my hand and the porcelain skin of her face that's so precious to the Republic's upper crust begins turning purplish blue. Rage and grief and knifing betrayal slip me into that pitiless, destructive place that makes me want to annihilate everything in my path, starting with the former friend whose pulse flutters beneath my fingertips.

Selene squeezes out between one gasping breath and another, "Please, *Kenna*. Don't! Wait!"

Something inside me that I hate flinches, the image of dropping Selene's body at my feet, eyes vacant of life with their light snuffed out, making me recoil. I smother it because she does not get one sliver of pity, empathy, or compassion from me. "Stop calling me that," I snarl.

"You don't get to use that name anymore. You knew how things would be when you made your choices," I tell her. "I know you aren't stupid enough to think I'd do anything other than kill you. You've known me for far too long to surmise otherwise." *We've known each other for so long and were friends for so long that this shouldn't even be happening!* I hiss in my head but don't dare add. She doesn't get a front row seat to the anguish that I shouldn't be feeling about ending her in the first place. *Fuck. Her. FUCK HER!*

I tuck Grandfather's dagger in my belt and wrap the hand that fisted it around the hand already choking the life out of the Praetorian Donya of Rhysien War House turned Legatus Commander. I watch her eyes bulge while she increases her efforts to pry my hands away. Her nails—the same dark green from the press conference—dig into the flesh below my knuckles. They leave fine scratches behind when she drags them downward toward my wrist. Thin lines of blood well on my skin. I glance down at the blood that she's spilled then back up at her with a savage, ruthless smile. "That only makes me stronger."

She stops trying to fight me physically. Impressively manages to raise her chin, tilt her slender nose into the air, and cling to some dignity while I'm choking the life out of her. She manages to get another plea out.

I catch the words: *massacres, protestors, Elkspur,* and *Krashen.* They are the only things she could utter to make me ease the pressure and allow her to sip in gulps of air.

"What's more important to you?" she rushes out when she can talk. "Me or the Republic? Me or the Tribunal? I want them dead too."

"Rhysien's full of shit!" Caiman calls out.

"You *are* the Tribunal." I stab a glare at her garb. "You're Legatus now."

"Only transiently," she says. "As you noted, it's not as solid as it looks. I needed to prove I could deliver something to make it permanent. *Your death.*"

My fingers flex. "Fuck mentioning me," I snap. "Go back to the part about massacres. What was that about?" She might've been saying whatever she had to in order to buy a few additional precious minutes, but I've got to check.

I let her throat go all the way so she can speak easier. Selene stumbles backward, rubbing her neck. Glowering at me, she says, "The Tribunal is planning to hold a briefing from where they've fled in an hour and call the widespread protests in Krashen along with the Elkspur camp you're aiding insurrections. During that briefing, the bombing of Elkspur will occur as penalty for accepting your aid and harboring you. Praetorians will simultaneously march through Krashen and shoot all protestors. They wanted you to come after them first here, so they could crush the open rebellion that's brewing. Why do you think they *let* you strike at them first?"

It's Dane who curses. He's turned deathly pale.

"We knew they had a reason," Liim says, body rigid. "I never expected it to be this heinous, or for them to direct a strike at civilians."

"We are a nation indoctrinated from youth to operate according to strict hierarchies, duty, and discipline, *and* to hate the gods," supplies Selene. "Mass murder of Mareenian people *by* Mareenian leadership becomes much more palatable and digestible for the people to swallow when it's an act to cull the threat of the blood-gifted Zenith who brought Accacian warlords back to Mareen and only killed the former Blood Emperor so she could replace him and conquer us herself. The Tribunes know Accacian warlords flew in overnight, and they know how governing power really gets transferred among Accacians," she says directly to me. It rings odd because it isn't an accusation or said with the conviction that it's her belief too.

"None of that is right!" I cry, stricken. "The warlords flew in to kill me, and I'm not keeping the emperorship. I'm handing it away."

Selene draws herself up. "I'm aware of that and it's why you can't kill me and need me alive. The Tribunal doesn't care what the truth is, only that they can spin what they have to thoroughly quash the revolt

Mareen is in the midst of against them, and quash it with an indisputable reason to have exercised the force that they do it with."

"We need to get to them, *now*," Reed says, stepping forward. "Where are they, Selene? Will you really stand by and let a massacre occur?"

Selene's expression is cool. "I already said I wanted them dead too. Let me live and I will take you all to them straightaway. Send in a report that while Ikenna killed the rest of the Praetorians, I killed her. Tell the Tribunes I'm bringing her body for confirmation so I can have my Legatus seat, officially."

Of course that's what this is about for her. I've already pieced together what *her* play is and what she'll get out of flipping sides. "When you're permanently Legatus," I say, not phrasing it as a question, "you'll reverse the mandates and expose the Tribunes after you've used everybody as pawns. Make the people love you and support you as Legatus."

She doesn't dispute it. "It's a win-win. We both get what we want."

Except the part where she killed my grandfather. I don't get her atoning for that if things go how she wants. More critical is the fact that she is not fit to be anywhere near the office of Legatus; she's proven as self-serving as the old guard.

I narrow my eyes. "Tell me where the Tribunals flew to?" I ask it with compulsion, thrusting a good bit of my power behind it to be sure it works.

"No." Selene scoffs. She inclines her head, almost taunting now that there's space between my hands and her neck.

Why the hell is my compulsion not working?

"Did *you* forget the biochip experiments Chance mentioned?" she says, emboldened. "Your little mind-hijacking trick won't work anymore on biochipped individuals. We needed more time with Chance for the other adjustments, but that is one advancement Rhysien innovation has perfected beyond a test case. Agree to my terms," she snaps. "That's the sole way you get the Tribunes in less time than it'll take to *try* to torture their location out of me, *Ikenna*."

I really want to gut her. I rub my head. Survey the team. An unspoken discussion travels among us that says we all are aware there's no choice here.

"Okay," I grit out to Selene. "Take us to them."

Her offered deal leaves me with another concern. She's known me, closely, for over a decade. There's no way she thinks that once the Tribunal is taken care of, I'd let her stay Legatus or escape the blood debts she owes me. It's why I gaze at her warily as she says we'll take a private Rhysien stealth jet, trying to figure out what else she will pull to cover her own flank.

She believes she has a way to neutralize me after the Tribunes die.

"This won't be how you imagine," I warn up front.

Selene Rhysien shrugs. "We'll see."

And I'm no longer confident this is the best path forward . . . but I go with it anyway.

Because that's what you do when you let your instincts lead.

33

I STARE UP AT KRASHNA'S Citadel, eyes narrowed. Selene, gratingly, has been proven right. I never would've found the Tribunal, who dropped off-grid from even Dannica's contacts and retreated to the sole place we wouldn't have checked.

"They really are afraid if they fled here," Reed says tersely.

I roll my neck. Try to let my own tension bleed out. Selene claims the Tribunes have dared to come here because they held knowledge of a rune Ajani used that dampens the magic that attacks trespassers. If she's telling the truth, it's a comfort to know why the former Apis took the risk of establishing a stronghold at the citadel before our treaty forced him to relinquish the holding; it assures me no attack will be hurled my team's way, at least on that front. As for my own protection . . . I'll have to hope Kissa's former vow holds.

Ritual or no, the Khanaian goddess holding her brother in check or no, the prickling sensation of wrongness, of danger, of alarm that we

382 + N.E. DAVENPORT

should not enter skirts over my skin as we approach the citadel's doors. They bear the protective glyphs Ajani placed there, and I try to use the meshwork of sharp, crisscrossing lines etched into the ancient stone to settle my nerves. The doors' carvings appear similar to the marking on my left shoulder blade that Ajani had inked there too. The likeness helps me lay some of the unease to rest. Accacia's methods at tackling a problem *have* proven effective, I remind myself. Now it's time to use *my* methods.

We pass through the doors, the rune on my back reacting to *something* when iciness floods it. A step behind Selene, I lead my squad toward the same great hall I formerly stood in with Ajani, and hold tight to faith in his adeptness with runes protecting my team and Kissa covering my ass—both leaps stretching the incredulity I feel at such unlikely allies.

WHEN WE REACH the room, my targets sit around the tabletop that's propped up by the tree of life. All twelve Tribunes are present, including Sutton Rhysien. Despite the power struggle going on between him and his daughter, Sutton stubbornly and haughtily remains clothed in the maroon-and-gold wartime dress coat of a Tribune General's rank. There's an empty chair at the head of the table that I presume was grudgingly placed there for Selene to occupy as Legatus Commander, even though I'm sure they never expected her to show up.

I clench my teeth merely thinking of her plopping in it. Forgetting her for the time, I scan the faces of the Tribunal Council. None of them bear startled, stricken looks at beholding me very much alive— and glowing the gold of the gods—that I honestly thought would be quite delicious sights.

In fact, Sutton looks me, Invictus, and his daughter over with a superior sneer. His eyes tighten in vindication—not fury—at the corners when they linger on Selene. "I warned you not to count on her," he says to the Tribunes. "My daughter is too much like her mother: contumacious, shifty in her loyalties, and out for herself above war house and country."

"'Contumacious,' Father? Don't use words you don't understand." Selene pushes her shoulders back. "Besides, you say it like it's a bad thing; like I didn't get it from my *father* as well."

Sutton finally turns angry. He pushes to his feet. "I take it you were unable to fulfill what you promised this council and you've switched sides, bargaining for your own life over that of the Republic. So don't condescend to me, *daughter*, when you couldn't do a single thing you set out to do. Instead, you brought the impure, blood-gifted akulu who threatens the persistence, values, and integrity of this Republic directly to us! You're as traitorous as she and the rogue Praetorians are and sentenced to die as they will." Despite his anger, he displays a sense of calm that is almost amusing. It's as if he believes anything he says from here on out has any bearing on his life, the life of the Tribunes, or the country he purports to serve ever again.

Echoing my thoughts—if not my enjoyment of his bluster—Selene says, "No, Sutton, you will die." Her words have all the venom that I always wanted her to show toward her damn father. She sweeps a hand toward me. "Ikenna will kill you, all of you, and afterward, as Legatus, I will leverage the authoritarian wartime rights *this Tribunal* voted in to be able to handpick the council that serves under me. They will be individuals with much more progressive outlooks on women's roles in war houses."

I'm not so sure about all that, but I let her say her piece for now. There's no point telling her that pretty much *nothing* the Tribunal decided before their—very imminent—executions is going to play a role in the world Invictus is going to help establish. She got us here . . .

We'll take Mareen the rest of the way.

She's not the only one who doesn't quite see the future as firmly as I do. "We will persist as will the Republic," Sutton hisses. "I and my fellow Tribunes have assured it! There's a reason we retreated here, girl. It's time you found out that you are attempting to play a game you still don't know all the rules to."

I listen to the exchange and don't go for the Tribunal immediately on the chance that in her back-and-forth with Sutton, Selene lets slip what her plans are for me and Invictus. How she walks out of the citadel with everything she wants. She proves smarter than that. Doesn't venture there. Only crosses her arms over her chest and stands her ground against her father.

"Kill them, Ikenna. What are you waiting for?" she says, and it is more than grating that she thinks she can simply point me in the direction and I'll oblige. Like I'm *her* weapon. The funny thing is, she could've just asked. She could've trusted me, accepted my blood-gift, confided in me from the beginning, and we would've ended up here, truly aligned, regardless. She didn't. She chose different. And now that I've gotten what *I* want, it'd be stupid for *me* to make any choice that leaves her alive a moment longer because she is a wild card.

A blood axe is immediately in one hand, a blood dagger in the other. I let the dagger fly at Selene while I run for Sutton. Invictus moves with me, gunning for the rest of the Tribunal Council.

Mocking, throaty laughter whips around us before we reach them. "*I can't let you kill the beginning of my new* dutiful *and* obedient *flock,*" comes a disembodied voice that makes my skin crawl with a familiarity that almost makes me stop in true fear. An icy power slams into me a beat later. It must smash into my team, too, because we're all ripped from our feet and thrown backward. The laughter persists. It slides against my senses, comes from everywhere and nowhere at once as I shoot to my feet while my squad mates do the same. Before I process what it means, an ivory-hued male with eyes that are frost blue materializes in the empty head seat and answers my question. The god of war's golden armor is locked in place, exactly as before. The maroon cape he wore the last time, too, drapes over the arm of the chair he occupies as if it is a throne seat. Krashna stares directly at me, harshly beautiful features cool and amused. Phantom touches skirt along my skin, causing an internal hell similar to the effect of his laugh. I stiffen, and his smile broadens. That's all I need. I blink rapidly. Follow Kissa's instructions to close my mind and kick him out of my head. He is tormenting me at the worst time, and fucking with my team, as well, which pisses me off beyond endurance. I shove a mental window open. Imagine drop-kicking Krashna's ass out of it. I expect to see him flying.

My heart hammers when he doesn't budge from the chair I will him to vacate, and my blood plunges with a knowing.

I grip the blood axe, don't dare take my eyes off the god of war. I step back. Take *several* steps backward, actually, giving him a wide berth. Urgently tell the others to do the same. "That. Is. Krashna," I croak.

Before I completely get it out, Invictus closes rank around me, weapons brandished, without questioning it, all while looking like they behold the worst terror we could've encountered in the citadel—exactly like we have. Something drives me to glance toward where Selene stood when I lobbed the dagger. She's down, bleeding from a wound closer to her shoulder than heart, and gaping wildly between Krashna and Sutton. She appears genuinely bewildered, which means she didn't know about this.

"What in the Republic did you do?" Selene says hoarsely to her father, voice trembling and disbelieving. She instinctively goes for a blaster at her hip, but she doesn't have any weapons. We stripped them from her. "What did you all *do*?" she says to the Tribunal. "*Are you insane?*" she cries while scrabbling back against the wall and as far away from the god of war—who has manifested on Iludu in physical form, such that my mental wards do nothing against him—as she can get.

For the first time in a long time, I agree wholeheartedly with Selene Rhysien. Of all the shortsighted things the Tribunal could do—of all the stupid, evil, narrowly self-serving things they could do—this is so bad I couldn't even imagine it before, and am still having a hard time processing it now.

Sutton clearly has no such issues—he being the chief asshole who facilitated this little theological crisis—and he waves her off, casually returning to his seat. "I am quite the opposite. Very rational, very shrewd, and very able to discern the most prudent, preserving course when presented with limited options. The god of war came before us, saying he returned at the end of the war. Said it was because of the war itself, actually—I didn't quite understand all the mumbo jumbo, but got the overall gist. We were given a choice to serve and enjoy the privileges and ranks we currently do . . . or die.

"We chose the obvious."

"You chose death," I gasp, even as my head swivels between Sutton and Krashna.

The latter hasn't spoken yet. After tossing us away from the Tribunes, he's remained leisurely in the chair watching things with a sportive curl to his lips. I clench my hands, breathe in slow through my nose, driving away the instinctual terror, the programmed need to run. I plant my feet apart, remaining light on the balls; the Xzana stance helps center me. I forget Sutton, Selene, and the entire Tribunal. I level the blood axe at the only true threat in the room and remind myself not to make the mistake of taking my focus off him again.

"How the fuck are you here?" I demand. "How did the war help you break free of whatever hellpit contained you?" Hopefully, his arrogance and need to hear himself talk—as so many godsforsaken men have the need to drivel—will compel him to impart details about what is going on and, hopefully, show us a possible weakness to exploit. Some way to combat Krashna. To combat a *god*.

Because I sure as hell could not kick his ass the last time.

Krashna's grin widens, becomes every inch that of a predator playing with prey, as if he's plucked my latest thought from my head and deigns to oblige me with a response. "I did promise we'd get our clash in the flesh. Here I am," he says silkily. "Thank you, by the way. It was your actions during the war, Ikenna, that helped me return. You created the perfect discordance among the cosmos with your Stitching. It resulted in a rip that brought me straight to you, pet. Well, not straight to you. I stopped to bring these heretic Mareenians back into the fold." He croons this all in that noxious combo of sensuality and cruelty. It sets my teeth on edge. It takes all the fight I've got to remain unruffled and not give the bastard the satisfaction when his nightmarish phantom touch coasts down my back as if we're lovers and I should be welcoming him home with open arms. He abruptly unfolds from the chair and stands tall at his full, towering height. The broadness of his shoulders seems to expand, too, the god of war filling the space with his brawn as much as he crowds everybody else in it with his suffocating power.

There's a moment when I step back once more. When my mind shoves away the stark revelation that he's imparted. *I* made a way for him to return. The inward laughter is bitter. Caustic. My stomach drops. Ajani said himself the rite had the possibility to disrupt the order of the cosmos. I have no idea how it made a way, but here Krashna stands, claiming he does so because of my Stitching with Nkosi. I inhale a sharp breath then place the gnawing guilt aside—made a little easier when I recognize I didn't have a choice in the matter, that one way or another Nkosi was going to initiate the Stitching, and ultimately, his death *was* a good thing.

I just hope it outweighs this terror resulting from its aftershocks.

I pull on bravado. I pull on strength. I pull on a determination not to let Krashna leave this hall, no matter what I've got to do to get it done. I gift the god of war my best smile. "I am so much more now than I was when we last met," I inform him, letting my power suffuse the room, letting the red-and-gold glow fill it corner to corner and replace the unnatural chill with blazing heat. I bare teeth. No more smiles. No bullshit. Just a feral promise. "I did tell you I'd find a way to slaughter prick gods, did I not? I didn't think I'd feel this way, but I'm elated you're standing here in the flesh so I can carve you apart.

"Do not engage him. Let me handle him," I tell my team. They haven't spoken a word yet, and I'm proud they aren't cowed. Rather, they've remained tight at my side and have been cataloging Krashna, sizing him up, assessing when and how best they might go about helping me cut him down.

"Wasn't planning on it playing out any other way than you killing him," Caiman mutters, and for some reason, that little vote of confidence from my former nemesis is exactly what I need.

I step a few feet in front of Invictus, placing Krashna and my cohort farther apart.

At least I attempt to. They take up position back around me.

"This is not the time," I stress. This time no one says anything, not even to argue. Only flick me looks to tell me I got this, then go back to whatever they're each individually strategizing.

I want to thank them and warn them off but Krashna has decided in this moment to stop toying with me and starts striding toward me in earnest.

Toward me and my friends.

I don't think. Just slash out at the god of war. I use the blood axe to drive him back and away from my squad, who are damn good in battle but *human*.

He will not touch them.

He will not get close to them.

Except . . . he's a god. And while I haven't quite found a way to completely turn my will into reality, Krashna has no such issues doing exactly that.

He manifests his infamous blue-steel sword after my blood axe strikes against his gold armor. He meets my downward arc that's in line with his neck with an upward swipe of the enormous, unshatterable sword gifted by Kissa in an age when she wasn't so opposed to her twin. The magic-imbued blood blade striking against magic-imbued blue steel cracks out like thunder in the hall. The collision sends shock waves up my arms with enough force that I nearly drop the axe.

Don't you fucking think about it, I snarl to myself. And put all the weight and strength and power I've got behind keeping my blood axe locked against Krashna's mythic sword.

He leans into my ear during our struggle for one of us to knock the other's blade aside and says, roughly: "I don't like that you have another's scent on you. This doesn't end in your death today, so we can play, but it absolutely ends in Kissa's mongrel's death and the rest of those where I clearly see bonds traveling between you and them." His words are laden with warped jealousy, lust, and affront, and I remember how petty the gods were in all the stories.

Turns out those were true.

It also turns out that a non-magical short sword can punch through the god of war's chest. His eyes widen, awash in disbelief he's been struck.

"None of that happens on my fucking life, asshole!" Reeds snarls from behind Krashna.

Krashna spins around quicker than Reed has the chance to yank the blade out; he hammers a kick into Reed that sends him flying backward, slamming against the far stone wall. "That's what I just said, you insignificance!" Krashna grips the hilt of the short sword, yanks it from his flesh, and rotates it in one hand while he levels the blue-steel sword in his other. Enraged, he waits for Reed to get back on his feet. Stunningly, Reed *does* and stares the god of war down with an ice-cold fury that's as frigid and cleaving as Krashna's own glare. Still, Reed's inhale is the ragged way you draw breath when a rib is broken and has punctured a lung, and my heart skips beats, remembering the war camp. The difference is, he's not alone now. Invictus draws up alongside Krashna, shooting a spray of bullets he dodges in a blur of speed nobody could hope to match. It's a distraction, though, which Reed uses to cursedly advance *toward* the god of war instead of maintaining distance with his attacks like the others.

Somehow I pry my attention away from Reed, which is something

Krashna seems incapable of. While he's laser-focused on Reed, I run at the god's back. I raise my blood axe above my head, aim for his spine to hack into and then carve out his heart. If he's present in the flesh, I imagine even an immortal god can't remain upright and fighting without those important body parts. Even if he has the ability to regenerate or heal somehow, the axe will certainly take him down long enough to decapitate him and that should permanently put down a god.

Again, though: god.

Krashna spins and catches the blood axe by the arm, wrenches it from my grip, and casts it aside. His massive hands wrap around my neck. He lifts me off my feet, dangling me in the air, and squeezes. Clearly, this is one of the shithead's kinks. Well, I have things I like to do over and over again too. Quick and dirty, I bury blood spikes into his thighs and groin. He snarls. Drops me.

I scramble backward for maneuvering room, forming a new blood axe in my hand because I won't make it to the dropped one on the other side of Krashna. Invictus, save Reed, converge upon the god while I do it. The five of them are impressive blurs of blaster discharges and lethal blade swipes when they do move into closer range. They're attempting to take him down together. Do enough damage combined that it exacts a toll. It's as solid a plan as I can think of, considering my Zenith-ass has had no seeming impact on Krashna, and I sync my assaults with theirs. Reed does too. As a perfect unit, as a Praetorian cohort, complete with all that is supposed to mean, as brothers and sisters who will not die—or let each other die—in this damn citadel, as *Invictus*, we move together. We attack and strike and fight like the tight-knit *family* we've become, that will not lose another member, and that will defend and safeguard one another and Mareen and maybe even the world from every threat.

We are better than good. We are extraordinary. We fight like the best that Mareen, the best that Krashen Academy, the best that each of our graduating classes had to offer. We fight with our combined prowess, ferocity, and skill. It works to keep us mostly intact, even though we become bloodied and battered and visibly sporting numerous broken bones.

All against a god.

Krashna doesn't slow down any more than he did at the beginning.

We keep at it.

We keep striking.

We keep going.

We keep fighting.

However—and I think I've mentioned this—Krashna is a *god*. I am only half god, and only just coming into that divine half. The rest of Invictus are fully human.

And we begin slowing down.

The god of war does not.

There's an accursed, gut-wrenching shift in the group. I see it in the grave, furious, wretched looks we pass one another. *He kills us, eventually, in this citadel.* We all know it. More than it is evident in our grim gazes we exchange, it's evident in the stubborn, pissed off way we continue to fight—like people who know they are hurtling toward death and refuse to let it claim them easily. Who rage against letting the darkness take them readily. We will all keep fighting until there is no more fight. Until our last breaths, or last heartbeats, or last vestiges of strength fizzle out.

It's not defeatist. It's not even just perseverance. It's . . .

Love.

We will do this because we love one another. Because we love our people and want to see the world that Invictus has promised them.

If I die with love in my heart, that's not so bad, right?

Not at all, I hear Grandfather's voice say.

Reed parries a sword strike that Krashna tries to drive through his eye. The next one impales Reed through the thigh that already bears a dozen holes he's bleeding from. Reed grunts, fiercely trying to remain standing. Yet drops to one knee.

Caiman fires a flurry of UVs at Krashna's head, turning his attention away from Reed and buying me time to sprint to Reed and haul him to his feet. He staggers but stands. Manages to push off me and stay upright. Gripping a slim stiletto—one of the few blades he's held on to—he limps toward where Krashna and the others clash. "Take this too," I say, pressing one of my Khanaian daggers into Reed's hand that I've barely remembered I'm armed with because it's become as natural to slash and thrust and parry and hurl with my blood blades as it is to breathe.

He takes the blue steel. Nods. There's a torment in his cobalt stare, a tightening to his shoulders, a flicker of a second when I see gut-wrenchingly plainly that he fights viciously not to be *Ikenna and Darius* in this moment. Not to whip around to me, kiss me, tell me he loves me one last time.

"I love you too, Darius," I say softly, mourning and cherishing what could've been if things had turned out different, and let it be enough of a good-bye between us. *Cosmos-damned, I want that last kiss.* I want the future we won't have. The peace he promised to hand me, that he has gone to war with something on the same cataclysmic scale of the cosmos—*a living god*—to try and give me.

"I love you, Kenna," he says back on a tortured exhale as we burst into movement in perfect harmony at the same time, two warrior souls linked.

I will find you in the After. I make the silent vow to Darius Reed when we reach Krashna and our team. *I will find you.*

Then, if Invictus is going down as ferociously as we've endured hell in a martial academy, the brutality of the trials, grim lives consumed by death and blood, and a rearing as children bred for war to become . . .

I give a last enraged war cry at the injustice and unfairness of *everything*—of being robbed of a better past and more tranquil future— and then I resolve to die with strength and resilience and the fucking nerve to continue battle with a god in the face of the inevitable.

Krashna *will not* easily win this. Planting myself directly in front of the god, I shove my blood-gift outward. I send shock waves after shock waves after shock waves of power, alongside unswerving blood daggers, at him. I am tired and I am grieving and so much brutally hurts, but I keep doing it. Keep making Krashna expend the focus of countering me while my team continues their strikes. Krashna doesn't get to kill them and drag my death out. He doesn't, out of simple rage and pettiness, get to have this end the way he wants. He has to kill me in the great hall too. Right here. Right now. And I force that as his only choice when I stand in the midst of the full barrage of Krashna's power and throw mine right back at him, relentless and merciless and refusing to let one fraction of it dwindle.

Giving myself over to the thrall of the immense red-and-gold power that pours out of me, flows around me, and thunders at Krashna, Ikenna shrinks away, similar to when I'm submerged in the worst of a blood rage. I *become* destruction and chaos itself when she vanishes. I become the blood and murder and savagery I've been bathed in since birth. That I was anointed in. Cursed in. Blessed in. Swathed in. Gifted in. I give in to all the parts of me that are dark and deadly and petrifying and monstrous. I grasp on to the deep-seated roots inside me that make me *Ikenna*, but also make me so much more. An inner knowing tells me what I curl a firm fist around is the gold in my blood, the power source and essence of whatever makes me a Zenith.

And that essence might merely make me *close* to a god, but I hold on to it anyway, wrench hard in a stubborn attempt to pull it to the surface and throw it at Krashna until the bitter end. In that moment I transform into the most *me* I've ever been: the Ikenna Amari who is suffused with the arrogance to try to take on a god at *his* level. I will die but I will go out as fucking strong as I could possibly be. It's a matter of fucking pride. It feels like something dislodges from within me when I do it. Solid gold light that I didn't intend to display, or even knew I could without the red, streams around me. As it does, I experience a surge of more power. Again, an inner knowing tells me it has nothing to do with my blood-gift. Everything to do with being a Zenith. They are things that are similar, yet wholly different—as this new surge effect feels slightly different. I'll have to take the time to be amazed later.

Right now, I do what I've always done best: wing shit and trust my gut when I do it. I imagine the gold around me shaping itself into daggers, like I can do with my blood-gift. It obeys, same as my blood, and a dozen gold daggers fly at Krashna. He dodges them. But something about me using the power that way makes him startle. It's only a flicker of a reaction, but I see it in his ice-blue gaze nonetheless. He narrows his eyes on me, bellows, and seems to forget about my squad entirely. His own power comes back at me in the same manner.

When a gold dagger embeds between my ribs, I understand why he's enraged. Searing fire erupts at the site like nothing I've ever experienced before. I feel like my insides are being dissolved by acid. Being eaten away at. Being destroyed. I drop to my knees when three more slam into my chest. Greysen drops beside me—I don't know where the hell he came from because he was farther away from Krashna a second ago. I am terrified for him as he lifts me up. Or tries to lift me. He buckles under my weight, too injured himself. I glance up. See Krashna's eyes shift to him. See the irrational, territorial anger that he's moved so close. I see the gloating when Krashna's attention slides back to me. His eyes remain on me, projecting I failed and I don't get to die alongside my team. A gold dagger zooms at Greysen. I know—I *know*—that if one hits him, he won't survive whatever it was doing to me. I shove Greysen out of the way, hurtle my own dagger back at the god of war. It doesn't lodge into his heart, like I want. But as he sidesteps it, Krashna moves straight into the line of Dannica's blaster. Caiman has his trained on him too. So does Liim. They form the points of a perfect triangle, with Krashna in the center and their bullets aimed up to rip through his skull in unison. They pull their triggers. When they do, Reed lunges forward with the Khanaian dagger from behind

Krashna, and I hurl a simple blood dagger that he won't be trying to dodge so ardently at his heart in case Reed misses.

None of us do.

The blood dagger sinks in. The shots splatter Krashna's brains in all directions. Reed's lunge sends a gleaming blue blade thrusting out of Krashna's chest a moment behind my blood dagger punching into it. Reed yanks the Khanaian dagger out, thrusts it in again, face splattered with blood and twisted into a mask of fury. Krashna roars, hemorrhaging gold blood. It's only then that I guess at what the blue steel impaling Krashna might help accomplish. Understand what I should've considered before: if another god's magic forged the sacred metal, then it very well might inflict further lasting damage on Krashna in tandem with my gold dagger.

Thank the cosmos Grandfather's prized blade handed down to me does exactly that.

I stagger to my feet and form my blood axe as the god of war finally takes damage that sticks. Krashna drops to his knees. Braces a hand against the floor, pushes back up. I don't give him time to stand *ever* again. I fly at him, and this time, my blood axe swings true. It slices through Krashna's neck. His head topples from it, rolling to a stop at the base of the tree of life beneath the tabletop the Tribunes remain seated at.

I wait, wondering if a god can survive that. Wondering if those eyes will blink back at me in mirth, and somehow the head reconnect with his body.

I wait . . . and nothing.

Krashna, the god of war, is fucking dead. He. Is. Dead.

Before that crashes down on me, I search for Selene. I need to see her face, see if she registers just how much of this she caused, and how much worse it could have been. But I don't see her—Selene is missing from the great hall.

"Where'd she go?" I croak out. Liim tells me she ran during the battle.

Of course she fled. She's the slipperiest person I've ever known—or, at least, thought I knew. But I don't have time to dwell on her or even process the feat we've accomplished, because I have something more pressing. I wipe the blood from my face, glare at the Tribunes who were going to readily yield Mareen to Krashna, who were going to murder hundreds of its own people, who murdered my grandfather, and who no longer get to make piss-shit choices.

"It is your turn," I say, prowling toward them, blood axe in hand.

They blanch, practically in unison. Comically and delightfully.

Fantastic.

I do not give the majority of Mareen's Tribunal Council time to do anything other than remain in their seats and reap what they have sown. The twelve of them die as the Accacian warlords died: by the blood-gift both sides despised and detested me for possessing. Myriad blood daggers punch out of the bodies of eleven Tribunes' chests and they slump in their seats.

Sutton Rhysien, whom my team makes sure is held at gunpoint until I get to him, gets a more personal death. He deserves nothing less. "You spearheaded the assassination of my grandfather," I say when I stab a blood dagger into his gut, pull it out and spill entrails his hands try to stuff back in. "That is the chief reason you were always going to die a rather horrible death." And it is the only thing I care to say. The only expenditure of energy and words directed at him that he gets. I manifest more blood daggers and slice every major artery I can think of (and if there's one thing the Republic taught me, it's where the vulnerable parts of a body are) simultaneously, letting him think he's going to bleed out until one last dagger punches into his heart, the same organ he made stop beating in Verne Amari. The same organ he destroyed in me when he did. The same organ that was broken when he started Selene down the path toward her betrayal.

I stare at him until the life drains completely out of his damnable, hateful, vile gaze.

I leave the last blood dagger in place. We are torching this hellish citadel to the ground when we depart anyway. I'll figure out a fucking way. It and what the god of war started, the rot he initially sowed into Mareen and then the Tribunal Council kept up while ostensibly casting his tyranny off, gets to stand on Mareenian soil no more.

But Sutton's last moments of being a physical presence in this world will be with my blood dagger sticking from his chest.

All around me the Tribunal lies dead.

Krashna, the god of war, lies dead.

Somewhere, Nkosi and his warlords lie dead.

It is time for the Republic of Mareen to see a new age. A different way of life. It is time for all its citizens to have peace from the rot and sickness that have polluted Mareen for too long.

I've had my revenge. I've proven every doubter wrong. I've been victorious.

Invictus, my squad *and* I, have been victorious.

34

LIKE WHEN AJANI SIGNED THE peace treaty in Accacia, I find myself front and center of a press conference during the signing of a second accord. However, this one isn't a promise of permanent peace, and it has little to do in the immediate sense with the rest of Iludu. This accord is one that's only about other Mareenians and how we'll be governed moving forward. But it gets broadcasted to the rest of the world so all can see the beginnings of the first change of guard that's come to Mareen since the war house system and Tribunal Council were established during the Pantheon Age centuries ago. The planet-wide transmission is important to help soothe nerves and lingering reservations among citizens with darker complexions, the common ranks, the elite ranks, and the rest of the Minor Continent about what the Republic will evolve into, what the Mareenian people's future will look like, and whether Iludu needs to one day fear *me*. Hopefully, the public broadcast of a monumental governing decision—when such things have only ever previously been done inside private Tribunal chambers—will serve as confirmation in triplicate that Mareen will never be like it was before, the Republic is seeing critical change, and the foundation is being laid for that change to last. The broadcast should additionally affirm that I only have good intentions and only mean to aid Mareen with achieving a new and better future.

Gathered in the rubble of what used to be the Pinnacle Tower, standing tall and at attention among what used to be Krashen Base, the seat of governing and military power for the Republic of Mareen, are me, Reed, Caiman, Greysen, Dannica, Liim, Dane, the Republic's entire class of Praetorians, every surviving war house scion, and common-rank heroes who galvanized Mareen's masses toward rebellion, prepared to die for a better life.

Conspicuously absent is Selene Rhysien. A matter I will deal with at some point, but not now.

With Invictus having exposed the full, horrific extent of the Tribunal's planned massacres, it was fairly easy to negotiate a bloodless regime change that didn't descend into civil war with the scions and prominent legacy families. Especially given the fact that the Rossi heir lives, has been proven a champion of the people instead of a traitor, and the elite ranks would follow a Rossi to the farthest edges of the cosmos. There's also the crime that many among the second tier of elites were never actually distributed the resources the Tribunal's restoration mandates made it legal to seize. The war house heads handed down nothing to the scions outside of their immediate kin. So in the end, nobody is truly too aggrieved about seeing the old regime die and something new replace it. The war houses will remain whole and scions who'd otherwise fight against change will retain their enjoyed pedigreed standing and titles—a compromise, as there was no way to keep them from rejecting the new regime outright. Invictus would have been there to put down any such recalcitrance, but it would have cost too much. And we realize it doesn't matter. Because the Republic of Mareen won't be dominated by a Tribunal Council anymore. It'll be ruled jointly by an elected Senate of Scions and an elected Senate of Commons.

I present this compromise via live vidfeed. The fifteen war house heirs, including Caiman, sign the paper document that expresses the agreement when I'm done. An equal number of community leaders from among the present common ranks sign the Reformation Constitution next. Eight of the fifteen are what some among the Republic would spit the slur "akulu" at. Those mixed-lineage men, women, and other persons who descend in part from ancestors bearing darker skin and ancestral homes beyond Mareen's borders sign the Reformation Constitution to also outlaw discrimination based on said lineage or skin color. I'm aware that won't erase the bigotry that has pervaded Mareen from day one—ink on paper very rarely upends systemic abuse so easily. But it's a vital start that so many of us who've suffered the oppression, slurs, violence, debasement, and stripping of humanity that comes within a Republic where bigotry runs deep never imagined could happen. My chest squeezes watching people who look like me sign a governing document for the Republic while the world looks on. Tears prick my eyes, and I don't do myself, Grandfather, my Khanaian-transplant great-grandfather, or the rest of my fellow mixed-lineage peoples in the Republic the dishonor of supressing them.

After representatives from the common ranks sign their names, the leads helming each of the Praetorian cohorts sign the Reformation Constitution, too, beneath an article that expresses Mareen's Praetorian Guard will safeguard, fight, and uphold the freedoms of the Republic itself and the Republic's people, bearing a duty to those citizens and no duty to the body that governs it when and if that body acts against the rights and welfare of the people. It furthermore specifically says that Praetorians *must* serve the will of the Republic over the will of their respective war houses, a stipulation that no amount of whining from those houses would make me back down on. We will *not* go back to a country of private armies.

When Reed signs for Gamma, his sea-blue eyes shine with a fiercely proud, triumphant outpouring of his immense love for all the Republic is that's good and all it will become. He also makes no attempt to mask the bittersweetness that's evident about him. Signing the accord is Reed's last and final act as Gamma's lead after only resuming that rank in an official capacity in the fourteen days that have passed since the Tribunes died.

A twinge of guilt squeezes my chest for why the quiet regret clings to Reed. However, I shake it off; I know that a little tranquility, for a change, is what *he* wants as much as I do.

As for me and my role among the proceedings during the signing, I'm Mareenian, but I am also a Zenith. Which means I can't be involved in anything other than sharing the news and then to look on as Grandfather's surviving kin, suffused with my own fierce pride and love for the Republic.

Grandfather, are you watching this? I ask Verne Amari, the man whose life's work was toward this end. I'm certain he is, from whatever place he occupies among the Light Fields. *Your dream is being realized. We did it.*

You *did it*. His baritone voice crashes into my head. More than any other time I've felt this way, Grandfather's words, his very voice, seem so damn solid and real and like he is actually somewhere near talking to me. It's ludicrous, but I glance around as if I'll see the king among men who was the formidable, matchless, fierce Verne Amari actually present. I know I won't see him. But when I think about that, that he's long passed into the After, a tide of grief no longer threatens to drown me. I still miss him with a keen ache—I always will—but delivering death to the people who schemed to murder him and the signing of these accords allows me to claim a measure of solace. Even sizable joy. So I make peace with Grandfather's death and tell the great, venerable, esteemed Verne Amari, *my hero*, Legatus, hensei, and parent, "I'll see you in the After, Grandfather."

When I utter it, I swear that Iludu's scorching, regal sun, which will continue to shine down on its peoples and nations every day and step aside every night for its extraordinary, otherworldly moons to shine for as long as the planet spins, increases in wattage a little bit brighter.

At the end of the press conference, I step out of view of the drones and make my way to the idling transport. My entire squad and friends—Reed, Dannica, Caiman, Greysen, Liim, and Dane—do the same. My Invictus family refuses to let me travel back to Accacia and complete the Claiming rite alone, although I have little worry about it or Ajani. Accacia's future emperor's proven caliber as a leader who cares about sparing his people suffering, not enhancing it, has left me more than untroubled to be handing him the liegeship formally. However, each member of Invictus has separate, important stops to make prior to heading to the Principal Continent. So, although we leave the press conference together, we'll be boarding jets taking us to different corners of the planet.

Before I climb into the transport alongside my team, I scrutinize the gathered crowd. I look for a familiar shade of flame-red hair and gunmetal-gray eyes. Selene hasn't turned back up since the citadel, and wasn't involved in the reformation of the Republic, but it wouldn't have surprised me to see her show up today, to start trouble if nothing else. But she isn't here. Her eldest brother assumed steerage of Rhysien War House, and he hasn't heard from her either. After everything— all the blood, the death, having my vengeance on the Tribunal, battling Krashna, finding peace—part of me sort of wants her to just stay gone. Find her own peace somewhere too. I'm not sure how I feel about those sentiments, but they're something I don't need to sort out unless she does turn back up in the Republic and makes another play to be involved in its governing.

I exhale, making a knee-jerk decision to keep the trend going of claiming solace, peace, and joy, while relinquishing the heaviest burdens of grief. I smile slightly at nothing in particular. *Find your freedom and the Selene I loved in the academy,* I tell my former friend wherever she is. I truly have no desire to hunt her down. I've got more blissful things to do—like Darius Reed over many, many, many nights that do not get interrupted by the next op, or the looming battle upon the coming dawn. Darius and Ikenna are going to enjoy an eternity of nights—and days—being unconcerned with anything else.

We have paid in blood.

Given the world refuge.

We've earned a forever that transcends the stars.

EPILOGUE

Over the next week, I tell Ajani to fuck off since we can't do the Claiming ritual for a little while longer. Reed and I gift each other seven days of uninterrupted bliss. Of enjoying and living out the peaceful future spanning before us after Edryssa comes through again. She delivers on an opulent, secluded seaside villa in Lusian, and Reed and I spend seven days fucking on every surface, not bothered by a thing, and deciding we will purchase a similar villa by the ocean in a rebuilt Cara and repeat the experience. It's the Light Fields incarnate and leaves my body deliciously spent, muscles heavy with an exhaustion that has nothing to do with fighting. Well, not the bloody and gruesome kind anyway.

Our week ends and then we have to drag ourselves away from heaven to take care of the last bit of business. The others—who went their separate ways for indulgences of their own in the peace we just won for Iludu—meet us in Lusian. Together, Invictus finally heads to

Accacia. Ajani greets us, brooding and prickly about us all being *children* as soon as we land.

What else is new?

That same evening, when the sun dips below the horizon, Iludu's moons reign in the sky in their vanishing gibbous stage. The truncated spheres blaze crimson, as Accacia's royal augurs forecasted. As always, no matter what phase they present in, be it crescents, quarters, or full-body orbs, the trinity of Blood Moons is imposing and oozes portent. But for me, at least, they've always ushered forth good things: necessary change and positive evolutions. So I go into the Claiming rite at ease, my hard-won tranquility something precious that I'll hold on to and guard fiercely. The fact that I believe Ajani will stick to his pledges facilitates this.

He and I stand beneath the Blood Moons in one of the courtyards of the palace, wearing crimson-and-black ceremonial robes to perform the Claiming. Invictus forms a semicircle at my back. It's a relaxed form that underscores they don't mark Ajani and his people as threats either. Iyko and fellow marshal, Sol, stand a few feet behind their leige, mirroring my squad's leisurely stances. Each time I glance at Ajani's marshals, I'm struck by the way the pair gaze at him—with open fierce pride, unwavering loyalty, and the unflinching belief that the man who Accacia *needs* and *deserves* to call Blood Emperor finally helms the Empire. And I can't deny it: seeds of that same ferocious belief about the necessity of Ajani to the Empire have taken root in me too. I blink and turn away from Iyko and Sol, shaking my head because I refuse to let Ajani glimpse even a glimmer of my harboring that sentiment. His crowing will never cease.

I focus my attention instead on Odion and the remaining four royal augurs who stand in front of Ajani and me. They look upon their liege with more neutral—and highly *less* unnerving—expressions. Well, all of them do except for one. The dark-skinned woman from the Accacian press conference eyes her *betrothed*, as it turns out, with a similar pride as his marshals and with pure adoration. She lays a hand on her belly, which is beginning to swell. I smile, despite myself. I am happy for Ajani and have no doubt he will make as good a father as he will an emperor—more judgments about His Imperial Majesty that I will never utter out loud.

Seriously, the know-it-all smugness will make me have to relieve him of his tongue.

I cut off the musings when Odion steps forward, presumably to begin the ritual. "My liege," the augur says, bowing low to Ajani. He straightens, turns to me, and bows too. "Sacred Zenith," he says reverentially. His words and actions toward me add to the growing heap of disconcerting things accruing here since I serenely went into the ritual.

I gape at Odion most unprofessionally, inelegant, and undignified. The elder augur chuckles and takes my hand. He draws a stiletto from his silver-and-gold robes. "Kneel, my liege and my Zenith," he instructs.

He draws blood from the inside of my right wrist and Ajani's. As he had communicated to me to do, I raise my wrist and let my blood spill onto the dirt in front of me and repeat the Accacian words that Odion has begun to speak. Ajani does the same, letting his blood drip in the same spot on Accacian soil as mine.

I brace for what comes next. According to Ajani and Odion, it'll be a tug on my power similar to what I experienced during the Stitching with Nkosi. When I do feel it, it is similar. Though it isn't a violent or violating sensation as it was the last time. It's the complete opposite— more akin to a peaceful request carried on a soft, gentle pull that then waits for permission. I'd already decided to fully trust Ajani, and the marked difference in the feeling of this transfer of power versus what Nkosi tried to force confirms he's the far better choice to rule mighty Accacia. So I don't hesitate. I give over my claim on Accacian lands that the tug is trying to take.

When it's complete, Odion's body goes stiff. Red washes into the gentle brown of his eyes. He hisses as if in pain.

I glance wildly at his fellow augurs, but their expressions remain unperturbed.

"Is this supposed to be happening to him?" I ask Ajani. "Nobody said anything—"

Ajani curses. "Gods—*fuck*! This needs to come now, old man?" Ajani bellows at Odion. He emits a string of further curses.

All right . . . that supplies my answer.

Yet, none of the Accacians move to help Odion or look surprised.

"What the hell is going on with dude?" Dannica says behind me.

I'm wondering the same. My eyes swing among a ruffled Ajani, a hissing Odion, engulfed by a glow of red power, and the remaining, serene augurs. "Is he going to be okay?" I ask.

Ajani laughs caustically. "As the leader of Accacia's order of augurs, Odion has his own connection with the magic in the land. It sometimes hands him prophesies." He scrubs a hand over his brow and curses again. "I do not wish to know what damnable thing he's about to prognosticate. It can't be anything good if it's arriving at this moment."

Before I can entirely wrap my head around that and ask further questions, a voice that sounds like Odion's, yet not and bleeds power, pours from his lips. And perturbingly, his eyes that shine entirely red pin me in place when it does. *"You may not be ready yet to assume a role and responsibility in the Empire because of a commitment to other duties,"* booms Odion. *"But you, Ikenna Amari, have much to learn about your importance to Accacia, the blood-gifted, all Pantheon-blessed, and the larger world as one of the last remaining Zeniths hailing from the Pantheon. You will have a great war to fight. When it comes, you will be the blood blade that fights for us all. You will either prevail and Iludu will ascend grand, permanently peaceful, and prosperous into a new, unified age. Or you will fail and Iludu will descend into carnage and ruin that the planet and its people will never recover from or escape."*

As Odion speaks the spine-chilling words that my mind struggles to make sense of, the ground beneath us shakes, and a seemingly ancient, alien, enormous power that doesn't feel like it's coming from me or Odion cracks through the night air.

When Odion stops speaking in the otherworldly voice, his red glow dissipates and his eyes return to untainted brown. The primordial, freakish power persists in the air for several long moments, however.

As it does, every stare turns to me. I blanche, the full forecasting and ramifications of Odion's prophesy hitting me.

"What new war is coming? *When* is it coming?" Ajani asks rigidly.

"The gods," I say hoarsely. "The gods are coming back to Iludu. The Stitching allowed Krashna to return, and Amaka certainly said she intended to use my Stitching for her own agenda when she gave me the power to overcome Nkosi in the Stitching." My voice is barely a whisper by the time I finish. I rub my temples. Hiss out a breath.

Without my needing to vocalize what's truly wrong, Reed steps to my side, collects my face, kisses me, calms me down.

"I'm sorry," I tell him. "I am sorry," I say again, this time for shattering Reed's personal slice of claimed peace and to the planet for only giving it the illusion of quietude. It. Is. Always. Something.

Reed kisses me again. Slow and ardently, like we have all the time in the world to stand in the courtyard and just be us—when we don't anymore. "We fight them," he says when he raises his head from mine. "We killed one god. We can kill another. We can kill them all. And afterward, we go back to this—" I'm treated to a third kiss. One that makes my toes curl and that holds heated promises of right this moment, later, and forever still.

I place my hands into Reed's, lace our fingers together, hold on tight, and admit the truth because I know I have his strength, support, blaster, and love behind me and can be vulnerable for a moment. "That sounds nice. Probably doable. I'm still terrified of what comes next."

He pulls me into his arms, kissing the top of my hair. "So am I, but we've got this. You're fucking spectacular in everything you do, remember?" he says with the ghost of a smile, throwing the wiseass, arrogant, stuffed-full-of-bravado words I've said to him at me.

The banter helping, I pat his chest. "Smart man to recognize such truth." I kiss the proud line of his jaw, drawing strength and confidence from the fact that I'm not going at this new fight alone, as I didn't go at my last fight alone. Reed will be with me again. Apparently, so will the rest of Invictus because they all chime in and assert exactly that. I turn in Reed's arms. Place my back against his chest and nod to our team in the affirmative. We ended two monsters. My squad and I can end the new ones trying to rise.

I don't get to stop playing general just yet, it seems. And since I don't, I might as well extract the perks where they come from this fresh shitstorm.

"I want a war table night this time around too," I let Reed know over my shoulder.

In my peripheral sight, I catch his cobalt gaze darkening. "I promised you every night and you can still have it. Wherever you want, Kenna."

Dannica makes a gagging noise. "*Seriously, y'all?* I'm envisioning shit that's gross with Darius as a participating party, and it's traumatic as fuck. Thank you for that—not one bit."

Caiman coughs. "Oh, I need to hear this story, Amari."

I flip him off. "You never will, Golden Boy."

He shrugs. "We're about to go track down and kill some gods; I've got the time to wear you down." I get a winning Rossi grin.

Greysen, Dane, and Liim laugh at our antics.

So do I. This time, I'm heading Invictus on an op to kill numerous terrible gods, but an easiness and a comfort settle over me as our camaraderie and bonds present strong. It's what got us through Nkosi and Krashna alive. It will get us through the rest of the Pantheon alive. And while we're doing it, I decide I can have both. I can go to war again and still claim my peace while I kick godly ass because what I have with Reed and Invictus *is* my peace.

Amaris are as strong as Khanaian steel, I remind myself. It has never been truer because I find that I am not so afraid of this next battle, after all.

I am forged by adversity. I am tempered in perseverance. I will not bend. I will not break. I will not bow. I will not yield.

Once the mantra I have proven many times over is finished, Grandfather's voice adds: *Not even to gods, Kenna.*

Give the Pantheon hell too.

I will, Grandfather. When they come, I will be ready.

DRAMATIS PERSONAE

PLAYERS IN THE REPUBLIC OF MAREEN

IKENNA AMARI: a warrior with elite Praetorian rank; mixed Mareenian, Khanaian, and Accacian heritage; former Gamma Cohort squad mate; granddaughter and sole surviving kin of Mareen's murdered Legatus Commander

The child of an unknown Accacian father, Ikenna is infamously blood-gifted and her illegal magic has been exposed. She's become the leader of a rogue Praetorian cohort whose members broke from the Republic alongside her. Ikenna aims to assassinate the tyrannical Blood Emperor of Accacia, end the war with him that Mareen's government instigated, then return to Mareen to execute its Tribunal Council, getting justice for her grandfather and overthrowing her country's own despots.

If that isn't enough—the goddess of blood rites, which Ikenna's magic stems from, has taken a keen, shadowy interest in aiding our beloved Murder Girl.

*VERNE AMARI: Ikenna's half-Khanaian and half-Mareenian grandfather, former Legatus Commander of Mareen (44th), war hero who wounded Accacia's near-immortal Blood Emperor to end the first war between Accacia and Mareen, a Xzana combat arts master and strategy genius, the most brilliant combat mind the Republic has ever seen.

Verne raised Ikenna from birth and kept her blood-gift a secret from his government, which would execute her for it.

*MAIIKA AMARI: the daughter of Verne Amari, a woman who had an affair with an enemy Accacian and was subsequently killed by Accacian warlords while pregnant.

The baby, Ikenna, survived the execution after being cut from Maiika's womb due to Ikenna's blood-gift sustaining her newborn life.

DARIUS REED: a half-Khanaian/half-Mareenian orphan from eastern Rykos, graduated first in his cadet class, top-tier Praetorian, former Gamma Cohort squad leader, transition officer and co-lead of the Praetorian Trials, Verne Amari's Xzana student and protégé, Ikenna's co-general in their rogue Praetorian cohort

KADIYA DANNICA: a Praetorian from eastern Mareen, traces of Khanaian ancestry in her lineage, formerly Gamma Cohort's third-in-command, transition officer of the Praetorian Trials, fiercely loyal to Ikenna and a member of Ikenna's rogue cohort

HAYNES: a Praetorian from western Mareen, formerly Gamma Cohort's second-in-command, member of Ikenna's rogue cohort

CAIMAN ROSSI: a northerner born in the mighty capital of Krashen City, "Golden Boy" of the Republic, heir to Mareen's most powerful and venerated war house, formerly a Praetorian in Alpha Cohort, fights alongside Ikenna in her rogue cohort

GREYSEN HUNT: a legacy Praetorian, formerly served in Alpha Cohort, Caiman's best friend, a squad mate of Ikenna's rogue cohort

LIIM: former Alpha Praetorian and trials transition officer, loyal to Caiman and Rossi War House, a rogue cohort member

DANE: former Alpha Praetorian, loyal to Caiman Rossi, a rogue as well

*ZAYNE DRAKE: Ikenna's and Selene's best friend, who died in the Praetorian Trials, born of labourri parents from the Southern Isles

SELENE RHYSIEN: Ikenna's former best friend, war house scion, duplicitous

SUTTON RHYSIEN: Selene's father, head of the war house that developed a way to neutralize magic use in warfare, the Tribune General who convinced the rest of the Council to sanction the assassination of Ikenna's grandfather

*HAYMUS ROSSI: Caiman's father, a Tribune General and former head of Rossi War House, the 45th Legatus Commander, murdered by Ikenna in vengeance

*RUDYARD BROCK: Verne's brother-in-arms, helped raise Ikenna, a Tribune General and head of Brock War House, the Tribunal Council's former spymaster, murdered by Ikenna in vengeance

*ZEPHYR CAAN: a young, newly minted Tribune General and war house head, murdered by Ikenna

LYKAS CHANCE: skilled Praetorian, Alpha Cohort's leader, former transition officer and co-lead of the Praetorian Trials, sadistic and hates Ikenna

PLAYERS IN THE EMPIRE OF ACCACIA

NKOSI: the Empire's feared Blood Emperor, purportedly godlike, has conquered most of the planet and vastly expanded Empire territory, a bloodthirsty warmonger who seeks to conquer Mareen and the rest of the Minor Continent nations that held out against his former expansion campaign

AJANI: one of the Red Order warlords, a member of the Blood Emperor's inner circle of men whose power is only a step below their liege's

RIGAUD: a Red Order warlord

IYKO: Ajani's second-in-command for the unit of legionnaires he leads

ODION: a gentle Accacian holy man with the gift of augury

PLAYERS IN THE KINGDOM OF KHANAI

MUSTAPH GYIDI: Grand Monarch of prosperous Khanai, Verne's good friend, an uncle figure to Ikenna who becomes estranged from her following her assassination attempt on his life

ENOCH GYIDI: Crown Prince of Khanai, childhood friend of Ikenna, enemy to Ikenna after his father's attempted murder

AKASHA GYIDI: Queen of Khanai

PRINCESS NISHIA GYIDI: Enoch's younger sister

PLAYERS IN THE FREE MICROSTATES

TARIYAL: Queen-Sovereign of Ska'kesh, former lover to Verne Amari, confidante and friend to Maiika Amari

EDRYSSA CYPHIR: Lady of Lusian, Cyphir Syndicate crime boss, reigns over the City of Thugs, ally to Ikenna

THE ILUDU PANTHEON

KRASHNA: god of war, created the lands of Mareen and its martial-minded people, once handed down war gifts in the population along with ruinous ideas about purity

AMAKA: goddess of blood rites, created the lands of Accacia and proliferated blood magic in her devoted flock, preached similar ideas of superiority

KISSA: goddess of arts, riches, and wisdom, Khanai's beloved patron goddess, the sole benevolent entity among the Pantheon, twin sister to Krashna, creator of sacred blue steel—a metal Khanaian blades are forged from that is unshatterable

HASANI: god of the After, legend purports he's served by twin hellserpents who collect recently deceased souls and drag them into the After

Hasani buried the entire civilization he created alive under ice in a fit of rage at his flock daring to rise up against him. This gave rise to the notorious Ice Waste that encompasses the harsh mountain range known as Hasani's Wrath.

ONEI: goddess of the hunt, creator of Onei's Expanse—a Pantheon-cursed, hellish forest prowled by undead cannibals and myriad other magical predators

VA'IA: goddess of beauty and love, used both to trap the unwise into eternal servitude

NANWI: god of trickery and illusions, a penchant for cruel games and crueler jokes

IMU: goddess of chaos and the crossroads, sower of discord

DAJA: god of the sea, populated the Tumultuous Sea, which stretches between the Minor Continent and Principal Continent and is filled with an array of monsters

MALIYA: goddess of fire, history recalls her engulfing whole cities in flame on occasion

*Deceased

ACKNOWLEDGMENTS

DRAFTING A SOPHOMORE NOVEL IS brutal. Drafting a finale to a series is harder. I had to do both with *The Blood Gift*, and there are so many individuals whom I'd like to express my infinite thanks to for keeping me grounded and confident I could pull this sequel off. As always, Caitie Flum, you are a rock-star agent. I couldn't have brought Ikenna's story to life from the very beginning without you championing it, reading countless drafts, and chatting with me about the myriad ideas I had for the potential directions the story could go. Likewise, David Pomerico, you are an exceptional editor, and I am continuously in awe of your skills. You have a gift for being able to cut to the core of the narrative I am attempting to tell when I hand in an initial draft and provide incredible insight as to how I might enhance the story to really make what I most want to relay shine. You're proof that great editors are worth their weight in gold. Vicky Leech Mateos, the same sentiment one thousand percent extends to you as well. Thank you for seeing something special in Ikenna and her world and working to bring *The Blood Gift* duology to a wider audience.

To Mireya and the entire HarperCollins team, who have displayed tons of support for this series since the beginning, the biggest THANK-YOU. Julie Paulauski and Emily Goulding, you've been phenomenal publicists to work with. Your high energies, warmth, and dedication to helping boost this series and increase its visibility has been super heartening and exceptional. Deanna Bailey, I really appreciate all the work you've poured into things on the marketing side. You're amazing and your ideas are always just so brilliant and spot-on. Raymond Sebastien, you are a gem of a talent. Your cover art on both books helped bring Ikenna to life in a way that still leaves me breathless. You rendered her exactly how I imagined her *and* made her even cooler!

To my husband, Courtney, and oldest daughters, Carmen and Cydney, you three were LIFESAVERS while I drafted and revised this book. I owe you an entire galaxy's worth of praises for pitching in to help with the babies and keep them entertained while Mom worked. Janee, Elana, and Lauren—you are the greatest sisters a girl could have. If I don't say it enough, I feel immensely blessed to have you in my life as women who are always there for me in any way I need. Mommy, you have been amazing since the day I was born and continue to be. Thank you for helping out with the babies too, hanging with the older girls, and taking shifts for school pickup and ballet drop-off while I drafted this book.

Dhonielle Clayton, Tracy Deonn, Roseanne A. Brown, J. Elle, and Ronica Davis—all of the publishing advice and experience you've generously lent has been invaluable and so very appreciated. Susan Dennard, Hannah Whitten, and Kalynn Bayron—I super appreciate you three agreeing to participate in my launch events for *The Blood Trials*. Our chats truly made launch week magical! Dhonielle, our in-person conversation at Kindred Stories on release day was more than

I ever could've asked for! Mark Oshiro, Julian Winters, and Saraciea Fennell—a big thank-you for rolling with Dhonielle to my release day event. It was such a delightful surprise to see you.

I saved this for last, but it is certainly not of the least importance. It's simply because I am going to cry while typing this next thing. To my writing fam—Traci, Jonathan, Shari, Kwame, Brent, DaVaun, Alaysia, Liz, and Jamar—you all have been along for Ikenna's journey and my larger writing journey for so long now. When I've needed advice, cheerleaders, a kick to get to work, peeps to talk plot and story with, or a second opinion/read on pages, y'all have been there every time. Traci-Anne, you are my sister. You're *family* family; you're stuck with me—and all my writerly chaos—legitimately forever. Sorry! Jamar, the same goes for you! We've been friends for many years now and it means so much to always have you there no matter if it's to squee over something good, gripe about something not so great, or just talk through whatever I need to.

Finally, I can't end these acknowledgments without taking a moment to humbly say thank you to the readers who found the Blood Gift Duology, fell as hugely in love with Ikenna as I have been since I first conceived her, and helped shout about her and her story to the world. Thank you for all the cool pics and words of excitement that I was tagged in on Instagram and Twitter. You all made the weeks leading up to *The Blood Trials*'s launch, launch week, and the months following launch something that was joy-filled, magical, and really freaking cool, while keeping the usual angst of releasing a book into the world at bay. To B²Weird Bookclub, chatting with you all during release week was so amazing and wonderful. It was a literal dream come true to have the opportunity to talk with readers who enjoyed *The Blood Trials* and came READY to discuss the shenanigans, the bloodshed, the spice, and the heavier issues woven between its pages. Briana and Dani—our chance meeting at Politics & Prose was a highlight of debuting! We must meet for shots again sometime soon! Your hype for Ikenna and the world of Iludu starting even before publication made release day immensely less scary. It boosted my confidence that *The Blood Trials* would find its readership, and the individuals I wrote it for would love it, see Ikenna, and get what I was trying to accomplish! Veena, you, too, have been so generous and kind with your support for this series. I can't express how much I appreciate it. To Kindred Stories and the Book Bar—Black-owned indie bookshops—I admire the hell out of your work. THANK YOU A BILLION for existing within the book community, supporting Black authors, and championing stories reflective of the diaspora and our multitude of experiences.

ABOUT THE AUTHOR

NIA "N. E." DAVENPORT is a science-fiction/fantasy author who has a penchant for blending science and magic. She possesses undergraduate degrees in biology and theatre, as well as master of arts degrees in secondary education and public health. When she isn't writing, she enjoys vacationing with her family, skiing, and being a huge foodie. You can find her online at nedavenport.com, on Twitter @nia_davenport, or on Instagram @nia.davenport, where she talks about bingeworthy TV, fun movies, and great books. She lives in Texas with her husband and kids.

DISCOVER THE BLOOD GIFT DUOLOGY BY N. E. DAVENPORT

Blending fantasy and science fiction with Afrofuturistic inspiration, N. E. Davenport's fast-paced, action-packed debut kicks off a duology of loyalty and rebellion, in which a young Black woman must survive deadly trials in a racist and misogynistic society to become an elite warrior.

"Davenport debuts with an ambitious epic that blurs genre lines, setting futuristic technology against a historical fantasy backdrop...this invigorating debut marks Davenport as a writer to watch."

— *Publishers Weekly*

"Davenport's ambitious debut is gritty and bloody, and balances emotional arcs with fast action. Fans of Pierce Brown's *Red Rising* and Evan Winter's *The Rage of Dragons* will find similarities in Ikenna's journey."

— *Library Journal*

"*The Blood Trials* is one of my top reads of the year—a riveting story with richly-drawn characters caught in a tangle of political intrigue, systemic racism, and nonstop peril. Don't miss this one!"

— Melissa Marr, *New York Times* Bestselling Author of *Wicked Lovely*